A SPYMASTER
MIDAS

By
Roger Bensaid

Book Four in the Spymaster Series.
A Major Brown story.

Published by New Generation Publishing in 2024

First Edition

ISBN
Paperback	978-1-80369-837-3
Hardback	978-1-80369-838-0
eBook	978-1-80369-839-7

www.newgeneration-publishing.com

 New Generation Publishing

The Plot

Major Rodney Brown, invalided out of the Army, finds himself in an independent section of the British Secret Service. Their remit is to deal with matters that do not fall neatly into the Foreign Office or the Home Office or that neither Office wants to deal with.

This fourth Major Brown adventure concerns corruption and the billions of pounds diverted by fraudsters. A mode of corruption that invades three main sectors of British life. Fact is stranger than fiction and entry into the KGB world is driven by a highly placed Treasury civil servant and his KGB handlers. The idea for this story was generated by the humble traffic cone, the plague of our motorways, and the discovery of its secret life by the Treasury Compliance Officer from hell. As ever, the Major's nemesis Brigadier Carl Tsygankov, KGB, retired has much to answer for.

The Author

Roger Bensaid spent twenty-four years in the Army and a further seventeen years in the gas and oil industry before becoming a specialist consultant for ten years, which took him to many parts of the world and into conflict zones. He was often working in support of the British and other Armed Services, one way or another, for which he retains the highest regard. Once asked why he did it he said, 'To give something back.' His children Julien, Christian and Chloe have now grounded him. No more adventures and living on the edge. And he misses it.

Roger now spends his time mainly writing and painting. Mac and Bob, retired veterans both, would have added 'And was tending his grapes in France.' Regrettably, Brexit made it too difficult to live in France and the UK, so the UK won. Still, he has a few vines in his Hampshire home and squeezes the odd bottle out of them.

Acknowledgements and Foreword

Thank you, New Generation Publishers, for getting this book out and David for his patience and support. And thank you, Kate, who can unlike me can tell when a full stop or comma is needed and where a capital goes.

I hope that the reader will enjoy this fourth soldier-spy tale. The idea that spurred it? It is my protest for all the unnecessary hours we spend on the roads in traffic works. To highlight the lamentable way we work our road repairs compared to our continental counterparts, I hope it may raise a wry smile from you as we all suffer. Our 'will to win' in this context seems to have evaporated.

So why do I write at all? It is hard work, I am mildly dyslexic, spelling is torture. Could be just to prove to myself that I can produce books and for others that find writing difficult that it can be done. For the support of many people and anyone who buys and reads this book – thank you. To Kate, for putting up with my mental absences and lack of response when I am deep in thought amongst the plots in play, and the others yet to be worked out and hatched.

Roger 2023

My Motivators

Bob Coveney (plays the head of SO13 Anti-Terrorist Branch, keeps insisting that I should promote him, but I don't think that I will.

'Get on and do it. Never give up. Focus on the barriers to achieving your mission; innovate, improvise and overcome. Just get it done!' And Bob would always want me to add, for those who know this, thank you.

'We are the pilgrims Master; we shall go, always a little further; it may be beyond the last blue mountain barred with snow, across that angry or that glimmering sea.' from The Golden Journey to Samarkand by James Elroy Flicker, 1884.

Pat Jones (plays one of the SIS team.)

'If it's under the bridge it is gone forever; only *the next bridge counts, so step carefully.' Pat plays one of Major Browns' SIS team.*

'The only ones truly free of the daily struggle, strife and war, are the dead.' Apologies to Plato.

The family.

Contents

SPYMASTER MIDAS

List of Players

Players in this Story

(And I need to remind you the reader that it is only a story – to while away your free time but also to amuse you "players" and my long suffering "friends and acquaintances." All characters appearing in this work are fictitious-almost. Any resemblance to real persons, living or dead is purely coincidental.)

> *"The beginning is the most important part of the work."*
>
> Plato

Executive Players

Mrs. Thatcher – Prime Minister and First Treasury Secretary

Sir Geoffrey Gilmore – Cabinet Secretary

Neil Ashchurch – Senior Treasury civil servant

Special Advisors to the Prime Minister – Dan and Shaun

The Russian Cast

General Polyakov – Director 1st Directorate KGB

Brigadier General Carl Tsygankov – The Spymaster Deputy of the 1st Directorate KGB. Retired, enjoying his Dacha and its vineyards

Brigadier General Shabarshin – Spymaster Deputy of the 1st Directorate KGB

Colonel Pushkin – KGB Operations Illegals Directorate

Major Carla Kazimira Tskhovbova – KGB Intelligence Officer 1st Directorate

Major Vasily Vladimirov – KGB Intelligence Officer, – 1st Directorate

Major Vladimir Servo –Russian GRU Special Forces Spetsnaz Alpha Group – Seconded to the 1st Directorate KGB

Tamara and Mac Suraj – Tsygankov's housekeeper and her ex- GRU Airborne Special Forces engineering husband, Tsygankov's dacha engineering estate and maintenance manager.

Galena Vorakova – Russian mafia boss running the KGB 'off-book' London operation. Returned after expulsion back to Moscow to London as official declared Cultural Attaché

Leonid and Dimitri Abakumov – KGB enforcers stationed in London.

Third Party Double Agent Players

Jenny Woo – Head of a Triad operation in London.

The British Players

Brigadier Robinson – ex-Guards, now Director of the Secret Services Covert Intelligence Section SIS

Jean (Salomon) Saied – ex-contract mercenary working for Brigadier Robinson, seconded to the SIS

Major Rodney Brown – ex-SAS – Deputy to Brigadier Robinson, Chief Intelligence Officer Covert Intelligence Section SIS

Mr. Reid – ex-SAS/Ordnance, Senior Field Operations Agent Intelligence Officier SIS

Patrick Jones – ex- RMP/Fire Service (Resources and Planning) Intelligence Officer SIS

Graham Swain – ex-Ordnance, Agent (Coordination Field Admin and Logistics) Intelligence Officer SIS

Andrew Harrison – ex-Oman Forces officer (Weapon Contract and Legal Specialist) Intelligence Officer SIS

Ms. Jane Christine – ex-Special Branch/MI5 (Communications and Intelligence Specialist) Agent SIS

Mould – Field – ex-INF Operations Agent Intelligence Officer SIS

Sharky – Field – ex-INF Operations Agent Intelligence Officer Field SIS

Fred Jones – ex-Guards Watcher Field Agent SIS

Lewis Jones – ex-Guards Watcher Field agent SIS

Dr Jules Christian – Department's Forensic Scientist and Man Friday SIS.

Colonel Jimmy Raymond – Royal Army Pay Corps retired – Compliance Officer, Treasury

Mr. John Brown – investment banker and money laundering specialist on loan from the Bank of England

Sgt Laurie Burns – (The Invisible Man or The Ghost) Behind lines off-books freelance operative. (Russian cover name Oleg Nicolai Kowalsky)

Armand – ex-French Special Forces

Sgt George – SAS

The Third Parties Players in support of Brigadier Robinson Covert Operations Section

The General of Special Forces

Colonel George Laurie Handyside – British Army Counterintelligence

Commander Robert Coveney – SO13 Anti-Terrorist Branch London Metropolitan Constabulary

Chief Inspector Christiana – Special Branch

Simon – Somalian warlord, sub-clan tribal chieftain

Carol Windsor – FBI London Liaison Officier

William Murphy – FBI London

Ms. Reid – M16 and SIS liaison officer to Major Brown's team (ex-Royal Signals and Mr. Reid's daughter)

Fate whispers to the Warrior "You cannot withstand the storm!"
The Warrior replied, "I am the storm!"

SPYMASTER MIDAS

Spymaster Series Book Four

PART ONE

Chapter One

The Compliance Man –Ruislip, North London 2000hrs

He looked and dressed like any other largely nameless and unmemorable civil servant in their middle to late fifties. The Colonel was only average height, maybe a little less, at 5 feet 6 inches or thereabouts. His custom was to have his shoe heels lifted, not exactly Cuban heels but more discreet. A touch of vanity, his wife always told him. And which he dismissed. At fifty-five, Colonel Jimmy Raymond, formerly Royal Army Pay Corps, now well retired, held the senior compliance post in the Treasury.

Using compliance as an audit tool to keep the idle, simply lazy, undisciplined, cavalier and unscrupulous, honest and toeing the line was not new. But in this case both the PM and the Chancellor were intent on making a show of it. Small contractors and suppliers were squeezed at contract stewardship meetings and the style between contractors and the officers of the various government contracts agencies was increasingly confrontational. Not pleasant for either side and increasingly the contractors pushed back. They were grown-ups after all and with the exception of the very few, honest and wanting to deliver. After all, contract renewal depended on performance and price. CEOs of companies began to question this new mood of 'us and them' and not a few were balancing the rewards against the hassle.

Colonel Jimmy, himself a cold fish of a man, was not happy with the outcomes he had experienced at contractor meetings. It was small fry in his mind being penalised, he had set his sights high. He was not satisfied; the big fish were not being taken to the cleaners. He knew they were protected and had influence in high places. It became a passion to bring them to heel. Give him his due, he had worked tirelessly and already cracked open one ring of corruption. He had learned to be devious, and it had paid off.

Colonel Jimmy Raymond had never been that popular in the Army. He had served in the Royal Army Pay Corps. The RAPC was a small

Corps of the Army and as such was protective of its promotion pyramid and demographics was paramount. In effect, this meant that someone had to be promoted to fill any post that became vacant. There were in fact very few in the potential pool of officers able to rise to the rank of Colonel to begin with. As the years went by, the many in his peer group dwindled, leaving just him. His contemporaries were either dead or had left the service for more lucrative financial posts in the civilian market which had left the coveted Colonel position open and the promotion slot available.

Raymond was intelligent, no question, and so had easily passed his promotion exams. Rank by rank the slots fell to him in order to enable his Corps to fill the chains of command. Despite his annual confidential reports invariably stating, '*Ready for promotion in his turn or not yet ready*' – a coded message to the promotion board meaning '*never*' – in his case it failed to stop his advancement to Colonel. It was an anomaly. The Colonel Commandant of the Corps was spitting blood when he heard that Raymond, who he thought of as an overbearing little man, had got the promotion. Raymond's arrogance and ignorance blinded him to the put-down when it had been explained to him that whilst he was technically qualified, in fact there had been no one else!

Raymond himself thought that his boat had come in and drove his junior officers and his other subordinates even more and without a jot of empathy. The Colonel Commandant of the Corps could only look on in dismay, hoping against hope that he would leave. Some younger officers said they would swing for him, but they never did. By chance, two years after his promotion, a change in the promotion pyramid affected him adversely when, a number of high-quality younger officers from other regiments and Corps were transferred into the Royal Army Pay Corps. Raymond was first out of the door with a handshake to sweeten the pill. When he had protested, the then Colonel Commandant told him that if he stayed his future was going to be very bleak. His retirement was not an option.

He left and set up house with his family in Ruislip, North London and took the promise of a Civil Service Treasury job in town. Now, six years later, he was the Treasury's new compliance hatchet man; he was good at it and it suited him.

In the Army, his officers and men had called him 'B4'; thankfully, there were not many B4 personnel in the Army. An army recruit, after basic training, will seek a trade and the first step on the career ladder could be a B3, before further training to achieve class B2, B1 etc. He was less than a B3 basic recruit in their eyes. Hence 'B4',which was also a coded name as: one boring, two bombastic, three bumptious and four a bully. Some wag wanted to make him B5, a bastard, as well. Did Raymond know? Of course, he did, well, probably. Did he care? Not very much.

The small band of civil servants now reporting directly to him were not quite so imaginative, they just thought of him as the 'Fat Controller.'

He swept his hand over his balding dome before putting on his hat so that the remaining dark brown hair on each side of his head was disciplined. He strode out of one of the many Treasury buildings and headed for the nearest Underground station.

After a satisfying day at the Treasury – at least in his eyes – he had spent some time after official office hours working on his Ministry laptop. He was astute enough to realise that the report that he had helped compile and that Mrs. Thatcher was reading was a dangerously damning document. He didn't want the evidence to go missing. He organised and created files of all records of his findings, the evidence backing them and the workings on a series of discs, three copies in all.

One copy he would lock away with his laptop in the security cabinet, satisfying the Treasury rules on the clear desk policy. Nothing was to be left out for the curious cleaner, the security guard on his rounds, authorised or otherwise visitor.

The second he put in a double envelope and addressed to himself. He left this with the front desk security guards to hold safe until he arrived next day when he would retrieve it. He simply told them that he was going out for a drink and didn't want to carry the disc with him in a public place. They knew him well and were happy to oblige.

The third he had hidden, taping it securely to the back of the steel locker of one of the men in the office whom he strongly suspected of being in league with the fraudsters he had uncovered. He had no proof, but the man had shown an unnatural interest and curiosity in his work recently. That was unusual as the individual had nothing to do with his Compliance section so that hiding place would be the last place they would search if they came looking. He thought of the saying 'Where do you hide a leaf? In a forest of course.'

The lateness of the day meant that he had an uncrowded and comfortable Tube journey to Ruislip Station. He was pleased with himself and that his precautions in making copies of the damning report would defeat the fraudsters getting at the data and protect himself at the same time.

Alighting from the Tube and making his way to the exit, he melted into the crowds as they flowed in and out of the station entrance like a disturbed ant heap. He checked himself as he passed a shop window. Still trim, at least in his mind, for his slightly below average height, he thought. He was in reality a stocky, short man.

He preferred to walk home in the evenings and to the station in the morning. He ate frugally and seldom drank (except if others were offering food and drink), an all-together tight-fisted, mean, grey man.

For all his relationship failings and the lack of empathy with his fellows, what everyone had to acknowledge was that he was a good family man and that he was both intelligent and clever. He had a first-class degree from Oxford in Maths and Accounting. In another life he could have been an exceptional mathematician. He could have competently held a Finance Director post in any company. Perhaps not in the 'City' though, he would simply not have fitted in. As it was, he could read pages and pages of spreadsheets with the speed of light and dissect the most well-presented account. If it had an error, he would find it, much to the dismay of many an account holder or accountant who may have thought that their efforts were a work of art. The Colonel didn't do art.

He was a godsend to the Treasury. They didn't care that the good Colonel was not a team player or had very limited empathy when dealing with his seniors, peers and juniors, they just wanted his accountant's brain power. Many feared his zeal.

His life as he knew it was about to change.

He developed sophisticated verification software that ran data from one stream against the same data from other sources. This very verification program had in the first instance picked up the massive fraud that was even now on the Prime Minister's mind as she glowered at the gathering of the business great and good at the Mansion House.

The result of his discoveries presented him with a 'get out of jail' card given to him by the two financial guru advisers in No10. To him it was 'pennies from heaven'to be allowed to dig deep into the affairs of the corrupt.

This talent was the one and only the reason he held on to his current post as a senior civil servant, and his growing reputation had made him a natural target for the two Prime Minister's advisors. They saw in him a man who could, with his verification tool, audit the Government Agencies handling Government contracts and their supplying companies. Many of the largest contractors and companies were, on the face of it, apparently robbing the country blind with overspends and delays to deliverables.

An early surprise was a massive army of people double tapping, charging men and materials against one contract and the same men and materials found to be working on multiple others. These findings were to the amazement of many who were not implicated. The heads of Agencies, CEOs and quangos were sworn to secrecy under the disclosure of state secrets on pain of death, by the Prime Minister's advisors. Nevertheless, many of the presumed innocent were quaking in their well-heeled boots giving a truism to the saying, mud sticks!

Despite the need for a covert enquiry, which the advisors had emphasised to Raymond time and time again, his ingrained behaviors made it hard to disguise the real task from others.

Alerted to the Colonel's mission late in the investigation, he was deemed to be a direct threat to those who cheated the Exchequer. To be fair, the bent CEOs, contractors and others had been warned early on about the compliance campaign by a handful of well-placed civil servants who were in hock to them.

In the beginning, the fraudsters in their turn had been confident enough in their cover to continue their activities. 'Too big to be caught' was the mantra.

As for the well-placed servants of the state who were in one way or another crooked, some others were victims of a sort and had simply been corrupted, some were just plain greedy, others had been blackmailed. At the end of the day, they were all betraying the hard-pressed British taxpayer, Queen and country. Colonel Jimmy was on their case.

Eventually, when the fraudsters were alerted to the damning report that was being presented to the Prime Minister later in the day, they set up a hurried mid-afternoon secret meeting of the senior heads of some of the 'miscreant traitors'as the PM was later to call them.

At that meeting was a top Treasury civil servant, Neil Ashchurch, the titular head of the scheme. His advice was to leave the two specialist advisors alone and go for the Colonel who knew as much, if not more, than them. The Colonel was the problem, and the other advisors were lightweights who could be discredited. The Colonel would not be missed and was after all the main instrument of these difficulties. The advisors, it was decided, would be left for Ashchurch to neutralise.

The main decision taken by the team of five men and one woman who led the massive, organised fraud operation, was that the Colonel had to be interrogated to find out how much was in the report, who he had named and what else he knew. Like the Prime Minister they saw the immediate task had to be to limit the damage and cover their tracks.

A parallel and concurrent task was to get hold of the report, any copies and destroy the trails of evidence wherever they led. Task Two would be to see that business resumed.

They had then unanimously agreed that once the Colonel had given them all the intelligence that he possessed he was to be neutralised.

As the retired Colonel left the bustle around Ruislip Station, he began walking briskly until ten minutes later he turned into his road. A sleek, black ministerial-looking car, engine running, drove from where it was parked, moved to meet him and quickly pulled up next to him.

A smartly turned-out younger man jumped out of the car and stopped him with a raised hand.

'Sorry, sir, but you are requested to come with us. I've been told that they need you back at the Treasury urgently.'The man held the rear door open, smiling encouragingly, inviting Raymond to enter the car with a wave of his hand.

The Colonel hesitated, dumbfounded for a moment, looking from the man to the car and to his house some fifty yards away. 'What?'He automatically took a step towards the car and stopped.

'There's a panic on. They need you.'

Whilst this was music to the Colonel's ears, he was still perplexed, this had never happened before. A sudden gust of wind picked up dried leaves in the gutter and from the roadside; they rustled, brushing against his shoes and trousers. He had a sense of foreboding. Was he in trouble?

'Er, my wife...'Raymond began.

'Taken care of, they called in and explained the situation to her.'The man's smile began to slip. 'Now, come on, sir, they are waiting for you.'He then said again, encouragingly, 'It's been a long day and my dinner is waiting for me.'

'Yes, but...'The Colonel took another step towards the open car door, removed his hat, bent his head and raised his leg to get in. He sensed more than felt the man move quickly to his side. He went to straighten up and push back but he was too slow. The man cracked a pistol against Raymond's skull and pushed him inside. Looking round, the man checked that he hadn't been seen by anyone. Clear; the street was dark and empty, and then he followed the dazed Colonel inside the car.

The Colonel was only stunned and began to shake his head to clear his mind. He felt a gun pressed painfully into his side and the man's order somehow reached his still befuddled brain.

'Sit up, shut up, and belt up.'

' Who are you?' The Colonel grimaced, rubbing his head. 'Do you know who I am?'he blustered. 'What do you want of me?'

'Relax, Colonel. Others will answer your questions. What our job is…'he nodded to the chunky thick-necked driver, 'our job is simple. We deliver you. How we do that is up to you, as long as you are alive.'His pleasant Oxford accent had given way to pure Eastern European. 'Now, shut the fuck up. Sit still or I will damage you.'To emphasise his point, he pressed the gun forcibly into the Colonel's side again.

The Colonel winced. Then he sat up straight and stared ahead. He relaxed, taking in the route and set his clever mind to work out how he could escape at the earliest opportunity. He had taken part in enough escape and evasion exercises in the Army to know that it was important to pick an early moment before the enemy had had time to make the capture holding arrangements a fortress with no chance of escape.

They drove northeast until they hit the M25 and then after a while the driver took the exit taking them east towards Chelmsford. Afterwards, the Colonel judged fifteen minutes, they turned south into the countryside before finally turning to the southwest onto a winding unmetalled rutted track.

They stopped the car and the man guarding the Colonel pulled a blindfold from his pocket. He passed his gun to the driver in the front seat and roughly tied the blindfold onto the Colonel. The man retrieved his gun before pressing the barrel under their captive's chin.

'Stay still and you will not get hurt or dead.'

The man nodded to the driver who started the car and drove carefully until they ended up at a dilapidated, isolated farm complex housed in a shallow valley.

The Colonel had taken a series of memory snapshots of his route by looking out of the car window. He also tried to rationalise roughly where he was on his memory map of this part of southern England. He knew the area slightly and so knew approximately where he actually was. Orientation is, even for the Pay Corps, one of the well-honed basic skills every soldier must be proficient in.

The fact that they hadn't blindfolded him until they were on the rough track and the farm complex had come into view was not a great sign that he would be let free anytime soon, if at all. He coldly calculated that his current situation was precarious and his future bleak.

The farmhouse was in poor shape. The rendering was cracked and stained. The roof was sagging and some of the tiles were missing. The windows and doors had not seen a lick of paint for years and the windows were grimed. The farmhouse was supported with decrepit barns, animal pens and some other miscellaneous ramshackle wartime outbuildings. They tumbled the Colonel out of the car into the sudden chill of the night. The cold didn't cover the strong smell of animal detritus.

They made him kneel in the mud among the droppings of the chickens and other beasts and put his hands on his head. He shivered and could hear the squeal of pigs, the lowing of the cattle and squawking poultry settling in for the night.

Two large hunting dogs ran up, barking and snarling aggressively, sniffing at the legs of the two thugs and the Colonel's face. He kept his head down and forced himself not to look at the bloodshot eyes of the hounds; he didn't want to show fear.

He was pulled roughly to his feet and they tested the blindfold around his eyes. It was a token gesture and he knew it. He could see underneath it. He cursed them silently and worried for a moment about his wet knees and the knife edge creases in his trousers which were now destroyed. Foolish, he thought.

What the Colonel saw by squinting from under his blindfold was that a lean countryman whom he took for the farmer had emerged from the farmhouse with a broken shotgun cradled in his arm.

You found him then?'

The voice was gravelly with an Irish lilt. The farmer's face was lined, thin and wasted. His overlong black hair was greasy and streaked with grey. The craggy face showed the ravages of time and whisky. Colonel Jimmy wrinkled his nose as the farmer came close. The farmer smelt unwashed and of cannabis and urine.

The man who had forced Raymond into the car was holding onto the captive and nodded at the Colonel.

'No problems with this one.'

'Good. They just called me tell me that they're sending men down in the next hour or two to question him. Until then, lock him up in there.'He pointed his shotgun to a lone Romney hut forty metres away. The hut was ten metres wide by thirty metres long and four metres in height. The old wartime Romney had originally been painted with black bitumen but now it was badly weathered and rusting corrugated tin sheeting showed underneath.

The farmer gestured with his gun again towards the hut. 'When you've done that, come in for food, it's ready. When you've eaten, you're to disappear until they call for you.'

One man dragged and kicked the reluctant Colonel towards the Romney. It was used as a storage building for machinery, other miscellaneous farm materials and rubbish. It had an acrid smell of stagnation and old spilt diesel. The other man, the driver and the heavier of the two, ran ahead to open the door. Dirty fluorescent lights dimly lit up the interior. Apart from a few rusting chairs and tables, the rear of the hut was almost full of the accumulated junk of years.

The Colonel was forced into a metal chair bolted to a steel upright that formed part of the building's structure. His right hand was handcuffed to the chair and although his blindfold was tightened and readjusted, he found that he could still just see underneath. No one spoke. He listened carefully and heard the men disappear; the door of the hut was slammed shut.

He felt fear, but not despair. The lights were still on so he could take in his surroundings if he raised his head and looked out under the tied blindfold. He was alone in the hut. He confirmed that it was an old, converted wartime Romney. After a moment he decided that it had fallen into serious disrepair.

It was certainly cold and damp with an all-pervading spent diesel smell that assaulted his senses. He was grateful that they had left him with his coat, and he thought he could last at least until the morning without worrying about exposure. Pragmatically, he didn't that think he had that long, he needed to escape as soon as he could. He reminded himself from his military training that the best chance of escape was early in the capture.

He twisted in the chair and stood up. Inexplicably, they had only handcuffed him to one arm of the metal chair so he had a free hand. He assumed that they had thought that they wouldn't be long, or they had simply made a mistake in the rush to get to their dinner. Whatever the reason, he needed to capitalise on it now. The first thing he did was to remove the blindfold with his free hand. He was able to stand easily and put both hands together. He tested the metal arm of the chair using the strength of his arms and hands. It gave a little. He tried again. He used extra leverage by placing his foot on the other arm. He was conscious that the men could be back soon. A cold sweat broke out on his forehead and he could hear his heart thumping.

The metal tubing of the chair frame began to bend more easily as he worked it back and forth. Frantically flexing it backwards and forwards whilst looking over his shoulder all the time, the metal arm began to give way.

As quickly as he could, he continued to attack the rusting metal, up and down, backwards and forwards, desperate now, in a panic until he heard the satisfying sound of it parting. He then bent it so he could release his handcuffed hand by slipping it down the arm's tube. The retired Colonel was sweating profusely, bent over with his hands on his knees, he half-stood, panting. He spent a few seconds listening to hear if his frantic actions had alerted his captors.

With his heart still pounding, dangling the handcuff from one hand, he ran to the door. At the last moment he thought better of it, stopped and went back to the side of the hut near the rear wall.

Desperately he ran round the building checking out the old riveted curved metal panels. Almost immediately he found a loose panel where it had rusted so badly that the rivets were mostly free of the metal sheeting.

It was now only just secured on one side in a few places. The fear of discovery gave him the strength from somewhere deep inside him to bend the wriggly rusting tin sheets back, defeating the overlays which gave the hut its structural strength. He worked the gap, drawing on a strength that he didn't know he still possessed. When the gap was big enough for him to squeeze through, he struggled out but only with difficulty, ripping his coat and trousers and picking up scratches to his hands, forearms and neck, all of which stung. He hoped that his regular Army tetanus jabs would still offer him protection from 'lockjaw'as he thought of it.

Out into the night, heart pounding in his ears, adrenaline running, he was free. Searching his immediate surroundings and trying to decide quickly when he should move and which way his escape route should take him. Certainly, he wanted to be away from the danger of discovery. Unconsciously, his basic military training kicked in. Checking round the corner of the hut, he glanced at the house and saw the lights blazing away in the lower rooms, throwing alternating shadows and light out onto the farmyard.

Decision made, the Colonel would work his way in a large right hand semi-circle to the back of the farmhouse and then strike south. First, he needed to pause for a second or two to choose his moment. The last thing he needed was for the dogs to kick off.

He ducked involuntarily, a reflex action, as he heard a vehicle tortuously making its way down the track to the farm. Headlights bounced off the hedges and at times pierced the night sky. The noise of the vehicle's engine rose and fell. The dogs started up. This was his chance!

He ran.

Chapter Two

The 1989 Issue 10 Downing Street 1800hrs

There was a chill in the room and a silence so profound there seemed to be an all-enveloping shadow being slowly laid on the whole room. Even the highly polished, rich, wood-panelled office of the Prime Minister, normally warmed by its patina, was dulled. It would seem to an observer that both parties in the room were holding their breath. The only movement was the dust that danced in the late afternoon sunlight streaming from the large casement windows into the Prime Minister's roomy office, the dust dancing fuelled by generating gently rising thermals from the central heating.

Mrs. Thatcher sat upright in her studded, high-backed chair, stony-faced, oddly for a moment dwarfed at her large kneehole partner desk. She was white-faced, drained of colour, head down, staring at the dark red leather top of her desk. Her Cabinet Secretary sat in a red club leather chair mirroring her posture, at least as shaken as she was.

But his experience and position meant that he'd ridden out bombshells before, not least the Falklands War and he was already focusing on solutions and options open to them. Mitigation was high on his list as he ran down his mental checklist of things to do.

The Prime Minister was deep in thought. It was not that she was reticent out of fear of upsetting or even alienating big business and organisations which caused her to prevaricate over the report that lay in front of her Cabinet Secretary. She was, for the moment, simply frozen by the shock of it.

It was merely a case, she was thinking, of how she could possibly manage the intelligence that the two independent special Treasury advisers, both Inland Revenue gurus had, in the form of a report marked 'most confidential', slapped on her desk earlier that afternoon.

The Labour Party opposition would crucify her even though the records would clearly show that they were as guilty of overlooking the disaster long before her Tory administration took power. Not only the

Labour Party, she was also thinking about her enemies in her own Party, they would have a field day at her expense.

The report showed in starkly uncompromising clarity that the UK taxpayer had been unknowingly funding billions of pounds of deliberate fraud for the last twenty or more years. The Prime Minister knew that the report would eventually be leaked, she could almost guarantee it. She could just imagine the headlines in the tabloid rags.

She had, after all, she grimly reminded herself, dissenters in her own inner circle of Cabinet Ministers, never mind backbenchers. She could picture the circling cabals of her own grey suits ready to hang her out to dry. No matter that the fraud had been ongoing for as long ago as the recorded investigation had so far shown so graphically.

Her government, which was growing increasingly unpopular, could fall because of it. Hers would be the first head to roll. She moved to stretch her aching muscles and stood, moving to the windows through the dancing dust particles. She took a cursory look outside, wishing for a moment that she could just be an ordinary member of the public and anonymous enough to join the throngs in the busy streets. *Fat chance*, she thought, *what would I do with my handbag?* She smiled before a steel shutter came down on her momentary lightness of mood, but the colour had returned to her face.

She began to slowly pace the floor of her carpeted office in Number Ten Downing Street, hands clenched behind her back, chin jutting forward. She ground her teeth and shook her head slowly from side to side. She used an index finger to run lightly over the surface of her rosewood meeting table, inspecting for dust. Finding none, she moved on. Occasionally she glanced up at the Cabinet Secretary who sat quietly, speed reading the document for a second time.

She glanced at the French clock on the mantelpiece. The face of the ornate clock, a gift from some long-lost French president, blurred as the Prime Minister held back the tears of frustration that suddenly threatened to overwhelm her.

The clock was a favourite of hers and reminded her with some amusement of the matter in 1816 when the Emperor Napoleon Bonaparte had arrived on board a British man-of-war expecting to be given residence in Britain, and she imagined Wellington sitting in this very room insisting to the Admiralty and civil servants that 'Boney' should not land on our soil and instead be exiled to Saint Helena. Ah, those were the days; how she would like to exile a few of her own ministers to such an island!

She fingered and thumbed the double string of pearls round her neck for which she was famous, a sure sign, Sir Geoffrey knew, of her nervousness or angst. He thought in this situation probably angst. At the same time, he discerned that her mood was impenetrable, dark and brooding. The atmosphere seemed to make the late afternoon shadows suddenly lengthen and bring a new gloom to the otherwise normally bright and airy room.

Sir Geoffrey felt someone walk over his grave and shivered. He got up, crossed the room and switched on the lights before returning to his chair. He resumed his study of the document and while he was conscious of his boss still prowling round the room, he ignored the distraction.

When he had finished reading, Sir Geoffrey looked up and softly asked, 'Your first thoughts please, Prime Minister?' He had rarely seen the PM look so angry. Anger was good as far as he was concerned, it meant that his Prime Minister was ready for a fight.

She sighed with exasperation, then growled, 'Geoffrey, how could these miscreants betray their country so blatantly?!' She was not looking for an answer; she gathered herself. 'I want it stopped! Quite apart from me wanting to personally publicly castrate, hang and quarter these people, I want to get the money back. I want all of it,' she added furiously, 'and with interest!'

She suddenly smiled. Her eyes crinkled at the edges as they had alighted on a plate of curling sandwiches and crumbling cakes left on her rosewood table. She picked up a sandwich, sniffing at it before taking a bite. A piece of a tomato shot out of the side, the morsel dropping unnoticed onto the carpet. She picked up another two to take to her desk. Despite her obvious shock the PM was softening. She said with a grin, carefully clearing a crumb from her lip before waving her sandwiches in a defiant gesture, 'Dammit, Geoffrey, I still want to be the PM of the governing Party when this mess is sorted out. I really want my manifesto seen through before I go, and to the letter.'

Uncharacteristically, she slumped back into her high-backed captain's chair. She took her glasses off slowly and gently placed them on the desk. She was back in control, cold, calculating the odds and seeking ways of damage limitation. She finished her snacking and brushed more crumbs from the front of her dress. She looked up with a smile.

Very much the Iron Lady now and thank goodness, thought her Cabinet Secretary. He could hear the gears whirring.

Sir Geoffrey shook his head. 'Big ask, Prime Minister.'He chewed his top lip. 'Assuming that this is all true, it has to be proven and that it isn't some convoluted plot. What we need to do now is to decide how we are going to work through the problem. Who is going to do that, and who is going to be your, or rather our, champion?'

Mrs. Thatcher leaned back in her chair, put her glasses back on. 'I would appreciate your thoughts on just that.' The PM jabbed at the report. She wanted to confirm that she had the Cabinet Secretary's buy in. The PM knew that her Whitehall mandarin was the key to sorting out this problem – if anyone could he would be the man; she needed him on side and fighting for her.

Sir Geoffrey looked at the vintage clock on the mantelpiece that he had seen the PM staring at earlier. 'This problem is a little like your beautiful clock up there. There's an awful lot of camouflage, fluff and ornamentation to clear away before you get at the people and the fraud itself, the very mechanism of it. First, we need a team who can cut through to get the heart of the matter.'He slapped his knees. 'It's getting late and we still have some matters to close out tonight. Let's not get diverted by it this evening. I'll think on it overnight and have our suggested detailed strategy for you to consider first thing in the morning. I'm already thinking of a way forward. How does that suit you?' '

'Early would be good and with your way forward.'

'Yes, Prime Minister, first thing. I'm going to ask the two report authors, Dan and Shaun, to be here, say for seven thirty. We should meet ahead of them at seven. I'll bring Brigadier Robinson. Not I think at this stage the compliance man, a retired Royal Army Pay Corps Colonel who was the first to discover that something was amiss.'He saw the PM brighten at the mention of Brigadier Robinson and smiled to himself and added. 'I think that the Colonel could muddy the waters at this first meeting and it may in any case not be appropriate. Are you OK with that?'

The PM screwed up her eyes and pinched her nose. 'That would be very acceptable to me. Thank you, Sir Geoffrey, you are, as ever, a pool of calm in a storm, and what a storm this is.'

She allowed herself a chuckle. Her Brigadier Robinson and his team as she thought of them, sorted problems that neither the Home Office, M15 nor the Secret Service M16 wanted to handle and/ or were so sensitive that they needed a team that was for all intents and purposes invisible to the powers that be. Above all, they were capable of handling complex issues without a fuss. Mainly comprised of retired soldiers,

Robinson's team was without *'side'*, their loyalty was to themselves and Queen and Country. 'Country'for them also translated into the elected leader of the country, currently the Queen's First Minister, the Right Honourable Mrs. Majorette Thatcher.

'Yes, Prime Minister. Now, let's address today's business as best we can. A half hour should do it. Then you will have some time to yourself, a rare luxury I notice from the diary that your Private Secretary showed me earlier this afternoon. Some time to relax I think, and why not, before your dinner tonight at the Mansion House.'

Sir Geoffrey liked this PM. She was more honest than most, worked hard for her country and most important of all, she listened with attention to her ministers, civil servants and advisors before taking her own decisions, which might or might not coincide with theirs.

He could not have asked for more. 'And may I suggest that any names in this report that are at the dinner tonight you treat with your customary "hail-fellow"? We don't want them going defensive'. He paused. 'Not just yet anyway, and at least some of them may of course be innocent of the charges and may later support us enthusiastically.'He added wryly, 'The innocent will be quick to realise the commercial advantage of doing so, if only,'he added wickedly, 'to eliminate the competition.'

'Sir Geoffrey, that is very perceptive of you. As for giving the game away at dinner tonight, as if! Now, let's get on.' She grinned and mimicked rolling up her sleeves.

Chapter Three

The Colonel Runs

Bending low in a half crouch, Colonel Raymond went wide as he circled the farm complex. He had to take care with his footing on the churned ground surrounding the farmhouse. His leather-soled city shoes skated more than once in the mud and he had to quickstep a few times not to fall over. He then struck south as fast as he could, exploding into the field at as fast a trot as he could manage, his London greatcoat flapping around him.

He headed towards the far lights of the giant Greys industrial park. In the distance he could see the Thurrock Bridge brightly illuminated with the southbound motorway running on and off it. He fancied he could see northbound traffic accelerating out of the Dartford Tunnel. He saw the north and southbound carriageways with traffic over to his quarter right. Traffic on the bridge and from the tunnel was heavy and to him the headlights of the vehicles represented normality. A normality that he desperately wanted to become part of.

The Thurrock Bridge stood out tall against the night sky and the additional lights of the vehicles made it an easy target for him, some four miles to the south he calculated, maybe a little more but not much. He fancied that in the still night air he could hear the rumble of the traffic.

He stumbled through the night as fast as he could, over rough farmland tilled after the winter crops and not yet sown with spring vegetables. Mud glued itself to his shoes and clogged the turn-ups of his pinstripes. The tails of his heavy London overcoat were soon caked with mud and it all combined to weigh him down. After about half an hour, tiring now from his frantic burst of energy, he felt the adrenaline rush dip. He made for the edges of another field. Here the going was firmer underfoot and he began to move faster.

He now kept to the edges of any woods and fields he passed; he was learning fast. He thought that he saw golf links on his right. He felt a pang of disappointment as the club house seemed to be in darkness, but he let it go, no help there. He crossed Fen Lane and then into the wilds again.

The large well-lit town of South Ockendon came up on his right. The Colonel made a beeline for it to seek help. Somehow, exhausted, he conjured up a new urgency. He was not so naïve to think that they hadn't discovered his escape by now and would be out, looking for him.

He smiled to himself at the shock they would have experienced when they discovered he had escaped. He glanced around and dropped to the ground. His night vision was by now well established. A sixth sense told him that this was a time of maximum danger.

He needed a moment to think. In the distance he heard dogs. They were tracking him. 'Fuck!' His brain went into overdrive. He shrugged off his coat, throwing it into the field as far as he could. Then he was up running, stumbling, gasping for breath. Without the weight of the coat, he began to make distance. But without it he felt the chill of the wind against the sweat on his body. He pulled the lapels of his suit jacket up and bent his head down, seeking to warm his ears. It had been a long time since he had jogged. *Never mind, just bloody run!* he told himself. His lungs burnt with the effort, his heart pounded and his breathing became more and more laboured. He took great gulps of air, his throat burned. He broke out in a fresh sweat. Raymond could feel his legs cramping, trembling with the effort and the insidious inevitability of weakness creeping upon him.

Dragging up memories he suddenly remembered the old sergeant beasting and yelling at him when he was a young officer cadet. 'When you can't go any further, say to yourselves as you take your next steps: left-right, left- right! It's all in the mind. Keep the rhythm going. Move, you idle man. Left-right, left-right.' The memory gave him hope and he pressed on. He was now in 'rag order' but he didn't care, he felt buoyed, lightheaded, as he repeated the old mantra. 'Left-right, left-right!'

Now he could just see the bright lights of a petrol station on the B186, maybe a mile away. He turned right, took a chance and headed straight for it.

Suddenly he was unexpectedly falling, silently and into blackness. He didn't know why; he couldn't understand what was happening. He was in freefall. Was it a heart attack? He twisted round in the air, scrabbling in a panic for a hold. Something, anything he could grab at. As he tumbled, his feet hit something solid. It jarred his body through to his spine. As he tumbled head over heels his mind's eye registered the edges of a gigantic crater against the night sky. His racing brain rationalised that he had fallen into a large quarry as his feet again suddenly hit a scree slope. He was going too fast to gain traction; his heavy body overtook his racing legs. He saw large rocks pass him as he continued to tumble, praying that he wouldn't collide with one. His legs collapsed and he catherine-wheeled the last dozen feet down to the floor of the quarry. He lay immobile as if dead, winded and gasping for breath.

It took a minute for the initial shock to wear off. Shaking all over, whether from the fall or the chill of the night he didn't know or care. He gingerly moved his limbs, one by one. *Lucky; nothing seems to be broken* was the thought that flashed through his mind, but there was pain where long unused muscles had been stretched and pulled. His head and chest hurt. He blinked to clear his vision; there was sticky blood covering one of his eyes. Shakily, he wiped it away with a trembling hand and carefully felt his head for the source of the bleeding. The blood seemed to be coming from a gash on the side.

He found a large flap of skin with some of his thinning hair. It was bleeding badly and by now he had a splitting headache. He screwed up his eyes in pain. He used his handkerchief to hold the flap of skin against his scalp to staunch the flow of blood. He knew head wounds bled a lot, so he wasn't unduly worried, just annoyed at his bad luck.

Next, he took stock of his suit. The trousers were both ripped at the knees and his white legs protruded. The Colonel sat up and twisted round, taking in his immediate surroundings. At the same time, he could hear the dogs getting closer.

The farmer jogged easily over the fields following his dogs, loping ahead to the point where the Colonel had discarded his coat. The dogs milled around, smelling the ground and the air before they resumed following the trail of scent on the ground, baying as they picked up the scent again and increased their speed.

The noise of the dogs made the Colonel look round desperately for something, anything, to hide in.

Raymond saw a pile of rusty corrugated metal sheets and beams strewn close by outlined in the mud. The sheets and timber were from a long-abandoned and collapsed site hut. He crawled over to the pile, then with desperate urgency but as silently and carefully as possible he crawled under them to hide himself from his pursuers. Puddles of water and mud lay underneath the pile and Raymond cursed his luck.

The farmer caught up with his dogs milling around the lip of the quarry. They had lost the scent. The dogs sniffed the air, turned and followed the man's faint airborne traces blowing west to east but it was uncertain, and they soon lost interest in the hunt. They mooched around round seeking other game – rabbits perhaps or a juicy pheasant.

The farmer angrily called them to heel, walked to the edge and looked down. The quarry was in shadow, dark and uninviting. He switched on the torch strapped to the barrel of his shotgun and swept the beam down the quarry slopes and floor. His beam passed over the pile of metal sheets where momentarily the Colonel tensed, frozen as the light shone through the fixing holes in the metal sheets. He stopped breathing until the beam swept over him and on.

The man grunted and switched off his torch; there was no evidence that the Colonel had climbed into the quarry. Why would he? Resigned, he accepted that the prisoner may well have passed this way but he was probably even now somewhere in South Ockendon raising the alarm.

His priority was to see to his own future and hang the others. He had to get his own story straight for the authorities. At the end of the day, he had his farm and animals to care for; they couldn't look after themselves. If he had any feelings of empathy at all it was for his dogs and his livestock – as far as he was concerned, the human race were less than nothing.

He had a plan. He would say that he had been forced into the situation. He would think of the 'how' they did it and 'why' he had agreed. He would have to make the story life-threatening, maybe a threat of poisoning the animals and land.

He grunted as he thought of the men from London. Idiots! They had got back into the cars as soon as they had discovered that the Colonel had gone, but not before the man sent to interrogate the prisoner had cursed the incompetence of the two abductors, promising them dire consequences. The farmer turned, jogged, retracing his steps back to the farm. The dogs ran effortlessly by his side, enjoying this unscheduled late-night excursion, barking at the darkness.

The Colonel, pent up with nerves and adrenaline, sensed that the farmer and his dogs had gone. He listened to the barking fading into the distance, back the way they had come. He ran his hands over his skull and felt around his head wound. The flow of blood had all but stopped but it still oozed and was congealing into a jelly on the side of his head.

The night was cool, almost cold, but he didn't believe that either the loss of blood or the loss of his coat would lead to exposure before the sun rose. Looking at his watch first light was still many hours away. He began to worry as his clothes were muddy and wet and they only added to his misery. He knew that wind, cold and wet would be the enemy overnight.

The sweat from his frantic dash and the unaccustomed exercise was now drying, adding to the chill he felt creeping into his bones. He needed to seek shelter at the far side of the quarry to laager up. He hoped that he could wait there for an opportunity to make a dash for safety.

He stumbled across the alien landscape, strewn with the rocks and detritus of the working quarry. More than once on his drunken progress across the quarry Raymond only just avoided stepping or falling into pools of water of unknown depth. The sharp outline of a structure loomed out of the darkness a few hundred yards away. It was the hut like shape that caught his eye. Suddenly buoyed by the prospect of shelter and more, he made his way slowly towards it as best as his poor physical state would allow.

The hut was raised on cement blocks and was a large modern Portacabin. He tried the door but the cabin was locked. Cursing, he scrabbled round for something to help him break in. There was a skip nearby with rubbish in it and he found some sawn-off scaffold poles. He made short work of smashing the lock and made an entry into the hut. The door opened inwards. He jammed a chair under the internal handle to prevent anyone else following him in.

He stumbled around. The red standby lights on the hut's radiators were his first focus of attention. He turned the radiator thermostats fully up and immediately felt a dusty heat envelop the space. Next, he found a sink and running water. There were tea bags, sugar and a kettle. He boiled the kettle and having found the makings he made a brew.

He didn't dare put a light on, but with some further exploration in the gloom of the cabin he found a working site phone on the manager's desk. The presence of the phone calmed him for the first time that evening. It was a lifeline out of his predicament and a way back into civilisation. He dialled 999.

While he waited for the police, he sat on the floor nursing his hot drink, trying to rationalise what had happened to him and why. Even in his mildly fuddled state he fought the idea that it was something to do with the fraud he had uncovered.

He was in denial but only for a moment – he realised that the knowledge he held on file and in his head was dangerous for many people. Would people kill to protect their investments? On balance he thought that they might.

The flashing blue lights of a police car bounced round the cabin and the Colonel struggled to his feet. When he judged that the police had found him, he switched the cabin lights on and opened the door. He all but fell out of the entrance in his eagerness to meet them. The police car parked up and two officers got out, looking round and then back at the dishevelled figure that shambled towards them.

'Help me please; I was kidnapped. I escaped but I'm injured and in a mess.'

One of the policemen, Jimmy Howell, moved towards the Colonel and shone his torch on him. He was shocked at the state of the man. He was checking if the Colonel was a rough sleeper but the damage to his head and the overall state of the man convinced him that he had suffered a crime.

'Not looking too good, sir. Let's get you into the hut and sort you out, shall we?' He took the Colonel's arm and helped him back into the cabin.

The other policeman joined him shortly afterwards. 'I checked around Jim, there's nothing out there. I've got the triage pack.' He looked at the Colonel. 'Who do we have here?'

Colonel Jimmy sparked up. 'I am Colonel Raymond, working for the Treasury. I did a report, it is very sensitive, and I now believe that it led to me being kidnapped. They locked me up in a farm hut about three or four miles to the north of here. I managed to escape; they did chase me with dogs but I fell into the quarry. I lost them then, found this hut to hide in and called you.'

The first officer Jimmy Howell, a Sergeant, scrutinised him. 'Well, Colonel, the first thing we have to do is clean you up and get that head wound attended to. And in view of the work you do I'm going to phone up an old boss of mine. He is in Special Branch and I think that this is going to land on his desk anyway.'

'Thank you. I think that would be best.' Colonel Jimmy could not keep the sense of relief out of his voice.

Sergeant Jimmy Howell turned to his partner. 'Open the first aid kit and clean up the Colonel and get his wounds disinfected while I phone Commander Coveney to get a heads up on the way forward.' He had a thought and called after his partner. 'Just tell the desk that we are investigating and will get back to them. Let's keep the identity of our man here between ourselves for the moment.' He got a nod.

Chapter Four

The Other Running Man

At first light, the Ministry Jaguar, originally beautifully valeted, with well-padded black leather seats, darkened windows, midnight-black paintwork and containing two men, pulled in and parked in the empty beach car park. They could see out of the tinted windows but nobody could see in. They had found the car a pure a joy to drive, floating at high speeds like the high-end, powerful limousine that it was.

Sharky groaned as he saw the crumbs and other debris that both he and Mould were leaving on the seats and in the footwells. They had stocked up on drinks, crisps and sandwiches for the journey and the remnants were all too evident.

Mould just shrugged. 'Nothing that the boys in the Ministry garage like more than a challenge when it comes to a valet.' He grunted. 'It's the only excitement they ever get.'

Both men looked around. The beach car park at Perranporth was empty, covered in sand that had blown in from the storm overnight. Litter was strewn around from the car park waste bins that had been tossed in the wind and rolled, spewing their contents.

They climbed out and stretched themselves. Overall, it had been a good drive from London, fast with little traffic, but it had still taken five hours adding in the two stops to replenish their rations and grab coffee.

Chilly in the early morning sea mist after the warmth and comfort of the Jaguar, they shook themselves to get their circulation moving, then shrugged on their bulky bomber jackets, which were ideal for hiding the shoulder holsters with loaded short recoil-operated, locked-breech loading automatic Glocks and two spare full magazines in pouches apiece.

Before they moved off to the west, Mould went to the boot and grabbed a day sack containing the Major's necessities. Keeping the beach on their left they picked up a small lane, Ramoth Way. The lane ran alongside the shore, separated from the beach by a humped sand dune. The lane gently climbed as the dune gave way first to rocks and then to a low cliff. The cliff was capped with a line of old fishing and labourers' cottages. They made for the last cottage before the lane petered out and the ragged track took over leading to the moor and the western high cliffs at the headland of the bay.

The detached cottage they were after was larger than the others. It was made up of two modest semi-detached fishermen's cottages, now extended further by adding a two-storey comfortable dwelling. Slate-roofed and whitewashed, it was well maintained. A very desirable residence, both men judged as they approached it.

The secluded house had a large, tanked, reinforced cellar for use as a safe room. Above ground, the rooms had bullet proof windows and two large picture windows which looked out to sea. The cottage had a seven-metre garden which ringed the property. The beach was a further ten metres away with a rocky cliff escarpment which dropped precipitously fifteen metres to a rock-strewn beach. The rocks led onto the sandy bay. A two-and-a-half-metre high solid, stout and difficult to climb fence around three sides of the cottage kept tourists and ramblers from accidentally stumbling too close to the property. The fence also prevented anyone looking in at the lower rooms, which was in any case made difficult by impenetrable grey bomb blast lace-curtained windows.

Special Operations Officer Sharky, the leaner of the two, rang the bell while long-time partner Mould looked outward and back along the Ramoth Way. The door was opened by a tall woman in her early sixties. Still upright and surprisingly for this time of the morning fully dressed, her short, grey hair framed her face with an urchin cut that was nevertheless well-groomed. A touch of makeup emphasised her high cheek bones, intelligent dark eyes and full shaped mouth. There was a hint of amusement on her lips.

'I wondered who they would send for him. The terrible twins,'she said and followed her rhetorical statement with 'Come in.' The voice was cultured, no accent, a little husky and all the better for that.

The two men entered, bowing their heads to get under the low lintel of the front door.

'Hi Jane, you look well. Suits you down here?'Mould commented.

'Love it and I'm staying. I've been promised that this safe house is mine until I retire, with an option to buy. Got it in writing too. I'm just waiting for a policy to mature, this year in fact, before I pounce.'She laughed.

'Good for you. Is he up?'Sharky questioned.

'Up and out for his morning trot on the beach. He should be back in a short while. He runs every morning for an hour, sometimes more.' Jane gestured to the kitchen. 'What can I get you? Tea, coffee, breakfast? You look as though you've been up all night.'

Sharky smiled. 'That's about right. Tea for me and yes please, a full English. All we had on the journey was some gross travelers 'fodder.

Mould said, 'Happen, same, same, but I think I'll go and meet him. Which way does he normally come in?'

'Usually from the beach, then up into the car park and a last 100-yard sprint along the lane. Well, a fast jog anyway.' Jane thought for a moment.' 'He's in good shape now. It stretched my nursing knowledge in the beginning, but with the help of the company doctor the difficult phase thankfully, whilst intense, was short.' She clasped her hands one on each of the forearms of the men.

'Mentally he's strong, doesn't have flashbacks or any of that crap, but you both need to take it easy with him. Just occasionally he gets really pissed off and I'm not sure if it's as a result of breaking up with Julia or if he's just heaved off at collecting another scare to add to his score.' She hesitated. 'I'm forgetting that neither of you have seen him for months.' She paused. 'Well, the face healed well after the plastic surgeons did a near invisible mend. Sure, if you look you can see the faint line of the scar from his right chin running through to his eyebrow. Lucky boy, eh?' There was a hint of her almost long forgotten Belfast accent. 'He could so easily have lost an eye if the bullet had been a couple of millimetres lower or deeper.'

'Probably just needs some action to get him sorted out.' Sharky stated seriously. 'We're here to collect him and get him back in the saddle with an offer he can't refuse.' Sharkey paused. 'Or so we've been told. We shall see.'

Mould slapped Sharky on the shoulder. 'Right mate, I'll go and get him, you can help Jane lay the table and get the meal.'

When they were alone Jane asked how Mould was and about Mr. Reid as well.

'Mould...' Sharky mused, 'absolutely fine, got a steel plate in his head, which he claims he gets the BBC breaking through on. I call him "receptor", others have other names. As for Mr. Reid, the bullet that broke his arm made him a bit miserable for a while. In his case more than miserable.' Jane laughed before Sharky pushed on. 'I actually thought that he was feeling sorry for himself. He blamed himself for the terrorist shooting us up. But it turned out what he was really pissed off about was that his wounds bled out over his new suit which Mrs. Reid had just bought him. He just soldiers on but I know he misses the Major.'

'Well, Sharky, he needs to be careful for what he wishes for. A wound like the Majors can change a man.' She shrugged, lightening the moment. 'What do I know? Come on, let's sort the breakfast.'

Mould stood on the sand, earth and rock mound below the car park. The mound stretched out leading down to a wide expanse of wind-driven beach. The sun's rays stabbed the sky. The orb of the sun itself was still just below the horizon. The rays lit up the base of the clouds racing towards him. He could see in this late pre-dawn a mile or more up the bay and the stark cliffs of the western headland to his right. To his left and east he saw the eastern headland and town perched on it. To the east the cliffs climbed from the beach to high craggy cliff faces framing the land to the left. To his front a jumble of black rock formations rose out of the sand. He watched the rising sea reach round them. The sea swirled round them and then losing strength was rapidly sucked back to the ocean, disappearing behind the largest of the rocks. He stretched his eyes to the horizon, the dark sea far out and despite the rays of the sun now sparkling on it, the water still looked glacial. Mould shuddered and wrapped his coat around himself. He turned up his collar and shrunk his neck into it, shivering for a moment.

He could just make out a runner maybe half a mile or more to his right, jogging slowly in and out of the tidemark as the sea flowed up the beach and then rushed back to be engulfed in the pounding surf. The runner sidestepping the wavelets, a game? Where the retreating water met the incoming tide, the water was turbulent. The water was then whipped into white foam that the wind blew up the beach as spindrift before it lost its frothiness. The following waves crashed down on the retreating water. Thumping down, sending up plumes of spray before the force of the tide forced the sea to race up the beach again. The whole wild circular process of the following sea, the surf and the receding tide repeated itself, repeatedly over and over again. A relentless motion. Mould was spellbound, feeling exhilarated and, in that moment, envied Rodney his recuperation in such a setting.

Mould continued to watch the sea, fascinated. He was distracted for a moment as a stray dog wandered onto the car park and nosed amongst the spilled bins and their scattered contents. Mould studied the dog; it was an old boy that for its own part studiously ignored Mould. It had straggling, matted and mainly grey hair & was thin at the hips – probably renal problems, Mould thought. He felt a pang of sympathy as he watched the dog dig into the rubbish. With a characteristic toss of its head, it clamped its jaws on a discarded fish and chip meal and disappeared into scrub to his left as two seagulls landed nearby. Noisily, the seagulls crowded the dog in the hope that they could steal the mutt's meal.

Mould shrugged, he felt sympathy for the hound but knew he couldn't do anything to change the situation. He grinned as he imagined the scene if he decided to adopt it and took it home, or better still into the office; his other half would have him committed and worse still, Mr. Reid would probably have him put down and keep the dog! He struck a match, cupped it in his hand and with difficulty lit a Hamlet cigar in the breeze, tasting the sweet acrid smoke at last and feeling the kick of the nicotine. He felt warmer in the smoke although the nicotine dropped his body temperature by a degree.

The onshore wind blew the smoke into his eyes, making them water. By the time his eyes had cleared, the runner on the beach had disappeared. Bewildered and disorientated, slightly concerned that he'd lost his target, he searched the beach, quartering it left to right until he found his man. Mould let his breath out, relieved.

The man, Mould could now determine in the growing light, was definitely the Major. Major Rodney Brown was sitting on the big rock formation two hundred yards to his front, looking back at him, arms folded over his chest. Mould raised his arm uncertainly in welcome. The man detached himself from the rocks and jogged effortlessly towards him. Mould could not make out the customary limp from a bullet wound that had dogged the Major for years.

Rodney grinned as he came up to Mould and gave him a bear hug, lifting his six-foot frame of sixteen stone and some, effortlessly off the ground.

'It's bloody good to see you, Mould. Mr. Reid tells me that you're fighting fit.'

'Yeah, well,'he said, embarrassed, pulling his ruffled jacket back over his gun before taking off his woolly hat and tapping his skull. 'Mr. R is now calling me Metal Micky. As ever, he's all heart.'He shook Rodney's hand. 'You look pretty fit yourself judging from the way you were chasing around the tide and racing up and down the foreshore?'It was a question.

'Got to say, mate, I'm fitter now than I have been for twenty years or more. I've even almost lost my old limp. But am I ready for work? Not sure.'Rodney pondered that thought and gazed back at the beach. 'I'm not sure that I really want to leave here for a while.'His mood darkened for a moment, and then lightened as he smiled and added, 'I've taken up board surfing too, and I'm not bad at it.'He was suddenly enthusiastic. Rodney jumped into a standing surfer position.

Mould laughed. 'Well, that's tough, Boss. Sorry to be a damp squib on your hopes to become a beach bum because Sharky and I have orders to get you back to London PDQ.'

Rodney was uncharacteristically annoyed. 'Bollocks. I can't for the life of me see what the team can't handle without me?'he quizzed his junior intelligence operations officer.

'Clearly the Iron Lady doesn't agree with you.'Mould said gently.

It took a moment for Rodney to work out who Mould was talking about.

'What? Are you sure? You mean, it was actually herself that asked for me?'Rodney was torn, half disbelieving. He was an ardent fan of the PM.

'Yes, herself no less, she wants the team together. And, I might add – yesterday!'Mould emphasised, at the same time indicating the path and road to the house. 'Breakfast is waiting and time's wasting. We have a chopper arriving at the local golf course in an hour or two. It's a pain that they couldn't get us a flight down, it's a real flog from London by car even in that beast.'Mould pointed at the Jaguar, pinched his cigar and put the unsmoked half back in the packet.

'Waste not, eh?'Rodney studied Mould. 'What's the panic?'

'The missus has rationed me. Come on, I'm starving.'Mould added. 'As for what the panic is about, I haven't a clue. The Brigadier just said to Mr. Reid late last night,"Fetch Major Brown. I want him in my office by lunch time. How you do it is up to you." The Brigadier did tell Mr. Reid that if you hesitated, we were to tell you it has come from Mrs. T.'He grinned. 'And Mr. Reid also said if you tried to wriggle out of the summons, he would make your, and more importantly our, life hell.'

'Interesting, so what's new?'He didn't expect an answer; Rodney was intrigued even though he knew that Mould wouldn't know. Reluctantly he sighed, regretting his outburst. 'Sorry mate, better get sorted then, eh?'

Chapter Five

Brigadier General Tsygankov

General Tsygankov was to work in the dacha's winery with Mac. Mac was the General's ex-Russian special-forces estate manager cum-maintenance engineer and sometime minder. Earlier that morning they had decided that now was the time to sample the oak barrels holding last year's wine, prior to its possible bottling.

There had been much discussion between them about when to bottle the wine. Mac lent towards waiting till June to give the wine more time to oxidise in the barrels. Tsygankov favoured bottling sooner rather than later. So, they had decided to sample the barrels that morning and let the wine speak for itself.

They slid back the full-height doors on the low-roofed warehouse, pushed back the heavy translucent plastic thermal curtains that swung closed behind them and surveyed the contents. The warehouse was well insulated and kept at a constant temperature. Large fans lazily circulated the cooled air. It had been a great harvest. Barrels ran two deep both on the left and right the whole length of the building, leaving a broad walkway down the centre. Plenty of room to quadruple the holdings by double stacking if there was ever a need.

The General continued to be amazed at what he and Mac had achieved in the few years they had been at the dacha. His greatest regret was that he hadn't begun this venture as a younger man. He sighed, but then he thought that he wouldn't have had the money to do the building and renovations on the house and grounds. With a shake of the head, pragmatic as ever, he turned with a smile to join Mac.

'Shall we start on the left and work round the barrels clockwise, sampling every fourth barrel and see how far we get before we fall over or your wife calls us into lunch?'

'Tamara has promised us a lunch heavy enough to sober us up.'

Mac went to the first barrel, wriggled out the cork and used a thief to draw a quantity of wine. He released a small measure of the wine into two wine glasses held by Tsygankov and a quantity into a tall slim measuring jar, just enough to float the hydrometer. Mac let the rest of the wine out of the thief, dropping it back into the barrel under gravity and then banged the bung back in.

They looked at the wine in the light that streamed through the translucent curtains and roof lights; it was blood-red and heavy in the glass. They swirled the glass to release the aroma, smelled the wine and took their first sip. The wine was full-bodied with a hint of blackberry at the back of the throat. Long on the lingering tasting. Ideal.

Tsygankov waited for Mac to pronounce.

'Got to be said, General, this vintage is a triumph, even if I may say so.'

'Not bad at all.' The General was grinning, obviously delighted. 'Let's test the gravity and alcohol content.' Mac took the thieved quantity in the sampling vessel and readied the hydrometer. Tsygankov took the privilege of spinning the hydrometer. They eagerly waited for it to stop bobbing and settle, giving the reading. This translated into a specific gravity that gave a content of 14.4% alcohol. They were both silent for a while; this was a great result.

'Well, Mac, do we bottle and sell some or leave it for another month or two?'

'Hmm; certainly, we could bottle and sell right now. Still, can I suggest that we bottle this left side now, subject to sampling the rest? Then leave the right-hand side of the store for another two months. That way we can compare the early bottling with the later. It could give us a marker for the future.'

'Tell you what, Mac, let's hedge our bets even further. Bottle the left rows now. Then in three months' time bottle the first row on the right and then in the following three months bottle the second row. Just in time for this year's harvest.'

'I like that idea. It spreads the work of bottling all the wine at once and the risk if I'm wrong!' Mac spread his arms. 'And now, my General, let us sample the rest of this harvest.'

The sampling began in earnest. They sampled, swirled, smelt and tasted. The collection of glasses used to sample grew, laid out on a wooden bench in the order of the barrels. Tsygankov had followed Mac round with another thief, drawing out enough wine to fill his measuring jar with the hydrometer to check the specific gravity. He made a careful note of the reading against the barrel number and then poured the drawn-off wine back into each barrel and replaced the bung.

It had been a great year for the grapes. They had got to the point in the tasting when the heavy wine was beginning to take its toll, congratulating each other on the new wine as it made them heady, when Tamara, Mac's wife and the Brigadier's cook and housekeeper, interrupted.

Tamara told the General that he had a call from England which he needed to take. She giggled as she saw that the two men were clearly beginning to wobble.

'General, you need to sober up anyway, take five and deal with this call. The Englishman sounds in a panic.'

The General headed for his study, clearing his head as he went. He span his study chair and sat down. He took out paper and pen before he lifted the phone.

'Tsygankov.'

'General, this is Neil Ashchurch. We have a problem.'

Brigadier General Carl Tsygankov didn't like Neil Ashchurch as a human being. He thought him greedy, an upper-class snob and unprincipled to boot, the sort of Englishman he would go a long way to avoid.

'Mr. Ashchurch, I am retired. I don't have problems, only opportunities these days.'

Ashchurch rode over the General's comment. 'We understand that, but we were hoping you might at least call the centre and alert them. We could do with a liaison officer who we can deal with and support us whilst we sort this mess. The goons we have been allocated for enforcement are not what we need at this time.' Neil waited for the General to respond.

The General was annoyed and he was abrupt with Ashchurch. 'I am busy, so make it short and to the point.'

'Thank you. I am grateful for your valuable time. We have a Treasury compliance officer, a retired colonel. He has got into the very heart of our business and drilled down into the fine details of our operations. He, along with two cabinet advisors, put together a damning report which may even now be with the Cabinet Office. We kidnapped the Colonel to find out where the report actually went and what was in it. We lifted him around eight last night and by ten he had escaped. He has been missing for over twelve hours now.' He paused for breath. 'I secured his laptop and disc but they are encrypted and we are working on that, but I am worried.'

Tsygankov swore under his breath. 'Listen; and listen well. I am retired and I will not get involved, but I will call the centre. They will no doubt contact you after my call. Until they do, in the interim, I want you to ensure that the Colonel is found. Get what you can from him and then get rid of him. The two advisors I think on balance should disappear permanently too. Above all, get hold of the report and that means recalling any stray copies that may have been distributed. Then, after you have analysed the contents, make the necessary adjustments to nullify and discredit any issue that it raises. I am sure the centre will want that action from you at the very least.'He paused to make a few notes. 'I don't need to tell you that the operation was important to Moscow for the intelligence that was collected. Whether that is still the case I don't know and the money was useful in its own right. You need a liaison officer. Use Galena, she's in London."He paused to let the second veiled threat sink in. 'I am not, repeat not, involved anymore. I am retired and you knew that, so I am not sure why you called me and not the centre. Consider me unavailable to you and your team with immediate effect. There is no margin in it for me now that I am retired and I don't intend to get involved. Is that understood?'

From the quietly insistent manner that the General had used Ashchurch was now under no illusions that his future was in the balance, if not his and the lives of others. 'Yes, General.'

'Then let us hope for all your sakes that the laptop you are trying to break into contains the report. I expect that you'll need to secure the advisors' laptops too. So, get that sorted out.''He paused. 'Expedite. I will call the centre so expect a call. Message me when you have resolved this mess, as a matter of courtesy only. If you fail, don't bother.'

He got up and gently cradled the phone. He stood for a few moments, thinking the problem through. He knuckled the top of his desk. Not a real problem for him. He was, after all, not involved anymore but did justly receive a share of the booty from time to time when the centre thought it prudent. He didn't need the money and often wondered why he was still on the payroll, probably a gift from Polyakov?

More perplexing was why they had phoned him and not Moscow. But he would need to speak to General Polyakov to make sure his friend wouldn't be exposed if the report came to light. It was important to give General Polyakov the opportunity to grip the Moscow and London teams to get them to bury the problem. He mused, 'Definitely not a problem for me, just an unnecessary diversion.'

He lifted the phone and spoke to Polyakov. Typically, his response was what would be expected, and he was, as ever, the perfect gentleman. Polyakov listened patiently to his old friend without interruption. He took a moment to think and then put his old General at his ease.

'Just leave this to me, Carl, and get on with your retirement.' He laughed. 'I think that we'll find that someone got too greedy. A pity really, it's been a great scam and helped out our Divisional budget on occasion; not a great deal of money but a gentle domestic income and a lot of foreign currency in world banks is always welcome. It was too good a scam to last forever. I've constantly been amazed that the Brits and the others, bless them, haven't twigged the frauds before now.'

Polyakov sat in his office twirling his silver pen between his thumb and forefinger. He watched it as it shone in the reflected sunlight. It had been a gift from his mistress, who was his personal assistant. He smiled to himself, he was a lucky man when all was said and done. He cleared his throat and addressed the problem, thinking through and bouncing his thoughts off his friend. 'The truth is, Carl, that in the overall scheme of things the return for effort with the British after everyone has had their cut, is now not that great compared with the past and diminishing I am told by the team running the fraud. You know, time moves on as does the world and politics. It may be that this could just throw up an opportunity to help the Brits out, in exchange for a bigger prize for us of course, by closing down this operation. I need to think and discuss this with my immediate team and then the chairman. I will, as Ashchurch asked, get one of my people to call him and send a fixer to help him, although I may have someone in play there already, your friend and mine, the beautiful Galena Vorakova.' He heard Tsygankov chuckle. Polyakov concluded the exchange by asking, 'And what, my dear friend Brigadier General, are you up to today?'

'Truth is, my dear General Polyakov, Mac and I are sampling before bottling this year's wine. It is exceptional I promise you. Will you come and drink some with me? Your partner is always welcome too, or would you like a case sent to you?'

'Carl, both offers are of course welcome! A case of wine, if imminent, would be appreciated. As for a visit, we'd love to as soon as I can clear my desk, which may sadly be a month or two. It's just manic at the moment, as you know.'

'A case will be with you within the week. As for busy, since I retired, I haven't had a day off yet!'His dry humour brought a guffaw from Polyakov as he, the Moscow KGB chief of the First Directorate, gently placed his phone down, cutting the contact.

For his own part, General Tsygankov knew that Polyakov would run with the problem and he dismissed it from his mind. 'And now, let's get back to my wine.'

Chapter Six

Major Brown and the Brigadier

Mould and Sharky dropped Rodney at the entrance to Thames House. Before going in, Major Rodney Brown looked at the entrance steps where he had been gunned down six months earlier. He shuddered, tracing the scar slowly from his jaw to the eye. Then he shrugged and squared his shoulders as he remembered the shooting. *Shit happens*. He dismissed the memory.

At the security desk he was welcomed back with smiles from all the staff who knew him well. They asked after his health, and he assured them that he was absolutely fine and glad to be back, even if inside he was still not sure that he wanted to be there.

He had to disengage, excusing himself with handshakes and a smile, claiming truthfully that he was due at a meeting and couldn't be late.

At twelve o'clock midday he knocked on the door of Brigadier Robinson's office.

Unusually for him he felt a moment of nervousness and hesitation. It had almost been six months, but still. He took a deep breath, put a smile on his face and entered.

The Brigadier hadn't changed a bit since Rodney had seen him last – if anything Rodney thought that he looked slightly fuller in the face. When the Brigadier looked up, he grinned and stood up.

'Damn good to have you back, Major.'

He came out from behind his desk, grabbed Rodney by the shoulders and scrutinised him for a moment. He noticed that his deputy looked trim and fit as well as tanned.

'They tell me that you're fully repaired. But we both know that physical wellbeing is not the whole story.' He held Rodney's gaze. The Brigadier thought that he detected something in Rodney's eyes, a flicker perhaps, but it passed quickly and Rodney's quiet stare was impenetrable.

Rodney said seriously, 'I'm fine, sir. It wasn't the first knock I've had, and I don't expect that it will be the last.' He grinned, putting Brigadier Robinson at ease.

Robinson dropped his arms from Rodney's shoulders, turned and returned to his desk. 'Bring up a chair; we have much to talk about and a lot of ground to cover. I've asked Mr. Reid to join us at twelve thirty with food and drink, but I need to talk to you about Servo and Saied before he arrives.'

He reached into his desk and pulled out a bottle of single malt and two glasses. He poured two generous doubles and handed Rodney a glass.

'Hope that it's not too early for you but I thought that we deserved it. You especially for what you did.' He toasted Rodney, adding, 'You're looking awfully trim and fit, Rodney. Clearly the Cornish life suited you.'

Rodney could not help laughing gently. 'You could say that, sir and I have to say that I have very reluctantly relinquished my beach, surfboard and Jane's ministrations to be here.'

Brigadier Robinson frowned. 'An understatement, I suspect.' He raised his glass once more. 'Missed your sense of humour this last half year, Rodney.' He unlocked and opened his drawer, took out Rodney's logbook and spun it across the desk with a pen and pencil. 'You're going to need this.'

Rodney took the book, studied the cover for a moment and flicked it open to a new page.

'What's the panic, sir?'

'Well, Rodney.' He hesitated. 'But first I do need you to tell me again that you are ready, in every regard, to return to the fray?' Robinson was if nothing astute and knew his staff. He was still troubled after reading Jane's last report that, while she felt Rodney was physically A1, she was mildly concerned about his mental wellbeing and motivations but only in the context he had, albeit short, quiet and moody unexplained distant moments.

Rodney sipped his drink and dropped his head. 'I have got to say that I am stronger and fitter now than before the incident. Mentally I don't believe that I have any issue that would stop me resuming my duties and responsibilities. But do I want to return? That is really the question that I've been wondering myself on the trip back up here. Just that, nothing else, sir. I do enjoy my time and the lifestyle in Cornwall, perhaps a little too much. I even learnt to surf.' He smiled and paused 'As the French might say: "l'herbe est toujours plus verte ailleurs".

Robinson was still, upright in his chair. 'The grass is always greener. Apt. What was your answer to that question, Rodney?'

'I'm in.' What else could he say?

Robinson, finally convinced, let out a whoop, grinning. 'In that case Rodney, please pick up your pen!'

He shuffled some files on his desk until he found the one for Servo, the Russian Spetsnaz Major who had been turned by the promise that he and his partner, the talented Major Carla Kazimira Tskhovbova, would find a welcome in England at the right moment.

Opening the front cover of Servo's file, he began. 'Rodney, I picked up and ran with Servo after you were injured. Only three points of note. He earned his freedom by silencing the IRA quartermaster as you requested. You can get the Jones brothers to tell you when and how it was done. Second, Servo then initially went to Tsygankov's dacha before being recalled to Moscow. Thirdly, he knows that you are on the mend and awaits your contact as and when. Carla and Servo may well be able to help us on this mission as I can't believe that the Russians haven't orchestrated this problem we have somehow. I feel it in my water. They are both at the heart of the First Directorate and have access to data we may need. And they may just earn their freedom and get that first-class British Airways one-way ticket in the process.'

He reshuffled his files. 'As for Saied, well, like you he's up and running and delighted with his new multi role. Today he is lecturing to a final term of young officers at Sandhurst. He's adopted us with zeal. I think that for the first time in his life he feels that he belongs and is at home.

'It's amazing what he brought to the tables of the Secret Services, Special Forces, even GCHQ. The man is an encyclopedia of terrorist and other dissident organisations; their structures, peoples, capabilities and aims. On that, he rocked us with a few revelations which SIS is still checking out.

'At our request he retains contacts with many of his past masters. We are getting more current intelligence from him than we could have wished for. For all that, he remains below the horizon, incognito, adopting multiple identities. As for the various guises he maintains, he's a chameleon. Technically he works out of a MI5 cell that runs a small group of people like him.

'You were right, Rodney; he is an excellent leader and team player. He's on the books and, he tells me, looking forward to his Civil Service pension in due time. I was able to get him a dozen years' seniority and pension credit which he was really grateful for. He said that you and I have given him a sense of security he has never experienced before.'

Robinson continued, laughing. 'He gave a talk to the heads of sections for both of the Secret Service organisations, dressed in a full burka outfit to start with. He terrified them with his revelations; I'm told that they left the lecture more motivated than they had been since leaving training school. Russia, thank goodness, believes so far that he died of his wounds. He had, by the way, a splendid funeral.' The Brigadier pulled his files together, put them into his desk drawer and locked it. They would go into his safe later.

Rodney commented, 'Good for him.'It was enough for him that he had four Russian assets under control – Saied here in the UK and three others in play at the heart of the Russian Security Services: Servo, Carla and Vasily. Vasily was so deep in cover that Rodney wondered if he would be of any use until he decided to come out.

'I'm delighted, of course, that it's worked out for Saied.' He finished his whisky. 'And now to this business that was important enough to call me back from my adopted paradise. Mould and Sharky had no details at all, so I guess that it's sensitive?'

'Let's wait for Mr. Reid, he's due about now. I can brief you both at the same time and bring you up to speed. It goes without saying that the team can't wait for you to return to the section. So be ready to ward off the mob! I need about an hour to tell you what's what, and then you can go and sort yourself out.

'On the domestic front I sent Graham and a facilities team to your flat overnight to clean it throughout and re-stock your fridge, check the utilities etc. You should be able to walk in and function immediately.'

Rodney was surprised and grateful. 'Thank you. I was wondering about the state of the flat.' They had arranged to have his mail forwarded when he was in convalescence so on that front he was up to date. 'It was very good of you to fix that for me.'

'Not at all, Mr. Reid insisted.' Robinson grunted, before grinning.

There was a knock on the door.

'And here he is, I think?'

Chapter Seven

The Task Ahead

After a delighted Mr. Reid had joined Robinson and Rodney, the food and tea and coffee arrived on a trolley in short order.

There was much to catch up on between the three men and the consumption of the food and the refills of tea and coffee meant that it was a good hour before they got to the main point of the meeting.

Robinson held up his hands. 'OK, let us move on to the issue that had me recall Rodney at this time.' He turned to Mr. Reid. 'This is in no way a slight to you, for I couldn't have wished for a more able deputy in the Major's absence.'

Mr. Reid waved the Brigadier's compliment away. 'A pleasure, and in truth we've had a pretty light six months.'

'Thank you, appreciated nevertheless.'The Brigadier cleared the cups and plates off his desk so that they had a clear field to work on. 'We've been given a massive task to do from the PM and Cabinet Secretary. I will go into it in some detail but before that let's hear from Mr. Reid about Colonel Raymond.' He turned to Mr. Reid. 'The floor is yours.'

Mr. Reid opened his notes, glanced at them once and began.

'A most curious case. Well before two this morning, I got a call from Commander Bob Coveney, Special Branch who we all know only too well.' Reid checked his notes. 'The Essex police had had a call from a Colonel Raymond, claiming to be a key member of the Treasury, who had been kidnapped yesterday evening. He had been held hostage for a short while before he managed to escape. He was chased and had made his way to a quarry that he fell into. He had lost his pursuers and wanted help. Two local Essex policemen who responded to his call soon realised that the good Colonel was indeed in some trouble and was who he claimed he was. They gave him some immediate first aid to a head wound and called in the situation. The police sergeant at the scene called Bob. Both he and his Chief Inspector on duty had worked for Bob in the past; they made a quick appreciation that the situation needed sensitivity, so alerting Bob was a good call. Bob was assuming that the kidnap was likely to be terrorist-related but he wasn't sure. Bob immediately alerted me. Between us we agreed that they should bring the Colonel in and to me. He is enjoying medical aid and our hospitality in one of our secure guest rooms in the cellars on level one.'

Reid looked at his notes again before looking up. 'After we patched him up further, I interviewed him.' He related the Colonel's story.' Here is what I've done so far. I got the Colonel to mark up a map of the area that he had been taken to and we identified the farm where he was held. I've sent the Jones boys, Pat and some of Bob's men to search and interview the farmer if he's still there. Their brief was to find out the names of the other men involved. I persuaded the Colonel to talk to his wife and get her to disappear for a couple of weeks to friends until we sort things out. She was very cooperative, must be that Army wife thing. Bob sent her a couple of men to help her sort herself out.'

Reid hesitated. 'His initially default was to claim that he can't work out why he was taken. Not sure that he completely believed that himself. He seemed to be reluctant to acknowledge the reason even to himself, so it has to be sensitive. He mumbled something about a report but wouldn't elaborate. He's an arrogant little bugger and strangely innocent. But, more positively, he agreed to spend a night and some with us to recuperate and for us to get to the bottom of this.'

The Brigadier held up a hand to stop Reid going on. 'I think that I can fill in the gaps. Here's the problem and it's one that we have to solve; only God knows how!'

He began by telling them of his early morning meeting with the Cabinet Secretary and Mrs. Thatcher and the report on the fraud and money laundering prosecuted by a plethora of individuals and organisations. He told them of the two advisors, Dan and Shaun, who had put the report together but were only able to do so with the Colonel's valuable input. 'In truth, I suspect that the Colonel found all the evidence and they used it. As you say, the Colonel's character would have led him to be flattered by the attentions of the two special advisers. I suspect that the Colonel is our ace in the hole.'

Rodney and Reid looked at each other, mesmerised by the revelations.

'Of course!' exclaimed Reid. 'They kidnapped him to find out about the report and what was in it.'

'Yes, correct, and now we have him.'Robinson said. 'They must be worried sick and they'll try again unless we defuse the situation in his case.'

'Could be that the two advisors are in danger too. 'Rodney put in. He looked at Mr. Reid who nodded his agreement. 'We'd better get them undercover after this meeting.'Reid made a note on his legal pad.

Reid looked up. 'Vis-à-vis the Colonel, my gut instinct told me that it might be something serious. As a precaution, until we know the extent of the threat to him, the Colonel has been confined with a multiple button-coded locked door to his room. It has a new code which only I, Andrew and Graham have at this time and the nurse housekeeper, whom I trust.'He gave the code to Rodney on a slip of paper. Rodney scrambled it and put the number in his logbook. Reid continued. 'I have also posted two guards in the corridor of Level One for the next twenty-four hours. They have a list of four names – that's us three and Andrew Harrison. Nobody else is to be admitted, outside of the housekeeper nurse. They will be escorted by one of the guards when they enter the suite. I also told them that food or medication had to be tested on the provider. That should deter any attempt on the Colonel, at least for a while.'

Rodney was scribbling in his logbook as he listened to the Brigadier and Reid add depth and colour to the situation. Both men fell silent; he finished making a list of questions and other notes before addressing the Brigadier. He ran his hand through his unruly hair, a gesture the other two knew well.

'First, do we have a copy of this report?'

'Yes, but it is supposed to stay in my safe except when we study it. Extracts can be taken but only data specifically relating to the operational task. This is a hypersensitive task that we've been given and I promised herself that we would only release intelligence to the team in order to achieve the mission.' He pulled the report out from his desk and slid it over to them. 'It is well written, short and concise, backed with a large number of annexes detailing the evidence. But, having read the report, it seems to me that its contents are only the tip of an iceberg in the context of the mission facing us.'

Rodney and Reid groaned. They had been here before and this was going to be a nightmare to resolve, considering the constraints.

Both men spent ten minutes speed reading the report and its findings. When they had finished it took a moment or two for them to rationalise what they had read. Rodney stirred first.

Rodney pursed his lips. 'Seems to me that we need a quick success – get some low hanging fruit picked, plucked and in our basket. But at the same time, I'm not rushing into this as we need to shape the team for this mission. Having said all that, I would like to get three actions underway immediately – first, secure the two advisors, this to be executed after this meeting, this will give us a breathing space; second, I want the Banker in on this, working with Pat and Andrew apropos the accounts stuff. I want our trusty Captain Freire to get GCHQ to monitor any calls out of the Treasury that relate to the Colonel within the hour, let's say from two o'clock. And I want to put our Colonel in play tomorrow morning, even better, if he's up to it, this afternoon and see who reacts to his reappearance.'

'Interesting gameplay, Rodney. I just wonder if it's premature?'Robinson looked worried.

'I thought about that, but on balance it's the way to go. At the moment they are on the back foot. We might just get an early result that gives us a lead into the labyrinth that we are going to have to negotiate. We just need to find one plump, corrupt, unsuspecting individual or individuals to get us in the game and we can begin to unzip the fraud cartels.'

Robinson immediately saw the plus points of Rodney's idea. 'All right Rodney, let's do it. Have you thought about how you're going to protect the Colonel?'

Rodney looked at Mr. Reid. 'I suppose that we could get our men disguised as contractors doing something meaningful around the Colonel while he sits benignly at his desk, acting normal. Let's say that we put him in play and then bring him back here. In reality, all he has to do for a few hours is to act as though nothing has happened and make up some story about the wound on his head. Or we could simply mind him for a quick visit to get whatever he needs from his office.' He turned to the Brigadier, giving Reid time to work out what to do. 'Are the SIS Directors in play? We need them to clear it for Captain Freire to stand up GCHQ.'

Robinson responded, 'The Cabinet Secretary briefed them this morning. I'll handle them and Freire.'

'OK,'Reid said, grinning. 'I'll set up the minders to escort the Colonel in and out of his workplace, quick time. Let's keep it simple. The Royal Corp of Signals motto meets the need. Certo Ceta. Be Sure and Swift. Bit like our Major Rodney on his surfboard, so I hear.' His Scots accent was strong, and he inclined his head and gave Rodney a knowing wink, raising a finger to the eye and holding the eyelid down for a second.

'Freire is going to be impressed that you've taken the trouble to remember her Corps motto.'Rodney countered, hoping to move the game on.

' Good to have you back, Rodney.'Reid closed down the exchange. They all laughed.

'Thank you both. That frees me up to shape a plan and to speak to the Banker and then get him in. I will, sir, need him to analyse the annexes along with Andrew and Pat. Are you OK with that?' His boss nodded.

Rodney continued. 'I would like to see Graham and the Colonel immediately. I need to reacquaint myself with my office, if I still have one?'He glanced at Mr. Reid.

Reid laughed. 'Oh yes, it's waiting for you, never fear. It has been repainted, dusted and bulled to within an inch of its life; they even found you some new furniture and pictures, so hope you like the team's choices. I was thinking of turning it into a conference room for a while, but the team nearly lynched me.'

Rodney grunted. 'Good for them! Now, on balance, I want you, Mr. Reid, if you're free and Andrew with me when I see the Colonel and I think that I would like to do that as soon as we have finished here. Then I need to see Graham, go home sooner or later and shake the moths out of my wardrobe.'

The Brigadier stood and shook his deputy's hand. 'Good to have you back. OK, Rodney, off you go. Leave Mr. Reid and myself to sort out the arrangements. Shouldn't take long and then Mr. Reid can rejoin you shortly.'

Mr. Reid flourished the code for the Colonel's suite again. Rodney studied the alphanumeric code and nodded to Mr. Reid.

'Thank you, got it. Full team meeting tomorrow or maybe later today even.'Mr. Reid made a note. Rodney shook their hands and added a throw away remark. 'Good to have a mission to keep me off the street.'

Brigadier Robinson responded seriously. 'Well, collectively I remind you that you need to be careful what you wish for!'

Chapter Eight

The Major and the Colonel

Rodney went from the Brigadier's office to the main office to meet the team and to collect Andrew. As it was, it took Rodney a while to extricate himself from the well-wishers and he could only do so by promising to return after he'd seen the Colonel. He beckoned to Andrew to join him and together they made their way down in the lift to the underground suite of cells and accommodation.

When they entered the Colonel's suite of rooms he was sitting at the desk, writing. He looked up, clearly annoyed at the interruption.

'Yes? And you are?'

Rodney and Andrew calmly introduced themselves to him. They were two old hands, quite used to handling difficult people. Rodney immediately understood Mr. Reid's description of the man as being both arrogant and with an over-inflated sense of his own self-importance. Rodney very much wanted the Colonel on side and took the unusual step of asking him if he wanted to be referred to as 'Mr. Raymond, sir, Colonel or your Christian name, Jimmy?' Rodney added, 'You are going to see a lot of us so a less formal arrangement would be preferred.'

The Colonel looked from Rodney to Andrew, both still standing and dominating the room. Summing them up, he was he decided, not in the best position to demand anything. His quick brain sought a solution.

'Why don't you choose?'

'In that case,' Rodney smiled, 'we'll call you Colonel Jimmy. How's that? Sort of makes you one of the team.'

'That will do.' Secretly Raymond was pleased. It still had an element of respect for his rank and at the same time he felt that after last night he wanted to be part of a team. 'What can I do for you?'

Good start, thought Rodney, and Andrew allowed himself a silent *Well done, Boss.*'

'What I would like to know first is how are you in yourself? Are you up to helping me this afternoon?'

'Well, as you can see, I'm a bit battered, certainly stiff as hell and sore, but OK in myself. Tell me what you want.'

Rodney studied him. 'I should think that your laptop is with them by now. Did you secure the information on the frauds elsewhere in some other way?' He waited for the Colonel to answer.

'I did take precautions so that should my work be lost stolen or corrupted I could resurrect it in its entirety. Before leaving the office last night, I ensured this by backing it up in a couple of different ways. I am glad that I did, I had no idea that they would go to such lengths to get hold of it.' He paused. 'Or, as I now realise, my life was and probably still is in real danger.'

'How do we get hold of the information you've saved?' Andrew asked, joining in the conversation for the first time.

'I did three backups. One I hid as a disc in the office where no one would think to look; one I locked away in my steel locker – that one, I expect, is long gone along with my laptop. As I left the building, I gave the third one to security to hold it for me until I got in today. The files are encrypted so that only I can unlock them as far as I know.' The Colonels shoulders slumped and he stared at the floor. 'I suppose that you want me to go and retrieve the information?'

'Not alone, but yes. What I want them to see is you walk into the Ministry, bold as brass, collect the information and leave. Just be a "hail fellow well met"to anyone who wants to talk to you. Let them know that you had an accident last night but you're fine. Give nothing away about your ordeal, pretend that it simply didn't happen. Andrew will go with you and there will be others, armed and dangerous, close by. You can say that Andrew is a cousin or whatever and is with you because of the head injury to drive you about today.'

'So, when is this all to happen?' Colonel Jimmy wanted to know.

'Well, Colonel Jimmy, I see it like this. Due to your unexpected escape – well done on that by the way, they'll be nervous and on the back foot. They have no idea where you are or who, if anyone, you might have spoken to. Your family home is deserted, you can be sure that they've checked and will continue to do so. Andrew tells me that Special Branch have eyes on your house 24/7. I am told whoever and whenever they show interest in your property, whether by driving by to check your house or physically on the ground doing close target reconnaissance, they'll be sorted, one way or another.'

Rodney let the information about the care they were taking to protect him sink in. 'My team is being updated regularly from our trusted partners in Special Branch. I'm waiting any minute to hear when we have a tap set up on the Ministry for any call that mentions or alludes to your good self, as soon as that is confirmed, we go. So, now it's time for you to get ready to go with my team and retrieve the data.'

Rodney turned and spoke to Andrew. 'Phone upstairs and find out if we have the communications sorted and ask Mr. Reid if he would pop round and get the disc left with security, I am a little concerned that it might go missing.' Andrew left the room.

Rodney, left alone with the man, looked at 'Colonel Jimmy'as he now thought of him. He looked in fairly good nick despite his ordeal. The clothes that he'd been given were smart enough not to attract attention. He had on dark blue trousers with a white shirt and blue crew jumper and his shoes had been dried and polished. He would find an overcoat for him and Rodney decided that that would do. He grinned at the Colonel.

'Just think of the consternation you'll cause when you march in. I would certainly like to be a fly on the wall when you do. They are going to be out of their minds with worry. And it might be of some, even if small, immediate grim satisfaction for you. Revenge is best taken cold and I give you my word you that you will get it that in spades in due course.'

The Colonel studied Rodney. He saw a man in the prime of his life, radiating an inner strength. He knew that he could trust this man.

'OK, Rodney, let's do this. Sooner sorted, sooner mended.' He allowed himself a sigh and half smile and held out his hand. Rodney took it. To Rodney this simple action meant that the Colonel was on board.

Andrew knocked on the door before entering.

'OK, Mr. Reid is on his way. The phone tap is set up and our favourite Captain, now Major, is managing that from GCHQ but will travel to us ASAP and switch the monitoring over to here. She promises to be here this afternoon with a half a dozen of her trusted staff. So,' Andrew turned to the Colonel and said, 'Colonel Jimmy, would you follow me please?' It was a command.

'Andrew, grab an overcoat on your way out for Colonel Jimmy just to give him a bit more cred. Who do you have with you?'

'The Jones boys are back from the farm so I have them. Mould and Sharky went with Mr. Reid. The three of them are going to wait for us at the Treasury so we'll have plenty of cover on the way back.'

'All armed?' Rodney queried.

'All armed.'

'Will I be armed?' the Colonel asked anxiously, looking at Rodney.

Rodney smiled, understanding the desire as an ex-soldier to have his weapon – or maybe not in this case.

'Not today, Colonel Jimmy, but we'll check you out on the range over the next few days which I'll sort for you. As part our team, as of now, you need to be in a position to protect yourself and others as long as you are in danger and in our care.' This explanation seemed to calm the Colonel.

Andrew drew the Colonel away and left Rodney in the suite, pondering the task ahead. He ordered his priorities. He must get hold of the Banker and then talk to Graham et al.; he just knew that this task was going to be a bitch of a mission. He couldn't yet see a clear way forward. But strangely enough he could imagine the shape of the two large rooms that made up the team's operation base on the first floor of the MI5 building and how he would arrange the cells of disciplines he would need in there. What they were going to do he had, at this stage, no idea.

Chapter Nine

Graham's Control Centre

Back upstairs, Rodney joined the members of the team that were not out on the hunt for the Colonel's data. Only Pat Jones, Andrew's sidekick on many missions, Laurie Burns alias 'the Ghost'and Graham were fussing about in the control room, re-ordering the IT, desks and battle boards.

'Tea, Boss?'Laurie asked Rodney when he entered the large double room.

'Definitely, Laurie. Thank you, and I think that my energy levels just crashed so I'd like something sweet, biscuits or cake, to get on with it,'Rodney replied.

'No change there then.'Graham gave a small chuckle, before asking the question on all their minds. 'Good to see you and you're looking mega fit too. So, Rodney, what have you got us into this time?'

Pat was equally pleased to see the Major. 'It has, in truth, been a little pedestrian without you rattling around the place and it's time that we had a mission to test us out.' He put his hands flat on the table, jutted his chin forward and looked around at those present. 'Think that I'm rusting up. So, I hope that it's going to be something challenging. We suspect that it must be for the Brigadier to think it necessary to recall you away from sun, sea, sand and the beautiful lady Jane.' Rodney blushed red at the mention of Jane's name. The blush did not go unnoticed but was not commented on out of respect for Jane and their boss.

Laurie Burns, alias the Ghost, was not so inhibited. 'Hope it is, or my boss will think that I've got another girl on the books,' he called out loudly as he was heading for the team's kitchen area.

Rodney waved Laurie off. 'He and Pat are right about one thing, this mission has the potential to be at best difficult, at worst way above our capability. That reminds me, Graham, can you get the Banker on the phone?'

'No problem. Short code 25.'He grabbed the phone on the desk, selected the number and waited for it to ring before passing over the handset.

The phone rang only once before it was picked up. The Banker answered with a 'Can I help you?' Rodney recognised the gravelly voice with its slight Dublin burr.

'Good afternoon, Mr. Brown. This is the Major, wishing you well and asking for your help.'

The Banker, John Brown, chuckled.

'Ah, Rodney my son, all mended, are we? Back in circulation are you, and causing me trouble again?'

'Could say that, Sir. I've been given a task way outside my experience. I simply don't have the expertise and can't even begin to grasp the ramifications and labyrinth of dark avenues this mission promises to lead the team and myself into. 'He searched for the right phrase to win over the Banker. He kept it simple. 'I really need your help.'

'You have my attention Rodney, that's for sure.'He was serious. 'Want to tell me what's it's all about?'

'Would you consider attending the team briefing at eight tomorrow morning?'

'I would consider it, if you gave me something. I take it for granted that it's sensitive.'

'Suffice to say that it's very sensitive. I can tell you that it involves fraud and also, I'm convinced, money laundering on an unimaginable scale.' Graham, Pat and Laurie let out a collective if polite gasp.

'I'll be there at eight. Don't disappoint me.'The Banker cut the call.

'Your tea and cakes, boss, as ordered.'Laurie, standing behind the Major, held out the tea tray. Rodney thanked him. He liked the fact that Laurie had not only found a variety pack of half a dozen small cakes, but also made him a pot of tea, not just a mug. He took the tray and walked to a desk at the rear of the main operations room, setting it down and calling over the team members who were present.

'Join me for a heads up.'

He opened his logbook whilst Graham, Pat and Laurie took their seats and looked on. 'And now, gentlemen, here are my initial thoughts.'

He took his time, running his left hand through his unruly hair. It was overlong and now, streaked fair and bleached from the action of sun and sea, made him look like a refugee from Bondi Beach. Six months' exposure to the salt-laden Cornish sea air, with his daily runs and surfing, had tanned him and he looked to the team fit and ready for action.

'Graham, I need two things from you. First, prepare for a full team briefing at eight tomorrow morning, second, rejig this main room for a mission and prepare the adjoining room for the Banker. '

'Plus, I need to add, the annex room, now the Banker's room needs to be got ready for...' He stopped to compute in his mind a possible force led by the Colonel and John Brown and the resources needed. 'I don't know, let's say for up to eight bodies, maybe ten. They'll need desks, phones and IT linked to our own intranet. Plus, I think, one long wall completely corked and whitewashed. Three sets of free-standing whiteboards and pads, marker pens, SOP. Can you get it done for tomorrow?'

Graham pulled his lower lip. 'Sure. It might be possible. Not doing anything tonight, Laurie, Pat?' Laurie grinned and Pat leant back in his chair, putting his hands behind his head.

'I'm in too,' he said.

Rodney continued. 'Secondly, I think that we will need, even at this early stage, lockdown security 24/7 and a communication, co-ordination and admin cell. Freire will join us later this afternoon and needs space for six running into your admin and co-ordination cell. The signallers can help you set up.'

He gave them a moment to digest his requests. 'Just retracing what I said on the ops, team, bear with me. I want, if possible, an area for the operational field team in here. Stick them in one corner of the room running along the wall, so that they don't get under our feet. If they become a distraction then stick them in my office when they are just hanging around awaiting tasking. I want at all costs to avoid them becoming disconnected from developments as we move forward and they need access to the intelligence gatherers. And we need a conference table not too far from Laurie's food stall.' He moved on, on a roll now.

'So, apart from that, Pat, the area next door prepped for probably two to four analysts, with yourself, Andrew, the Banker John Brown and Colonel Jimmy. Also plan for two consultants and so that's my eight. In your team is Colonel Jimmy. Currently, and until this is over, he will live in the guest suite downstairs. It's likely that two consultants, Dan and Shaun, are going to be guests too. More on Colonel Jimmy later. Suffice to say that he is the key to this mission. He's not the most loveable cove and will likely need a lot of attention, so, in a word, high maintenance. TLC from you all. Make him a team member. Graham,

Colonel Jimmy needs a code name for external communications etc. etc.'

'Hmm. I think Midas would be appropriate as a code name?'Graham looked round for approval.

'Good choice Graham, make it happen please.'Rodney thought that the name said it all.

'Here in this room.'Rodney waved his hands around the fenced off conference and quiet area. 'A desk, conference table and ten chairs, one for me too, all as far away as possible from the action. Think that that's enough for now, don't you?'Rodney finished off.

Next, he turned his attention to Laurie Burns. 'Laurie, I don't know what you're still doing here when you should be in Baku with your wife but I assume that you have an excuse?'

'Yep. Not guilty. Got a call from Mr. Reid last night, to my wife, not to me, you notice. He had a word with the Boss lady herself who gave me straight off a four-week leave pass. She's busy anyway with several acquisitions so here I am. I flew in on the early BA flight this morning.'He shrugged his shoulders. 'Here to serve, no charge to the Crown.'

'We'll see about that. I was always taught that a man is worth his hire.'He sipped his tea. 'As you're here, immediate task – set me up the 24/7 hot food supply. Add a sandwich and high-energy snack bar. Rationing for all the team from early tomorrow, starting with full English for everyone at the briefing. Might use you initially for liaison between field ops and Graham's communication and admin team and yes, his other staff, analysts etc. I see the analysts as having a major role digging into people's backgrounds, the companies they work for etc., etc. You all know the score.'He got a nod from Laurie. 'We'll see.'

Rodney turned to Pat. 'Pat, I don't need to tell you what's wanted but I do want you to work with Mr. Reid when he gets back. Hopefully he'll have the data discs and set up some laptops in your area. Say five, no six, linked by an intranet for information sharing in your adjoining room. No access to outside networks at this stage please, but we'll review that edict tomorrow.

'Amendment, new item. Add a separate single PC linked to MI5 and a single PC at this time and link it to GCHQ. Major Freire can advise. Graham, in your room please add two secure stations for the purpose of getting on the internet, mail etc., password and key-controlled. Freire will sort herself out but may need support and will be arriving at the run and will be operational later this afternoon. All of you, get some sort of feel for what's coming and what we have to do about it.'

The team were scribbling frantically in their report books. Rodney gave them a moment.

Graham said to Rodney as an aside, 'Freire spoke to me. I'm putting her and her team up at my house and Laurie will join us. Laurie will sort out soldiers'comforts for her and her team. Food and refreshments etc.'

'Thanks for that; what a team. Now for Colonel Jimmy. Pat, as I said, he is both your and Andrew's baby and he is to be escorted everywhere with at least two armed men. I also want him checked out on the range and we will arm him as and when, Pat please fix. My reading is that he's in real danger, they've already had one go and it suggests that he's on our enemy's hit list.'Rodney looked at the three men at the table. He could see that they, like him, were now switched on. They had an enemy and they could understand that. He continued. 'Add to our Colonel Jimmy the two special advisors Dan and Shaun who worked with him. I want them out of danger and installed in the same secure accommodation. OK so far?'

Pat was scribbling madly in his logbook. 'Stop, Boss, let me get my head round this.'He scanned his notes for a minute. 'OK, sorted. We need to crack on if we're to get this done by eight tomorrow morning.'

Graham had been taking it all in and like the rest knew that now was not the time to ask questions. He waved to the team.

'Well, guys, help me rearrange the centre; sooner started, sooner finished as Rodney said. Main room – ops, admin, field team, conference and Rodney's area and soldiers'comfort-food counter. Side room is for Pat et al. Think, Pat, that we'll want the walls dedicated to organisations, individuals and track and trace. Let's break out the battle boards etc., while we have time. When the rest get back, they can pitch in too. Cry Harry and Saint George; game on!'

They left Rodney to his tea, cake and biscuits. He watched his men begin to reorganise the rooms at warp speed. He wanted time to scribble in his logbook and sketch out the forthcoming operations. How he was going to execute them, he wasn't sure yet. But, he thought, reordering the team's rooms in the way he had asked for would be a good start. Feet on the ground and all that. Most of all, he needed to speak to Mr. Reid. He took out his mobile and called him.

'How are we doing?'

'Good so far. I got the disc from the security staff but only after some minor hassle. Tell you about it later. Andrew has just arrived with the

Colonel in the armoured Land Rover and is in the building with him now. We are going to huddle around the entrance and make sure the Colonel makes it safely from the entrance to the protection of the Rover. The targets are bound to have eyes on, but they're not obvious or we'd have seen them. Speak later.' Reid cut the call.

Rodney stared at the phone. He wanted to go home, sort himself out and prepare for tomorrow but his sense of duty meant that he needed to wait for Mr. Reid and Colonel Jimmy to get back or he would not be able to rest easy.

To fill his time and to get out of the team's hair, as he waited, he decided that it was time to see Dr Jules Christian, the section's scientist, to prepare him for the mission ahead and how he might fit into the operation. Another area he needed to sort out with the Brigadier was trusted bodies.

Colonel Jimmy and the two consultant gurus would understand the organisations of the HMRC, the Treasury, the Paymaster General and any ministries or Government Agencies of whatever shape, size or status that had the authority to sign off work and authorise payments.

He felt that he needed to understand the systems and organisations in his own way. It would be another life changing, vertical learning curve challenge for him.

Chapter Ten

Mr. Reid sorts a problem.

Mr. Reid had had little trouble bouncing the security guards at number 11 Downing Street into action. When they prevaricated, he had his SIS identity card and a note from Colonel Jimmy. Flanked by the two silent, intimidating figures of Mould and Sharky when they began to shuffle their feet and limber up, the guards could not comply soon enough. Mr. Reid took the envelope offered by the building's Sergeant at Arms with a good grace and started to examine the package.

True to form, the Colonel had signed over the joins of the envelope before sealing the edges with inch-wide Sellotape. Reid examined it closely and was satisfied that it hadn't been tampered with. He tore open the outer envelope and found the inner envelope intact and similarly sealed. 'Careful man, our Colonel.'Reid approved. He tore the cover to check that the disc with the Colonel's signature on it was intact. Reid wrapped the disc in the torn envelope and tucked it away in his inside jacket pocket.

'All in order sir, the Colonel isn't ill, is he? Or is he in trouble?'The Sergeant at Arms bounced on his toes and rocked back forwards and forwards on the balls of his feet. He inquired more curiously than anything else.

Mr. Reid decided to be kind to him and forthcoming. 'Yes, thank you. All is in order, Sergeant. The Colonel is in rude health, if a little bruised, but not in trouble.'

Confidentially, the Sergeant at Arms added, 'He's a strange cove, not, as you might say, open to a friendly word or welcome.'His accent was strongly West Country. He shook his head. 'We had a chief like that once, when I was in the Commandos. Stingy, aloof, greedy bastard had a heart attack on a battle run. He'd overstuffed himself with our steaks one breakfast time before the run, or so they say.'

Reid allowed himself a laugh. He held out his hand, which was taken.

'My two men and I are going to hang around outside for a while. Some more of my men will arrive shortly with the Colonel and I'd appreciate it if you could get them in and out as quickly as possible. Would you have time to escort them through to his office to speed the visit? The rest of your men should stay alert until we have gone for good.'

'Expecting trouble, sir?'

'Hope not, could be though. Nevertheless, let's hope for the best and plan for the worst.'Mr. Reid's Scottish accent was stronger now and Mould and Sharky shared a grin which drew a scowl from Reid. 'Let's go.'

On the steps of the Treasury, Reid took pole point duty on the top of the steps so that he had good visibility over Hyde Park, the building to the left and the road to the right. He sent Mould across the road to cover back to the Treasury and the road left and right. Sharky, he sent down the steps to patrol his left and right on this side of the road.

The three men had just settled when a bulletproof armoured Land Rover pulled up and the Jones brothers climbed out, followed by the Colonel and Andrew. Rodney's men formed a box round the Colonel, hustled him up the steps and into the reception area of the Treasury.

Three minutes later a dusty, muddied black BMW pulled over against the kerb along from Horse Guards between the parade ground and number 11. Under the dusty exterior the car sported metallic black paint and smoked tinted windows. Sharky glanced casually at the car which was stationary around forty metres from him. The car was a 7 series, but an older model. The rumble of the engine exuded power. He could just make out two men in the front, outlined as shadows. The men seemed intently interested in observing the Treasury entrance. The car's age and its dirty state sparked Sharky's sixth sense.

Sharky caught Mould's eyes and he in his turn Mr. Reid's.

A silent alert message between the three men had Mould reaching into his jacket. He brought out a Hamlet cigar. Lit it, sucked the acrid smoke into his lungs and wandered off down the road towards the BMW. Sharky shuffled off, paralleling Mould. Mould was stopping now and again to tie a lace or pat his packet as though he had forgotten something. Passing the BMW's rear door, he bent down again to tie his lace.

Mould saw the driver and passenger crane their necks back to look at the man half hidden by the rear door.

What happened next, Mr. Reid would relate to Rodney later, was in the moment, as everything seemed to happen at once.

The Jones brothers appeared on the steps with the Colonel following and Andrew bringing up the rear. They were barely out of the door.

The movement at the top of the Treasury steps must have caught the attention of the two men. They straightened up and quickly wound their windows down. Throwing the BMW into gear, the driver accelerated away to intercept the Colonel.

Sharky had crossed the road and was approaching the driver's door. The car passed with a roar leaving him in its wake but not before he glimpsed the passenger reaching for two automatic pistols, passing one to the driver before aiming the other out of the window.

The BMW men had broken off their observation of Mould as they drove away towards the Treasury. With his window now down, the passenger thrust a gun out of the window. In one lighting movement Mould stood up, bringing his Uzi machine pistol up, firing and shredding the passenger's arm and shoulder. The passenger's automatic pistol clattered onto the road. Running now, Mould scooped up the weapon as he passed, whilst turning his fire onto the driver. He felt rather than heard his rounds hit the man in the shoulder and he slumped over the wheel in pain.

Sharky spun right, weapon out, firing from the hip he took out the BMW tyres with well-aimed shots. The BMW slewed to a hard stop just short of the Land Rover.

Running, Sharky and Mould reached the car in seconds.

Sharky pulled out the passenger out of the car and dragged him onto the road. The man was in shock and groaning with pain, but apart from an arm covered in blood he seemed otherwise unmarked.

Mould smashed out the driver's window and pointed his own Uzi at the driver. The rounds had caught him in his shoulder and the top of his chest and he was in a bad way. Mould opened the door, grabbed the man who was the older of the two and a bull of a man. He grabbed the man's coat collar and dragged him out. He ignored the man's grunts of pain. Mould then kicked him down onto the road.

The Jones brothers, covering the Colonel, had hidden him behind the solid balustrade of the Treasury steps as soon as they saw what was going down. At a shout from Mr. Reid, they lifted their charge by his armpits, ran and bundled the panic-stricken white-faced Colonel down the steps and into the Rover and took off.

Andrew went left and Mr. Reid right along the road, both men with credentials held high to calm the running Police who were reacting to the gunfire and arriving in ever increasing numbers.

It was impressive, Mr. Reid told Rodney, after the police officer in charge agreed to call Commander Coveney at SO13, the speed with which the incident was contained and the evidence removed.

'Commander Coveney now has the BMW quarantined in a nearby police pound. He will get the vehicle tested to see if it was the one that drove the Colonel to the farm last night but he doesn't think so from what he was told. We can, if we wish, inspect the car in concert with his scientific officers. I thought I would grab Christian and have a look this evening.'

'Yes, good idea. Please take Christian with you. What about the shooters?'Rodney had asked. 'Where are they?'

'After the paramedics sorted them out, bandaged them up and stuffed them full of antibiotics they were good to travel and I brought them back to the cells below. Got our medics settling them in, in custody on Level Three. They're not going anywhere soon and or until we have their details sorted, how they fit in and who sent them.'He grunted. 'Wounds not life-threatening. Even the driver that got one high in the chest, the bullet went straight through into the dash.'He thought for a moment. 'I will get a quick polaroid taken to see if the Colonel recognises them from last night. Worth a try.'

Rodney was thoughtful. 'What about collateral damage, public outrage, stuff like that?'

'Sorted. No stray bullets, not even a scratch on anything or anyone except the car and the enemy. In that regard Sharky had them swearing blue murder. Chances are that they're Eastern European rather than Russian, not that that means much.'

Looking at his watch, Rodney said, 'As ever, Mr. Reid, you seem to have everything in hand. I am grateful to you. Today has been a real welcome back.'

'Boss, what can I say? Great to be in the game again. As for you, Major, it's been a long first day. Think that the best thing you can do is get home and get sorted. Get an early night and prep for your team meeting. Eight tomorrow, I'm told.'

'One last thing, how is our Colonel Jimmy?'

Mr. Reid shook his head in bewilderment, followed by a low throaty laugh. 'Let's just say that he wasn't impressed and that he didn't want to play anymore! Andrew put him right. He told him he could either play with our gang or we could set him free and put him back on the street. He's staying. Andrew got all the data discs etc., everything and he'll give you an account tomorrow before the meeting. In the meantime, Pat, Andrew and Colonel Jimmy will work through the files and load them on their part of the intranet.

'I have to say that the Colonel's appearance did cause quite a stir. A few people were incredulous when he strode into the room. Andrew is pretty certain that telephones will be ringing off the hook so let's hope our Captain Freire, sorry now Major Freire, and her team are on the ball. I'll see the Brigadier to update him before he goes. So, just disappear, Boss. Day over. Sort yourself out as the team are assuming that it's 24/7 from tomorrow.'

'And some.' groaned Rodney ruefully. 'You can sort out Major Freire when you see her. Going to be a late night for us all but Graham is adamant that the operations centre will be ready for the morning.'

'I should stay and help.'

'Not a chance. You'd only get in the way or fuck up the smooth workings by making last minute changes as we progress. True or false?' Mr. Reid tucked his elbows in and spread his hands, inviting comment.

'Yeah, true.' Rodney mimicked Reid's posture.

'As I said, Boss. Fuck off and get yourself sorted.' Reid put a hand on Rodney's shoulder and spun him round to face the door.

Chapter Eleven

Rodney at Home

Mr. Reid saw Rodney down to the basement with his bags and helped to load them into one of the section's Land Rovers manned by Andrew. In the car, Andrew passed Rodney a loaded Browning automatic pistol and two full magazines.

'Brigadier's orders. The new SOP (standard operating procedure) now states that when on Ops or heightened state of alert we are to be armed at all times.'

Rodney checked out the gun. He liked the Browning as a man-stopping weapon. Despite its weight, it would serve you well within its operational limits if you practised enough with it and looked after it. Rodney had had a lot of practice and always looked after his weapons.

He took out the gun magazine. He checked the safety catch, a honed automatic reaction. Rodney pressed the bullets down in the magazine against the spring to check the resistance and ensure that the shells bounced back to the magazine top. Happy that the shells were properly loaded, he racked the slide back, checked the barrel and firing pin. He put the magazine back and made sure it was fully home. Then he slid back the slide again and let it fly forwards, carrying a round into the chamber. He pulled the slide half back to reveal the bullet nestling in the chamber and carefully let the slide go just fast enough for the mechanism not to feed another shell from the magazine into the waiting breech. Finally, he canted the pistol over to work a check on the safety catch.

'Good to go, Andrew.'

'I decided that I would drive so that it would give me the chance to tell you about the visit to the Treasury. There was little trouble getting into the room that Colonel Jimmy was working from. I hadn't realised that some of the rooms were massive. There must have been sixty desks in there. And they seem to have corralled some of the best works of art that I've ever seen on the walls. Anyway, we went straight to Colonel Jimmy's workstation, a few raised eyebrows and a few half-stood to get a look at him and us. A few words of sympathy as we passed desks, they could see he had been in an incident. He is a rude, arrogant bugger. He just batted any kindness off without any thank yous or with at best a grunt. Mr. Reid had cleared the way and initially collecting the stored data was without resistance, despite a few curious glances and not a few more sympathetic words by those I found out later were his immediate staff, which the old boy probably doesn't deserve. As expected, they'd removed his laptop and disc. Without turning a hair Colonel Jimmy went to retrieve the disc he had hidden behind a possible target's locker. The man and some union rep or other and another posh bugger, whom I took to be the room mandarin, objected to him taking the disc out of the office without checking it. Give Colonel Jimmy his due, he told them forcefully to fuck off. I was quite surprised and saw another side of our man. I don't think that he's a pushover, which might augur well for us, but then again maybe not. Still, don't think that he's a team player, so I'm hoping that the Banker and Pat and their natural gravitas will keep him on side. Anyway, it was his property, and he brandished the disc with his name on it. He told them that if they had any problem to take it up with the Secret Service i.e., the Jones brothers and me. It was enough for them to back off, thank goodness. I think that the presence of the Sergeant at Arms also helped to defuse the situation.' Andrew smiled. 'Know what I think? The problem with Colonel Jimmy is that he has some form of Asperger's. Most people are familiar with the lack of empathy that many sufferers exhibit. Doesn't mean that he doesn't have feelings, just that in his case they are mainly targeted on his family and his maths. Problem in his case is not being able to communicate or comprehend feelings or the feelings of others. Therefore, his emotional experiences to others tend to the non-existent. So, it's hard for him with his Asperger's to relate to others i.e., on a scale of empathy of zero to ten he scores about a half. The plus is that people with his problem can be incredibly gifted in some areas. Good for us, eh?'

Rodney smiled. 'Time will tell, Andrew. Time will tell. You've been studying Sigmund Freud.'

'No,' Andrew was offended. 'He's all about sex. I worked this one out for myself.'

Rodney chuckled. 'The little that I know about Asperger's, you could well be right. Maybe it's simply that we are the first people in his life that have allowed him to join a team.'

The two men chatted, catching up on life and the universe. The traffic was light so it only took ten minutes before the Land Rover pulled up at Rodney's apartment block.

'Want a hand up with your kit, Boss?'

'No thanks. I'm good. You'd better go home, get a leave pass from the wife and lend her the credit card for the little luxuries in life. Think that we're going to be busy for a while.'

'Happen, later; but Graham has other ideas for me tonight.' Andrew shook Rodney's hand. 'Until tomorrow.'

In the reception of the flat complex Rodney was pleased to see Joe, who was the concierge and an old retired soldier. He didn't seem to have any other home but the reception desk and the small two-room flat behind it. He always seemed to be on duty. He welcomed Rodney back enthusiastically. Joe, who knew everything about his 'guests'as he liked to call them, wanted to show his concern and insisted on taking up Rodney's bags for him; whilst Rodney prevaricated, Joe grabbed the bags and called the lift.

He ushered Rodney into the lift and followed him in. 'Good to have you back, Major. You know, you hear things in this job and rumour has it that you got shot up badly, sir; is it true?'Joe was intent yet sympathetic. Rodney nodded, running his forefinger down the faint, raised white scar running down his face.

'True, Joe, but all's well now. It's just another souvenir to add to the collection.'Rodney grinned and ran his finger again down the scar on his face, feeling the slight ridge. 'And how about you, Joe? Well, what's the gossip?'

'Well, you know me, sir. I just let stuff wash over me. Keep to myself what passes for gossip, but from one old soldier to another there is a new tenant in the flat below you who gives me some concern. Well, maybe not concern, but more a puzzle. A mature Russian lady who is, nevertheless, I think, very beautiful in her own right. Mind you...'he continued quickly. 'Very smart indeed, expensive clothes and jewels. Probably middle fifties, could be older but doesn't look it. Clearly got a lot of money, drives the latest Mercedes coupé. Mind you, she's always pleasant and courteous to me. She's been here for the past few months.'He paused and keyed the door, throwing it open before carrying the cases into the main room of Rodney's flat. 'It's just that I can't square her with one or two of the people that visit her, or her living here.'

Rodney's curiosity was raised. 'Tell me, why? And what about these visitors?'

'So, there are a couple of regulars. They always come together. Well turned out, but thugs, nevertheless. Quick of movement and armed; seen the bulge of a gun more than once. Both early middle thirties, brush cut haircuts. Most of the time they escort the lady, following in their own car when she goes out for a drive. They never speak to me or give me the time of day. They are definitely Russians too; I hear them talking to each other and Madam. Then there's the three ladies, sometimes together, sometimes separately. Always formally dressed like solicitors. They, that is the ladies, are a mixture. One of them is Eastern European and the other two are educated English ladies. Some of them stay overnight, sometimes even for a few days. Could be nothing but it doesn't sit right in my mind, Major. She could afford to live at any Mayfair address or, if it's the view of the river she likes, why not a penthouse somewhere along the bank? Sure, she has the view of the river, St Paul's and that. But why would a woman like her, who could clearly afford to live at a better address, no disrespect, Sir, but I think that you'd agree that this block caters for the more conservative clientele. So, why would she choose to live in this building?' Joe was silent, thinking of something else, Rodney thought, but he was knackered so cut him off.

'Very interesting, Joe and I agree, as you say, puzzling. Give me the lady's name and her car registration number and I'll find out what's what to put your mind at rest.'

'Good enough. I'll slip the information under the door. You look a bit knackered. Good to have you back. Your keys, Major.' Joe respectfully closed the door to the hall behind him.

Rodney, alone at last in a flat he had not seen for six months, let out his breath and looked around. He was well and truly weary and just wanted to crash.

The flat hadn't changed a bit, but it was, he decided, much fresher, cleaner and tidier than it had ever been since he moved in seven years ago. He felt unexpectedly buoyed and spent ten minutes sorting out his kit; there wasn't much that he'd brought with him but it gave him the opportunity to flick through his wardrobe. They had even taken his suits to the cleaners and they hung pristine in plastic bags side by side and colour-coded – he laughed as he imagined the team sorting them out.

All day he had half expected to be going back to Cornwall sooner rather than later, but now he wasn't so sure. He chose and hung up his clothes for the morning. He threw the kit that he'd worn and the stuff from Cornwall into the laundry basket, then thinking better of it, into the washer dryer machine and flicked it on. Preparation and chores done, he suddenly felt hungry. He thought of going out but couldn't be bothered. He thought with some regret of the pleasure that he had had with Miss Jane preparing his meals at the Cornish cottage.

He opened a bottle of 'The Guvnor,' a smooth, strong Spanish wine which was a favourite of his, from his floor to ceiling free-standing wine rack; poured a generous measure into a large goblet and left it standing, to breathe.

He then attacked the freezer, searching for a frozen meal that would appeal to him. As the Brigadier had said, they had indeed stocked it up. He chose a chicken Balti and a large punnet of saag aloo. He searched the cupboard for a packet of poppadoms. He cut the packet open, took out three and put them in the microwave for one minute.

He had a taste of the wine and, as ever, it suited his palate. He read the instructions on the food packaging. Portion sizes said that they were both for two people which he reckoned should be just about right to assuage his appetite.

Twenty minutes later, whilst he ate, he pondered on the day and the mission ahead. It was, he decided, just too difficult for his tired brain to compute and sort out mentally tonight so his mind turned to what Joe had said about the new tenant, an easier subject.

Joe's report that evening didn't really ring any alarm bells for a moment. Then he suddenly thought of Galena Vorakova, femme fatale and one-time girlfriend of Tsygankov or so they said, and also an off-the-books ex-KGB colonel. He thought that he had chased her out of the country last year. *Couldn't be, could it? Could it wait till tomorrow? – definitely.* Nevertheless, after he had cleared away the dishes, he checked the windows and doors for security, took his pistol and slipped it under his pillow when he went to get his head down for the night. His last thought was, 'If it is Galena, the beautiful Russian cat woman [as he thought of her] or one of her ilk in the flat downstairs then it isn't a coincidence. And as such the matter would have to be taken seriously and sorted.'

Chapter Twelve

Neil Ashchurch – A Very Senior Treasury Civil Servant

As the Colonel had been collecting his data discs, Neil Ashchurch was alerted by the senior civil servant whom he had watching out for him. When he buzzed to tell him, Neil called forward the takedown crew, who were parked just up the road by Buckingham Palace. Then he immediately called back his man to find out exactly what had happened while the Colonel was in the office and who was with him. What he heard angered him. He was going to have to stand up his contacts as necessary to get rid of the problem. Neil, the perfect gentleman, had thanked his man politely for his vigilance and quickly delivered a report to his top team.

Neil had grown extraordinarily rich over the years and needed to consider the various options open to him and his colleagues. He could run to his Costa del Clog flat in Amsterdam and live well for the remainder of his life, but even with a new name and papers he would be forever looking over his shoulder. Status, family and friends, all important to him, would be lost forever. He could, as they say, turn Queen's evidence but he would almost certainly lose his pension, family and friends and in all probability have to pay back his loot. Or he could cover his tracks and carry on with his fellow fraudsters.

He needed to confer with three others key members: the one from Customs, the one from Excise and the one from HM Paymaster. Also, of course, the senior KGB liaison officer available to him in London.

It had all been so easy when they began, but now in this computer age when machines were gaining more and more credence, with more and more intelligence shared and that damned Colonel, their perfect money-making machine was in danger of falling apart.

It had taken years to infiltrate the numerous various Government agencies and quangos, to cultivate their own people in positions where bills could be authorised and extensions to contracts, as well as rework and overruns, would be allowed to float through the system, be rubber stamped by ministries and paid out by the Government paymasters.

He didn't even want to think about the myriad of private and public companies that were in the scam with them. He didn't want to think either about the money launderers that moved the money into his account even though it paled into insignificance compared to the KGB's ever-growing offshore bank accounts. He especially didn't want to face the thugs that the KGB could put his way.

Chapter Thirteen

A Meeting of Minds

Rodney woke early. He felt, to his surprise, refreshed and rested. He growled, 'Time to clear the brain for the day.' He dug out what he called his exercise box from the bottom of his wardrobe. He pulled out his tracksuit bottoms, struggled into the trousers and pulled one of his old favourite tatty washed-out blue sweatshirts and put it on over his head. A baseball hat, also from the box, completed his outfit.

The wide pedestrian boardwalk running along the South Bank of the Thames was a disappointment for him after the light, fresh sea breezes and sand under his feet that he'd become accustomed to. He ran, his mind in neutral, dodging the other joggers, who annoyed him purely by their presence. He was used to having a sandy beach and it being mainly to himself in the early hours.

Was he simply intolerant or turning into an old grouch? He smiled to himself and knew in his heart that he had to guard against becoming fixated on returning to Cornwall or it could impair his functioning and by default the team's.

He jogged back into the flats and ran up the stairs, glancing at the door of the new occupant on the first floor.

Showered and suited, he took the lift to the ground floor. Breakfast could wait until they got into the office. He had ordered Laurie to rustle up a full English for all and he had an appetite to satisfy.

Joe had been waiting for him when he walked through the flat's reception. He had the new tenant's name and her car registration. Rodney thanked him and struck out for the office. He glanced up at the curtains of the target's flat, which were drawn back, but there was no presence showing in the double full-length patio windows.

In by 0700h, he retrieved his notebook from his office and headed for the operations room. He was pleased to see that the team had arranged the working areas and that the battle boards were up and running. How Graham and the rest had got all the communications and IT in overnight he wouldn't ask, but he would acknowledge the effort, say thank you and give the team a 'well done.'

He found the desk that they had set aside for him to work at, threw his working tools down on it and put his suit jacket on the back of the chair. *Space claimed,*'he thought to himself. He stretched, shook himself, straightened his regimental tie and went over to the team's mini canteen. Laurie had set it up as Rodney had asked and he chose the full English breakfast he had been looking forward to and made it into sandwiches. Pouring a large mug of tea, he called Laurie over.

'Good effort, Laurie. Can you do me a quick search on this person and her car from this registration?'Rodney fished in his pockets for the note on the neighbour that Joe had given him. 'Russian lady. She may be a person of interest to us, could be false name. She's moved into the flat below me. According to Joe, the concierge, she had armed bodyguards, so be careful and discreet.'

Rodney rammed as much of his breakfast as he could between two slices of bread.

Laurie watched him before he replied in fluent Russian, in the northern Moscow accent he had perfected and, as always, on key.

Rodney grinned, patted Laurie on the shoulder and went to begin his rounds of the office, sandwiches in hand and a mug balanced dangerously in the crook of his arm. He had a chance to talk to everyone present and then returned to the conference table and settled himself down. He had a half hour before the meeting, so he applied himself to writing quickly in his logbook.

Rodney cleared away the remains of his meal and grabbed another mug of tea. His return to the conference table was a signal for the team to join him. Rodney took the top of the table and the team arranged themselves around it in their operational speciality groupings.

Looking round at the team he steeled himself. He wasn't ready for the mission, which on reflection he thought was a job for the police, which pissed him off. Grudgingly, on the other side of the coin Mrs. T had asked for the team and he didn't want to let her or them down; he owed them. Bottom line, he didn't want to be there. His long-honed, deep-seated self-discipline and loyalty simply meant that he had to dig deep. Rodney could not let the team see that he was less than 100% committed.

Mr. Reid sat on Rodney's right and cascading down the right-hand side followed Andrew, Pat and The Banker John Brown, Colonel Jimmy, who was looking pensive, and the two special advisors, Dan and

Shaun. As always, Graham sat on his left; cascading down from him was Major Freire, Royal Signals, followed by the Jones brothers and Dr Jules Christian and the two section analysts, Jill and Jamie. Laurie filled the last seat on the left. Moments before, he had set a teapot of Earl Grey and a cup and saucer at the end of the table.

Rodney sat silently. The others around the table, sensing his stillness, gradually ceased talking and the shuffling of papers stopped. The table members were now silent and expectant. They turned their heads as they heard confident footsteps, quarter steel on the heels, clattering on the Civil Service's highly polished brown lino. The footsteps came closer as they approached the screened-off conference area. They stopped and Brigadier Robinson appeared, wishing them all a very good morning. He had a pile of files jammed under one arm like a Guards Officer's pay-stick.

'Major'

'Brigadier, your team is assembled.'

'Thank you. Now, Graham, would you pass round the information files to everyone? Listen in. Here is what I can tell you. Colonel Jimmy has unearthed a fraud against this country that is costing billions of pounds. That is your and my money by the way.'Robinson smiled. 'Your mission...'is to get the money back, every penny. Further, as instructed, by our ultimate Boss, with interest.' He repeated the mission so that there could be no misunderstanding. 'And I want the perpetrators of this crime hung, drawn and quartered!'This brought a chuckle from the table.

'My aim is to support you and I have set a target of thirty days to complete this mission without embarrassment to Her Majesty's Government or Her Majesty. Do I make myself clear?'He eyed Colonel Jimmy and the two advisors. He could be sure of his own team, but he wanted to ensure that the three newcomers understood the stakes. 'Nothing, absolutely nothing, of the work that you are about to undertake or its outcomes is to leave this room, both now and for the rest of your natural lives. Now, let me set the scene.'The Brigadier spoke cogently for thirty minutes. The lecture, as he had promised, was like a Texan steer: a lead in, the 'head', a conclusion, 'the tail' at the end and a lot of bull (meat) in between. He finished and leaned back in his chair.

'I had a long talk with Colonel Jimmy overnight.' He acknowledged the man with a nod. 'And I found the story of the way he discovered the fraud both amusing and enlightening. I am going to ask the Colonel to retell it to you. The story that has brought us to this point started with the humble road cone in protracted and ongoing road works. Intrigued? Well, I was. Replenish your plates and drinks and be back in five minutes.'

Rodney could but smile. The Brigadier was on form and all the better for that.

Chapter Fourteen

The Road Cone

Colonel Jimmy had put up a whiteboard and chart. As soon as the team had reconvened, he started. He spoke carefully and Rodney heard for the first time the slight Welsh accent with a baritone timbre to the voice.

'One day, two years ago, I was commuting daily on a motorway and had to negotiate roadworks ten miles long with the attendant slow-moving traffic, sharing the frustration of other drivers. Especially when, at times, there appeared to be nobody working in the roadworks. The question was why not, and for that matter why were they not working 24/7? I tried to calculate the cost to business, and the hire costs and or depreciation against the idle capital equipment etc., etc.

'I noted the men and plant, either working or as many times, not. I noted the cone population separating the lanes. I started to take photographs to make a record of the works. What turned a driver's idle curiosity into a serious investigation was the behaviour of the humble traffic cone.

'There were about 1000 cones per kilometre for each lane in these particular roadworks. My commute went on for about three months. What I noticed was that the cone population varied from time to time. My curiosity was raised; I looked up the construction company. In my position I was able to get a look at the motorway construction contract and the promises made at the tender clarification meetings, penalty clauses etc.'

He wrote the name of the company and the motorway on the board.

He continued. 'I was staggered at the sums involved for materials, manpower, plant and infrastructure. Not least the hire or purchase price of the humble traffic cone. On my next few drive-bys I continued to count the men and mobile plant equipment, site huts etc., and, like the cones, these items also varied. Something wasn't right.'

Colonel Jimmy warmed to his task. 'I was already frustrated beyond measure as I could not for the life of me understand why they didn't operate the way the French do. The French advertise that they are going to sort a section of motorway between two dates and they achieve it by having a road gang, with everything pre-prepared, men and material etc. etc., lines of vehicles with cement and tarmac held on wheels, ready to go in and be replenished. Fast, efficient, inconvenience minimised, good for business and the country.

'By now my blood was up and I became fixated on my suspicion that there was skullduggery going on. I looked up the company and what other road construction contracts it had ongoing. There were three funded by the taxpayer within the same county. So, I visited them all; one was within days of completion and the others in various stages of work. I continued to photograph and record men and machines etc.'

He paused to regain his audience's focus. 'You won't be surprised by now if I tell you that men and machines and cones were transiting between jobs. This was despite the fact that all the contracts called for dedicated materials, men and machines and so on. They were double, triple and quadruple charging. You might conjecture, as I did, that small but nevertheless significant works other than the motorway had to be finished before the motorways work which was facilitating them, and so it proved.'

He paused again as emotion overwhelmed him, which Rodney put down to the man's stress over the last twenty-four hours. 'Appallingly, I recorded frequent rework. Road laid, dug up and re-laid with the excuses that a cable or drainage needed had been forgotten for instance. All this prolonged the various jobs.'

The Colonel took several deep breaths to calm himself. 'Initially, I wasn't prepared to accept that this had been just allowed to happen, but what other explanation was there? So, I took all the data I could get hold of from a myriad of government contracts and analysed it. I was appalled at what I found when I mapped out the possible links to people in organisations that had to be complicit in a massive fraud.'

He looked round the table. 'Any questions at this time?'

The Brigadier asked the question that all the team wanted to hear. 'Does this mean that other parts of industry are involved?'

'Yes, every part of our principal industries from Defence to the National Health Service and providers.'

The group round the table moved in their chairs, realising just how big this mission was. Rodney asked, 'How far have you got and how much have you documented on these matters?'

'A great deal.'He sucked his lips. 'I need to explain; I used computer models to run and compare invoices with demands for payments, deliverables with contracts, and company payrolls with work and locations; also with who authorised payments at every level. I also looked at the Government agencies that bid for funds for work from Government ministries. I found that the fraud was so sophisticated and disparate that in the ordinary way the Government's own audit agency would have failed to find non-compliance.'

John Brown the Banker asked, 'Can you give me a simple example of a scam?'

'Let's say poor practice. The Health Service buying in, say, a non-perishable item, millions of pairs of rubber gloves with a near "use before"date, leading to them being dumped to wholesale dealers who then sell them on at massive profit, and then of course the Health Service has to buy more. A real merry-go round.'

Sharky wanted to know 'But how do the companies move or hide the money from these frauds?'

The Banker smiled and told the meeting. 'They make the money disappear by laundering it in various ways. Unravelling this will be the most exciting and motivating part of the mission as we recover it back to the Treasury. Colonel, you feed us with the data, and we will do what we do best.'

Colonel Jimmy beamed.

Rodney brought the meeting to a conclusion. 'Colonel Jimmy, thank you for a fascinating story, it certainly painted a picture for us. Brigadier, with your permission we'll go to work now.'He stood. 'There does seem a lot to do if we are to meet your thirty-day target. Unless we break the back of these frauds and can pass it back to the authorities, the Fraud Squad etc.'

The Brigadier mused about Rodney's last sentence then stood, followed by the rest of the table group, calling out 'That could work, let us to it then. Rodney, come and see me later, around five would be good.'He turned on his heel and was gone.

'To work then, I think.'Mr. Reid hustled the staff away from the conference table in the sure knowledge that they would gain nothing by delaying the start of the task.

Rodney started to clear away the debris from the meeting and breakfast. He wanted a mindless task to give him the space to think through tactical and strategic operational matters. For example, did he deal with each fraud as it became obvious at a contract level, or wait until they had all the evidence to roll up the lot at ministry level? Not least, how was he going to do it with the discretion that the PM would wish?

Chapter Fifteen

The Shooters

Rodney made his way down the building to the cellars at Level Three that housed the two men the team had wounded, to have a look at them. Rodney knew that it was a displacement activity, but he was not yet in the mood to get down to the task. On the other hand, he might just get a nugget of intelligence out of them.

He felt grumpy, tetchy, an unusual feeling for him. He needed to shrug it off with a bit of fun, as he saw it. Travelling down to the cells in the third-level basement, he wanted to speak to the shooters. In the back of his mind was the idea that he might find out who they were. They were not on any database, which was unusual in itself. They must have got a call from someone in the Treasury when the team visited to get the Colonel's discs. Rodney wanted to know who that was. He also wanted to know whether they knew Galena Vorakova and if she was in the UK. For sure, the public capture of these two would now mean that the Russians would know about their detention.

At the first cell, he got the guards to let him in to talk to the man. It was the driver and he was going nowhere soon. Strapped up and drugged against the pain, he was laid flat and was very pale, handcuffed by an arm and both legs to his orthopaedic bed. The man was fitted with food and fluid drips and life measuring monitoring equipment.

The man turned his head as Rodney entered. Buzzcut hair and with Slavic features, the man's cold eyes, yellowed from his injury, radiated contempt. Rodney just smiled.

'I really don't think that I will hurt you, but I am thinking about it. Did Galena send you?'

Rodney watched the man intently. He saw him blink. The man gave Rodney a mouthful of Russian invective in a hoarse, croaking voice. It was enough. Rodney knew that the man was lying and wished that he had brought Laurie with him.

'I will be back to you, with others and you will talk. Everyone breaks eventually. Think on this. You are not in police custody so no one will miss you. As of now, you don't even exist.'Rodney knocked the door to leave. The man turned his head away, blanking him. Rodney thought that the man was trying to suss out if he was serious. For his part, he took out a small digital camera and took a picture of the man. 'Smile.'

In the second cell, the man sat at a table. His good hand was chained to the table centre ring, his injured arm was in a sling and taped to his side. He didn't look up when Rodney entered. Rodney sat opposite him and took the man's picture.

How are you feeling?'Rodney started, brightly. 'Looking after you well, I hope?'Rodney was relaxed.

The man raised his head. Rodney noted that he was younger by some ten years than his partner; early thirties, maybe a little more. Tall, fit and fair-haired. The man's bright hazel, intelligent eyes studied Rodney. 'Well?'

'Good, so far.'The man's English was good, if accented, but Rodney thought that he was naturally suspicious of Rodney's motives and cautious. Rodney looked around the room. Whitewashed breeze blocks, security grilles over the lights, a metal bed screwed to the floor. Wet room floor with a shower and toilet in one corner. A chain from the table just long enough for the prisoner to get to the bed, shower and toilet.

'Good to hear. I will be seeing Galena later. Do you have a message for her?'Rodney studied the man. Rodney thought it was worth a punt. His body language seemed to indicate that he was confused. Rodney decided to move on. Rodney was a good judge of people and thought that he saw something in the man that he might use.

'Galena Vorakova and I have a long-running relationship. I am sure that she would have discussed that with you?'

'I don't personally know Galena. Of course, I have heard of her, how could I not have?'

I'm confused.'Rodney questioned. 'I was told you were seen visiting her flat; isn't that so?'

'Not me, sir. Maybe Dimitri.' The uninjured hand held up in total innocence.

Rodney didn't believe him but changed tack. 'How do you see this ending for you?'

'I expect you will charge me and then a court appearance, a sentence. Not too long if I am lucky. Perhaps there will be an exchange, me for one of your people, in time? I have no real idea.'He hung his head. 'It all seemed so easy in the beginning. A minder job in the UK, good money. But then it as you English say got heavy. Kidnap, then an order to assassinate the man you were protecting. We were threatened and set up.'

Rodney had some sympathy for this young man but he didn't show it. But he did realise that the man was not a habitual dyed-in-the-wool villain. He was just another sap hired and abused by the bastards that promised the world, got likely lads off the street to do the dirty work. Rodney sighed. 'As for your future, probably none of those things you mentioned. You see, you are not in the care of the police so the law as you think of it may not apply. You don't exist anywhere. I could sell you to the Americans.'Rodney thought for a moment, paraphrasing a well-known saying. 'They do say an enemy can neither be created nor destroyed, only changed to some other form.'

'I don't understand you.'

'Well, think on. One option is that you work for me.' Rodney held the man's eyes. 'I will be back for your answer sometime soon. If you are interested then we will discuss the offer further.'Rodney stood and called the guard. 'Do you have a name?'

The man looked at Rodney's open face. He sighed. 'Vladimir, Vladimir Petrov.'

'What about Dimitri? Does he have a second name?'

'Dimitri Sokolov. How is he?'

'Vladimir, I can say that Dimitri is alive but badly wounded. He will live.'

He smiled at the Russian. The guard held the door open for Rodney to leave. Rodney wanted to get back to the ops room, show the pictures to Colonel Jimmy and find out if Laurie had any news. With the two men's names now known he would get them investigated. Laurie had prudently as a first stage given the information to Graham for a desk-based investigation, so he wanted to know if Graham and his analysts had discovered anything about the mystery lady in the flat below him.

Chapter Sixteen

Operations Room and the Sections

Rodney found that the operations centre was buzzing, and many of the staff sought his attention as soon as he set foot in the place. They had a hundred different questions for him to clarify and give his approvals. He groaned inwardly but put a brave face on it. After it calmed down, Rodney had a few words with Graham about the lady in the flat below him. Graham was still waiting for Special Branch to get back to him.

'They promised to come back before four this afternoon. And Commander Bob Coveney asked if he could see you tomorrow morning.'

'Did he say where?'Rodney was interested. He wanted to talk to Bob urgently about future joint ops.

'He suggested his place. He thinks that his office is more conducive to, as he said, a deal.'Graham smirked.

Rodney laughed out loud. 'He's right, he serves a supposedly exceptionally smooth old single malt Scotch from some obscure distillery. As he never runs out of the stuff, I suspect that it's a customs seizure he bought at one of the government auctions. It must have been one hell of a haul.'

'It was probably made in Taiwan.'Graham commented dryly.

'Could be, could be.'Rodney moved on. 'How are we getting on with the phone taps?'

'Major Freire and her team want to talk to you about that.'

'Where is she?'

'They are through there, in our annexe room.'Graham pointed at the entrance to what was the old board room.

'I thought that we were going to keep them in here and let the Banker etc. have that room?'

'We were, but we are within touching distance of each other anyway and Freire has a desk next to me. All joined up. And both teams reckoned that it would be more efficient if they are together. As you would say, flash to bang time is speeded up, and we don't exactly have a lot of time.' He was pleased that Rodney didn't push back. 'So, in this room is admin and control, food, field teams and the conference table as before. Are you OK with that?'

'Yes, happy. This is your centre and I trust you implicitly in these matters.'

'Thanks for that, Boss. Follow me then.' Graham led the way.

As he left Graham, Rodney gave him the two names of the prisoners, Dimitri Sokolov and Vladimir Petrov. 'May be worth asking Ms. Reid, Doug's daughter in MI6 what she can find out?'

Tucked behind the shoulder of a wall between the two rooms was Freire and her team, with communications set up feeding back and forth to GCHQ. It was already well established, operating and her battle boards were deployed. Her team of four, two less than Rodney had expected, were busy. Some had headphones on, and the others were shuffling signals and emails. Files of incoming data and messages were being created and matrixes of cross-referenced intelligence were building up on Freire's battle boards. Her area was a little cramped but not too much as the old boardroom, now annexed and knocked through to the original ops area, was a massive room. The room had previously been the boardroom for the head of MI5. But, he thought, better and with more legroom than working out of the back of a long base Land Rover.

'The height of luxury, don't you think, Major?' Rodney asked Freire.

'Oh yes, Rodney, much better and warmer. Just so you know, I have other men and women on standby if we need them, but for now I think that a small team as we build up the system is a plus.'

'Happy with that. Let's talk later?'

Rodney got a thumbs up from Freire before she turned back to the task.

The Banker, John Brown, had placed Graham's analysts and the two Prime Minister's gurus' PC workstations along the wall from Freire. His remaining team were then spread around the room. He had his boards up on three walls and already they were being populated with names and companies. Strings were being arranged to link the ministries and agencies to appropriate companies.

Rodney stood, fascinated, watching and observing Colonel Jimmy standing in the middle of the room directing the team with a fistful of sheaves of papers which he waved from time to time to make a point. Rodney nodded approvingly; Colonel Jimmy was in his element. *This is what the old boy should have been doing all his life. Waste of talent.*

Rodney decided that he would find a slot for this odd character after all this was over, in some organisation that would really benefit from his skills. MI5 analysts perhaps, as there was no way that the old Colonel could go back to his old job.

He turned back to Freire who had her head down again. 'Sorry, Freire, I meant to say how good it was to see you once again, and I hope for another interesting mission, perhaps. A Major now I hear, well done, I hope this doesn't mean your boss thinks you are carrying too much rank now to work with us?'He held out his hand and it was shaken warmly. Freire had a sparkle in her eyes, she was clearly glad to be back. 'Better tell me quickly, what do we have so far?'

'Well firstly my boss is quite happy with my working with the team, thank you. It's a feather in his cap and he will get some brownie points too. Well, what have we got? Quite a lot actually. Colonel Jimmy's escape and the shoot-out, coupled with his unexpected visit to pick up data, has really got them rattled as the mails and calls clearly show.'

Freire put her hand on a stack of paper. 'These are the transcripts of telephone calls. Very interesting they are too. When you have the time, read some.'She tilted her head to one side. It was a question.

'I will as soon as I catch up with myself. I'll be back later after I've got the whole ship on a course, that's a promise. I can understand how important it is. I will run through the data. Give me an hour or so. Anyway, as important, soldier's comforts. How about the admin arrangements for you and your team, are they OK?'

'All sorted. We're all staying with Graham, in his big old house.'Freire smiled over at Graham. Rodney raised an eyebrow. 'Don't forget, Boss, Graham is a fine chef, and the quarters are better than anything we can get on our allowances, even adding the London weighting supplement!'

'Oh yeah, do you know I'd quite forgotten the Army's insistence on wanting detailed expenses made out for everything from paperclips to food. Bring the forms to me weekly; I'll sign them off and get the Service Imprest Account holder we fortunately have in house to pay you and the team quickly. Don't forget.'He waggled a finger at Freire and her team.

He wandered off to speak to the Banker. He found him absorbing the data going up on the boards. Rodney pulled up a chair and sat alongside him.

'Looks as though we are building a spider's web?'

'It is, and a very expensive one, that's for sure. Pity our poor bloody taxpayers. What a game, my old soldier.'He grunted then confidentially in Rodney's ear. 'You know, son,'–His Irish accent was evident now – 'one of the many things that saw me through many sticky situations at the height of the 'Troubles'was that I'm a good judge of a person's character and his persona.'The Banker looked at Rodney. 'Now, I perceive that you're not fully quite with us yet. Mr. Reid also agrees with me. He's concerned, like me, but is too loyal to tell you.'He held eye contact. 'Not good enough, boy, you need to commit, or you must walk away. This task,'he waved his hand at the boards. 'It needs your total commitment. So, what's it to be?'

Rodney felt his gut tighten and a flush fill his cheeks; he held his breath then finally, he exhaled. He chuckled and hung his head to one side, eyes to the floor. How could he have been so transparent? He raised his head, eyeballing the Banker.

'You're right, of course. I am conflicted, but not for the reasons you might think. It's not the shooting or the aftermath, that comes with the territory. I'm pining, a sort of grief for what I had in Cornwall these last six months, and the last few months in particular. For the first time in my adult life, I was looked after 24/7 and I liked it. Not even that. It's the lack of freedom that this task imposes on my newfound free spirit persona. Selfish, self-indulgent even, eh?' He grinned. 'Could have been any task, not just this one. I have, I admit, been brooding for a month or so about having to get back into the harness of the daily work routine. Not that what I do is ever routine. Now that I have a task, I think that I resent it, simple as that.' Rodney put his head down again, resting it on his hand, he felt uncharacteristically emotional. 'On the other side of the balance sheet, who would want to pass up the opportunity of working with a team like we have and to ride the adrenaline rush that comes with the job again? Just give me time to think this through for a minute, John.'He gently punched the Banker on the shoulder.

The Banker got up without looking at Rodney and went to have a word with a turbocharged Colonel Jimmy. When he finished with the Colonel, he returned to Rodney.

'What's your answer, son?'

Rodney slowly moved his head from side to side and rolled his head on his shoulders.

'You're a hard man, John Brown, but I'm in, totally, body and soul, for the duration of this mission. Cornwall and my surfboard will be there when this task is over.'

'Good lad. Now, let's put your brain in gear. Come with me.'He directed Rodney to one of the boards. 'See here. This is a complete chain for one fraud, in fact the one the Colonel used as an example earlier. What do we do with it now?'

'My mind hasn't been completely in neutral. I've been giving a lot of thought as to the way we handle the next phase after we identify discrete or partially complete fraud cells data. Either we go after each one of the frauds as they materialise, or we save them all up and do a grand sweep.'

'Likewise. So, what's your take on the two options, Rodney?'

'We find a way to roll them up one at a time. But concurrent activity at all times with more than one fraud team as needs dictate. We keep the lid on each investigation, separate and apart from the others which need to be rolling at the same time.'He ran his hand through his hair, a habitual action which all knew meant that his brain was in overdrive. 'We don't have the resources yet to do this any other way, more for the Mr. Reid's ops cell side than yours in some ways. We have to keep this tasking discrete. Stay in control, one foot on the ground at all times. I'm thinking too that when we lift a group, we need to quarantine them from others while you recover the money.'

'How are you going to do that? The detention rooms downstairs don't have elastic sides.'

'There's a way.'Rodney smiled and tapped the side of his nose. 'Just need to get it set up and be ready for the morning, before the first one goes into the bag.'

'Going to tell me?'The Banker really wanted to know.

'Absolutely, but I need to do three things beforehand. One, read the communications that Freire has. Two, have a word with Mr. Reid, followed thirdly by a full brief from your team, in two hours from now – make that a fixed time. Focused particularly on the people involved in this particular fraud.'Rodney pointed to the board. As an aside he added, 'I take it that the two advisors Dan and Shaun are pulling their weight?'He raised an eyebrow.

The Banker put a hand on Rodney's shoulder again and squeezed. 'Good enough for me, Rodney.'He touched the side of his nose. 'As for Dan and Shaun, well, it took me no time to get them to understand that their adviser days were over. What I wanted from them was the facts. I told them that if they didn't have them, to go find, or work out how to get them, or they'd be out on their ear. That seemed to do the trick, so it did. And now they seem to relish the challenge of getting fully involved. They are not just pushing papers and using other people ideas and knowledge, so no worries at this time. I think they will work out just fine.'

Rodney looked at the Banker. 'Good. I'll have a word with Graham to speak to some of his contacts. I will get them checked out for background, just in case we need more guns. See you shortly.' Rodney was off.

Chapter Seventeen

Major Freire

'Hi Freire, can I see what you have?'

Rodney was back to her and took the chair next to her and she and her staff made room for him.

'So now that you're a Major, what do I call you, Major or Ma'am?'Rodney asked.

'Freire will do just fine. Can't have more than one person called Major in this office, what would Mr. Reid say?'Freire smiled and Rodney allowed himself a polite laugh.

'OK, let me show you the more interesting communications that we've intercepted.'Freire shuffled the stack of intercepts on the table. 'The key man in this web of fraud, or at least the man in the centre of the spider's web, seems to be a senior Treasury official called Neil Ashchurch. He has had loads of calls to his office number and his personal mobile.'One of her staff reached over and gave Freire a list of names. 'Here are around sixty names that we've identified so far. We've checked a lot of them, and they are all, at least so far and with few exceptions, suspicious. Half a dozen are important officials in the Government, various departments and ministries. The others are principal officers in some of this country's leading companies. Graham's analysts, with Colonel Jimmy's help, are marrying the companies to government contracts and to the men and women we have identified.'

Freire paused for breath. 'We are now moving down the food chain. I'm using half of my team on that investigation based in GCHQ and I am going to add a couple more to my team there. Here we'll focus on firming up current findings and continuing to receive new intelligence which is pouring in. I may need to get a couple more staff squeezed in here if the attrition gets even more frenetic.'She gazed round at her team area. 'No pressure then, Rodney, eh?'

'Speak to Graham about space, he can sort you out, I'm sure. I don't suppose that any of the targets gave much away on the phones?' Rodney thought out loud as he studied the list.

'You'd be surprised. They are either so confident in their scams, panicking, or they have no idea what we can do these days. Some of the conversations are very revealing. To a man, they are concerned about interruptions in the money flows. By the way, we can do amazing things once we hook on to them.' She brought up on one of the large formats screens a spidery network with different colours for several traces.' What you see here is a call to one person or another. You can see that many of the callers speak to the same man and or others in the web. It gives us an almost perfect view of the hierarchies of the fraud network and the principal players. Good, eh?'

Rodney studied the screen for a moment and then looked over his shoulder to the wall of growing data. The Colonel and his team, as Rodney thought of them, were adding data minute by minute. He looked back at the screen. He pointed to a trace.

'Wow. Have you got a key for all this? For example, who's this?'

'Sure, if we go to the next screen, you will see it's colour coded again, but with all the data we have on the particular person. I've already linked some of the Colonel's targets to our trace matrix and it's looking very promising.'

'How so?' Rodney was intrigued, despite the lethargy he was having difficulty shaking off.

'Well, look at this lot.' Freire pointed to the screen. 'They are the top ten on the Colonel's list. Not only do some of this top ten communicate with each other but all are in daily contact with this very senior Treasury civil servant and other contacts in Her Majesty's Custom and Excise, the Audit Office and some contract-awarding Government agencies and the Ministry of Defence. Not that in the latter case that it would be unusual to communicate with the project, operations and engineer contracts managers, but they are working backwards and forwards with the CEOs and the men who have the authority to sign off the work.'

'This is outstanding.'

Rodney was amazed, suddenly brightening despite himself at the progress Freire's team had made.

'Add to the links and some of the conversations which, without a doubt, prove the level of corruption. I am passing copies to the Colonel, he's over the moon. He now has a separate chain of evidence that confirms all that he claims.'

'And for me, it gives me the confidence and the impetus to crack on. Yes, really well done!'Rodney rubbed his hands together. 'Good work, keep it coming.'He spun on his heels, scanning the room.

He had thought that what was wrong with him was simply that he was grieving for his lost life in Cornwall. He smiled to himself. He would focus on that thought and overcome this lethargy which, he had to admit to himself again, could well be a form of depression for the loss of the freedom of his lifestyle of the last six months. *Well*, he thought, *Fuck it.*'He had a cure for that. *Just get busy! Get involved, innovate, improvise and overcome! The surf will always be there after this is over*.

He felt Freire tug his sleeve and hold him back. 'Not so fast, Major. I saved the best till last. As Ashchurch is the prime suspect, we've analysed the calls from his phones – office and private mobile – going back seventy-two hours. Guess who he called the morning after Colonel Jimmy's escape?'

Rodney shook his head, laughing. 'I couldn't begin to guess. Surprise me?'

'Your friend and enemy, Brigadier General Carl Tsygankov, brackets on, retired, brackets off.'Freire waved a paper at him. 'I have just received the transcript of their conversation from GCHQ.'

Rodney was stunned, speechless, frozen in the moment as the ghosts of the past raced through his mind. He jerked himself out of his daze and tried to snatch the paper out of her hand.

Freire pulled the paper out of his reach. 'Ah, not so fast. A please and thank you would be good.'She frowned, pretending annoyance.

'OK, I give in, and really, really, please. Wow, I can't believe it. Don't want to believe it. Well done, you lot.' Rodney was recovering from the revelation. 'A game changer.'He was grinning from ear to ear. 'Thanks, team. His mind was spinning, and he would have given his eye teeth to know what General Tsygankov would think if he knew they had this transcript.

Freire presented Rodney with the transcript with a flourish.

'Feast your eyes on that, senior retired Major'.

Rodney received the two pages of close-typed message with gratitude. He scanned it and patted Freire on the shoulder.

'First class job of detection, my dear Watson, or should it be Holmes?'

Knowing Tsygankov as he did, he could imagine the old General, whilst initially being amused that Rodney had the transcript because it clearly showed he was not now involved, would nevertheless want to protect his long-time friend and protégé General Polyakov. He would probably rage at the stupidity of Ashchurch and Rodney had a fleeting half wish that Moscow would send an assassin against Ashchurch to save Rodney from a problem which was growing by the hour.

He wandered away, head down, reading the papers and deep in thought.

Chapter Eighteen

Mr. Reid

Mr. Reid's L-shaped operations empire took over most of the far, and half of the road front walls of their large forty by fifty-metre square main operations room. This arrangement left ample room for Graham's square-shaped admin and co-ordination cell, which abutted onto Mr. Reid's, leaving a generous area for Rodney's day desk and conference table to the rear of the room and Laurie's screened-off food and refreshment's area. Rodney thought it was a very military thing to have as one of the team's priorities. Soldiers' comforts in the form of food and drink available 24/7. Budget? What budget. The civil servant housekeepers had long given up any pretence of trying to recover money for Brigadier Robinson's team's eccentricities as they saw it.

Mr. Reid was hunched over his desk. His desk was in the corner facing outwards so he had a view out of the window and could also survey his empire. Members of his team were busy, either shuffling files or making up the battle boards and large planning maps. Whiteboards were fixed on the walls with the maps. Flip charts on their stands were much in evidence.

Mr. Reid of course had his own. Mr. Reid had his phone clamped to his ear, getting an earful of grief from somebody and oblivious to Rodney as he walked over to him. Mr. Reid looked up, rolled his eyes and mouthed, *'food and drink,'* emphasising the urgency for refreshments with his free hand. The old Army field craft sign to 'hurry up', a clenched fist making a quick up and down stabbing movement. Rodney got the message.

Rodney had a look over his shoulder at the refreshment and meal area that Laurie had set up. It was well stocked with provisions and Laurie was fussing round the table, clearing used cups and food wrappers.

Laurie caught Rodney's movement towards his little empire as he approached.

'Hi boss, hot or cold food?'

'Tea for me and an egg and bacon sandwich. Can you heat it up? And for Mr. Reid whatever you've been feeding him and a mug of tea for him too.'

Laurie opened one of the insulated heated hay boxes and passed Rodney four foil wrapped, bulky sandwiches. Then he poured the teas. Rodney looked round the room.

It had had a makeover since he was last here, the walls were pristine, done in antique white with the woodwork in brilliant white. He guessed that after the last mission the two rooms had been in a pretty bad state with the walls needing some TLC after the battle boards and damage from papers stapled or worse to them. *Looks like it will need doing again after this task*, he smiled to himself. He drew his attention back to the sandwiches, following Laurie who soon placed them and the teas on Mr. Reid's desk.

Rodney unwrapped the foil from his sandwich and took a bite out of the piping hot bacon and eggs. Laurie put the tray under his arm and saluted. 'Don't let the teas get cold, gentlemen. Enjoy.'He got a thumbs up from both men, which pleased him.

Rodney chomped on the sandwich. 'Good sandwiches, Laurie. If you have a couple more, can you bring them over? Thanks.'Laurie tugged his forelock. Rodney rolled his eyes. 'Good to have you with us, Laurie. Don't push it!'

Tray in hand as Laurie headed back to his refreshment area Rodney asked if Laurie had had time to find out anything about his neighbour.

'Sorry, Boss, been a little bit hectic up to now but I'm on my way in ten to do a recce of your flats. Check with Graham, he should have something for you by now.'

Reid had finished his call and sat back on his chair, grabbing the tea and food as Laurie landed a replenished refreshment tray on the paper strewn desk. Reid had a smile on his face.

'Banker gave me a nod, Major, says that you're in.'

'Was there any doubt?'Rodney said blandly, and took another bite from his sandwich, egg running onto his fingers. He raised his eyebrows. 'Had a moment feeling sorry for myself and interruption to the life that I'd become used to. No issue, Mr. Reid. Just had to grip myself – like the old days in the Army, eh? Could be I just needed a mental refresher. Needed to visualise a run over Pen y Fan in miserable weather with a weight on my back with you behind me all the way kicking me to get it done. Remember, the cry, *just get it done*, so I am. Back in the game for the duration.'

'Thank fuck for that! I admit that I wasn't sure for a while, but you do seem to have bucked up. Still, life as a beach bum has some attractions I suppose, eh?'Reid's Scots accent was strong and he pulled one eyelid down. The laying on of the Scots accent was in this case not a sign of tension from Mr. Reid but amusement at Rodney's expense.

Rodney grinned. 'Truth be told, I was pissed off that my toys had been taken away. But now,'Rodney said languidly waving his hands round the room, 'I have a new basket of toys to play with! But I admit the basket looks a little overfull.'

Both men laughed and any tension or awkwardness dissipated.

'Very funny Boss,'There was a hint of a smile on Reid's lips. 'Now, let's get down to it. What's on your mind?'

'Gut feeling for the way forward as I see it now. Here goes. This Neil Ashchurch from the Treasury seems to be a linchpin around which others rotate. Reckon that we leave him and his top table associates in situ for the moment, or at least until Freire and the Banker have all his contacts tied down. But as we ring-fence a particular contractor, we take him out of the equation. I think that if we do that, Ashchurch and his mates will get begin to get agitated enough to reveal more of the network. Even if we don't know from them by then, the way Freire and the Banker are working together and the intelligence is piling in I would be surprised if we can't see it. We may need to pull in Ashchurch now for his own protection. I will explain shortly.'

'OK so far.'

'And,'Rodney added, 'We now have a cast iron lead, thanks to Freire and her team, on who is or was behind the scheme.'

'And who is that?'Reid sat up. Rodney passed the transcript to him. His deputy took the papers and began to read. He took in the first few sentences and then shot out of his chair and wandered round the room, reading the papers and muttering to himself.

Rodney calmly munched his sandwiches, supping from his mug of tea. He was analysing the implications. Tsygankov was clearly retired from any active involvement. The odds were therefore that General Polyakov, who was still in post, would naturally be the next in line and natural key player. This could be the time to bring Servo and his partner Carla into play. If they helped him to get what he thought might be in their wish, they could earn their passage to a permanent stay in the UK. He would think on it, at least he thought, until Mr. Reid had finished his round of the room.

Mr. Reid returned to his desk, slumped down in his chair and gently placed the transcript upside down on the table. He took up his mug and had a good pull at the tea.

'Makes some sense now of the whole business. A KGB operation to undermine our economy. Typical operation for them. Keep their borders safe by screwing up others. Anchors the mission somehow.'He looked at Rodney for a lead.

'In one way it does, in another way, Mr. Reid, it throws up a whole lot of questions and some not so easy options. 'He shook his head. 'I think that I need to talk to the Old Man.'He took a breath. 'This doesn't immediately affect my thought on the UK in-house fraud. I think that I'd like to keep new twist of the KGB involvement low key for a moment.'

'You are thinking about Servo and Carla, aren't you?

'Sharp, Mr. Reid, sharp.'

'Could mean a trip to Moscow?'

'Could be.'

'You?'

'Hmm, maybe, maybe not.'Rodney rolled his head over to Laurie Burns. 'Our Ghost.'

'Anything to stop him playing canteen manager, he's driving me crazy. Anyone would think that he was after a Michelin star and service manager award of the year.'For the second time in the last hour Mr. Reid allowed himself a chuckle, before he reverted to his normal dour, serious demeanour. 'Still, could be a dodgy trip.'

' Quite.'Rodney looked at his watch. 'Now, it's time to see what Colonel Jimmy and the others have for us. Have a word with Freire and Graham for me and tell them to hold off on the revelation about the Russians at least until I've spoken to the Brigadier.'

Chapter Nineteen

Colonel Jimmy and the Banker

Chairs had been pulled into a semicircle and they were all filled by the team players bar two until Rodney and Mr. Reid took their place in the middle two seats.

The Banker John Brown stood at the centre point of the semicircle and Colonel Jimmy stood behind him and to the left with a pointer. He held it ready to mark out the data when instructed on the boards behind him.

'Well, ladies and gentlemen, we have our first target to go for. Not bad for a first day, eh?!' The Banker beamed. 'Now, I want to remind you, whilst we have identified the key reprobates in this particular major multinational construction company, let's consider what is possible. Sure, we can pick them up, but that's only a third of the story. Another third is to analyse how they have fraudulently stolen the money. This we have done because of the work previously carried out by Colonel Jimmy and then the team working flat out today. No mean feat, I can tell you. The final third of the task is to get the money back and impose a fine.' He paused, turning to the Colonel. 'Jimmy, give us a run down on the board.'

It took a good half hour for the Colonel to explain the intrinsic nature of the company fraud. He read out the names and the positions of the key company stakeholders who were perpetrating the fraud. A total of twenty-two staff including the company sales, operations and financial directors. He made it clear that the CEO and MD were not involved.

'Help me get my head round this. Can you go over again how they perpetrated the fraud?' Mr. Reid's head was spinning.

'Let's keep it as simple as we can. First of all, simply accept they charged for more men than they put on any one job. And they confuse the poor auditors by swopping men around between all the contracts. Add to that that they have two or more sets of identity for each of the men as far as billing is concerned. And they have phoney subcontractors invoicing for hours worked. These subcontractors are in fact limited companies within the main company. And they have dummy equipment, vehicle and manpower supply companies and agencies purporting to supply men and materials.'The Banker paused, seeing that Mr. Reid was still lost. 'Again, let me put it as simply as I can. The firm charges the Government agency for more engineers, workmen supposedly working than there actually are. The Company charges the agency for more materials – things used to complete a task – than there is. The company charges for more expensive, let's say building material, for example wood, than it pays a supplier. The company repeatedly asks the Government for extras due to rework. An example would be, they lay or repair a section of road motorway, whatever; then, due to a supposed surveyor's oversight or say a late need identified to put in more culverts or a cable duct than they contracted for. And we can show other selected corrupt third parties are involved to make the accounts look real. For example, they buy cheap and charge high against the contracts. Two sets of invoices are produced by each party. The third party gets a kick back. OK?'He directed his attention to Mr. Reid.

Mr. Reid asked, head in hands, 'But how do they get the money into the company? It must show up for a company as large as this when the independent auditors inspect them?'

'Well now, there we are at the heart of the matter. How indeed? They have two sets of books for a start. And this we can prove from published accounts and monies paid in and out. And we have a correlation between the delta for declared income shown in the false company accounts and money channeled into subcontractors who in fact get paid twice; their books are equally falsified and not checked by the auditors. They only check invoices raised and invoices paid. And so, it goes on and on like a one-armed bandit going round, spitting out money. And some subcontractors aren't even registered in the UK. This little twist helps them to launder the money.'

' So how much money for this particular company are we talking about in this instance?'

'Let's say, give or take, £263 million over the last five years. And we are looking at the preceding five years and we are almost there. Another hour or two should see that exercise complete. It seems that they weren't quite so greedy in the early days, as far as we can see.'

There was an audible gasp from the room.

Rodney was taken aback. 'And you can prove this beyond doubt?'

'Indeed, we can, oh yes. Every last penny for the last five years and more to come.'

' Even so, where is the cash and how do we get it back?'

'That, Rodney, is the third part of our task. In this particular company I am proposing a two-phased approach. Firstly, we fine the company itself twice £263, that is £526 million. They get to keep trading, but only after they probably sack the rotten apples and blacklist them. And for where out and out criminal activity of the kind that can't be overlooked, they get their just desserts. We'll then take on these rotten apples and persuade them to reveal where they have stashed the money. We won't get all of it back of course, as some will be out of our reach or spent. Some will be in assets that we'll need to liquidate. But I think overall that it will be a good contribution to what I would like to call "interest and super-profit due to the Crown."'

Rodney got up from his chair and walked over to the board showing the fraud network. He spun round to face the Banker's team.

'OK and whilst I have been thinking on how we should play this, I want your ideas first. Colonel Jimmy?'

'Our agreed position is that John, Pat, Andrew and myself call in the CEO and MD and present the evidence to them tomorrow. Present the evidence and then fine them on the spot and give them only a few hours in our company to pay the Crown. They will need this time to accumulate and move the money. There is likely to be some resistance and prevarication by banks and legal, but we will overcome them. Concurrent activity: the operations team roll up the fraudsters and do whatever you need to…'He hesitated. '…to recover as much money as possible. Andrew, Dan and Shaun will be available to the operations team with supporting evidence as necessary. How do you feel about that?'

'I can run with that. However, I think that Brigadier Robinson, maybe even the Cabinet Secretary, may want to be in on the interview with you to look the CEO and MD in the eye. Mano a mano. We are talking about one of the three biggest construction companies in the UK. The phrase *too big to fail* is running round in my simple brain. What's the company turnover, anyway?'

The Banker took up the conversation. 'I see where you're coming from. And much as it grieves me to say, you are right from every perspective. What we must avoid doing at all costs is getting bogged down as we have at least another half dozen equally large frauds with different companies to crack on with. And, I remind you, the heads of these organisations control a multifaceted spidery network of goodness knows how many third parties. We only have thirty days. This company's turnover is year on year around twenty-five and half billion, with profits of two billion and assets of three billion. They can afford the fine without turning a hair.' He took a breath before continuing in his soft Dublin accent. 'Don't forget, Rodney, that there is no evidence trail whatsoever that the MD and CEO have any involvement in this fraud, quite the opposite. And there will be hundreds, thousands even of foot soldiers who are not just innocent but being taken for a ride but will have suffered because of it in one way or another, financial at least. We need to protect them, their families and livelihoods. Talk about state within a state; never seen the like.'

'I understand. We will do our best to protect the innocent and victims. Now, let me have a word with Brigadier Robinson and I'll be back to you within the hour. Before I go, can you confirm now that say by 0700hrs tomorrow that you could confidently interview the CEO and MD and get a result if I can get a go ahead?'

The Banker and the Colonel looked at each other for confirmation and both nodded. From the sidelines, Andrew and Pat caught Rodney's eye and both gave a confirmatory nod. The Banker said, 'The truth of the matter is that we are in a good position now. Let's go for it, Rodney!' The Banker was adamant.

Chapter Twenty

Major Brown and the Brigadier

Rodney sat quietly, neither tense nor relaxed, just expectant in the armchair, listening closely, waiting patiently while Robinson talked through the situation with the Cabinet Secretary, Sir Geoffrey Gilmore.

The two men's' relationship was one born of mutual respect. Sir Geoffrey, for his part, was at the top of his profession. He had nothing else to prove and was as apolitical and straightforward as a mandarin could be. The Brigadier, for his part, was as straight as they came. He could be devious as any spymaster was expected to be with the enemy but apart from that he was totally committed to his master and his team.

Robinson replaced the phone with a smile on his face. 'He wants in. He'll be with me at the 0900 Banker's fund-raising party.' He chuckled at his little joke. 'Ahead of that, at 0800hrs we'll both come to your ops room for a full briefing to get us up to speed and then try to ask the questions that the CEO and MD may use to defend themselves. Sort of play devil's advocate'.

'Fine, good idea. What I want to do is to lift them early, then hold them incognito in one of our rooms, say my office. Just before nine I'll get Bob's Special Branch with Andrew and the Jones brothers to arrest them. Handcuff them, blindfold them and bring them into the data room. We'll screen the rest of the operation so that they only see what they need to see.'

'OK with that. If it goes wrong, I will of course do my bumbling old codger with apologies and promises of compensation and sackings etc., etc. But I don't think that that will be necessary, do you?' The Brigadier's eyebrows were raised in question.

'From what I've seen, I really don't think so. On another matter, I have something else to brighten your day.' Rodney produced the transcript of the conversation between Ashchurch and Brigadier General Tsygankov, retired.

Robinson adjusted his glasses and took the transcript. He read it carefully with a smile gradually spreading over his face and his eyes crinkling at the edges. He looked at Rodney.

'And why am I not surprised?'

'A development, that's for sure and one that I want to make the most of.'

'Does seem that he's retired from the field though?'The last thing Robinson wanted at this stage was Rodney running after Tsygankov.

'Yes, it seems so, but I'm betting that his old boss General Polyakov is in it up to his neck.'

Robinson turned in his chair to face the wall. He looked over his shoulder at Rodney. 'Polyakov, hmm; I do like him as a man. OK, what do you have in mind?'He was relieved that Rodney seemed to have put his nemesis on the back burner, at least for now.

'Well, what if Servo and Carla could get their hands on the KGB files relating to this fraud? It may just give us the key to the whole operation and its history.'

'Hmm. It means burning not one but two major assets. You would have to bring them in.'

'I know. I know. I am balancing what they might bring to the table against what we can achieve without them. It's a hard call, Brigadier, but given the time constraints and the size of the task if we can shortcut the investigation somehow, it may be worth it. I am of course making the assumption that Polyakov's division is handling the file. Got to be him, I don't think that there is any other part of their organisation that would. I am also assuming that Servo and Carla, who still work for Polyakov, can get file access to what we want, or that they can somehow get close enough to the action to make a killing for us.'

'So, what do you want to do?'

'Send Burns to Moscow to make contact with Servo and Carla and talk to them. Plus, in his care, two open first-class tickets to London for them; just in case. Don't see that Burns needs to stay any longer than necessary. They'll either tell him that they can help, or they can't.'

'That would work.'Robinson turned back to face front. 'I'll get the tickets for you by tomorrow.'He made a note on his pad. 'We're moving at a very fast pace. Can you and the team handle all this without more support?'

'Now that, sir, is the third and final big ask of the day. 'Rodney flipped open his logbook. 'This mission is massive. I'm only beginning to realise just how big after only one day. It's mind boggling. My immediate and overriding concern is around not getting bogged down, whilst remaining fleet of foot. We need the support of Commander Bob Coveney and his team from Special Branch and we desperately need a discreet secure facility for say up to two hundred fraudsters. Initially say a couple of dozen. They will need to be secured, fed and watered. Whilst some of these individuals are simply pen pushers, some will be dangerous and desperate.'Rodney looked at his notes. 'Prior to the 9 a.m. meeting with the construction company, which will be successful as I have heard nothing that might lead me to believe otherwise, I have to pick up a dozen or more of the key players. Discreetly enough for others not to be suspicious and to disappear before we can get at them.'

'How can I help?'

'Please call your friend and drinking partner the Commissioner and ask him to get Bob in and to us within the hour. I did have a meeting with Bob scheduled for tomorrow, but we need to bring that forward if he is going to help us lift the targets tomorrow morning. Second, can you and the Commissioner find me a place to put the fraudsters? Ready from say 0900hrs tomorrow morning?'

'Don't think that that'll be a problem. Leave that to me. Now, anything else on your mind? Some well-meant reticence to ask for more resource perhaps?'

'In time, perhaps as soon as tomorrow, we'll need a few more analysts if we are going to run the ship 24/7. But not today, the team is fired up, shaking itself out and I don't want to disrupt the flow at the moment. What I do need, and thank you for asking, is that Fraud Squad officer, the one we used before. Freddie Howelle, that's the name. We want him and his crew to shake down all the third parties, their networks and businesses. That would be of immense help to stop us getting down into the minutiae of money and asset recovery. This would greatly allay my greatest concern of getting bogged down, and they are after all the experts.'

Robinson made a note. 'Good idea, Rodney. I'll fix that. I'll get Freddie within the hour too if possible. I remember that our Banker has a good relationship with the Fraud Squad, so he can be the liaison body going forward. Are you sure now that there is nothing else?'

'I don't think so, we're good. Just a couple of first-class tickets and of course a return for Burns, I have to get him back or face his wife. Authority for Bob the Fraud Squad officer to play with us. Both will be here within the hour, and a secure facility for tomorrow. That really sums it up for now.'

'Game on, Rodney. Can I offer you a stiffener? you really look as though you need one.'

'Hah, yeah you could say that. Much as I would like to, I don't think that I'd be able to do justice to your whisky.'

'End of the day then, after you have sorted your team and given Bob et al. the good news.'

'Bob, at least, will be pleased to see me back, or possibly not?'Rodney pulled a wry face which brought an open, generous smile to Robinson's normally unreadable expression.

PART TWO

Chapter Twenty-One

Major Brown

As he walked back to his team, he worked out how to handle the next hour or two. He looked at his watch; it was nearly 4 o'clock and he was hungry again.

Rodney grabbed food and tea from Burns and called Graham over.

'Got a fast ball for the team. I need you, Mr. Reid, the Banker, Andrew and Freire. Logbooks all, please. 'As Graham went to get the principals together, Rodney called after him.

'Any news on my neighbour?'

'Nothing yet.'

Rodney spotted Burns loitering around the conference area and went over to him.

'Laurie, I need to talk to you.'

'Thanks, that's good for me as I'm just back from your place, having a dig around about your neighbour.'

'Me first mate, if you don't mind, Laurie.'Rodney held up his hand to block Laurie speaking further.

If he was surprised or miffed, Laurie didn't show it.

'Not at all. Go ahead, Major.'

'I'll be brief, and we can talk again later. I would like you to go and see Servo and Carla in Moscow. OK with that?'

'Hmm, that's a fast ball, but sure.'

'I'll sort the "how to contact"and give you a briefing before you go.'Rodney pulled him to one side. 'As ever, for your safety, this is between the two of us, Mr. Reid, Graham and the Brigadier. '

'Got it, Boss.'

'See you later.'

Rodney restocked with more sandwiches and tea and headed for the conference table where the key players were arriving and settling in.

'Thanks, and sorry to interrupt your work, but I have information which I need to get over to you now, and quickly. Questions at the end.'He took a sip of his tea, then for the next few minutes told them of his meeting with Robinson and the support he had asked for before asking for any clarification questions. Lastly, he reminded them that they would bring the MD and CEO into the operations centre and that he needed Graham and his team to screen off all but the data relating to the fraud in question.

'Mr. Reid, you first.'

'For clarification, my boys with Bob's Special Branch teams, raid and detain the twenty-two individuals identified as the construction company's economic terrorists. Preferably as they leave for work but away from their house. Names and addresses on a list from John, Pat and Andrew.' Mr. Reid looked at Pat. Pat held up five fingers, meaning in five minutes and got a nod from Mr. Reid. 'Good, then I will get my team to plot them on the map before Bob arrives.'

'That's correct, Mr. Reid.' Rodney went on addressing the team. 'They are to be taken to a facility, of which the Brigadier will give us details of shortly. The facility, I hope, will be secure with all the comforts of home. The primary aim is to get them to identify where the money is or has gone. If we can quickly and easily recover the money – John, you can have that pleasure. If it's a protracted and difficult issue, say assets, offshore stuff involved, then maybe, maybe not, so hand them over to the Superintendent, Freddie. He will run his team of specialist officers and be liaison between you and the Fraud Squad. SOP is proper hand over, get the Fraud Squad to sign for the targets so that the handover is clear. The Fraud Squad can spend time sucking them dry and picking over the bones. Mr. Reid, the map is your immediate task as Commander Bob should be here within the hour. Take them round for a briefing from you all so that he knows what he is up against. Same applies to your man from Fraud, Freddie Howelle, John. OK so far?'

'Yes, for now no issues to raise, except what time is this all to happen?'

'You need to have eyes on the targets from first light. As soon as you get the go ahead from me, have them lifted. The action that will trigger the confirmation of the lifts will be when the CEO and MD of the construction company are taken around 0600, in the sure knowledge that they will acknowledge their liability; hopefully tie that all up around mid-morning. OK?'

'Who will lift the MD and CEO?'

'I'm going to leave that to Bob and you, Mr. Reid.'

'What if the CEO and MD don't cave in?'

'As a default, you'll lift all twenty-two fraudsters anyway and we add that pressure to the pot.'

'Happy with that.'

Rodney turned to Andrew and the Banker.

'I 've asked for the Fraud Officer that you've worked with before, if you remember, to be here within the hour. As I said just now, I'm going to leave the detailed briefing and tasking to you. You know what's on Mr. Reid's plate, so you need to dovetail. Andrew, I suggest that you set up a coordinating cell with Graham. It has to work for everyone involved, not only to be able to check where all assets, friend and foe, are at any point in time, but also what they're doing. Any questions, Graham?'

Graham nodded. 'Got that. I'll set up the architecture and battle boards etc. for not only Andrew but Mr. Reid to feed into. Major Freire's intelligence will also feature. And we will reinstitute a dashboard for everyone to see. Think that that will be helpful. Happy with that, Andrew?'

'Happy,' said Andrew.

' Guess that we'd better get on. Anything else, Major? 'Graham asked.

'Not at this time. I'm available to you all if you need more input. Otherwise, I'm going to my desk to write up today. Which is, gentlemen and lady, by any measure a massive step forward. Thank you.'

Chairs scraped and the team dispersed to their action stations. Mr. Reid lingered after the others had disappeared. 'What about Laurie? Need to know whether I can use him.'

'He is going fishing in Moscow first thing tomorrow. He will need some time to himself to prepare and organise for the trip. I'm going to brief him now.'

'Good, makes sense. Speak later?'

'Definitely, we need to do that after we get Bob and Freddie out of our hair this evening.'Rodney grinned.

' Bob is not going to be happy. You might get some heat.'

'Not looking forward to that.'Rodney grimaced. 'What we get paid for pissing off senior officers.'He smiled but he was dreading the encounter.

Chapter Twenty-Two

Respite

'Phew.' Rodney slumped down into his chair and got himself comfortable. He opened his logbook and began to scribble. He desperately needed to get his notes of the orders that he'd given down on paper. It was a discipline born of practice and experience and, he reminded himself, of fairness to the team. He was only too aware that, especially with a lot going on, the memory was fallible over even a short period of time. His shoulders were broad, and he was a believer in 'the buck stops with the Boss' i.e., himself. He wrote furiously for a quarter of an hour, covering four pages in what he thought was his best writing. No matter how hard he tried, his script always looked as though it had been done by a twelve-year-old. He read his notes quickly and then, satisfied, called Graham over.

'Copy these four pages for the ops room please, Graham. They cover the orders that I've given today.' He hesitated. 'Have a dekko and make sure that I haven't left anything out.'

He watched Graham disappear into his admin and coordinating area. Rodney was sanguine; he put his feet up on the desk, took his tea in one hand and a bacon and tomato sandwich in the other. His thought, as he ate, that he was lucky to have such a good team. His first full day back and they had gone along with everything that he'd asked of them, without pushback or argument. Or maybe, he thought with a wry smile, they can read me like a book, and they've trained me so well that I'm following their script without knowing it.

Graham was back. 'Good notes Major, you haven't lost your touch.'

'Brainwashed and programmed, you mean.'

Graham laughed, his lean frame and long face shaking with mirth. 'You might be right at that.' He passed Rodney his logbook back. 'Can I get you anything?'

'No, don't think so, just going to sit and relax until Bob gets here. On second thoughts, ask Laurie to come over on your way back. He seems to have taken over your desk.'

Graham looked across the room to see Laurie, deep in concentration, scrutinising Graham's over-large display screen. 'Cheeky bugger.'

The evening was approaching and the lights in the operations centre were activated. Rodney watched the team draw the curtains over the bomb-blast screened windows. He drew his eyes back to Laurie having his future told to him by Graham.

Laurie put his hands in his trouser pockets, stuck his head in his neck and shuffled over to Rodney.

'Bloody hell, Boss. He gave me a right earful for sitting in his place without asking. I won't be doing that again anytime soon.'

Rodney could only shake his head in amusement and waggle a finger at Laurie. 'That'll teach you.'

'Yeah. Guess what, she is back and is your neighbour. I don't understand it, we chucked Galena Vorakova out and now she's back. It's definitely her. And it can't be a coincidence that she's your neighbour, can it? I don't think so.'He paused and said with a grin, 'I was checking the database of declared and undeclared agents, stroke, whatever you want to call them, when Graham jumped me. In her case, she appears to have diplomatic immunity. Her car bears the DP badge just to emphasis the point.'

'Hmm. I wonder why she's here. Is she a declared bona fide attaché of some sort?'

'Yep, Third Secretary for Arts and Culture.'

'Well, I really don't know what to think. Bollocks. It's clearly a cover, but why me? I'll let the Brigadier know just in case, but otherwise I don't see that there's much I can do about it. Who knows, might get a season ticket to the Russian circus or something?'Rodney made a note. He would talk to Brigadier Robinson later. 'Now, Laurie, here is how you contact Servo and Carla. This is their address. They live on Tsentral naya Ulisa, off Moscow Oblast. Know it?'

'Yeah. What's the block number?'

'You're lucky. It's a small one near Uspeka Auto, just behind the garage. Block number 22A. You go to the block and stick a chewing gum wrapper in their post box. As far as I know, they are currently in Moscow. Don't ask me how I know, just accept it. They, or one of them, will be in Gorky Park for a walk from 0830 to 0900 from the day following your sign to them that we want a meeting. They will walk the park to check that they're not being followed and then go to look around the local church, each day for two days following the day that you post the gum wrapper. Got it?'

'Bloody big park, Boss.'

'Yeah, I know. You need to go to the church on the edge of the park. Tserkov Ioanna Voina Na Yakimanke. Make sure that you're seated in there by 0900hrs. 1st pew in, on the left. Sit at the far end and wait.'

'Got it. Not an issue now that you've pinpointed the location. I'm familiar both with where they live and I am sure the church. Think it is up near the monks' place, massive place.'

'Good. Apart from asking them if they can get the file on this fraud, the situation re the KGB involvement and who is involved, you have to give them the two first-class open tickets for a BA flight. They're grownups, they'll decide if they need to come. In all likelihood, they probably have an escape route already planned. It's up to them. I'm just trying to make it easy for them.'

'We'll see. Just leave it to me, Boss. Been there before and got the t-shirt.'

'I know, I know. Don't, under any circumstances, take any chances. I want you back here in one piece and ASAP. I need everyone on this job.' He sighed. 'If, and I say if, Servo and Carla can help us, it will be a bonus, otherwise we'll simply have to sort ourselves out like we are already doing.'

'I take it that I fly tomorrow?'

'Yep, the Brigadier should have the tickets by tonight. Passport and tickets in your Russian name, Oleg Nicolai Kowalsky, and of course you have your Brit passport in reserve with corresponding tickets. Should cover your needs.' Rodney returned to writing in his logbook as Laurie Burns bounced off, but his mind was partly on Galena. Should he call on her and pre-empt a meeting that could happen if they were living a floor apart? He thought that it might be amusing but, he had no doubt, potentially dangerous. Rodney relaxed, thinking about today and the Banker. He had said something that had been niggling him all day for some reason. What was it? Then he remembered, it was the remark about the construction companies having suppliers or sister companies abroad. Why, Rodney thought, was that information unsettling him so much?

Chapter Twenty-Three

Commander Bob Coveney

The Commander walked softly up to his old friend's desk. He smiled, looking at Rodney, who was head down, working furiously at his logbook task. The Commander had not yet decided whether or not to give Rodney a hard time for summoning him so precipitously. He banged his heavy briefcase on the desk, bringing Rodney's head up, frowning.

'Bob, so glad you could come so quickly. Got a real fast ball.'He looked at the taciturn face of the Commander, quickly judging the atmosphere. 'Hmm, pissed off with me. Fair one. I would rather that I'd been a guest at your office tomorrow. Unfortunately, this task that we've been given has taken off like a rocket so I can only apologise upfront. What can I say, I owe you one?'

Commander Bob, an old soldier albeit ex-BOSS, South African Special Forces, could see that his fellow brother in arms was in the mire. He shook his head and grinned.

'OK, Major, start paying – feed me.'

Rodney called over Laurie, who was hovering in the background.

'Can we feed the Commander and a mug of tea for me, please?'

'Hi Bob. Give me five and I'll give you a meal fit for a king.'Rodney held up two fingers, indicating a meal for himself too. Laurie nodded and left the two men.

'OK, what's this all about?'

'It goes like this.'Rodney briefed him for half an hour during their meal. He finished as both men clattered their utensils on their plates.

'Let me get this straight You want me to work with Jock Reid to lift twenty-two men, hold them and deliver them to a secure facility. Plus, a CEO and MD to be brought here tomorrow morning.'

'That's about it.'

The Commander shook his head in mock disbelief. 'Listen, my old friend. At the end of the day, I'm a policeman. A policeman works for the Home Secretary and is bound by the law. What you're asking is a stretch, even for SO13.'He raised an eyebrow. 'Admittedly, if the team show me the proof, then I could at not too much of a stretch, agree that this issue is, as you term it, an economic terrorist-related incident with violence.'

'That would be great. I'm expecting Chief Superintendent Freddie Howell, Fraud Squad any minute to get his briefing from the Banker John Brown. The briefing will give you the evidence that you want.'

'We'll see. I like Freddie so if he is in, I expect I will be too. In the meantime, I'll work with Mr. Reid to get my men and his stood up. I can always cancel them if you come up short. On past experience my old son, I think it unlikely,' he added, seeing Rodney's face fall as he mentioned cancelling. He looked at his watch. 'I need to get on if we're going to get this done tomorrow by sparrow breakfast time.'He looked at his watch again. 'Two other matters; I need your boss, the Brig, to square this with the Commissioner. I'm kicking the legalism upstairs. It will then be up to others if they want to bring in the Home Office ministers, even though MI5 is clearly in the know. It is, isn't it?'

Rodney smiled. 'Oh yes, and MI6.'

'In bad company then. I trust them about as far as their sloped shoulders will allow if this goes tits up. Now for my other needs. Don't care what time we finish, you, Rodney, can take me to my very favourite Chinese restaurant, run by the delectable and dangerous Jenny Woo.'

Both men laughed.

They had worked together on her arrest as the head of the London Triad and subsequent release in exchange for her help last year.

'Come on Bob, let me take you to Mr. Reid before he comes and rips both of us to bits for ignoring him. Bring your food and drink with you.'

The main operations room was, by any standards, a large room and was by now a maze of screens, Rodney noticed – how the hell had they done that? He shrugged. The screens separated the discrete operation areas run by Mr. Reid from Graham's admin, communications and coordination sections. They followed the sound of his voice which they could hear berating Mould and Sharky for some reason or other.

The reason was simple. Mould had spilled a mug of coffee over Mr. Reid's plan for tomorrow. He was shaking the papers free from the liquid as they arrived.

'Clumsy, my fault. I should never allow drinks on the planning table.'

Mould, head down, was drying up the spill. He rolled his eyes.

'Hi, Mr. Reid. Good to see you and the gang again. Seems that the Major has something even more challenging than normal. I'm up to speed. Just waiting for a briefing from the Banker when Freddie gets here. Until then, let's look at the plan, timings and geographies. What do you say?'

'Good. Rodney, are you staying?'

'Love to, but I need to see the Brigadier immediately to get Bob a "get out of jail" card. Shouldn't be long and I'll join you as and when. OK?'

Mr. Reid looked from Rodney to Bob and shrugged. 'Whatever. Not getting soft in your old age, are you?'

'I wish. We have more red tape these days than a barrister's clerk. I don't want to find myself in a scroll with a ribbon on it.' Bob's wry smile at last got a tacit grunt of approval from Mr. Reid. Mr. Reid knew the score.

Bob looked at the map and notebook strewn desks of the men in the operations section. To a man, those men who sat at the desk turned around, studying their boss and Bob. Sharky was the first to rise and offer his hand to Bob, followed by the rest of the team, Mould, Fred and the Jones brothers. After the initial welcome, Bob turned to Mr. Reid, his South African drawl evident.

'Skipper, ahead of the approvals looks like your team could do with some reinforcements. I suggest that I get four of my section leaders here pronto. How about we split up the hit list, five or six targets per team subject to geographies? We could make the four teams up of one of my men and one of these fine intelligent officers. How does that sit with you? Plus, another senior man plus one to work with you or whoever to collect the CEO and MD?'

Reid rubbed his chin. 'Sounds like a plan, like it.' Mr. Reid lifted the phone from his desk and passed it to Bob. 'Make the call.'

Bob spoke for five minutes or so with his deputy, explaining that they had been landed with a fast ball and who he wanted sent round in the next quarter of an hour. He put on record that he was going to need a bigger force for the morning so to get the men on standby and all the vehicles fully fuelled up. When he had finished the call, he returned the phone to its cradle.

'Job sorted. I just hope that Rodney can get the clearances. Right now, what I'd like to see is the geographic locations of the targets. Home and work locations if you have them, please. This will give me a picture of the task ahead.'

'We've marked the maps up and we're just about to hang them up so we can see clearly what's what where. Come on team, stick the maps up on the wall so the Commander can have a look.'Mr. Reid's team reacted and within a couple of minutes the maps were up, and everyone crowded round them. Mr. Reid stood back.

'Not too bad and Bob, you can see how your idea of forming geographic teams would work well.'He drew four imagined circles with his left hand.'

Bob and the others looked on. 'Going to be a bugger for the northern top circle and the one in the Midlands. It means getting up there tonight. The ones in the southwest and east should be able to be mounted early morning. What do you think, Mr. Reid?'

'I agree. Think we should concentrate on getting the North and Midlands sorted first so the teams can deploy asap.'He frowned. 'Let's get on it now, working out routes in and out, timings, arrest locations etc.'He turned to his team. 'Sharky take over and crack on, I'll be back soon.'He grabbed Bob. 'I've just seen Freddie from the Fraud Squad arrive and you and he need to link up and get the briefing from the Banker. I'll take you over.'

'OK, Doug.' Apart from Rodney and the Brigadier no one but Bob had the front to call Mr. Reid by his first name and then only occasionally.

Reid called out to Sharky as he left with the Commander. 'If Bob's men show up before we get back, give them the tour and start working out the detailed plan.'

Sharky nodded and waved Mr. Reid's team back to the task in hand. Sharky knew that help was needed and wanted to ensure that the SO13 support were met with a job that was well planned and achievable.

Chapter Twenty-Four

Eve of the First Liftings

It was a hectic time for everyone and it was late evening before they felt that they had done everything to make the lift of the targets as seamless and effective as possible with the least friction generated. The issue of keeping the reason for the action secret and the knowledge of the mission ring-fenced to as few people as possible was emphasised to all involved.

Even so, a couple of dozen had or would have full disclosure. Several dozen other players would get at least a peek under the covers. So, Graham had designed a mission chit for everyone to sign to say they could not discuss or disclose the activities of the ongoing investigation on pain of loss of livelihood and certainly pensions. Nobody objected, it was all part of the great game.

At around nine o'clock, Rodney, Bob and Freddie, John Brown alias the Banker and Mr. Reid met in the Brigadier's office for a dram of his special whisky. Rodney gave a summation of the situation and the next day's activities. John Brown added some points for clarification when the Brigadier probed, as was his way.

His next question to the team was to ask 'where to next?' The Banker smiled broadly.

'Well now, sir, that's above my pay grade. But we have made Rodney aware of two immediate prime targets we would like to have at, as they say.' The Banker's Dublin burr was seductive.

'And they are?' He looked at Rodney.

'Either three large Defence contractors or the organisations who buy drugs and other supplies for the NHS. Both have their challenges; both have political implications in their own right. What is not in doubt is the large-scale fraud and that needs the companies to have a good shakedown and sorting out. Either one at a time or we split the team, attack both at the same time and bring in some more forensic account analysts'specialists to help out. That maybe my preferred option, as it happens.'

'Because?' asked Robinson, as ever relentless in his questioning to get to the nub of the matter. He gave the floor to Rodney to carry on.

'For two reasons. The first is that we should get serious money back from both early on. Over time the Fraud Squad can get down in the detail.'He looked at the Fraud officer, apologising for the remark. 'Sorry Freddie but we simply don't have the legal authority, men or training to go digging for the pennies, seizing assets and liquidating them. Secondly, time is short and we want to move as fast as we can before the game goes to earth or our targets bolt.'Rodney's reference to the game was for the Brigadier's benefit, who, as a hunter, appreciated it. 'Having said all that, Freddie, I, John and the team see it as our remit to get the data and evidence one way or another and put it together in a form that leaves no room for maneuvers as far as legal and the villains are concerned.' He paused. 'Once we have had a quick go at them and hopefully ripped the low hanging fruit out of them in the form of cash, we hand them over to you and the system.'

Brigadier Robinson took back the baton. 'I hope that you and Bob can agree that is at least a way forward, a little crude possibly but its simplicity should fulfil the brief from all our masters as the matter stands presently. I see this mission as a collaboration between trusted partners. I am sure that as the job progresses there will be many twists and turns and the plan will be revisited many times.'He smiled. 'As simple soldiers we tend to want to operate in straight lines as far as possible, whilst we accept that we need to plan for the unexpected and redraw the direction as needs dictate. You will find us flexible.'He turned to the Banker. 'In the morning, John, can you and the team give me a single page on the Defence contractor and NHS frauds?' John Brown nodded his agreement. Robinson continued. 'I'll discuss this with upstairs and let you all know the outcome. I don't anticipate a problem. Now, let's toast to success tomorrow.'

After the Brigadier had refilled their glasses and had toasted them, Bob picked up his briefcase.

'Goodnight, Brigadier. I'm taking Rodney for a Chinese meal to overfill him with E numbers before tomorrow's marathon. Chief Superintendent Freddie Howelle is going to join us too. If anyone else would like to join us, you're welcome. I'm paying.'

'Fine offer, another day. I have a few more meetings tonight.'The Brigadier waved the offer away.

'Regrets, Mrs. Reid has a meal on the hob and I don't want to get detention and not be able to attend tomorrow.' A rare stab at a humorous aside by Mr. Reid and everyone laughed in appreciation.

'I'd like to join you, if I may,' John Brown said brightly. 'Not often I get out these days, being retired as I am. Whilst being retired is pleasant in its own way it means you never get a day off, so to speak. With my family long gone now, makes me a solitary old bird until dragged out of my hovel by you young thrusters.'

'Less of the young.' Brigadier Robinson chided. 'By the way, Shepton Mallet is on the short list of one for the detention centre. Just waiting for a final sign off.'

'So, you say, General, but I think that I can give you ten years,' the Banker responded. Everyone laughed.

'Off you go, all of you and let this old man get to his meetings or I'll be in danger of meeting you all tomorrow coming back to the shop as I head out for breakfast.'

Chapter Twenty Five

The Meal

The evening was well set when they left the meeting with Robinson. Bob's driver was waiting with the car for the three men when they exited the building. Bob gave the driver the order to take them to Jenny Woo's Dragon Restaurant in Soho. Minutes later, after driving through the lights of the London streets, they were in a narrow dimly lit street deep in Soho.

The driver pulled up outside the Chinese restaurant and parked. He quickly left the car and ran round opening the doors, letting out Bob, Rodney and John Brown. Bob thanked his driver and asked him what he wanted. 'My usual, sir, would be fine.'Rodney looked at the driver, this was obviously the regular haunt for Bob and his team. Rodney shrugged, and why not.

His gaze lifted to survey the surroundings, imagining how his team had managed that night they raided the restaurant last year in this gloomy street, badly lit with its old, grimy, dust-darkened windows in the continuous run of high buildings either side of the narrow one-way thoroughfare.

A few lights burnt in the windows of some of the street's establishments, casting weak yellow shafts of light into the street. There was music just discernible from some of the occupied flats that were confined where occupied to the third and fourth floors. The only bright point of the night street was the Dragon. True, in the daytime the street was a hive of noisy, busy small businesses where every conceivable commerce was practised. A transformation from dawn to dusk. Money changers, a tattoo parlour, a Turkish barber with attendant nail and beauty bar. Cash businesses for small-time money laundering, as were the pawnbroker and the antique and art shop.

Respectability was lent by a lawyer's practice, an accountancy practice and an upright private detective with a popular but questionable minder sideline. There were numerous small publishers and even a convenience store of sorts, a stationery store.

Jenny Woo had the only restaurant. True, there was a delicatessen but it did not attract her disapproval as it only served hot and cold snacks from early morning to late evening. It was in her interest to remain on the best of terms with her neighbours, using them as cover for her role as head of the London Triad. Jenny had inherited the leadership from her powerful grandfather and was more than amply secured by her father running his Hong Kong and American Triad-based businesses abroad.

'No problem.' Bob smiled and patted his driver on the shoulder. Bob would bring it out to him when it was ready.

The dining room was richly dressed in red velvet paper on the walls and ceilings. Golden dragons ran twisting around the walls. Subdued lighting picked out the highlights on the dragons, giving off richly burnished reflections. The atmosphere in the restaurant was one of calm; joss sticks gave off fragrant scents into the dining area and there was an expectation of the exotic.

Six strategically placed, six-foot-tall, highly decorated Chinese vases and the table layouts with smart dressings lifted the class of the restaurant out of the ordinary. The restaurant was not too busy and Rodney cast his eye round the diners.

A woman, dark-haired, turned round to see the men who had entered and momentarily caught his eye, and there was a flash of possible recognition between them. Rodney was not sure if he had imagined it. The woman was well dressed and her dark hair swung back hiding her features as she faced away from him, blanking another chance to look at her. Turning away, she spoke to her companion who glanced up. Both women were late thirties to middle forties. *They look expensive,* was Rodney's thought as his attention wandered elsewhere. Then he remembered Galena's side kick, Jane. It was a small world.

Jenny Woo, working on her laptop, looked up as she saw the men enter the bar. She closed the lid of her laptop and went to welcome them. John Brown, who hadn't met her before but knew of her reputation and her leadership role in the Triads, was impressed by her poise. She was above average height even for a westerner. He was the last to introduce himself and was pleased when Jenny greeted him with, 'Ah, the famous John Brown.' She put her hands on his shoulders. 'The notorious, mysterious Banker. Welcome.'

'You know about me?' John was taken aback.

'My dear John, everyone who has any connection with merchant banking and finance is in awe of the legend that is John Brown. At times I heard you have been quite naughty with some of my acquaintances, but then again, they shouldn't have messed with the man.' Jenny smiled and hooked her arm in his and guided the blushing elderly Banker and his companions towards the rear of the restaurant. They entered a plush private back room adorned with fine Chinese artefacts and paintings.

Chief Superintendent Freddie Howelle from the Fraud Squad was already there, head down, studying the menu. He got up as his dining companions entered the room. 'Hope that you haven't had to wait too long for us?' Bob asked.

'Not at all, just got here myself. Been prepping for tomorrow.' Noticing a smiling Jenny Woo, he stopped, looking guilty.

Bob laughed. 'No problem then. Jenny, can we have your late-night feast for us four and the driver wants the same as usual. Water, Chinese tea and Tiger beer all round for us, I think.'

'In a hurry, Bob?' Jenny picked up the vibes of a team wanting to talk. 'I'll serve you myself so don't worry about any other intrusion. Don't forget, life has been very dull for the last six months. It is good to see you all back together. I hope we have no reason to tremble. If so, save a walk-on part for me would you please, if you can, in whatever drama you are planning.'

Everybody laughed and Bob said. 'You'll be the first to hear from me if you can help.'

With an 'Oh good.' she was gone. Rodney watched her go, frowning. If anyone could give them a lesson on money laundering, apart from the Banker or Freddie, she was the one he would turn to.

The background enticing cooking smells of Chinese food filled the room, making the men realise that they were hungry despite Laurie Burns' best efforts to keep their sugar levels up.

As one, the men shook out their red napkins and looked at one another expectantly.

'Well, guys, I, for one,' Rodney looked round the table 'would very much like to know more about fraud. Any takers?'

Freddie smiled wryly. 'Where to start? That's the question. To start with, preventing it isn't always possible, so you need robust strategies to detect it. To detect it, you need intelligence and good analysts. You need to look at your business and do proper in-depth and honest risk assessment. When you detect fraud, you need to investigate it. In my humble opinion, companies or individuals get taken because they fail to do a proper risk assessment, leaving themselves open to fraud.'He paused. 'And it helps to have a whistleblower or two, which we don't currently have.'

'Hmm. A lot to consider. OK, so Felon A perpetrates the fraud and ends up with the money. How did he make the cash out of the company?'

Freddie smiled, warming to his subject. 'There are, say, eight main scams. The first is the most popular, billing fraud. For example, overstating labour and materials and, of course, any other equipment needed to complete the job. Then there is contract rigging. In this case a number of suppliers collude to fix prices etc. I personally hate this practice. There is bribery and corruption. This form of fraud is as varied as the grains of sand on the beach. Collusion, blackmail, incentives. This is a creeping, invidious form of fraud, to my mind. And opportunities to buy or acquire cheap and sell high. Then there are made-up vendors, for example companies who are fictitious or phantoms but who receive money. Individuals also use this scam for purchasing non-existent products or services.'

At this point Jenny Woo tapped the door and pushed it open with her foot, her arms carrying a heavy tray full of drinks. Rodney was quick to rise and take the tray from her. For a moment, their eyes locked and Rodney thought he could see fear flicker across her face. It was gone in an instant, but Rodney had seen it and Jenny knew that he had. She was momentarily flustered, but she covered it up with a diversion, or so Rodney thought.

'Your Mr. Reid, is he well? I heard that he'd also been hurt last year.'

'He's absolutely fine now.'Rodney smiled.

'You must bring him here.'A slight hesitation. 'Soon, please.'And then she was all business. 'Waah, must get your food. Excuse me, Rodney.'

Rodney put the drinks tray on the table and spread the drinks around, saying, 'Freddie, please continue with your talk, it's fascinating.'

'OK, quickly then. False representation. A beauty. Using undocumented and phantom workers, supplies, materials and charging for them. Falsifying reports, insurance certificates, all sorts. Then substitution of cheap materials for promised higher quality ones etc. Manipulation, for example, contracting a lump sum for time and materials and diverting this sum to expenses, billing time and materials to change orders. Cross-charging etc., etc., clever but complicated, a lot of work for the fraud account manipulators and something Colonel

Jimmy initially used in his investigation to crack the cases wide open. How's that?'

'Mind boggling,'Bob commented. 'But how do they get the mountain of cash they skim off out of the business?'

'Good question,'said the Banker. 'Fraud is the most commonly used crime in the UK and elsewhere for that matter and costs many, many billions of pounds a year. I think that Freddie would agree that, in the context of what we are talking about today, we could simplify the fraud into money laundering, a simple example of which could be buying an asset cheap and selling it on high. Then bank the money overseas. Could be buying dummy companies, all sorts, to give the money legitimacy. There are many forms, the second tranche involves tax avoidance. Cash in hand etc., and at the other end of the spectrum, clever tax lawyers beating up Her Majesty's Custom and Exercise.'

'Ah, our food.'Bob clapped. Jenny Woo kicked open the door again, laden with candle-heated trays and a huge bowl of Chinese crackers with dips.

'Major, will you help me with the trays of food please?' Jenny asked Rodney on the way out. The others looked at him, he shrugged and followed Jenny Woo out.

'This way, Rodney.'Jenny made her way to the kitchen and she looked back at him. 'I do need to speak to you and Mr. Reid about some rumours that my people are bringing me and a lady you will know. They may not mean anything, but they do involve you and your team.'

Rodney was stunned for a moment. 'Look Jenny, we're flat out tomorrow but I could get Mr. Reid here tomorrow night, say early evening?'

'That would be good. I can ask my people for more details. It may be nothing but then again maybe not. Food, or it will get cold.'

Rodney and Jenny collected two trays, each stacked with food. Rodney took a quick look for the two women that had caught his eye when he had entered the restaurant earlier, but they had gone. With the trays in hand, Jenny and the Major returned to the back room and were greeted with cheers from the others.

Left alone, the four men got stuck in to the crispy duck, satay chicken, battered king prawns and spicy beef dishes. Rodney's favourite was the Singapore rice with chicken and prawns embedded and with the hot 5 spices it was liberally cooked in.

Through mouthfuls of food Freddie took up the theme of money laundering.

'Generally, I look at money laundering as a three-stage process. First, they have to place the dirty money so they don't get caught with it.'He refilled his plate.

'We mentioned some of the ways before, basically moving the money into shell or subsidiary companies by paying for false services and goods etc. There is an opportunity here to move funds into companies based offshore and from offshore accounts into a near untraceable network of shell companies and owners paying out for whatever. They will likely have clients in some cases where the clients use money to invest in their own company for off- the-book projects or to pay, for example, cash in hand artisans and labour.

'To illustrate how diverse and weird this game can get, I had a case last year. Simple but clever. Basically, the criminals opened a network of cash businesses. A Turkish hairdresser network of a dozen shops and the same in nail bars. Punters normally pay cash. So, our bad lads load the day's takings with cash from their criminal activities, mainly drugs and prostitutes and the activities of others, in this case white-collar fraudsters. They then used the cash to buy up property and other tradeable assets. What they fell down on was a couple of alert bank staff doing the audit on local businesses doing well who couldn't believe how much the Turkish barbers and nail bars were raking in. So, they alerted us and the rest is history.'He took a drink.

'Second stage is layering. We touched on it just now, but this is reckoned to be the most difficult and complex stage. This is where they separate the illicit earnings from their source. The fraudsters we are dealing with will be, once the money is made, wanting to quickly begin to move the money offshore, electronically where they can. Suitcases full of cash going through Customs is a risk. Even the use of couriers carrying small amounts is risky and clumsy. They will be constantly moving money from one account to another, taking every advantage they can of loopholes in the regulations.'

He stopped to refill his plate. 'Lastly, a stage where the money is now unidentifiable and they can draw on the funds, pay off partners, for example the KGB or integrate the money into legitimate businesses.'

'How the hell do they do that?'Bob wanted to know.

'Diverse ways. How about high-end art for the boardroom? A luxury company holiday home on the Costa Brava? Make up any deficit in the pension funds? Directors and staff bonuses? A luxury cruiser, fast cars, property etc. etc. For some it is a drive to accumulate sterling and dollars, because they need those currencies to do business. Take Russia as a prime example.'

The Banker wiped his mouth with his napkin. 'What we lads are missing in this task is *Qui tam*. This is where a whistleblower can file a lawsuit on behalf of the government and share in the money recovered. The Latin expression for this is *Qui tam pro domino rege quam pro se ipso in hac parte sequitur*. The law dates from 1318 under King Edward and was fruitful for the Crown. But we don't have any whistleblowers, unless you could call Colonel Jimmy a whistleblower.'

Rodney pondered this for a moment.

'Do you think that we should put some greater emphasis on finding some? Goes without saying that for the men we pick up tomorrow it must be a priority.' He looked at his watch. 'Wow, it's almost today, gentlemen. We'll interrogate them, but it may be worth giving them the chance to turn in our favour?'

'Consider it a given, Rodney. Mr. Reid and I have discussed just that. Yep, right, I'll pick up the tab and see you in the car. Freddie, you could join us.' Bob stood and left them to say goodbye to each other.

At the car, Rodney and the Banker stood talking, Freddie hailed a cab and was gone. The Banker had the use of a flat nearby when he was in London and was going to walk but would wait till Bob joined them. They stood chatting in the street and listening to the background sounds of Soho, noisy at times from revellers enjoying all it had to offer even at this late hour. And it had a special smell, not unpleasant as it was mixed with the smells from the restaurant. A few minutes later Bob rejoined them.

'All done. Jenny didn't want to take any money but, as I told her, if she didn't let me pay then I couldn't come back. I'll drop you off on my way home, Rodney. What about you John?'

'I'll walk. See you both in the morning.' He waved himself off, leaving Rodney and Bob climbing into the car.

Chapter Twenty-Six

Revelation

It wasn't as though Rodney was thinking about the mission, in fact it was the last thing on his mind as he faced the morning chore of shaving. He fired a blob of foam into his hand, raised it to his face and spread and rubbed it onto his skin. As he worked it, some flicked off onto the sink surround. Why he had the random thought at this moment in time as he looked at the spilt foam he didn't really know. Perhaps it was the spread of the splattered foam or the slight hangover and sluggishness brought on from the late Chinese meal and the chemical beer, or it could have been the remark that in the USA fraud in the defence industry, health and others cost the taxpayer not multiples of millions every year, but many billions.

*What if,*he thought, *what we're facing in the UK is replicated in our nearest neighbours, France, Holland, Germany and or Spain?* A sort of United States of Europe being defrauded. It would make sense from a lot of perspectives, especially moving materials and money around. Now it clicked that was what had been on his mind all yesterday. He made a mental note to feed the revelation to Andrew and get him to dig around with the team. Feeling pleased with himself he had a feeling, an excitement even, that he was warming to the mission.

A few hours later Rodney sat in the annex room to the main operation centre, studying the complicated presentation set up to rock the lives of the construction company CEO and MD to the core. They had set up the area with two sets of chairs and desks. Rodney sat at the desk with three chairs. The other desk, set at a right angle, had two chairs. This formed two sides of a boxed area. The third side of the box was made up of the presentation boards. Forming the fourth wall was the massive six metres long by three metres high display of the spidery network of the fraud showing its depth and breadth. The scene was set. He tried to follow the threads of the networks but got lost time and time again and had to reset. This really was something outside his experience and he was not sure he would ever fully understand what the hell was going on and it frustrated him.

Rodney had spoken to Andrew about the fraud possibly being international and not just UK-wide. Andrew immediately grasped the significance of the revelation. In truth, Andrew realised, Rodney's lightbulb moment could answer some of the questions that he, Pat, the Banker and Colonel Jimmy had been wrestling with.

'Well, well.'Andrew scratched his head. 'This thought of yours definitely has legs. We'll get on to it after the presentation.'

It was half past seven when the Cabinet Secretary, Sir Geoffrey Gilmore, and the Brigadier joined Rodney as he sat at the desk. They were early and they apologised for that. Rodney stood to welcome the two men and introduced them to the team. While the team briefed the VIPs, Rodney excused himself, as he wanted to know how Mr. Reid was getting on. Rodney's vacant chair would be taken by Chief Superintendent Freddie Howelle in his absence.

In the main operations room, Graham and his team had done a good job of screening off the activities from 'civilians'but Rodney was not completely happy with the situation, albeit only for a few hours, until the CEO and MD had hopefully been justifiably fleeced and the Exchequer repaid. The screening disrupted the process flow of the task. Maybe they could do something differently with the screening. He would discuss that later with Graham if he had the energy. Not the biggest thing on his mind but he did wonder if he was suffering from OCD.

He found Mr. Reid lying back, relaxed, in his chair alongside Bob. In front of them were several large display screens. One was being worked by one of Major Freire's signallers. Another was a member of Bob's men from the Special Branch working the location maps as the various local police and Special Branch officers rounded up the fraudsters. His screen was split to see several operations going on concurrently and he toggled between operations. The third and final flat screen was actual live feeds of scenes from the field. A further desk had a signaller and a Special Branch officer working on communications between the field teams and the centre.

Rodney stood behind Mr. Reid, taking it all in and listening with one ear to the radio traffic. The team were so engrossed in the capture of the targets that it was a few minutes before they realised that Rodney was present.

'Hi Rodney, good that you could join us. This is a particularly key moment as we're about to lift the financial director.'

'Got a place to put him and the rest yet?' Rodney was annoyed with himself; he hadn't had a moment since he arrived to update himself on this critical piece of the jigsaw.

''Yep, and not a bad location. Could have been so much worse,' Mr. Reid said, with a grin.

'Where is that then?' Rodney had to ask as Doug Reid hadn't offered any other information.

'The old Shepton Mallet Prison as the Brigadier had predicted.'

'My goodness! Is that still going?'

'Yep, Cat C lifer prison. But mainly old boys, wasting out their time.' Bob swivelled in his chair. 'Takes about 200 inmates today, ideal for us and the situation at the moment is that it's more than three quarters empty. It has been under threat of closure for many a year since it was no longer needed as a military prison. They have three complete wings immediately available. Plus, they can redeploy the current inmates around the system over the next few days if they need to. By this time next week, we could have the place to ourselves with all mod cons and staff to boot. Brigadier Robinson did us a big favour sorting this one. Good, eh?'

'I take it that the Home Office didn't object?'

'They didn't blink, why would they? Win for them. The closure goes ahead when we're finished and it's now on someone else's budget. Win for us. Our own castle that we will not be sharing.' Reid was pleased.

' Brilliant. How are we getting on here? it all looks amazingly busy.'

'Pretty good so far and half the catch is on its way to Mallet. Take a seat and join us for a bit.'

'Nothing I would like more, but...' He looked at his watch. 'I need to collect the CEO and the MD from my office and bring them in for what I hope will be the most expensive cup of tea in their lifetime.' He patted both men on the shoulder. 'Thank you all. See you soon.'

He found two confused, well-groomed civilians sitting in his office with the two exceptionally large ex-Welsh Guardsmen, Fred and Lewis Jones, standing silently either side of the only door of the room. Hands clasped, folded left over right in front. The overall effect was intimidating.

Rodney didn't introduce himself.

'Good morning. Please follow me.' He swivelled on his heel and the Jones brothers made it clear that the two men should follow. Rodney walked quickly to further unsettle them as they had to shuffle to keep up. The CEO, short and over-fat, was soon breathing hard and perspiring. The MD by comparison was tall, lean and fit. *Just as well*, thought Rodney. By the looks of him the CEO could well have a coronary by the end of the morning. Suddenly taking pity out of consideration for the man, Rodney slowed as he approached the operations room and smiled at the two men.

'Gentlemen, the next few hours will be a revelation to you, of that I have no doubt. Stay calm. Stay focused. Listen very carefully to what is being said, it is complicated. Listen and evaluate the offers made to you that are in your interests. Now, shall we join the team?'

The men looked at each other, no wiser, warned of what, they had no idea.

Rodney led them into the operations room, past the screen closing off other activities not of their concern. The radio traffic could not be disguised behind the screens but that all added to the drama of the moment. Past Graham's screened area and the clatter of printers and photocopiers, into the den of the Banker.

Rodney walked them into the room, straight to their chairs and sat them down. He then went and stood behind the Brigadier and waited for the chill of the occasion to settle into the room. The Brigadier and Sir Geoffrey resumed their seats next to Freddie. Only when he judged that the men's attention was fully engaged with the displays and array of the Banker's team before them did he give the Banker the nod.

Chapter Twenty-Seven

The Banker's Parallel Universe

'Good morning, gentlemen. Let me introduce you to...' He picked up the shake of Rodney's head indicating that himself and the Brigadier were to be left out. 'Sir Geoffrey Gilmore, who you will know of course. Myself, John Brown. Chief Superintendent Freddie Howelle, Fraud Squad. Colonel Jimmy, Treasury. I think that will do for now. You will be wondering why you are here and that's perfectly understandable. It will help you if you imagine a parallel universe functioning all around you at work. By its very nature, a universe invisible to you but inextricably linked to every facet of your life and company. Rather like our world, your parallel universe operates every hour of the day, every day of the year.'He raised his eyebrows and paused for effect. 'We would like your undivided attention for half an hour while we introduce you to this new world and what it means to the two of you and the future of your company. To put your minds at rest, the frauds that we will show you are being perpetrated in this other universe. And yes, by senior and not so senior members of your company. You will be delighted to hear that we are quite convinced that this has been going on without your knowledge or approval. Relax, and please help yourself to the refreshments provided on your desk.'

The men nodded, worried but still uncertain how to react. On their desk was a percolator flask, cups, a milk jug, sugar bowl and a plate of biscuits. For half an hour they listened carefully with growing alarm and incredulity. Colonel Jimmy was in his element, he knew his subject inside out and if any man made his name that morning, it was him. What a player! Rodney was delighted with his performance and the Brigadier turned round more than once to nod his approval at Rodney's choice.

The Colonel finished off and the Banker took over, his Irish brogue adding gravitas.

'And now, gentlemen, you will have some questions. I want to give you a copy of the twenty-two principal names in your companies who

127

have masterminded the frauds with the connivance of other third parties.'He handed them the lists and gave them a few moments to scan them. 'Your questions?'

The MD sparked up. 'You can prove all that's been said?'

'Oh yes. The records are there to prove that all we have related to you is true.'The Banker waved his hand towards a table marked "evidence"with a stack of orderly labelled files.

The CEO stirred, pale-faced in his chair. 'This is incredible, gentlemen. I find myself in denial, yet you have clearly shown what I don't want to believe but know to be true. Let's assume that all is as you say: what do we do, what can we do, what do you want?'

Sir Geoffrey took the question. 'What we don't want is your company to stop trading and working. You've heard the expression *too big to fail*. It doesn't only apply to banks but to our country's key industries too. What I want is the money taken from the British taxpayer by fraud returned. That seems to me the minimum that you can expect. We can show you where every penny has been stolen from. Colonel Jimmy gave the figure in his presentation. We have,'Sir Geoffrey looked at Rodney, 'picked up and incarcerated the twenty-two men on the list in front of you.' Sir Geoffrey fixed the two men with a glare before looking up at the large Civil Service clock with its Roman numerals. The clock showed 10.30 am. 'Pay up by two this afternoon. That gives you three and a half hours, and you get to keep the company, your positions, reputations, pensions, bonuses and any government contracts currently in play.'

Both men threw up their hands.

'How can we do that by two?!'cried the CEO.

Sir Geoffrey was stoic, unbending. 'The Banker, John Brown, and his team are available to you until two. They have been working on how to make the payment happen. They will show you how the bill can be paid without damaging your company or both of your reputations. They will also take you through the evidence as and when if you want to clarify a point. I will return at two to close out this miserable affair.'He led the Brigadier out of the room, trailed by Rodney.

Once they were deep into the main operations room Sir Geoffrey let out a 'Phew, fingers crossed we have one in the bag.'

'Hmm we'll see if that's the case at two o'clock. Rodney, take us to Mr. Reid. Let's see how the other half are doing in the field.'The Brigadier was secretly delighted with the morning's efforts so far but would not show it outwardly.

'Of course. I just wanted to add that today's windfall is hopefully not the only money we want to get back. We, with the help of Freddie, will try our best to recover money and assets where we can sensibly get at them.'

'Good to hear that, Rodney.' The Cabinet Secretary was more than delighted, 'Don't suppose you have a feel for what we might recoup?' He checked himself. 'No, of course not, too early but good to know we might get something back off the villains!'

Chapter Twenty-Eight

The Capture

The operations team were heads down when Brigadier Robinson, Sir Geoffrey and Major Brown entered the team area. As they entered, Bob got up and welcomed them.

Sir Geoffrey shook hands with him and asked how it was going.

'Well, sir, I wish all operations went as smoothly as this one. What helped is that the targets had no inkling of what was going down. There were a few targets out of position, but they were quickly tracked down. Overall, 150 of our men were involved this morning, spread around the country. All twenty-two on the list are on their way and some have already arrived at the prison in Shepton Mallet.'

'Well done, Bob, and the rest of you. Please give my congratulations to all the men in the field.' Sir Geoffrey turned to Mr. Reid. 'Mr. Reid, what's next to do?'

'We're going to see them processed and settled in. We will probably do a preliminary review of the senior managers at the same time. The purpose of this review is to see if we can quickly identify if any of these men are assets we can use.' He smiled at Sir Geoffrey. 'Our review will be swift, crude but effective to give us a feel for the calibre of men we will be up against, and I would be disappointed if some useful gems of intelligence were not uncovered. Then Freddie Howelle and his people will begin the interviews from this late this evening. What we want from them is their contacts, what part they played in the fraud and how they operated. There are a lot of background soft issues to go at. Bob will set up mini task forces with the local police and CID as I understand it. They will support Freddie to get bank statements, undeclared assets etc. squared away. There will be the families to sort out, many of whom will be quite innocent of their partner's activities. A lot to do.' Mr. Reid pointed to a desk covered with paperwork. 'We were working on the plan to sort out the issues when you arrived.'

Bob looked at some of the maps, and frowned.

'It's quite a task they've given us. Nevertheless, we all fully understand the importance of it all. My people, along with Freddie's and the local police with the support of the Chief Constables, need to grip this from here, so by doing so freeing up Rodney and the team to move on to the next target.'

'We'll all share the intelligence that's gleaned with our partners as it will help us work our way into the root of the fraud and those at the top of the tree.'Rodney was thoughtful for a moment. 'The conundrum is when will be the right time to pull in the men in public service facilitating the money tree.'

'Very poetic,'chided the Brigadier.

'Agreed, sir, but I've been giving it some thought. Colonel Jimmy tells me that the two big organisations which make up 80% of the fraud are the NHS and the Defence contractors and they are ripe for picking. Could be a week or two and we did discuss going for both at once, or not, or one immediately after the other.'

'So?'Sir Geoffrey wanted to know.

'So, my preferred option at this time, knowing what we know, is to pull in the two major sectors and then go for the principals perpetrating this fraud.'

'What, if anything, Rodney do you think might deflect you from that course?'Sir Geoffrey raised his eyebrows, showing that he was interested in Rodney's analysis.

'Clearly, intelligence coming in that makes it necessary and if the principals suddenly start preparing to do a runner. We would know in their cases as they are under surveillance. Another matter is that of external third party's interference'

'Third parties?'Sir Geoffrey looked questioningly at Brigadier Robinson.

'I thought, Sir Geoffrey, that you might join me for a quick luncheon in my office and Rodney can explain. Must say, there are one or two interesting and unexpected developments that you should know about.' The Brigadier canted his head to the side.

'I am intrigued, my dear Robinson.'Sir Geoffrey turned to the team. 'I just want to thank you for your efforts today. I am sure that there will be many twists and turns before this is all over, even disappointments at times. These disappointments we will have to work our way through. I want you to understand that we consider this fraud as an act of economic terrorism of the worst kind and the men at the top as traitors.'He paused. 'Should you need anything, resources, authorisations, whatever and it is within our power, which is considerable, please pass your requests through Brigadier Robinson with whom I am working closely.' He shook everyone's hand before smiling at the Brigadier. 'Time for lunch, and you can tell me about these third parties.'

Chapter Twenty-Nine

Laurie Burns, the Ghost

Laurie watched, dry-mouthed with a growing excitement in his gut, the City of Moscow grow ever bigger as the BA 747 circled to land. He later rationalised and acknowledged that in retrospect there might just have been a hint of anxiety too. His mind was also busy, miles away, remembering his trips to the city in a past life, at the same time processing the task ahead.

He was certain of two things– the first was that the Russian security services would be as paranoid as they ever were, the second was that he wasn't going to take any chances and on entry he would use his British passport. Armed with and having the legendary letter of invitation from the freight forwarding company was in Russia as important as the passport. He would, of course, visit the company as a potential client. The letter had been put together hastily but it was sound. He was to pose as a salesman from a British freight company seeking a partner in Russia. The British freight company had supplied and organised the letter and had facilitated the secret intelligence services many times over the years in one way or another. If anyone checked he had the card from his contact in the freight company, a retired military man. Like many companies the freight company employed their ex-soldiers as they were thought of them. These ex-soldiers might wear many hats while holding down a regular post in the company. Not surprisingly, in a situation like this they came into their own.

Overnight the Secret Service sections responsible for documentation and letters had put together a past life – business cards, brochures and letters of introduction from a well-known company. The MD of the company owed the Service a few favours and was happy to play along. Laurie felt more than happy with his cover, it was certainly a far cry from his last masquerade in the dacha of General Tsygankov in southern Russia as a wine merchant.

He had made the decision early on to go directly to the Russian freight forwarding company at the airport to help build further credibility in the legend. The Russian company was conveniently located midway between the new international airport Sheremetyevo and the old airport serving mainly internal flights. Laurie preferred the old airport; it was decadently tired. He loved the old long bar with the crush of people that seemed to inhabit it, smoking themselves into oblivion along with their vodka.

He liked the Russian people, and was in awe of their humour in adversity. They had, to his mind, had a miserable hell of a time for most of the century, if not centuries. Maybe it was that they lived in fear of betrayal, loss of their freedom or worse, which made the average citizen want to live life well while they could.

Laurie had chosen the location of a hotel, wisely he thought, just south of the Volga, not too far, at a pinch, from both his immediate locations. Far enough out of the city to be of little interest to the security forces. Close enough for the first phase of his task which would enable him to walk to Servo and Carla's accommodation block this afternoon. The other advantage of the hotel location was Gorky Park was also within a brisk walking distance for the meeting that he hoped would take place the next morning, or if necessary, the following day.

The aircraft slid onto the runway of the gigantic airport, flaps down. The engines roared as they went into reverse thrust and slowed the Boeing to a speed that was slow enough for the pilot to feather the brakes and, using the residual momentum of the plane, coast into the docking area.

He had been woken from his reverie when the undercarriage hydraulics began to push out the landing gear before the wheels locked down with a clunk. Time to switch on. As the plane pulled onto the stand, Laurie was surprised at himself, he suddenly felt quite relaxed and at peace with himself. He did a quick review of his situation and the positives. He had booked into the Hotel Zhenchuzhna, roughly three miles from the meeting point, and less than two miles from Servo and Carla's flat and he had secured one of the two turret rooms where he had a great view of anyone approaching the hotel entrance. Sure, it was a little old fashioned but the rooms looked fine. As a bonus it was close to the Moscow water park. Laurie thought that he might take a look if he had time to use up.

Typically Russian, the passengers leapt out of their seats before the aircraft was settled and Laurie followed suit. He wanted to be in the middle of the crush going through Customs and Immigration, not at the front while the Immigration and Customs officers were alert, nor at the back of the queues where the officers had more time to scrutinise passports and paperwork. As it was, when Laurie got to the Immigration desk and handed over his documents to the stony-faced lady immigration officer who, with agonisingly slow due diligence, eventually with a dismissive, almost rude wave passed his papers and passport back, with not even a *'Welcome to Russia.'*Fair one, considering.

The lunch on the flight had not been filling so as Laurie walked across the disembarkation concourse, he spied a fast-food outlet and bought himself a cheese hamburger and a long coffee. The coffee was lukewarm so he drank it quickly and bit into the cottonwool bun, plastic cheese and slipper-hard, overcooked burger. He shrugged; this was real life, this was Russia.

Outside at last in the cold of the day, looking round he chose an old, battered taxi that had just pulled up and discharged a passenger. Other taxi drivers, waiting in a queue for a fare, shook their fists and shouted at Laurie's driver. The driver, with a helpless gesture, held up his arms in surrender. Laurie shouted out to them, 'Sorry guys, it's my father!' The other drivers swore and waved them irritably away. The driver, a white-haired old boy, was chuckling, cowering behind the wheel and ignoring the other taxi drivers, amused at Laurie's efforts to placate them. The driver himself was only too keen to have another fare without having to queue with the others.

Laurie gave the address of the forwarding company to the driver. The man was even older than Laurie had initially thought and Laurie hoped his eyesight was up to it. Old, certainly eighty plus if he was a day, unshaven and a scruffily dressed peasant of a man, short of a tooth or three. Laurie found that during his time with him the man chain smoked his way through life, the cab certainly smelt of strong Russian cigarettes, there were other smells as well intermingled with the smoke. The cab itself was dirty, years of grime and litter strewn both front and back. Laurie wouldn't have been surprised if the driver lived in it 24/7. The man's accent was coarse, throaty and difficult to follow at first. Laurie was up to the challenge and with his fluent North Moscow accent had the old man laughing before they arrived at the first stop. Laurie liked the ordinary Russians and had a soft spot for the not so well-heeled, as he had himself been poor once and knew the score.

Could be it was the memory of the always hungry, rag-arsed and difficult childhood and teenage years he had endured before the Army brotherhood had given him a home. He felt a kinship with people like the driver and thanked his lucky stars that he had found a way out of poverty.

Not that his Army career had been without challenges. He had been shot at, got at, been hot, cold, frozen and there was no cold like Army cold, he always thought. Stuck in a hide, trench or scrape for days with the bitter cold and freezing rain seeping through the layers of supposedly winter clothing.

At his destination the taxi shuddered to a stop. Laurie climbed out of the taxi and took in the area and the freight business to his front. There was a lot going on around him, the area was noisy. A couple of lines of container trucks stretching into the far distance were being loaded in turn with forklifts. Porters and other manpower were much in evidence supporting the operation. There didn't seem to be any attempt to clean up detritus generated by the activity and the area sported broken pallets kicked aside and polystyrene, paper and cardboard lay in piles everywhere. With the noise from the aircraft taking off and landing all adding to the mix it seemed to Laurie to be unorganised chaos. He was just thankful that for a fee the taxi driver had agreed to wait for him while he made his call.

The forwarding agency turned out to be a surprise in all the chaos, a pleasant one too. The agency office was housed in a large airfreight-filled warehouse. The office was manned by a team of attractive Russian ladies who were enthusiastic in their welcome.

They flattered him and were only too keen to welcome another international client. They discussed at length how they and the UK company Laurie represented could mutually aid one another.

Coffee, vodka and aptly named rich Russian honey cake were served to him. Russian honey cake, he was assured, predated Soviet times and was developed by the chef of Tsar Alexander. They also insisted that he try a slice of delicious nutty, sweet, rich Kiev cake by contrast, something very special, developed by the Russians in the austerity times.

He skillfully batted off personal questions and details of where he was staying. The last thing he wanted was the ladies turning up to host him when he was on a job. They did get a promise out of him to take him round Moscow on his next visit. Laurie saw himself out with difficulty.

They wanted to show him round the freight stores and other parts of the operation. Fair one, he thought and promised to come back before he returned to the UK but this afternoon he had a pressing engagement in Moscow. Laurie was relieved and grateful that the driver had stayed put, it would have been difficult to get another in this area and the last thing he wanted was to have to ask for a lift.

On the twenty-mile drive to the hotel Laurie learned that the driver's name was Sergei. Sergei told him of his early life in rural southern Russia, the hardships and his conscription into the Army in the Second World War.

He told him of the desperate times in the frozen steppes fighting the Germans and his eventual release back into civilian life but with little prospect of employment. No relatives or close family left and his father's house a casualty of war, but he had inherited a modest dacha just outside Moscow. Laurie made a note of this fact.

He travelled around and as he had learnt to drive in the Army and over the years with various driving jobs, he had scraped enough money together to buy a car and his taxi licence and the rest, as he told Laurie, was history. He told Laurie that in addition to the dacha he had a small community one-bedroom flat and was happy; the pensions here were rubbish so he needed to keep working. He was saving up now for a new car to see him out.

The taxi made its way carefully onto the main highway, driving on the snowy slush lanes made by other vehicles. The day at this early time of year was bitterly cold and the snow was piled high and had grown dirty by multiple trucks and cars spinning and spraying the slush from their spinning wheels. The drive was as he remembered from other visits. Nothing had changed; mainly tall grey flats built to the Stalinist model, interspersed with muddy supposedly front gardens. In these 'corporate condominiums'as he thought of the flats, a legacy from the older Soviet era, also applied to the green spaces in front of the flats where the State used to do everything and maintain them. It didn't look like that anymore. There were also other open spaces, shopping centers and small churches before the skyline gave way to the traditional Moscow suburbs and the centre of town. He was mindful that more than two thirds of Moscow had already burnt down or was burnt down when Napoleon occupied the city and that this was a city reborn.

Sergei drove straight to the hotel, telling Laurie that it was very well-known and that many of the famous people and stars from the Russian theatres and film stars used it as an escape. It was just far enough from the centre to protect their anonymity and he hoped that his stay would be interesting. Laurie took this as a good omen, confirming his earlier thoughts that it would mean that the Security Services, if they were around, would treat the hotel with a light touch.

He paid Sergei with a good tip and had a thought. 'Sergei, by any chance do you have a card? I would like to book you for a trip back to the airport in a day or three.'

'No problem, my pleasure.'He fumbled in the rubbish in the passenger seat well and came up with a grubby bent card with his number on. 'Just call this number and ask for me. If you need taking around during your stay, same-same. Call me.'Sergei waved, hit the gearstick and rattled off with a slight blue haze trailing behind him.

Laurie smiled after him – he liked the Russians. He then stood for a moment looking at the facade of the hotel. It was certainly different; old-fashioned, with towers either side of the steps leading to an inviting entrance. The overall impression was of a traditional, if overlarge, vintage Russian dacha. He shook himself, shivering in the cold and made his way into the hotel where the reception was comfortingly warm after the cold outside. The reception desk was in front of him as he entered and was certainly well-manned. The staff were efficient and he was in his room within five minutes. Great room, decent-sized TV, double bed. His thought that he'd won a prize with the turret room on the second floor, with its newly installed en-suite facilities which really was a pleasant surprise. A fridge stacked with miniatures, snacks and an assortment of Russian chocolate bars added to the luxury that he hadn't expected.

Laurie quickly unpacked the little he had with him. He calculated that it would take thirty minutes or so to get to Servo and Carla's and it was already half past three. He needed to get moving before they got home. Hurrying, he handed his key into reception telling them he was going out to get some air and would like to eat dinner around seven.

He threaded his way through housing and industrial estates until he found himself facing their apartment block. The early evening gloom aided his need for anonymity. As ever, the block was a grey edifice, not in the best repair with cracked cement cladding typically of the Russian flats in this area, and it was some four stories high. The entrance was a black, open scar against the grey cladding. He did feel a little apprehensive as the Security Services normally took on whole blocks for their personnel and they would be suspicious of a stranger. This was a moment of danger. He pulled up the collar of his long black coat, pulled the flaps of his Russian Ushanka Cossack hat over his ears, pulled its front flap forward in a peak and, now unrecognisable, marched purposely, hands in pockets, to the entrance.

Once inside he punched the timed light button and a dim overhead light gave off just enough light for him to get his bearings. He quickly found the block's post-boxes located by the lift shaft. Reaching into his pocket he found the empty gum wrapper which was the sign to trigger the meeting.

It took a minute or two to find Servo's box. Laurie was relieved and careful to make sure the wrapper was securely posted into their letterbox. He crossed his fingers that they checked the box every day and would find the wrapper and remember what it was for.

Spinning on his heels, he withdrew and retraced his steps back to the hotel, all the way checking carefully that he wasn't being followed. It took more than twice the time of the outward leg and it was nearly six when he got back to his room.

Laurie flicked on the TV and tuned into the Moscow news channel. He sat on his bed for some time, watching the news and getting warmed up before he took off his coat and hat. The three hours in the cold had chilled him to the bone. Russian winters really were a hardship for him, they had caught him out. The warmer climate of Baku over the last seven months had thinned his blood. Looking at his watch he saw that it was nearly seven. He took off his outer coat and hat, ran his fingers through his hair, checked that he had his documents secured in his shoes and around his body before he decided to go down for dinner.

He found the dining room to be a barn of a room. Heavy drapes were drawn and the old-fashioned flocked wallpaper seemed to insulate it from the cold of the night. The furniture was old, solid oak, and heavy enough to stand the test of time. He could imagine that the restaurant had seen many nights of festivities; it was the Russian way. The table settings were ready set for a silver service extravaganza. The waiters in their whites milled around adjusting the restaurant layout. The menu was extensive and in both Russian and English. The food on offer was solid Russian fare with an additional fixed menu boasting five courses. Laurie was delighted to read that the fixed menu was to be served with Russian and Kosovar wines. That suited him just fine.

He found a table in the corner of the room so that he could keep an eye on the comings and goings of his fellow diners. Taking his time over the meal, the first task was to decide what he wanted to order for (*uzhim*) dinner from the menu; in the end he went for the fixed option. For openers he laboured through a large bowl of *Borscht,* a hot beet soup they had spiced up, a speciality of the restaurant. The second appetiser he tackled was *Shuba,* a layered pie-like lump of potato and herring with mayonnaise which added to the heavy *Olivier* Russian salad and his bowl of rye bread was replenished whenever a waiter passed his table. Laurie wondered if it was true that *Shuba* was created by a landlord of a drinking house besieged by his customers who were threatening to destroy his pub if he didn't feed them with something. True or false, it was immaterial, Laurie loved it. For his main he chose *Kotleti* made with beef and mashed potatoes and vegetables. Admittedly, it was food for the masses but he loved it. He had enjoyed the wines with each course, in moderation. Finally, he struggled through an overgenerous slice of Russian honey cake stuffed with a sour cream filling. Tea was served, of course, to conclude the meal. He felt replete and at peace. When the waiter came and asked him if he would like anything else to eat or drink, Laurie had replied *spasibo* (thank you) patting his expanding waistline *ya nayelsa!* (I'm full.)

It was eleven before he got up from the table. During the evening the restaurant had gradually filled up with people and there were several noisy parties celebrating in Russian style, with lots of toasts. With live Russian string music throughout the meal and a Cossack dance act, it was for Laurie an entertaining evening all round. While he listened to the music, swirling his glass of heavy red wine between courses, he mused about Servo and Carla. What a pair of young lions they were: Servo, a Major, was GRU, in the Spetsnaz Regiment of Russian Special Forces and going places. Carla was a KGB Major, with a secure future ahead of her. And Carla was, he remembered from the report, an amazing violinist.

What puzzled him was where they fitted into the spymaster's acronym 'MICE'so favoured by the spymasters as an unfailing test of why a spy would succumb and want to work for the enemy. M for money – that wasn't an issue. I for ideology could loosely be applied to them in that they had lost faith in the Russian ideal. Not C, corruption or E, extortion. He needed for his own safety to be able to rationalise their reasons for ensuring they were committed to the Brigadier's cause. Sure, he understood that they were an item. That they had fallen in love with the UK and Ireland and proved themselves more than once. He felt that there was enough evidence of their loyalty if 'I' for ideology included love in inverted commas, which he reasoned that it did.

So, by his second glass of wine he'd relaxed back into the restaurant's evening entertainment and watched his fellow diners enjoying themselves – Russians in his experience were expert at that when they let their hair down and enough vodka had been downed.

No one bothered him or attempted to engage him in conversation. Nevertheless, he felt that the waiters were impatient for him to move on so he took a full cup of tea to his room to prepare for the morning as best he could. Preparation, he had learnt in the Army, prevented piss poor performance. He smiled at the memory.

The air tickets for Servo and Carla he slid into a seam that he had split in the lining of his winter coat. His passports, both English and Russian, and money he dispersed into the pockets of his jacket and his shoes. He then phoned down to reception for a six o'clock call and breakfast at six thirty. He calculated that if he left the hotel at seven it would take him a good half hour at a forced walk to get to the Church of St George next to the Monastery with its famous cemetery at the southwest of Gorky Park. Getting there around half seven, give or take, would give him ample time to recce the surroundings and church. A recce would give him comfort that the meeting place was not under observation by anyone wishing to do him harm.

Chapter Thirty

Brigadier Robinson's Luncheon

The occasional table that normally sat between the two burgundy-coloured, much used and loved leather easy chairs, cracked and creased with age, stood in front of the Brigadier's desk. The table had been laid for lunch and the three men in turn filled their plates. Rodney and the Cabinet Secretary took the easy chairs while the Brigadier took his place behind his desk in his high-backed reclining swivel chair. The Cabinet Secretary looked expectantly from the Brigadier to Major Rodney.

'You mentioned third parties. Is this good news or other than good news?'His eyes crinkled at the edges. This normally ever so proper head-of-the tree civil servant was enjoying himself in the company of the Brigadier's team. Such a joy for him to be with a group of individuals that had no hidden agenda, political or otherwise.

'That rather depends.'Rodney gave a brief overview of the KGB, Tsygankov's involvement before retirement and Tsygankov's boss, a personal and long-standing friend, General Polyakov. Polyakov was now clearly in the hot seat of the KGB First Directorate, responsible for overseas mayhem amongst other internal state duties. 'So, you see we're not dealing with an unknown third party; they are good at what they do and formidable opponents. And as they are based in Moscow, not exactly within arm's reach. But they will have their man here in London, with a responsibility to ensure the fraud continues, probably more than one, and they will have enforcers for want of a better word. Two we have captured already. If personnel are members of the Russian Embassy, we should be able to identify them. If one or more of these key players are illegal then it may be more difficult. On the other hand, our principal locally born bad boy, so far anyway, is Mr. bloody Neil Ashchurch; he will have to be confronted and we are on his case. Ashchurch, as we destroy this fraud base, could well be a target, if only to shut him up. This is a reason why lifting him is a balancing act, we need him to talk to us before they decide he is a risk to them. Difficult call we have yet to make.'

Sir Geoffrey took a bite of his sandwich and a sip of his single malt. 'Oh dear, Ashchurch. I have met him in the Treasury, he is a powerful civil servant in his own right. Not a man you would befriend easily and now I know why. How on earth do we square all this? No doubt you have something up your sleeve, I hope?' His left eyebrow went up and he tucked back into his food, clearly hungry. *Stress eating* was Rodney's thought and who could blame him.

'Before we get to what might be possible, I had something of a lightbulb moment this morning. What if the Russians have set up the same scheme in our near neighbours? French, Dutch, German, Spanish? And what about the American cousins? And we know or suspect that they are being defrauded with sums of money in the billions each year.'

Sir Geoffrey was only momentarily stunned. 'Wow, what an idea. Well, Rodney, what an interesting thought. That is a big leap into the unknown. Do you really think that it's a possibility?'

'My thought train was why on earth would the Russians only target us when they have developed such a brilliant and extensive fraud; why exclusively British? Other countries, you could argue, are potentially either easier targets or more lucrative. It would be a clever way to move products and money between crooked contractors from one country to another. If you think about it, it makes complete sense. When our Colonel Jimmy was going through the construction scam I couldn't for the life of me work out how this lot were buying so much of the construction material so cheaply from the Continent and now I think that I know. At best, it's a simple way of companies on the Continent selling at a devalued price to pay less tax. As you know, places like France pay tax in bands, greater the profits the higher the tax band. Or they are buying cheap imports from say China, smuggled in and sold to our contractor at a profit. The two invoices scam, one for the company and one for the fraudsters.'

Robinson had been quiet until now but suddenly brought his hands down flat on the desk in a rare show of emotion.

'My God Rodney, this is a revelation! I had no idea that this fraud could have wider international implications.'

Sir Geoffrey was sanguine. He picked up another sandwich and stood up, pacing the floor, slowly chewing as he went. 'Hmmm. This is a conundrum, I have to say. But let us look at it another way. If what Rodney is suggesting is actually the case, then it helps my Prime

Minister's position and I would welcome that. There are loose but supportive unofficial"brothers in arms"clubs of cabinet secretaries or equivalent ranks in our nearest neighbours. I could trust my Dutch and German equivalents for starters; the French, well, whilst the holder of the post is a good man, not sure that he would be allowed to be as discreet as the others. What would help is if we could get a link with the Americans then I could talk to the head of the CIA here in London. You've both met her before and as a lawyer she is used to discretion.'He looked at Rodney for a response.

'Big ask, Sir Geoffrey. I need to…'Rodney looked at the Brigadier and got a nod to go on. 'I think I need to keep on our present course of rolling up the main perpetrators of the worst frauds in the Defence industry and the NHS, local government but after that…'he paused and smiled wryly as though he had a solution. 'What I can imagine is splitting off a small team to run with the international dimension, at least to begin with. We seem to have a winning formula with Colonel Jimmy and he knows what he's doing, supported by my men and the analysts.'He rubbed his chin, head down before a smile appeared on his face. 'So, this is what I am thinking – the Banker, John Brown, will sit on both the Colonel's team and the new international team. I'll leave Pat with the Colonel. Pat has infinite patience and handles tantrums well. I'll put Andrew on the international task with two of my men to give the team some legs, Mould and Sharky, but I'd like to support them with Ms. Reid SIS, Mr. Reid's daughter and a couple of financial forensic analysts. Going to need more IT and comms but I will get Graham to handle that. I've chosen Mould and Sharky as between them they have command of most Northern European modern languages. Just thoughts at this stage, ideas which could be turned on their head, depending on how and what we know. When Laurie gets back from Moscow in the next few days, God willing, he can join the team as he is able to read and speak Eastern European languages and Russian.'

'Talent in abundance with your chosen men. I am comforted, my dear Robinson.'Sir Geoffrey was clearly impressed. 'You mentioned Moscow, Rodney?'

Rodney hesitated, as he was drilled in 'need to know'–- yet again he got the nod from the Brigadier. 'Indeed. I have a man out there who's going to see if we can't get some insight into this mission from two of our friends. It may come to nothing, but you never know. Speaking of which, I need to contact him shortly and expand his remit with reference to whether or not other countries are involved and if that is indeed the case it's going to be one helter-skelter of a ride.'

Sir Geoffrey was savvy and long enough in the tooth to realise that he had been given privileged information but then again, he was on the Joint Intelligence Committee by default of his appointment. He didn't press any further, he was more than happy that the Brigadier and his deputy Major Rodney Brown, ex-SAS, had got all the bases covered so far. He was now not surprised that the Major was gaining a growing reputation as the new deceiver.

'I will keep my counsel about one of your men being in Russia until he is safely back and we have a result one way or the other re international involvement until you give me the nod to tell the PM.'

The three men spent more time going over the plan until they were happy with its shape and had talked through any issues and difficulties that they could reasonably foresee. Rodney was the first to prepare to leave the other two men to return to the team. He needed to brief Andrew and the Banker.

But more importantly than that, he needed to speak to Laurie, he wanted to ask Servo and Carla to get not just the files on the UK but on any other country. Another recent thought was that he wanted Laurie to get the names of the KGB liaison officers running the fraud teams, wherever they were. If Carla and Servo could do that for him then they would have more than earned their residency in the UK, for sure.

'One last thing…'Rodney said before he left them, which engaged the two men's attention. 'On second thoughts, as soon as we've identified the KGB officer link man in the UK and for simplicity the second in command to Ashchurch then on balance I want to pull Ashchurch in, otherwise he'll simply disappear, so whilst it may shake them up it won't throw them completely. We'll make it look like he did a bunk or went on leave. OK with that, Boss?'

'I'm OK with that, and you, Sir Geoffrey?'

'Yes, OK. My goodness Rodney, you have got a lot on your plate.'

'Got a good team and a supportive boss, what else do I need?' He stood and collected his logbook from the Brigadier's desk before turning to the two men. 'Would you like to come with me and see if the team have finessed half a billion from our two unwilling sponsors?'

'You go ahead, Rodney.'The Brigadier looked at his watch. It showed quarter to two 'We'll be along in a quarter of an hour.'

Rodney nodded. He was right in thinking that the two men need a little time to themselves to talk through where he and his team were taking them. Outcomes were not certain and they needed to form a strategy to mitigate risk.

He was in a reflective mood as he retraced his steps back to his teams. He wondered how Laurie was getting on in Moscow and smiled. '*Just fine, probably.* Then again, the Russian Security Services seemed to have unlimited numbers to keep an eye on visitors. Hmm. He shook his head; there was nothing that he could do at the moment, the game would have to play itself out. But it was urgent that he speak to Laurie before tomorrow morning. He looked at his watch. Too early, Laurie would not be at the hotel until around three. He would try a call on the secure satellite phone and hope Laurie was in a position to speak to him.

Chapter Thirty-One

The Operations Room

Mr. Reid called Rodney over as soon as he had entered the Operations Centre.

'Good lunch, Boss?' Mr. Reid had a twinkle in his eye.

'Not bad, not bad.'

'Good, because we have a lot of work to do this afternoon and I'm proposing that you and I get down to the prison after an evening meal to look at our catch.'

'OK. I don't have a problem with that but you and I have a date for a meal with your mate Jenny Woo for high tea. We might need a decent meal.' Rodney tapped the side of his nose.

'What are you on about?'

'Don't really know, but Jenny was very insistent last night that you and I see her late afternoon. Don't think that it's an idle invitation, more of a command. She obviously has something on her mind. She wasn't going to say anything in front of the others. So, we'd better go and see, don't you think? Think about her food if nothing else. The meal's on me. I'll come back and see you shortly. I'd like to get an update but now I need to see the Banker and the team to see if we have a win or we're in trouble.'

'Interesting invite. But let's see Jenny before we go to the prison. We should get some take-away for later too, we could be at Mallet for a while.'

'No issue with that, speak later.' Rodney left Mr. Reid and his team. Truth to tell, he was both impatient and nervous. He just hoped that the Banker had got the money out of the construction company.

In the adjoining room housing the Banker's team all was calm, even business-like, but the Banker sat at the table supping a glass of red wine with the MD and CEO of the construction company. A near empty tray of sandwiches was between the three men and they were in deep conversation. The Banker saw Rodney enter his domain and nodded. Rodney felt the butterflies in his stomach settle. They had the cash.

He went to see Graham and got on the satellite phone to Laurie. He quickly explained the additional information that he needed and cut the call. He made his excuses to Graham and rejoined the finance team. He felt that he should wait for Robinson and Sir Geoffrey before he approached the Banker so went and spoke to a delighted Colonel Jimmy. 'My God, Rodney, the Banker was amazing. The banks fell over each other to oblige him. He sorted out the banks and HMRC. Never seen anything like it.'

If he was impressed by the Colonel's enthusiasm and the change in the man, he was bowled over when the Colonel told him the sums involved.

He made his escape when Colonel Jimmy was called away to clarify some point with the Banker.

He slid out of the finance room and was collared by Major Freire and Graham, who wanted some of his time.

'OK, OK, but be gentle, my brain's in overload!' Rodney grimaced.

'Ladies first.' Freire elbowed herself in front of Graham who placed his hands on his hips, pretending to be annoyed. 'We have to know our next targets so that we can focus on the traffic. At the moment we're running blind. Got lots of stuff but we need to, well, you know, have some direction.'

'Right-oh. Today I'm booked out with Mr. Reid till the morning. But I want to roll on to the main targets, so Defence contractors. Both manufacturers and the over-fat service companies. In addition, the NHS; context is the purchasing of overpriced drugs and materials. I am also interested in manpower providers like the service companies. I need you to link them with Ashchurch and his cronies. The construction company has coughed up and I want some more soft targets. I'm looking for low hanging fruit, so to speak. Got it?' Rodney inclined his head.

'Got it and ahead of you.' She smirked. 'We, that is Graham and I, have been building the matrix by business sector, by their principals communicating directly or indirectly with Ashchurch and other crooked civil servants. Even got two Members of Parliament in the bag now.'

'Sounds like great progress. Let's have a team meeting tomorrow around 9 o'clock, Graham. That will give you two the time to get a presentation together and for the Banker and his team to tidy up the files on the construction company in a form that can be handed over to the

Fraud Branch friend of ours. Then with your help the Banker needs to reset the room for the next take down. OK with that?'

'Yes, Rodney. Now, what about your neighbour? What are you going to do?'

'Think. See you in the morning.'Rodney was going to walk away but then thought better of it. 'Show me what you have so far and I can at least process your finds and mentally rationalise it as I plan forward.'

'With me, Boss.'Freire pulled Rodney and Graham over to her desk and sat Rodney down in her chair, pulling up another chair for Graham. 'Watch and learn.'She spent ten minutes flying through her screen of dates and tables. 'Well?'

Rodney could only but scratch his head; he felt his brain frying, overloaded. He needed space, so he said encouragingly in an effort to get away sooner than later, 'Not a bad start for the next targets, that's for sure. Can you go back to the overview schematic screen?'Freire pulled it up on the screen and Rodney studied it. 'Like the way this clearly shows the organisational tree of targets and the branches into other targets and the government departmental paymasters.'He rested his head back, thinking.

'Given any thought as to how you're going to present this to us tomorrow?'He looked at Graham. 'Got any ideas?'

'Well, we need Freire to present; I could get Dr Christian to set up some back projection so that the information could be projected on a big screen. Better than death by view foils and it would be live data that we could manipulate at the time.'

'Like that.'Freire said 'And I can get one of my team to run the screens while I talk and another one to do amendments in real time.'

'Great, so we're clear. My vision is that we first hover over the whole of the targets. A general big picture of the whole liability and then work down my declared targets, one by one. There needs to be enough detail to excite the Banker's team. Then, once we've been well and truly briefed, I'll let the Banker and Colonel Jimmy lead the second half of the meeting as they will have the best insight into best return for effort.'

'We can organise that. What about some of the key conspirators? Are we going to begin to pull them in? 'Graham knew that he was testing the Major's patience from the look that he got, but at the same time he wanted to prompt Rodney to at least consider them at this stage.

'It's a good question, Graham. Well, there are a few matters to consider before we arrest them and some things that I can't rush. I have Laurie in play and I need his intelligence feedback. Important as well is to balance and reward, in the context that if we pull them too soon the traffic Freire is monitoring will dry up.

'The Brigadier has set up physical surveillance with watcher teams from MI5 so they're not going to get away. I'm hoping to keep them in play until they begin to panic. Even then I am thinking, Freire, one point for tomorrow's meeting, if we can take over some of the operations by persuading some of our errant contractor key principals to work with us and to perhaps make the odd reassuring telephone call or email? We could even do some dummy invoices etc as they say, follow the money. Can you factor those processes in to meld with the Banker's help?'Rodney raised his eyebrows in a challenge.

Graham laughed. 'The deceiver, as ever. Would hate to catch you on a day when your brain wasn't busy.'Suddenly serious. 'I think that the plan to feed disinformation is a cracker. Did you really just think of that?'Rodney smiled and Freire laughed. Graham continued. 'Think that we need to keep it simple but I'll speak to the Banker right now before the CEO and MD disappear as we may be able to use them. Especially if you and Mr. Reid can turn a few key individuals tonight?'

'Brilliant. Now I must get to Mr. Reid before he throws his toys out of the pram; we don't want that do we?'He left them vigorously shaking their heads. Rodney wondered how come Mr. Reid could ever engender such fear in the team members as Mr. Doug Reid often did. Deep down he knew why, for Mr. Reid sure as hell scared him at times.

Chapter Thirty-Two

Mr. Reid's World

Rodney was whisked away as soon as he met up with Doug Reid. His field team's busy working area in the operations room was in full swing. Reid talked ten to the dozen, bringing Rodney up to speed as they charged through the corridors of the building and down into the underground garage. Waiting for them in a blacked-out Range Rover were Mould and Sharky. Rodney and Mr. Reid took the rear seats. Once strapped in, Mr. Reid gave the order to take them to Jenny Woo's Restaurant in Soho.

'Listen in. The Major and I will go into the restaurant. You two, get takeaways and munch them while we eat a banquet with Jenny and find out what's got her so worked up. And don't forget to get a large flask of her chicken soup and enough Chinese dishes in the sort of heated pans you plug into the cigar lighter, enough to feed us through the night if needs be.'

'But where do we get one of those, sir, in Soho?'Mould complained.

'Innovate, improvise, overcome.'Reid was merciless. He grinned at Rodney.

'But Boss...'Sharky started.

'Acch! Stop complaining, I sorted it out earlier with Jenny. Just make sure that you get them back tomorrow before she opens tomorrow night.'He sat back in the large comfortable seat of the Range Rover, smiling to himself and enjoying the wallow of the air suspension as it smoothed out the many potholes and sleeping policeman humps in the London roads.

Rodney closed his eyes. If he ever wondered why he enjoyed his job so much, it was the banter between trusted old soldiers, who wouldn't let you down, even if it meant going the extra mile and then some. And their presence gave him space and peace.

Mr. Reid broke his reverie; back to business as ever, into the order of things that were his disciplined world, epitomised by Mr. Reid's oft repeated mantra at the slightest sign of dissension or lethargy, *'Work first then play, that's the order of my day and now it's yours. Man up, and just get it done.'*He growled at Mould and Sharky; his Scots accent evident now. 'And don't forget that much as we love Jenny Woo, we don't want any surprises. You two make sure that Rodney and I are escorted in before you get your scoff. Time to make your guns ready.'Reid took out his Browning automatic, ejected the magazine to check it before clicking it back firmly into the pistol. He pulled back the slide and let it fly forward, taking a shell from the magazine with it into the firing chamber. He pulled back the slide gently, enough to see that the bullet was nestled correctly in the barrel. Gently, slowly, he let the slide go home. Checked the safety catch was on. Job done, he settled the gun back into his shoulder holster and watched the others sort themselves out with a smile on his face. Satisfied, he lost interest in his companions and watched London go by.

Alerted that they were on their way by Mr. Reid, Jenny had put out some traffic cones and they were able to draw up at the establishment's front entrance. She was waiting for them on the pavement.

'Safety's off, make ready.'Mr. Reid mouthed and waited, listening for the clicks of the safety catches from the others. Satisfied they were ready, he reached for the car door handle. The four Intelligence officers dismounted from the Rover. Mould and Sharky nodded to Jenny and immediately entered the restaurant to check it out. They found the restaurant empty of customers except for the restaurant manager who was waiting inside for them.

A soldier's code of first principles includes the one which is to look for anything out of place, or worse still something in place that shouldn't be there. In this case, with the closed sign on the door and Jenny and her manager relaxed and welcoming, they were satisfied. Sharky gave the nod to Mr. Reid, who entered before Rodney.

Jenny came forward and took Mr. Reid's arm. 'Been a while Mr. Reid, I have been feeling quite neglected.'

Mr. Reid coloured, an unusual emotion for him. He didn't quite run his finger round his collar, but he would have done if he could have done it without his grinning companions noticing and grinning even more.

'Come, Mr. Reid and Major, I have guests waiting to meet you and of course your food is on the table, ready for you. The cooks have excelled themselves today.' Jenny turned to the two silent, immobile figures of Mould and Sharky. 'My manager will look after you.'Jenny led Mr. Reid and Rodney down a corridor to the private room.

'Before you go in, I want to assure you that you are among friends today. Don't be shocked.' Jenny waggled her finger at them and turned the handle.

Intrigued, Rodney entered the room first.

Chapter Thirty-Three

Church of St George and Donskoy Monastery Cemetery, Moscow

The morning chill and mist carried over to Laurie as he stood still, looking up at the church belltower of St George's. The church was colourful and one of the many hundreds in Moscow. How they funded so many of them was a mystery to Laurie, even if to a man and woman the Russian loved their churches. He tried doing the maths for the two thousand-odd religious buildings in Moscow and gave up. What he did think, looking at the church, was that it lacked something of the magic of the Queen's chapel, St George's in Windsor Castle. He made a commitment and promised himself that he would visit it when he returned to the UK and spend a few private moments contemplating the regimental flags that hung in serried ranks and read the battle history on them. He would think of the soldiers that he had known and who had gone before him.

Returning to the present, the Church of St George, Laurie suspected that it benefited financially from the rich Donskoy Monastery next door. He had read up on the Monastery, which had been through some rough times since it was consecrated in 1591. The monastery had been the site of some spectacular events. Not least a famous battle when Cossacks attacked and were defeated under its walls. The Monastery's original purpose was the defence of Moscow from the south and it also commanded the highway to the Crimea, this much at least he knew.

His history was rusty, but he also knew that the monks were the beneficiaries of lands and peasants and from other satellite monasteries from the middle to late 1600s and the middle of the 1700s. Sure, Napoleon had ransacked them when he was in Moscow, which was a short-lived success.

The Soviets, he remembered, looked on the Monastery's cemetery as an asset and the Bolsheviks had dug a mass grave there. The Soviets added the treasures and artefacts of many lesser cathedrals and churches to the Monastery. The Soviets could bury embarrassments and those in disfavour quietly. Stalin preferred to put his enemies there too. So much so, there were several mass graves. He would take the time to visit Common Grave Number One with its contradictory messages.

Laurie pulled his coat round him and stamped his feet. He had been wandering round the area since seven thirty, keeping an eye out for any watchers. The walk from the hotel had taken a brisk thirty-five minutes and he was as sure as he could be that he wasn't being followed. Now, amongst the trees surrounding the church, he was on the lookout for anything and anyone out of place. As eight o'clock approached, he saw two priests, monks from the Monastery to his right, who were walking towards the church. He moved so that he could see the priests clearly but remain hidden. He watched them unlock the church for early morning Communion.

Shortly afterwards, for a quarter of an hour or more, following on the heels of the priests a straggle of more than a score of elderly Muscovites made their way into the church. All of them were well wrapped up against the cold of the morning and he pulled up his collar higher for warmth and was grateful for his great Russian hat and its warm flaps let down against the cold. Considering the number of churches these elders had to choose from, this one was popular. Time for him to move.

Against his expectations, the interior of the church was in fact relatively warm. The ornate interior and the stained glass with gold leafed ornamentation seemed to add to the warm feeling. Impressive, but not as famous or as old as the wooden Church of St George of the Victorious on Lake Yuksovsky in the Leningrad region, built around circa 1493 and added to later to celebrate a famous Russian victory up in the North of Russia. This younger Church of St George by more than a hundred years or so that he now sat in was as colourful inside and out as it was beautiful.

Moments after entering the church Laurie felt a brush past by one of the priests who thrust a small piece of paper into his hands. Laurie took an interested, respectful look round the church, before bowing to the altar. The other monk now had the service in full swing so Laurie made his way to the door unobserved and exited into the open air. The piece of paper simply read *Donskoy Cemetery SW corner* in small, neat Cyrillic writing.

Laurie Burns, alias the Ghost, made his way to the cemetery, pausing by the entrance arch to buy a bunch of flowers from one of the flower sellers. The flowers would help blend in with the local custom for a relative visiting a cemetery. He smiled as he thought about this very Russian unique enterprise being repeated by dozens of flower ladies at every Russian cemetery in Moscow.

He strolled rather than strode, giving whoever he was going to meet time to ping him. He took the time to reset his Russian hat, tying up the ear, front and back flaps so that the contact, who he hoped was Carla or Servo, could see his face clearly. He need not have worried. In the southwest corner of the cemetery stood a woman, with her head bowed over a grave, waiting for him. He let out an involuntary breath as he saw it was the beautiful Carla. He knew that Servo would be close.

He sidled up to Carla and stood beside her for a moment before handing over the flowers which now had the BA open tickets wrapped around them. She looked at the flowers and then up at him.

'Laurie, we thought it might be you.'She was serious, she didn't smile. 'Let's walk and talk.'

'The flower wrapper has hidden in it two open tickets to London. What Rodney would like is for you to come home if you and Servo think that the time is right. We have a problem with a scam being worked in the UK out of, we believe, Moscow by KGB Directorate One. Your Directorate. A contractor fraud and money laundering operation of massive size and complexity involving big business and Government agencies.'

Carla looked up at him. 'I know of it. Its future in the UK is uncertain.'

'Well, we want to roll it up, and fast.'

'I'm sure you do. Do I take it that you want names, dates etc. etc.?'

'All of it.'

'Could be possible for the UK.'Carla thought for a moment, smelling the flowers. 'Yes, it could be possible.'

'Now for the second request. Do you know if this scam is run in the other old European countries? Germany, France, Holland, Spain, Belgium, Italy? And what about America?'

'Of course it does. The model was too good just for one country. You were not the first one it was used on, but in the UK and in some other countries it has grown too big, too costly, too unwieldy.'

'My God.'Laurie was shocked.

'I do know that the UK business is under threat and there have been some top-level meetings on its viability going forward. As for the rest, well, my desk officers seem pretty laid back about their countries.'

'Can you get copies of their files too?'Laurie was warming to his task.

'I may be able to get what you need. I could manufacture the need for a full system audit using as the excuse arising out of the UK situation.'She thought for a while. 'It may be possible.'

'If you are successful, how will you get the data to us?' Laurie was lost in the narrative and almost missed the shadowy figure of a monk working his way towards them.

'One thing that we can do securely in our position is probably to email the data to your Major Brown. It will not be able to be traced back. Could take a day or two. No more, I will send the information as I get it rather than waiting for the lot to come together. It may be safer that way.'Carla was supremely calm, unnervingly so to Laurie.

'Will you and Servo travel to us then?'

'I don't know, Laurie. Servo and I have a lot to talk over.' She smiled for the first time. 'Timing is everything, you know that. You of all Rodney's team will appreciate that.' Carla waited for the monk to join them.

Laurie stared into the cold, dark, dangerous eyes of the Spetsnaz Russian Special Forces, now Major, Vladimir Servo GRU. 'And where would you like to lay your flowers?'

'I would like them to be placed on Common Grave Number One,'Laurie said solemnly, 'and then I will go home, tomorrow, first flight out.'There was a slight lifting of the lips into a warm smile from Servo.

Servo slapped him on the shoulder. 'Good choice, you will find many kindred spirits in there.'

Chapter Thirty-Four

The Unexpected Visitors

Jenny Woo opened the door to the private room and let Rodney and Mr. Reid move past her into the softly lit, richly ornate Chinese room. Adjusting to the lights, they made out three people, two men and a woman, seated on the opposite side of the table from the door. Two out of the three had an amused expression on their faces at the shock and surprise they had given to Mr. Reid and Rodney. The third, a stocky taciturn man, had a bland, neutral expression.

Rodney recovered fast but was still stunned. 'Galena, General Polyakov, this is a very unexpected...'He hesitated for a moment to catch up with his feelings. 'A pleasure of course, I hope? You will have a very good reason for this meeting, of that, I'm sure? Not defecting or anything like that, I suppose?'Rodney was pleased with his ironic question.

Polyakov laughed. 'Nothing is further from our minds.' His waved his hands indicating that the two British men should join them at the table. 'Let me introduce Colonel Pushkin, a name and face you will not be familiar with. The Colonel is supporting me on this trip.'

Rodney cautiously took a seat opposite the KGB Russian General and motioned Mr. Reid to sit down opposite Galena. His mind was still trying hard and failing to rationalise why Polyakov in particular was here. He shrugged and took the lead. 'Well, we have an amazing feast laid out before us. Let us eat and talk.'He rose again and took the wine from the chiller. Rodney poured drinks for the three Russians before pouring himself and Mr. Reid a glass.

General Polyakov raised a glass to all at the table and clinked glasses with everyone. He waved his hands over the feast and all helped themselves to the food on the dishes. Polyakov took a few mouthfuls of the aromatic Chinese food before starting his dissertation, breaking off now and again to take another morsel of food and sip of wine. He began. 'My dear Major and Mr. Reid – to business. Believe me when I say that

I am delighted to see you, and an admirer of your many adventures even if you have at times exasperated my dearest friend, Carl Tsygankov.'He chuckled. 'My God, you and your team have been a nuisance to him.'He smiled. 'And to me and Galena for that matter. But that, let us say, that's in the past.'

Rodney was studying him and decided that he liked this intelligent, well-groomed Russian General. Younger than Brigadier Robinson as the General was, there was nevertheless that special aura that made such men stand head and shoulders above the crowd. He decided that the two men would have liked each other and been kindred spirits in another world. Then again, they did speak to each other and had met.

'So, what we have is a conundrum, Rodney. May I call you Rodney?'Rodney nodded his agreement. 'On the one hand, I have a most tiresome operation in the UK, which others put in place years ago, with diminishing returns as the tail of hangers-on gets bigger and bigger. Simply too many mouths to feed and the consequences wrought now by your rather clever compliance man who has breached the scheme's defences.'Polyakov sighed and took some more food 'I have little doubt that Brigadier Robinson, you and your team will drill down into the scheme with devastating consequences. With Glasnost and our Chairman's wish to improve the state of affairs with the West, well, you can work out the conundrum for yourselves. I don't have to spell it out, do I?'

Rodney was watching for body language. Galena was smiling, her eyes had a sparkle, so she was clearly on board. Polyakov seemed genuine to a point. But Colonel Pushkin put his head down, clearly not on board.

Rodney swirled his glass of wine. He wanted to savour both the wine and the matter that he was in a position to press for ...what? He wasn't sure yet.

'What could you suggest, General, that could unlock this matter to both our nations satisfaction? There must be somewhere in the picture that you paint a chance for a win-win, don't you think?'He hesitated. 'That would satisfy both of our masters and save embarrassment for both parties. Certainly, my mission is to save the Iron Lady from her detractors.'

'Astute observation Rodney, thank you. Unusually, I will cut straight to the chase. You know how we Russians like to talk.'Polyakov stirred in his chair, seemingly to stare into the distance, deciding perhaps. It was a while before he continued. 'If we were to give access to names, the files even, to help you close down this operation, how would you manage that intelligence?'

Rodney stopped eating and looked at the General. Could this be true? What was the catch?

' No catch?'he said at last.

'No catch.'

'Nothing in return required from us?'

'Absolutely nothing. We have had our pound of flesh, don't you think, over the years?'

Rodney chuckled; he was almost convinced but needed to dig a little further.

'I have two or three imperatives. My primary aim must be predicated on the need to prevent embarrassment for this Government. Then, I have to stop any other taxpayers'money being ripped off by the criminals. ' Rodney saw Polyakov wince. Using the word criminal clearly wounded the General. Both men let the slur pass and Rodney moved on. 'We, or rather I, could have a problem with allowing some of the criminals to continue to live as free men in our society. Not the victims in the scheme, of which there will be many, but the worst of the worst. Can you help me there, do you think?'

Polyakov smiled. 'We will be delighted if you want to send any particular villains you identify to Colonel Pushkin. I am sure that he can find a corrective centre that will serve the need for justice in your eyes.'

'Happy with that, Colonel?' Rodney enquired, head tilted.

His English was stilted, slow and cautious, as though every word had been carefully weighed.

'Of course. This trip has been an eye opener for me, and an opportunity to see what an English spy looks like.'

Rodney nodded 'Fair one. As for the title "spy" applying to us, I regret that you will be disappointed. Neither Mr. Reid nor myself would think that we qualify. We are simple soldiers, doing what we are asked. I see it this way: the politicians and the Secret Services break things from time to time. As soldiers it is our duty to mend them when they can't.'

Pushkin gave Rodney a searching look. 'Hu-huh,'He waggled a finger at Rodney. 'A soldier, hmm, let us agree that then.'He smiled, sat back with his wine and toasted Reid and Rodney.

Rodney had to drag his gaze from this taciturn Russian, a dangerous man to make an enemy of. He toasted Pushkin in reply and said with a smile turning to Galena and Polyakov, 'You were talking of Galena, how is Galena here? And my neighbour to boot, I understand.'He smiled at the beautiful Russian lady.

'Well, Rodney, Russia needed a declared first-class cultural attaché for the London Embassy. One who understood the UK and its people and was familiar with the workings of state. Good choice, don't you think?'Rodney knew that as a declared asset Galena was now fairly untouchable. It rankled a little, all the same, but he was pragmatic and just raised his glass to her.

'How say you, Galena? Are you going to be good this time?'Mr. Reid narrowed his eyes and spoke for the first time. His tone was reasonable but there was an edge.

'Providing that you don't throw tea over my expensive clothes again.'Galena primly reminded Mr. Reid about the last time they had met when he had tipped a hot cup of tea over her when he was interrogating her. A wide grin spread over his craggy Scots features.

Mr. Reid nodded, accepting the rebuke. Rodney and Polyakov looked at each other – they knew that a deal had been struck. There was no more to be said, now only the need for Polyakov to hand over the intelligence.

The meal moved on apace now and small talk was the order of the day. Memories shared. Rodney asked Galena how she had chosen to live beneath him in the flats.

'Well, even as the first cultural secretary we have a certain living allowance and besides, don't we have a great view of the Thames? And the flats are warm in the cool weather and cool in the summer, roomy and comfortable. Not sure that our doorman completely approves of me?'

'I'll have a word with him. You'll find that he'll become your most loyal defender after that. How about you, General, Colonel Pushkin, do you have any plans while you're in London? I'm sure that Brigadier Robinson would appreciate the opportunity to host you, especially after you give me the intelligence that we need to close down the operation.'Rodney was nudging the General and it did not go unnoticed.

The General reached into his well-cut suit jacket pocket and slid three discs over to Rodney.

'My sincere regrets Major Rodney, but Colonel Pushkin and I flew in at noon and must fly out this evening before I am missed from my desk. But I did, in addition, bring with me three cases of wine from our friend Brigadier General Tsygankov. One for the Brigadier, one for you and one for Mr. Reid. Carl really has a growing business; his wines are popular and I am envious. He did wonder if you would have come and convalesced at his dacha, Rodney. He would have liked that. He sincerely regrets the attack on you and Mr. Reid, it was out of his control. He did tell me that the last time you visited, unannounced, never to return. Now he is truly retired he recants and extends an invite to you; he owes you, one could say. He likes the company of old soldiers and you should not underestimate his need to have intelligent people around him. I think that he gets lonely these days after the full-on life he led.'He paused.' I am sure Mr. and Mrs. Reid would be more than welcome. Not only the General himself, but Mac, his Man Friday. Like you, Mr. Reid, Mac is ex-Special Forces and would love to share a glass or two. I do see a rapprochement and loosening of the borders, but I do not think that we will as nation states be easy with each other for many years unless there is some event that brings us together.

'To understand us, you only need to read our history to realise our paranoia about our borders and social and economic insecurity. The Russian psyche, thanks to Peter the Great, is inbred in many Russians to expand beyond the borders. Ridiculous, really. Colonel Pushkin, however, may disagree that we are ready to move forward quickly as one, but we have an aspiration to do better. Now, don't forget Brigadier Carl Tsygankov's genuine and heartfelt invitations.'

'That's generous of him. I'll give it some thought. Thank you, General. Perhaps you might find time on another visit to see my Brigadier? I know that he would like that. He speaks warmly of you.'

'Perhaps.'Polyakov smiled. 'Perhaps. Now, I must leave you or we will miss our flight.'Standing, he reached out to Rodney with his hand. Rodney took it. The General's hand was hard, a strong man for all that. He shook Rodney's hand warmly.

'It has been a real pleasure to meet you.'He put both hands on Rodney's shoulders. 'You seem to have made a remarkable recovery from what I've heard. You look incredibly fit now.'He turned to Mr. Reid. 'Mr. Reid, what can I say but thank you. You will wonder why I didn't go direct to the Brigadier? Well, I could have, but I know him very well and I would not have had this chance to meet the powers behind the Throne, would I?'He winked at Rodney. 'You will both wonder how this all came about. Two of Galena's ladies spotted Rodney here last night with Commander Coveney and when you returned to your flat, the rest, as they say, is history.'

Galena helped the General into his coat. With a wave he was gone with Galena on his heels. Galena mouthed to Rodney that Jenny had the wine and to come and see her for a drink when he could.

The Colonel was the last to leave. He gave both Rodney and Reid a lingering look. It was cold, unreadable. He then said in poor English, 'I will remember you both. I know you both and the trouble you have caused us. Be certain of that fact.' Then he was gone.

Rodney flopped back into his chair. 'Bloody hell, Doug. What do you think of that?'

'Think? What I think is that the General may have given us a great deal with those discs but will they contain everything? I doubt that. So, we need to keep our focus and feet on the ground. Branch and root, I don't think so. Branches maybe, but the roots? Don't believe it for a moment. I hope that I'm wrong.'

Rodney grunted. 'If I was him, and I can believe him when he said pickings may be getting leaner to the point where effort for reward for many operations is not worth the upside and dangerous, I would keep the money and fraud pipeline infrastructure intact. So, we're agreed, we hand over the disc with an extreme caution label. There could be disinformation on the disc too, just to mess us about. Our side need to get corroborating evidence at every stage. Which they would do, I hope, anyway. And we also don't stop looking for what's not on the list.'

'I agree with all that. What did you think of the Colonel?'

'Dangerous, ruthless, but a clever man. Probably he is an idealist. Driven by what, I don't know. In a sentence, not an enemy I would choose. I have the feeling that one reason for giving this data could be to blinker us from a larger picture.'

Mr. Reid was sanguine. 'From Pushkin's negative body language, and it was negative at every turn so it's a bit late for that, Major, I think he pinged both you and I and we are on his bucket list of people he would like to bury. He is, I agree, dangerous, not to be messed about with. If we do come up against him, we give him no quarter.'

'Let's bear that in mind if we meet him again, we may still want something from him. I favour stringing him along as long as it's in our interest. I think he prefers straight talking as long as it's what he wants to hear.' Rodney laughed at his joke. Mr. Reid didn't see the funny side. Mr. Reid was unsettled, and Rodney knew from past experience to back off.

Chapter Thirty-Five

Shepton Mallet Prison

They arrived later than they had planned at the prison simply because after the meeting with Polyakov they had returned to the operations room to pass the discs and wine over to Graham and Freire, then Rodney and Mr. Reid briefed the Brigadier. They had lost an hour or more but it had been worth it. The weather was against them too. It was miserable, with the Land Rover and roads rain-lashed all the way.

Whatever was on the discs, Rodney had every confidence that in his absence the team would sort it for him and anyway the Brigadier had agreed to work with them as needs must until Rodney got back for the presentation in the morning.

When they arrived at the prison, Mr. Reid climbed wearily out of the Rover, shivered and looked up at the stone edifice that was Shepton Mallet while rain mixed with sleet pelted him. The cobbled courtyard was slippery and wet underfoot from an early evening downpour. Mr. Reid shivered again; the last time he had been here was many years ago when, as a young soldier, he was to witness the execution of an American soldier. He shook off the memory, it was long ago and he had had experienced worse, but the eyes of the hanged man still haunted him from time to time.

Rodney pushed his way into the reception followed by the others. The four intelligence officers checked their guns in at the keep before they were allowed into the wing holding the prisoners. They were met at the wing admin office by the leader of the Fraud team who had been allocated to the task. The leader was a lady Superintendent who introduced herself as Lara Speed. Mr. Reid was surprised at Lara's rank as she looked barely into her middle twenties, but was clearly older in order to hold that senior police rank.

Lara soon impressed him, however, with her grasp of the situation and her charges in the cells allocated after she had carried out an initial screening by interviewing the prisoners as they arrived. Lara had a good idea who would co-operate and who had resisted her efforts.

'I was wondering if you would interview the commercial, finance and operations directors? They seem to be the ones who may have the most to give us, but they are gently resisting my charms, but not a complete pushback.' Lara smiled at the four men.

'Delighted, and I am really looking forward to seeing these cheating economic terrorists.' Rodney grinned at Lara. 'What we need is an interview room. We'll see the financial man first, then the operations director and then the commercial man. I guess that in an old place like this the screams don't carry.' He said it with a straight face and only broke into a grin when he saw the horror on Lara's face. 'Only joking, but we have been known to make a bit of noise.'

'I was warned that you and the team were a little unorthodox. Please remember, Major, that at the end of the day we are police, and we have to operate within the law.' The Chief Inspector was semi-serious. 'I would hate to have to arrest you.' She poked him gently in the chest.

Rodney recoiled, hands up in surrender, smiling.

'Rest assured, Lara, we're not going to waterboard them or anything like that, but we do have our own style and Mr. Reid is a master of the art of making people open up with a little pressure and deception at times. Even so, it might be better if you are not in the room,' Rodney replied.

Lara put her hands on her hips. 'We'll see. I have just the room you need. It has recording facilities and a one-way glass panel. I will likely be in there. You can interview the men in the big chamber below my observation point. It was the old hangman's area. Terrible atmosphere, even has the ghosts of the hanged men who were guilty, or so I was reliably told by the prison governor.'

'Ideal, that should scare them into confessions if nothing else. Can you put the finance man in first and let us know when he is ready to receive us?'

Lara nodded to one of her team, who left them before going on. 'I think that, if you don't mind, I'll be behind the glass. I may learn something.' She was getting frosty and frowned, challenging Rodney to disagree. Rodney was perceptive and knew that he had some hearts and minds to work on.

The police were naturally suspicious of the men from the Secret Services, not that he saw himself and the team in that way. Not least as the police thought that where their hands were tied at every turn, Rodney and his like were free runners. In the normal way of things nothing could be further from the truth. They were as accountable as any other citizen and had to justify what they did. It was just, you could say, that if they had to go *off-piste,* they had to get caught first. Or eat humble pie if they were caught.

He tried to placate her; he wanted the relationship to be open and transparent.

'Fair enough, and by the way we have a boot full of evidence we brought down for you and your men. That should make your task a little easier. Mould, Sharky, would you take some of Lara's men down to the Rover and get the documents for her.'He turned to Lara. 'Lara, the Banker and his team with Freddie told me that they had arranged the files and contents in such a way that you and your people should easily understand them, but to give them a call if you needed something explaining. They'll be only too happy to help.'He put on his most welcoming smile.

He saw Lara thaw a little. 'That's great. Would you like a coffee or tea? We have a temporary canteen set up.'

'Absolutely, I'm gasping.'Mr. Reid, who had been watching the exchanges, was amused but wanted to get on and get home. Rodney and he had silently agreed that they would talk to the couple of men who were key players and who Lara was getting pushback from and then they would all get back and get some sleep before the briefing tomorrow. The briefing, Rodney felt, was critical for the planning of the future pathway and he needed to be there.

Now they had the files from General Polyakov and that information was as high priority as ever, he calculated that the Fraud Squad specialists could run with a lot of the dross from now on. He did, however, want to see the top men in the contractor fraud and look them in the eyes. Rodney wanted to get a feel for the sort of men he was going to meet in the field as they went forward with this mission.

They drank the tea offered and told Lara about what they were trying to achieve at their end of the operation. Basically, Rodney saw their role as getting the maximum payback in the shortest possible time, the 80/20 rule. He explained that in the normal way of things they had been allotted a finite time for the mission. But the real job, and far more difficult task for Freddie and Lara, was finessing the last 20% plus and then putting the criminals behind bars. Rodney tried to explain that it was regrettable, but they were not policemen and could not even begin to manage this task alone. The scenario that Rodney painted for Lara and wanted to discuss was where they could be of maximum help to her and the team in respect of gathering the evidence trails and documentation they uncovered.

Mr. Reid took notes and they promised again to put Lara directly in contact with the Banker's team and Graham's people. Mr. Reid closed up his notebook and after a moment's thought said to Lara, 'What I'll do as soon as I get back, Lara, is to ask Major Freire to remote a couple of screens down here. That will give you the ability to interrogate our database on this operation in real time. That should save time and effort. Now, let's go and see our criminals.'

They picked up Mould and Sharky en route to the interview chamber. They had belatedly decided to see the commercial, finance and operations directors together. Once the jailers reported back that the three men were in the interview area, Lara led them down a dank, stone-clad corridor. Lara peeled off to the observation room and Rodney's team carried on to the disused hangman's chamber. The three men were shackled to a stout table in the centre of the room and were watched over by four burly prison officers and a member of Lara's team.

The hangman's chamber was a miserable space despite its size. It was bereft of any warmth or features except a few metal-armed chairs facing the men across the long metal table. A series of barred security windows were let in high up the chamber wall, some twenty feet or more from the floor. Mr. Reid dismissed the guards, telling them to wait outside and told Lara's man to join her in the viewing room.

Mr. Reid and Rodney took the chairs and Sharky and Mould stood close behind the prisoners, crowding their personal space and intimidating them.

Mr. Reid and Rodney studied the three men sitting silently in front of them. All were well-heeled and carried a little extra fat from good living, or so they thought.

The finance director was a tall man with expensive clothes and shoes. No expense spared there. Silver haired and smooth skinned. Liked the good life, tanned and superficially fit. But scared.

They switched their gaze to the operations director. He was a big man, could have been rugby fullback in his time. Broad shoulders and broken nose with a pock-marked skin, unusual in this day and age. A fine pair of brogues, highly polished, showed a degree of personal pride. He was not ostentatious. Could be an indication of a hard early life, a hard grafter. He had a worldly outlook.

The commercial marketing director was moon-faced, short, fat and of the three was the only one casually dressed. He looked like he had been arrested on the golf course as he was wearing a pair of golfing shoes. Of the three he had his head down and was trembling.

'Would you like to introduce yourselves?' Mr. Reid was reasonable in his request.

The men looked at each other, then away and faced front, heads down, and said nothing.

'Well, if you won't be helpful, I guess we don't have to be either.' Mr. Reid voice was reasonable. He flicked his eyes to Mould and Sharky. As one, Mould and Sharky grabbed the men's heads and with surprise, bounced the men's heads off the table. Not overly hard but enough. The action brought tears to the men's eyes. Shackled as they were they could only shake their heads and try to rub the snot and tears from their faces on the shirt material at their shoulders.

In the observation room Lara was shocked at the violence and with her men as one started up from their seats, then they sat back smiling. How they would like to rattle the odd criminal who was abusive and reticent.

'No, let's try again.' Rodney complained. 'Just so you know, we are not police. I explained that to you all just in case you want to complain about police brutality. And I can't think who would listen anyway after what you have done, do you?'

'We want our solicitors.' The operations director was red in the face and angry. The finance director just looked askance. The commercial manager's shoulders shook as he sobbed silently.

'That really is the last thing you want at this stage and you are not getting one anyway. As terrorists and traitors, you're not entitled to one in my world.' Rodney leant back on his chair.

'We are not terrorists.'

Mr. Reid flicked his eyes again and Mould and Sharky bounced the men's heads on the table again.

Mr. Reid spoke quietly. 'Do not speak again unless my officer or I ask you a question. And you will answer him. I need to emphasise to you that this is not optional. The last time I was here I saw a man hanged in this chamber for treason. We don't have time to build gallows for you today.' His harsh Scots accent was getting through. He could see it in their eyes.

Rodney pulled a police notebook out of his jacket, tore out a dozen pages and passed them over with a small pencil stub.

'Write down the names of your contacts in the Treasury, HMRC, Paymaster General, Department of Transport. The contract branches. quangos etc. etc. who you are working the scam with. Start with Neil Ashchurch and his band of miscreants.' He smiled. 'Oh, I almost forgot, I want the names of the Russian liaison agents involved as well and include any enforcers too.'

The men sat back, astonished and felt the bulk of Mould and Sharky push against them.

Reid went over to the door, opened it and shouted for five large mugs of tea.

When Reid returned to the table, he was pleased to see the finance director scribbling frantically. The operations director sat, stony faced, staring at the wall. The commercial director was just a wreck. Reid judged that he needed to move the operations director on, needle him more perhaps, or he would close down on them completely.

Reid sat down and eventually made eye contact with the operations director. He saw the man's eyes flicker. This was his in.

'Tell me, Director, how did you get into this at the start?'

The operations director looked over at his companions in crime, working away. Shrugged. 'Hmm, it all seemed like such a good idea in the beginning. At the time, legal, even acceptable. Sharp practice perhaps, but it all made excellent business sense. Nods and assurances were given as to its legal status.' For his size and demeanour his voice was softly spoken, cultured and to Mr. Reid's surprise, Scottish – not what he had expected. 'What fools we were. Then they put the screws on. Threats to the family. Compromising pictures etc. The classic stuff you'd be familiar with, of that I'm sure. My poor old mates here were ensnared and they weren't the only ones.'

'Why didn't you all simply blow the whistle?' Rodney was as surprised as Reid at the confession of the man.

'Couldn't. They were too clever. They put in intermediaries, their own men, put into managing supervisor level positions to run the work and to keep an eye on us and our families and friends. They even threatened to do harm to the CEO and MD. That bastard Ashchurch is the man you should hang in here. He really is a cold piece of trash. We wanted out when we realised that we were being played. He came down to see us the three of us with his heavies. We were in it up to our necks and he made it plain that there was no walking away. We have a lot to tell you.'

'Just so you know, your company has paid back well over half a billion to the Crown. I left the MD and CEO in place and the contracts and banned you from working for them and now I am wondering if that was the right move. You are victims I am sure, foolish certainly. You should have gone to the authorities before you got so deeply involved. If you can prove to the satisfaction of the Fraud Squad that you are indeed victims, near innocent men caught up in this tangled web, there may be hope for you three yet. Let me speak to them. What you do have going for you is that you have the knowledge and expertise to help out the MD and CEO. They are cleverer than me and this game is way above my O-level Economics.' Rodney was going to talk to Mr. Reid, but Reid put a hand on his arm to silence him.

'Director, can you identify the men they put in to control you out of the men we picked up here?'

The director nodded. 'Not sure who you picked up. We were put straight into the cells so we haven't seen anyone else yet. Do you have a list of names?'

Rodney signalled to the one-way glass panel, calling Lara to join them.

Lara bounced into the room with her file and let the prison guards in with the tea. Rodney sniffed Mr. Reid's tea and his own, *proper brew*, he thought. The directors gratefully took theirs. Mr. Reid frowned, then smiled at Lara.

Lara was on form, she took Rodney's chair off him and sat down, scratched her forehead and said, 'Gentlemen, an obvious question is did you benefit from this scam?'

'That was another matter they hocked us with. Without our agreement they set up accounts in our names in various offshore banks, and not as a pension scheme as you may think. The bastards' purpose was to add to the blackmail trail that they were building against us. We were under no illusion that if this nightmare ever came to an end the money would simply disappear. So, no...' he said bitterly. 'We haven't benefited in any way, shape or form. Not so much as a paper clip.' The operations director spat out his frustration.

'Silly boys.' Lara was not yet showing much sympathy. 'Now, cast your eyes down this list and pull out the ones that work for Ashchurch and others. I take it that there will be others on the list that have been coerced, like you. So, identify them too please.' Lara turned to Rodney. 'I think, Major, that Freddie and I can take this from here.' It was not a request. Rodney smiled at her. Lara melted. 'But I must say that we are grateful and whilst we could not condone your methods, we do recognise that these are...' The rest of the sentence hung in the ether. Rodney and his men laughed. 'Away with you all, or I'll arrest the lot of you.'Lara laughed out loud and the directors felt free enough to tentatively join in.

Rodney gave a nod to the directors. 'Good luck. What a godawful mess you've got yourselves into.'He turned to Lara. 'Before we go Lara, just a thought, let's get our friends to look at the list of detainees we identified and see if we got the lot or there are some others involved that we missed. Might be crucial to the mission.'Rodney held her gaze.

'We'll make a detective of you yet, Major.'She held her hand out and her deputy handed over the list of detainees which she placed on the table between the two men.

The room held its breath as the two directors scrutinised the list. They conferred, then the operations director looked up. 'You've done a good job, no doubt about that.'He hesitated. 'But you've missed off two shadowy characters that appeared from time to time to put the frighteners on those who they were blackmailing. We called them the Chuckle Brothers. And they were indeed brothers. Russians, we thought, could have been Eastern European but we thought Russian. They were intelligent, well-heeled and more than once summoned us to a small, may be only a dozen rooms, but very posh private hotel for all that. North end of Bayswater. It was called the Blue Haven. Run by the harridan from hell to her staff but angel of service to the clients and guests.'

The accountant searched his memory. 'The two characters I dealt with were called… yes, the names were Leonid and Dimitri Abakumov. Interesting name for enforcers considering that the meaning in old Hebrew is *embrace.* And they certainly did that. Big men, broad shouldered, six feet at least, early forties, both sallow skinned, dark-haired. Leonid had a scar to his mouth and Dimitri had a chunk out of his left ear.'

'Useful and a good observation,' Mr. Reid commented.

'Most accountants, like artists, are observant. It comes with the territory.'

Reid grunted, turning to Lara 'We'll sort them.'

Rodney saw Lara stiffen. 'We'll discuss this with Freddie before we do but my guess is that these two men are enforcers not only for these operations but others. So, they'll be highly trained, potentially GRU operatives. I'll ask Freddie to keep you abreast of any developments.'Rodney bowed his head to Lara and the Directors. 'Time for us to go. Lots to do. Good luck to you all.'

Chapter Thirty-Six

Journey Home

They collected their weapons, signed out and made their way into the courtyard. It was still raining but the air smelt fresh after the cloying atmosphere in the prison. In the Land Rover Mould broke out the flasks and dished out the Chinese meal. They all sat in silence while they ate their late supper. Mould gathered the debris from the meal, stuffed it into a black bag and took it with the flasks and locked it into the boot.

Sharky fired up the Land Rover and put the heating on full blast. The evening chill had seeped into the car and in a minute or two the blast of heat warmed the cabin which was very welcome.

Mould opened the conversation. 'Boss, do you really think it will be wise to use the directors as friends?'

'Good question. Think about it; if you had been living under the threat year in year out of whatever and somebody comes and offers a solution of a normal life, I think that I would cooperate.'

Reid had been brooding in his car seat. 'On balance I agree but I think we need a short rein on the commercial man. He's a wreck. Did you notice he kept rubbing his nose on his sleeve? I would lay a few pounds on him being a cocaine addict and therefore completely untrustworthy. ' He folded his arms.

'Hmm. So, how should we use him?'Sharky looked over his shoulder.

'Face front, driver. I want to get home in one piece tonight. Mrs. Reid has her mum coming round for a meal. So, on second thoughts. Drop the boss then Mould, then me and with any luck and if the gods are smiling on me, the mother-in -law will have gone home.'There was a muted chuckle all round. They knew that the only two things which worried Mr. Reid were firstly getting in the bad books of Mrs. Reid and then secondly, her mother.

'I don't get it,'said Mould raising his voice over the sound of the high-powered engine and the road noise from the over-large tyres, 'How could they be so gullible? Particularly those directors, they didn't need the money, did they?'

'None so strange as folk.'Sharky was dismissive, 'More interesting to me is how they entrapped them. I can understand that they were given an apparent legal inducement, contracts they never expected to win. Honey trap could have been employed and in the case of the commercial director hook him on drugs and then feed his drug habit once he was hooked.'

'I was trying to put myself in their position.'Rodney mused, 'Trying for the life of me to find a reason why I wouldn't have shopped them.'

'Got to be down to the enforcers, innit. What were the names? Oh yeah, Leonid and Dimitri Abakumov, the chuckle brothers.' Sharky was nodding his head, persuaded of his own logic. 'How about Mould and the Jones brothers and me go round to the hotel tonight and lift them? Before they do a runner back to Moscow or wherever they came from.'

'Like it,'Reid said. He looked at Rodney. who was staring out of the car window at the road and the cars they left in their wake, thinking hard.

After a minute he said, 'Can't see a downside.'Rodney put his seal of approval on the idea.

'Mould, call the Jones brothers and tell them to be at the hotel and check it out but to wait for us.'He turned to Mr. Reid, 'Do you want dropping off or are you insisting on being in for the kill?'

'I wouldn't miss this for the world,'he replied with a grin.

'Thought that you'd say that. I want them cooling their heels in a couple of cells in our building overnight. Sharky, have them stripped down to their underpants and socks, lights off, total deprivation, no food, no water.'He listened to Mould talking to the office and then the Jones brothers.

'All set, Major. Think they wanted a break anyway from Graham and the admin stuff.'

Sharky finished setting up the Satnav. 'Estimated time of arrival 2330hrs at the Blue Haven Hotel.'

Rodney reached to the front. 'Pass me the car phone, Mould. I'd better let Bob know what we are going to do or he could get even more cheesed off. And he can find out for me if the hotel and occupants are on a list of interest.'

'Getting cautious in your old age,'Reid commented.

'Yes and no. Special Branch may have an interest in the hotel and even if not, Commander Bob may send some of his heavies from SO15 to lift them for us and hand them over. Bob would also be pissed off with me if I didn't tell him what we were doing on his patch.'

'True enough. Fair one.'Reid was happy.

Rodney's call to Bob took longer than he wished. He had to explain in detail how the hotel had come up. The others listened in. They could tell that Rodney was getting a little frustrated but admired him for keeping his cool. Bob obviously asked him to hold for five minutes as Rodney sat back in the seat and relaxed. Put his finger to his mouth calling for silence and held up five fingers. The men went silent. When Bob came back on the phone it was all good.

'Put me on speaker, Rodney,'Rodney leant forward and hit the speaker on the vehicle console. 'You all hear me OK?'They all acknowledged the Commander. 'Right, listen in. We are aware of these two jokers and that nest of some other villains of interest in the Blue Haven. So, we're going to mount a significant operation, lift the ones we want and your two. So, I don't want you getting caught in the crossfire, not that I think you would. So please sit in your cars and await my orders. We'll raid in force at midnight, that should give you enough time to park and get a grandstand view.'He paused, 'OK with that?'

'Yes, thanks; that all makes sense.'Rodney was relieved.

'Get a pen, you'll have to sign for your two. Got to go, lot to do. The first wave is already on its way to get eyes on.' He cut the call.

'Good call, Major.'Reid was pleased and surprised at how fast Rodney had picked up the baton. He grinned to himself. Beach bum to super soldier in less than forty-eight hours. *Must have been my training regime in those early days. Turning a rag-arsed, snotty lieutenant into a SAS soldier. Pedigree will out.*

Mould was not so pleased. 'Bollocks; I was looking forward to a good dust up.'Sharky gave him a look that shrivelled him.

Rodney had to laugh. 'Rest easy. This task has miles to run and I would be amazed if you didn't get the opportunity to test yourself against some other villains. At this early stage I can't afford to lose anyone or for anyone to get injured, we're a small enough team as it is. Remember I'm also going to plan how and when we take down the Defence contractors, they'll have a lot of boys on the books with the same training as us and they are younger; we'll have our hands full.'

'Well, just thought a bit of training to stop us getting rusty. A practice would be good.'Mould didn't want to let it go.'

'Be careful what you wish for.'Mr. Reid's Scottish accent was harsh. Mould took the hint.

Chapter Thirty-Seven

Blue Haven Hotel

Sharky pulled the Rover into the kerb on the far side of the road, three car lengths from the hotel. He parked facing the hotel. The Range Rover's height gave them an unobstructed view of the hotel entrance. The Satnav showed them the road at the back of the hotel. There was a small yard which was probably the hotel car park. That was the only conceivable escape route that they could see except the roof tops. The rain had stopped but the road and pavements still shone wet.

'What do you think?' Rodney asked Reid, leaning over towards him.

'Whilst I expect Bob's boys to do a good job, I think that we need to cover the back. We put the Jones boys there and they block the car park. Sharky, get them on the radio'. Reid looked at his watch, 2345hrs.

Rodney and his team could see the SO13 boys filtering into the area now. There were a lot of them.

Fred Jones, one of the brothers, came online. 'Bravo Two, radio check, over.'

'Bravo Two this is Sunray. Move to the rear of the hotel and prepare to block the exit to the car park. Roger so far. ' Rodney smiled to himself as he always thought that the call sign Sunray, designated to the commander, himself in this case, was a hoot.

'Bravo Two, Roger over.'

'Sunray. Bravo Two block the entrance from 2359hrs, don't care how you do it but don't get in the way of friendly forces. No targets to escape. Over.'

'Bravo Two, Roger Sunray. We will comply out.'

Rodney handed the radio mike back to Mould. 'God, I love this stuff.' Mr. Reid shot him a glance and shook his head in despair.

Mr. Reid looked out of the vehicle; all was now silent and still. It was going to go down in five minutes and he wanted to do something. He really didn't like not being in control of the events. He shuffled in his seat, grumbling to himself. Rodney could read him like a book.

'Why don't you go and find the ops van and Bob? They can't be far away along the road that the boys were coming from. That way you'll be able to keep us informed and we can respond if we need to. What do you think?'

'Thought that you'd never ask.' Sharky turned the interior lights to off. Mr. Reid was out of the car before Rodney could respond.

There was an audible relaxing in the cab. 'Good call, Boss. Thank goodness, he was about to explode. You know what he's like, needs to be in the middle of the mix or he feels unwanted.'Sharky chuckled. 'I am sure that Bob will value his input anyway and it's better that he's there rather than here giving us a hard time.'

'Talking of time, they seem to be taking their time.' Rodney wanted to understand what the delay was. 'Seems to me like it should be happening now.'

'Could be they are waiting for someone to approve the attack, or simply waiting for the lights to go out in the rooms?' Mould mused.

'I'll give them five more minutes then we go in and lift our men. Get ready you two. If we see anybody trying to leave the hotel in that time, we'll lift them and find out who they are afterwards.'Rodney took out his pistol and made it ready.

'You sure about this, Boss?' Sharky was not so sure; if they barged in too soon it had all the hallmarks of a disaster.

'Just get ready.'Rodney could feel the tension building. It had been a very long day and he wanted it to end. There was a bit of a breeze now and he watched a couple of newspaper pages get picked up by a gust, flap into the air and tumble down the road. Somehow watching the papers struggle with the wind lightened his mood.

The car phone rang. Mould put it on speaker.

'Reid. Listen up, it's happening right now. I suggest that when you see the boys go in you leave the comfort of your luxurious, over-warm Land Rover and get out on the street. Play long stop in case anyone legs it. I've spoken to the Jones brothers; they've blocked off the car park and are on foot. Bob sends his best. Good luck, see you later.'

'That man is all heart.'Mould shrugged on his coat. 'Hey up, there they go.' A stream of twenty black-clad officers steamed in through the front door. Rodney could imagine a similar attack through the back door. He and the others clambered out of the car.

Chapter Thirty-Eight

The Brothers

Rodney and his men watched the last of the police enter the hotel and then watched as police cars screamed up the road from both directions and blocked the road. From the lead car emerged Commander Bob Coveney followed quickly by Mr. Reid. Other policemen discharged from vehicles and set up a perimeter. The street was eerily quiet despite an ever-growing manpower presence, even if the noises coming from the hotel were noisy as the entry teams made themselves busy.

Bob beckoned to Rodney and with Mr. Reid they made their way to the hotel entrance. Inside they were met by the commander of the assault team who asked them to wait in the reception area for a moment and he would brief them. He spun the register round and pointed to the rooms held by Leonid and Dimitri Abakumov.

'We've sealed all the other guests in their rooms, with a presence of course. Your two men will be brought down first in a few moments. I'm going to bag all of whatever we can find in their rooms and get it over to you later. I'll also get forensics to go over their rooms inch by inch just in case.'

Bob screwed his eyes up. 'I suppose that I should thank you; I've had this hotel and its occupants on my bucket list for a while, just needed a catalyst. Anyway.' With his left hand he reached behind his stab vest and pulled out a sheaf of papers. He pushed them towards Rodney. 'Sign here, Major, that I will handing over two men, very much alive, into your care as requested.'

'Thank you, Commander, very efficient, 'Rodney acknowledged, taking the papers and placing them on the reception desk so that he could sign.

Two men appeared on the stairs with their escorts. The noise they were making preceded them. They were kicking out at the walls and stairs, shouting. Trying to headbutt the escorts who were having nothing of it. Once they had them on the ground floor the police pushed them onto the floor and one sat on them. Another of Bob's team came down the stairs with a handful of plastic evidence bags.

'Sir, just bagged all the mobile phones we could find and passports, several of, licenses etc. Bundles of cash in a separate bag. Something for you to work with till we get a full forensic search sorted. Please sign here, Major.'

Rodney rolled his eyes, put the evidence and a fist full of receipts on the reception desk. He leant on the desk again and carefully signed each document.

As he signed, he looked over his shoulder at the two prisoners. They were big, muscled men, thick-necked, similar in every regard and they almost looked like identical twins. There were distinguishing marks he noted, facial scars. These two had seen action so he and his team would treat them with the caution they deserved. Rest sorted.

'OK, think we are done.' Rodney tore off the duplicates of the paperwork he had signed on and passed them to Bob who smiled. 'Can we borrow a prison wagon and escort to get these two to our location?'

Bob looked at Mr. Reid. 'Doug, I need the van and my boys back ASAP; half hour max.'

'No problem.'

Bob called over one of his men who had been listening to the exchange. 'Get the nearest paddy wagon up here and a couple of heavies.' He nodded to his men holding the brothers, 'Let's have them up and into that wagon.'

The guards supplemented the plastic cuffs around the wrists by applying others, pinning the men's elbows together. The brothers grunted as the cuffs were tightened. They then applied other cuffs around the brothers'knees. This effectively hobbled them. With the additional cuffs the two men were pulled to their feet. They shuffled forwards with difficulty.

'Right, let's get off,'Rodney swept the evidence into his arms. 'Thanks, Bob. See you at the briefing if you're around; 0800.'

'Ugh!' The Commander looked at his watch. 'Yeah, all right.' He sighed. 'Rodney, please tell me you'll go back to your beach as soon as we are finished with this task. I am getting too old to run around with you. Only this morning I had a life.'

Chapter Thirty-Nine

The Cells

By the time the two brothers were in the cells and sorted out it was half past one in the morning and Rodney was a wreck but he wanted to see the two men before he was driven home. Reid had already gone with Mould and Sharky. The Jones Brothers would wait for Rodney and drive him home.

In the first cell was Leonid Abakumov. The warder let Rodney in. Leonid was shackled to a ring in the ceiling with enough chain to allow him to reach his ensuite shower, basin and toilet and his bed. He could also sit on the side of the table away from the door. This meant Rodney could safely walk quietly to the table, sit down and wait for the Russian to notice him.

Leonid was curled up in a ball, naked apart from his underwear, on his bed trying to keep warm. Rodney had a blanket under his arm and was determined to get Leonid to earn it.

'Do you want a blanket, Leonid?'

'Da, throw it over. I am freezing.'

'No, you come and get it.'

Grunting, the man clambered off his bed, walked over to Rodney and held out his free hand.

Rodney ignored him. 'Tell me, Leonid, everything you know.'

'Just give me that blanket.' His accented English was fluent but he was definitely Russian, Rodney decided.

'Afraid not. Unless you give me information for it.' Rodney smiled at him.

'Don't mess with me or you will regret it.' He roared and rattled his chain in anger.

Rodney was calm. 'Last chance, Leonid.' He sat stock still for a minute whilst the Russian yelled at him. 'Oh well.' Rodney stood and headed for the door taking the blanket with him. He banged on the cell door.

Leonid stopped his rant. 'Where are you going? Give me that blanket!'

'No.' Rodney turned as he went through the door. 'If you change your mind, just call out the information I need. Names, good guys, bad guys, bank accounts, addresses etc. If our men think you have given them enough to earn a blanket, they will give you one. If not, I suggest you do what exercise you need to stop freezing to death. Goodnight.' He paused. 'Ah yes, I am going to be a little busy till late morning. I am sure you will not miss the odd meal. See you then.'

Rodney repeated the scam with Dimitri. Dimitri was even less forthcoming, and said nothing at all.

'Right couple of bruisers,' the head guard said to Rodney. 'Think they will spark up in a couple of hours. We'll record whatever they say.'

'Maybe. Let's hope so anyway. How are my other two getting along?' Rodney was referring to the two men that they had arrested at the Treasury shootout.

'Good as gold, Major.'

'Ok, well I'll bring Mr. Reid with me in the morning, probably around 11.30, might be later. Let's see if they are more receptive after a miserable night.'

Rodney made his way to the garage where the Jones brothers were waiting. Lewis was in the driving seat and Fred Jones was lolling in the seat, head jammed up against the head rest. He climbed wearily into the vehicle. 'Home please.'

'Right oh, sir.' Lewis gunned the Land Rover. 'And we'll pick you up at 0700hrs. OK with that timing, Boss?'

Rodney opened the window to get some air through to help freshen up. At two am the air was chilly and Rodney shivered in the slipstream.

In no time at all the Rover pulled up at Rodney's block. Rodney tumbled out of the car and waved the Jones brothers off.

The apartment was pleasantly warm. Rodney hit the kettle switch and a minute later carried a cup of tea to the bedroom. There was a faint smell of a perfume that he recognised but he couldn't place it. Swigging the tea down, he crashed, fully clothed, onto the bed and was asleep instantly. His mental clock was set for 0630hrs.

Chapter Forty

The Morning Meeting

Rodney stood in the shower, letting the water cascade over him until the ravages of the day before were washed away. He felt surprisingly fresh and remembered that he had called the meeting for 0900hrs not the 0800hrs he had been working to. Time for a full English. The Jones brothers were on time, 0700hrs on the dot.

'Breakfast on me, guys,' Rodney said as he bounced into the Land Rover. He directed the Jones brothers to a café down a rear back street off Borough High Street. Parking was not a problem at that time of the day and they parked right outside.

'Nothing like a full English, cooked by an Italian, in the back of beyond in London.'Fred Jones was being philosophical, wiping his buttered bread into the egg with a good dollop of brown sauce.

'Cracking breakfast, Major and probably needed after yesterday. It's true what they say, a good Chinese meal will only fill you up for an hour. God, am I hungry.'Lewis Jones's Welsh accent was strong. Rodney wondered why Lewis's accent was so much stronger than Fred's, must be exposure to all good things English. He knew that Fred had an English wife.

They mostly ate in silence as there was nothing about their work that they could discuss openly in the café that was, at this time of the day, getting pretty full. And anyway, all three men were hungry, concentrating on their food. Merchants from Borough High Street market were also stocking up on calories in preparation for the day ahead.

Rodney was looking out of the bullseye glass window. Not a lot to see but the Land Rover and a red brick wall across the street. A few vehicles passed and sleepy people entered and left the café. They paid the three men no mind.

Rodney was absorbed with the day ahead. He was trying to see its shape and how it would work out. And truth be told he was feeling slightly guilty about the two men he had left shivering in the cells last night. He was really feeling guilty about the pressure he had put on the team yesterday in the context of preparation for this up-and-coming meeting, and he was concerned about Laurie Burns in Moscow and hoped that he was on his way back. He was staring into space, a thousand-yard stare old soldiers would have said.

Fred could see that the Major was away somewhere in another dimension; not sure where, but he was entitled. Hell of a job the Major had with this one.

'Boss.'

Rodney returned to the present at the sound of Fred's voice but uncomprehending what Fred had said.

'What?'

'Great breakfast, but time to move, Boss.'

Rodney yawned and then smiled and apologised. 'Sorry guys, miles away. Fire up the battle wagon and I'll get the bill.' The team gave up the table and it was immediately filled by other café customers waiting to sit down.

By the time they got to the office it was just after eight and the place was busy.

Chapter Forty-One

The Meeting

As expected, the team was hard at it and Rodney felt that he just needed to be around and let them get on with it without interference at this stage of their preparations. He retired to his desk, got out his logbook and wrote up yesterday's activities and conclusions and action points going forward.

He would have a short meeting with Mr. Reid and Graham after the main meeting to delegate any actions he felt necessary if they didn't get sorted at the upcoming briefing.

Graham had given him a thick briefing pack to be circulated at the meeting. After a quick read he was impressed with the comprehensive intelligence contained inside it. He decided to put it to one side; he had work to do himself and not too much time to do it.

He worked on his future plans as he thought of them at this time and how he thought he might need to steer the team. Much would depend on the meeting outcomes. He put down a set of bullet points and a list of *what ifs*. He converted his list of *what ifs* into a spidery decision chart. He now felt well prepared for whatever the team was going to throw at him.

Leaning back in his chair, he glanced at his watch; he still had ten minutes. Leaving his desk, he wandered round to the team's food and drinks table, made himself a tea and stole a breakfast bap from the table. He smiled and acknowledged members of the team as he headed for his seat at the head of the conference table. He settled himself and waited for the meeting to form.

There were a lot of faces from past operations arriving in the operation room and Rodney was not that surprised. Whilst he had been out, favours would have been called in by the Brigadier and Graham. What he saw pleased him.

A few minutes to nine Brigadier Robinson made his way in and sat to the left of Rodney. Rodney half stood.

'Good morning, sir.'

'Morning, Rodney. Ready for the thrash?'The Brigadier had also grabbed a breakfast bap and large cup of black tea. The tea gave out the aromatic aroma of Earl Grey.

'Yes and no. After I've set the scene, we'll get a report on yesterday and what happened. This is the chance for the team to brief us.'

'Very eventful, according to Mr. Reid.'

'You could say that, sir. The trick now is how to maintain the momentum and not lose control of the mission objectives.'

'Here to help, Major. Whatever it takes.'

'That, sir, is appreciated as ever. From the faces that have appeared it seems that you've been busy on our behalf.'Rodney grinned; he was genuinely grateful for the Brigadier's support.

The team were gathering.

Rodney had decided that first he would get the Banker and Mr. Reid to give a summary of yesterday's fun and games. Interested parties in attendance were Chief Superintendent Freddie Howelle heading up the Fraud Squad, Commander Bob Coveney SO13 Anti-Terrorist Branch, Colonel George Handyside, British Army Counterintelligence and the Cabinet Secretary, Sir Geoffrey, representing Mrs. Thatcher.

Graham passed out the briefing packs with the warning that they couldn't leave the room but notes could be taken. When Graham had finished, he raised an eyebrow to Rodney indicating that everyone was ready. He got a nod back.

'Did you want to say a few words, sir?' Rodney gave Robinson the opportunity to address the meeting.

'I think we'll just crack on, Major.'He held up his briefing pack. 'Think we have a lot to do. But welcome everyone. Rodney, let's go.'

Rodney got to his feet. 'Welcome. The shape of the meeting. Here is an agenda.' He passed handful of agendas around the very crowded table. Cosy, he thought, looking around. 'In brief. First, the Banker John Brown will give a short summary of the win from yesterday and then Mr. Reid will give a flavour of the operations undertaken with the help of SO13 and the Fraud Squad.

'Having rattled some cages, we had an unexpected visit from the KGB and I will talk to you about that meeting. Having looked at the past, we will move swiftly on to the future.

'The future will be in two phases. Major Freire and her team will show you a cat's cradle or spider's web of the corrupt principals involved in this fraud. We will break for refreshments served at the table by Graham's staff. Finally, John Brown and Colonel Jimmy will lay out their thoughts on the next two major contractor areas that we should target. I expect there to be lively debate before we settle on a methodology and time and space. I aim to manage the meeting to finish by 1130hrs so we need to push on. John, please.'Rodney resumed his seat.

The Banker stood and waved his sheaf of papers. 'Here, gentlemen, is well over three quarter of a billion plus recovered yesterday.'His Irish brogue fired the meeting's attention. 'Not a bad payback for a day's work!'He paused. 'Only made possible because of Colonel Jimmy and his investigation of the humble traffic cone.'A ripple of laughter ran around the table. 'Note, gentlemen and ladies, that construction is the largest sector of industry in the UK. Yes, we hit a mega company but there are other construction companies we now know of with links to organised fraud, waiting in the wings to be investigated. And, may I point out, this company may still have more to return. A detailed job for Superintendent Freddie and his team. More of that later.'He put his papers on the table with a flourish. 'As a team, our remit must be to race through those companies that we target. Our timescale is desperately short, so a second principle must be driven by the 80,20 rules. Low hanging fruit, gentlemen; don't get sucked in.'He nodded to Mr. Reid and sat down.

Mr. Reid took centre stage. 'Thank you, John. I will confine my report to the salient points. Although there are ongoing matters, I am not going to detail them. In that context, there is enough detail in the briefing paper for you to dig into. The focus of yesterday's operations was to corral the perpetrators and the principal players of the fraud. With the help of SO13 leading the police, we nabbed 32 people of interest. They are held in Shepton Mallet and are being interviewed by the Fraud Squad. The Major and I visited the prison. What I will say is that we had a word with the Operations, Finance and Commercial Directors and it is clear that all three were ensnared then blackmailed and are, in my view, victims; of that I am absolutely certain.'Mr. Reid's Scottish accent emphasised the point. 'The Directors gave us a very useful lead to the two enforcers in this sorry tale. Leonid and Dimitri Abakumov, two very unpleasant and ruthless Russian thugs. We have them being held below, awaiting interview, thanks to the Commander.

'The Major and I were called to a meeting early afternoon by a contact and we were in for a surprise. There is no doubt that this fraud is the brainchild of the KGB. The following is classified. Waiting for us was a senior officer of the KGB with another officer of the new breed, probably FSB, plus a declared Russian attaché. They wanted us to believe that they didn't feel the fraud was worthy of their efforts anymore, however we have our doubts.

'A disc was passed over purporting to contain the names of those involved. Graham and his team are working on the contents. More at a later date; wait out.'Mr. Reid exchanged a silent glance with Rodney. Both men knew Mr. Reid was asking Rodney if he should mention that they had an asset in Russia. Rodney shook his head. 'That concludes this part of the meeting. Major?'

Rodney stood. 'John, Mr. Reid, thank you. Time for a short break please and we will reconvene to hear about the intelligence report and future targets. I am happy to take any questions at this stage, but I believe that it would be better to leave them to the end of the meeting. Any questions?'

'Only one. where is the tea and nosh?'Colonel George wanted to know.

'Follow me, George. We can have a quick chat.'Brigadier Robinson waved George over.

PART THREE

Chapter Forty-Two

Moscow

Laurie Burns was about to make a decision. They had a tentative agreement that he would meet Servo and Carla the following morning; if not, Servo and Carla would come as soon as they could either with the data or having sent it on ahead.

Neither were at the rendezvous that morning. He felt uneasy and wanted to move on. He wasn't worried that Carla or Servo would be compromised, they were seasoned professionals after all. It was a personal thing he had. He didn't like the static nature of this task. Being in one place, even if only for a few days when on a job, made him uncomfortable.

He flicked the taxi driver's card with the fingers of one hand whilst he held it with the other. *Hmm, Sergei; I wonder if he's free?*

He called Sergei. Sergei picked up the phone and sounded hungover.

'Sergei, it's Laurie Burns. You picked me up from the airport the other day and I was wondering if you are free for the next two days. Do you remember me?'

'Oh yes, the English man who speaks such excellent Russian. Like a native. Yeah, I am free for the next thirty-six hours, only got one booking for late tomorrow to the airport.'

'That's great. How soon can you pick me up?'

'Hour be OK?'

'OK, see you then.'

'Where we going?' Sergei wanted to know.

'Sightseeing a lot, so fill up the tank.' He heard Sergei chuckle. Laurie had made his decision. Book out, get Sergei to move him around for the day in old Moscow where the tourists and FSB never go, and find a bolthole for tonight. Try to tie up with Servo in the morning then leg it for the airport and home, whatever the outcome.

Chapter Forty-Three

Graham and Major Freire

It took half an hour or more to get everybody back to the table with their snacks and drinks. Rodney wasn't fussed, he wanted them relaxed and receptive. He glanced over at Mr. Reid, who was clenching his jaw in impatience.

He guessed that Mr. R wanted to get on and thought that this briefing was just time lost. Rodney thought, as he looked at his longtime friend, that he was looking drawn and old. Rodney was suddenly shocked; he hadn't even thought that Mr. R was no longer young. Not the feisty, experienced SAS Sergeant Major, who at forty-five was a mega-fit soldier who had made his life hell. Hell for the six months when Rodney was doing his selection for the SAS as a barely twenty-one-year-old lieutenant. A 'Rupert', as they called the officers. He made a mental note that he would get the others to dash about and put Mr. Reid, who must be pushing his late sixties, in a more office coordination and control position. How he was going to do that he had no idea, but he owed it to Mr. Reid to make it happen, and soon. He also had to do it without Mr. Reid knowing that he had an agenda or his life would be hell.

The table came to order as Graham asked for their attention.

'Gentlemen and ladies, Part One, the intelligence briefing given by Major Freire Royal Signals with the support of myself and her team. Part Two, the future. I need you to remember that this intelligence is secret so treat it as such. Major Freire.'

'Thank you, Graham. Hold on to your seats for a helter-skelter ride through a bewildering maze of links and contacts that demonstrate the breadth and range of this fraud. Turn to pages fifteen to thirty of your briefing pack when you're ready. Right, here we go.

'Study page fifteen. Head of the tree is our Treasury official. Side bands feeding in are officials in the Paymaster General, Ministry of Defence, transport and infrastructure and health ministries, with links to the audit and fraud branches of government. Cascading down to the officials in the contract branches and quangos. A very busy network indeed. To help you, I'm going to project it onto the large screen so that you can see the detail more easily.'

The assembled meeting craned forward and twisted in their chairs to see the screen. After a few moments the Cabinet Secretary said, 'My God, it is a Pandora's box that we've opened.' He echoed the unanimous feeling of the people at the table. All were stunned by the revelations.

When Freire judged that the meeting had had enough time to absorb the data, she began again.

'We move on. The intelligence handed over by the Russians is incomplete. So incomplete that they have left, as Major Brown and Mr. Reid forecasted, a viable, slimmed down control set-up with businesses which can be built on and expanded again later. Sneaky.' This brought laughter to the table. Even Mr. Reid gave her the thumbs up.

Freire let them settle down again. 'We've blistered the intel onto the schematic in red. Watch.' On the screen now appeared the same schematic but with many of the connecting lines between the fraudsters and names shown in red. 'This schematic tells the story of either the Russians' duplicity or our fraudsters have expanded their own base up without telling the Russians. We don't know at this stage, but it gives someone-' She rolled her eyes towards Rodney, 'games to play.'

'Now,' Freire continued, 'what we will now show in a series of schematics is discrete to each business. For example, the Defence Industry, the National Health Service etc. Again, where the data we were given is from the Russians it's shown in red.' She hesitated. 'I want to point out that at times there are connections from one business to another as well as to the principal villains. There are other lines on the schematics to individuals in non-UK companies ex the mainland, that supply, for instance, medical requisites and drugs, machine parts or armaments. The name and the company name are shown where we have them.'

For the next half hour Major Freire went through the detail of each schematic. 'I apologise for the gallop through the information and I need to remind you that we are still gathering data hour on hour. It is also clear to us that many of these individuals we have listened into are definitely under duress.' She paused. 'That concludes this part of the presentation. Are there any questions at this time? If not, my team and I will resume our intelligence gathering.'

'Just one question please. Do you have the evidence to back up the presentation data we have seen?' Commander Bob Coveney was as shocked as everyone else. The breadth of the fraud and its complexity had left them bewildered.

'We have evidence to back up everything that we have shown you today; evidence of telephone connections and voice recordings of the conversations between parties. Nothing that you have seen today is not backed up with documentation. All the data, this presentation and briefing pack will be properly handed over to the Fraud Squad Superintendent today, signed and sealed. Plus future data of course.'

'Sorry. I wanted to learn briefly about the third parties, ex-UK?' Bob pressed.

'So far, we see clusters in fifteen countries with links to the UK, including the USA. I can say that the traffic of intelligence, money and products is two ways. We have examples of more complex networks for example UK to Germany, Germany to France, France to the USA and the USA back to the UK. Other principal European states too. At every transfer of, for example, the product, either there are price hikes and or the product gets smaller and so two items after a time become three and are sold as three items. Doesn't take a genius to see how the money is made.'

'Good enough.' The Commander smiled at Freire. 'One hell of a job, Freire.'

'Not a solo effort. This is the efforts of my team and Graham and his staff.'

'Well done, all the same. Another short break I think, before we get on the meat of the day, the next targets.' Brigadier Robinson rose and the rest followed him to the refreshment area.

Chapter Forty-Four

Future Way Forward

'Without preamble.'The soft Dublin Irish accent was to the fore as the Banker spoke. 'It became obvious late yesterday and in conversations with Brigadier Robinson relating to Major Brown's thoughts on our organization that we needed to make changes. Mr. Reid, Graham and I have come up with the following to manage two major targets and a few minis.

'Please focus on what I am about to tell you.'John Brown need not have bothered, the room was so silent that you could hear a pin drop. 'We will use Colonel Jimmy's methodology throughout as it has proved its worth. Overnight, the team developed and worked on an algorithm which looked at the turnover of two already identified major targets, and with the help of Major Freire they fed in communication traffic density as a measure of fraud. Major Freire's Information Technology Programmer is creating links so that as data is received the algorithm will be updated in real time for a myriad of businesses, large and small or within larger businesses the operating division where fraud has been detected or is suspected. The team is working on other parameters that will enhance the algorithm, for example anomalies in product traffic movements, quantities etc. We will feed in reworks, delays, contract escalation and any other flags that show that a possible fraud is taking place.

'We will capture data as of now, from all departments of the Government. Once everything is automated the upkeep and housekeeping will be minimal. A useful tool which we will share with Fraud Branch immediately and the Treasury and Audit Security Section once they have been cleaned up and the traitors cleared out.

'Please turn to page forty of your briefing paper which shows the proposed audit organisation. Team One, led by one of the PM's special advisors, Dan, for Primary Target One. Team Two, for Primary Target Two, Shaun. Each team has three financial analysts plus an IT specialist and a secretary. Team Three, led by Pat with the same support, will begin the work up of all the other target businesses as they are identified. Once a Primary Target has been worked up to a point where Mr. Reid and S013 can close down the operation, that Primary Team will be given a new target from Pat's clutch.'He paused. 'The point where we close down an operation is where we believe that we are able to recoup substantial sums of cash.'

The Banker looked round the table. Everyone was awake at least. 'Still with me? Good. Notice that Colonel Jimmy heads the three teams working directly to me. I have two other people who are instrumental to success. Andrew will work with me. He will lead a small team, initially of currency specialists from the Fraud Squad. We will follow the money and whether it's on shore or off we will get it back, one way or another. In direct support to Andrew and myself are three amazing ladies who have worked for us before. Ms. Reid, Secret Intelligence Services, Captain Chloe, Military Intelligence and of course Ms. Jane Christine, ex- Special Branch and now MI5. Please welcome them. Our very large working area has just shrunk, but I think that we'll manage!'This drew a laugh from all at the meeting.

'We have the team that we want and we will perform, gentlemen! All that remains is the choice of Targets One and Two. I'm going to hand over to Colonel Jimmy, who will tell you why he thinks our two preferred targets are the ones we should go with for now.'

Rodney looked at the Banker and nodded, saluting him. He had not been disappointed and he felt buoyed. He knew that the choice of targets was his and he would need to decide in a few minutes. But he was ready. He looked over at Jane with her flaming red hair. She felt his gaze, caught his eye and smiled. For himself, he was looking forward to working with her again and the other old hands for that matter.

Colonel Jimmy went to two whiteboards that he had set up on easels and removed the coverings on them to show a spidery network of links.

'Pages fifty-five and fifty-six of your briefing packs.'The Colonel directed the team to the relevant pages showing copies of the spidery data on the whiteboards. 'My task was to tell you where we should go next to recoup ill-gotten gains. Well, it's not that easy at this stage of our research. What I can tell you for a fact is that fraud in our Health Service kills as surely as a full metal jacket round or an artillery piece. Morally you may think that that's a good enough reason to hit the Health Service and accompanying pharmaceutical industry. On the other hand, you may think that we should hit the three Defence manufacturers and contractors identified in the document, which I hasten to tell you, go from everything from cleaners to tank builders. I would add that there isn't one simple Ministry dealing with Defence but also more than handful of quangos thrown into the mix. In a word, this is really complicated.' He tapped his pointer on the whiteboards. 'Beyond the talent at this table? I think not.' He beamed and got a smile from Rodney. 'But we need a few other tools in our armoury.' He paused. 'We may need a logistician. We need a couple of SO2s, even a SO1 animal.'

'What's an SO2?' Christine wanted to know.

'Hold that thought, Christine. But basically, an SO is a technical serving officer or could also be a retired officer who is re-employed as a civilian in technical MOD posts. A journey of a thousand miles begins with the first step. I want to deal with the Health Service for a few moments. Page fifty-five.'

Rodney and the Brigadier exchanged glances. They were both enjoying Colonel Jimmy's presentation and his real enthusiasm for the subject.

'Simplistically, we are assuming that there are fraud cartels who may or not be linked to the KGB operation and we have some links to the Treasury and Health Ministry already. But I have to tell you that there are many papers and studies done on fraud and many are heavy reading. Billions of pounds are fraudulently taken out of health budgets worldwide by cabals of greedy doctors, the thieves in the suppliers and stores, the pharmaceutical industry. The list goes on and on. Our mission is to find the fraudsters. So, let's keep it simple.'

The Colonel tapped his board three times with his billiard cue pointer. 'Here we have the Health system. Money goes in. Top of the tree is the Regulator; approves the norms and defines and controls equipment, drugs and construction equipment etc. Suppliers: two main categories; construction, that's engineering, operations and maintenance, and suppliers of drugs and equipment, iron lungs, scanner machines, ambulances etc. etc. A huge bill the Health Service carries. Private hospitals and physicians bill the Health Service and there is little if any incentive to save costs for either the private or public sectors; it's the patients who suffer. Over-billing, phantom patients, even ghost workers. We haven't even touched on informal payments, absenteeism at every level. Over-treatment, oversubscribing of drugs and, of course, blatant theft. Rerouting of Health Service supplies to gangs, the private sector etc. What about staff off sick in the Health Service moonlighting in the private sector? How many doctors employed for the Health

Service can hand on heart say they have never used some equipment or drugs paid for by the taxpayer for a private patient? Are our Health Service patients at risk where doctors and nurses moonlight in the private sector? If they have the time to do that, why are there waiting lists and the best physicians, nurses and support staff get too knackered to attend to Health Service patients? It's invidious. I could go on. Agency workers, why for goodness's sake, why are they proliferating when the Health Service is undermanned? HR inflexibility, T&Cs, issues with tracking staff, training. Who knows? The situation just seems to me to be a bloody mess.'

The Colonel smiled. 'Now look, I'm getting emotional and I promised to keep it simple. We need to hit procurement, storage of supplies and suppliers. We need to hit HR in the largest hospitals. Now, five-minute break please and then we'll look at the Defence contractors.'

Rodney went into a huddle with the Brigadier and Mr. Reid. As he listened to the Colonel, he had formulated the outline of a plan and he needed their approval.

The Colonel returned to the fray re-energised.

'Ladies and gentlemen. Here we go again, switch on to Defence contracts. Think BIEFIE – bribery, intimidation, embezzlement, fraud, intellectual and property theft, also extortion. I want you to think also of why some contractors seem always to win the majority of contracts. True, there are specialist needs; special metals etc., intellectual property and software rights. That's the BIEFIE part but these, let's call them projects, are overseen mainly by project officers, the SO2 and SO1s. Normally technical serving military officers. But there are a myriad of other contractors run by quangos and ministries where they hold the warrants to what I call service and construction. Service could include security, operations, maintenance, cleaning, transport, food and hospitality. Whatever you can think of, let's say, that's not metal or propellant'

'Confused, disappointed, depressed. Under normal circumstances you probably would be but not, I say it again, with the team that we have. But we do need to find the brick to remove that collapses the networks that fraudsters are using to steal public money.'He tapped the board with his pointer. 'Rodney, the floor is yours.'

'

Chapter Forty-Five

Dispositions

'Well, ladies and gentlemen, a real cat's cradle to unravel.' Rodney went to the boards and turned them over. He had two clean surfaces to fill. 'For both the Health Service and the Defence industry we need more data, more intelligence, more analysis. But perhaps not as much as it seems at this point. Our mission is to find the red cones.' This got a laugh from everyone. 'So, I am splitting the team for four days. Everyone except Mr. Reid, Mould and Sharky are to report as follows. I still need a small operational team for this week to come to tie up some loose ends. And in that context, I would appreciate it, Bob, if you could leave me a SO13 liaison officer to work with us this week.'

Bob grunted. 'Always a pleasure to help.'

Rodney couldn't make up his mind if the Commander SO13 was being sarcastic, so he chose to ignore him and nodded a thank you. Rodney drew the organisation on the board as he created the mission teams. 'Graham and his small staff and Major Freire's team will run the administration and the intelligence collection and data cells.' He moved on to the Banker and his men. 'The Banker has kindly agreed to form two primary research teams, one for Defence and one for the Health Service. The intelligence cell will feed them as they have been to date and as they acquire new avenues of intelligence as needs be. OK so far?'

The table was silent; they held their breath. This was Rodney doing what he did best, getting the chess pieces in place. 'Good. Now, I need a couple of willing bodies to help me parachute people into key points in both industries. To lead this amazing group that I'm calling "The Deceivers" I would like Christine to volunteer.'

'So that's what I am doing here.' Christine said.

'Was there any doubt?' Rodney replied. He drew more of the organisation on the board.

'So, drawing on Christine's experience, I want her team to embrace a new policing technique which is arriving on our shores from Canada.

That is *Geographic Profiling,* primarily used to find where the bodies are hidden in serial killer cases and where and who the perpetrators are.' Rodney could see the consternation on Christine's face. He would let her sweat a little longer. 'I want to co-opt Major James as our tame Procurement Officer, all things to all men re stores and storage systems and their management. Mr. Reid's daughter from 5. A couple of technical engineers, SO1s and S02s. Sgt George SAS. Freddie, could you lend me a couple of audit-trained officers? And our own Dr Jules Christian.'Freddie nodded, eyes rolling. 'Great. Christine, can you be here at five and bring Dr Christian with you for a half hour briefing and I'll explain to you and Dr Jules the main tenets of Geographic Profiling. So, questions now please?'

After a couple of questions to clarify a few points, Rodney closed the meeting and called the lunch bar open to those who wanted to eat with the team, which was just about everyone with the exception of the Cabinet Secretary who needed to get back and waved away the invitation. But he did thank the Brigadier and Rodney for a masterclass in the disposition of limited resources. As a parting throwaway line, Rodney addressed the departing bodies from the meeting.

' Don't waste this four days of research; we need to get our hooks into this, 24/7 please, two shifts. Who are the perpetrators? Who benefits from the fraud? Who sustains the fraud? Who are the willing participants in the fraud and who are the victims? Let's go to it. I'm available day or night!'

Rodney settled back into his chair, tidied his documents and closed his logbook. Only the Brigadier and Colonel George from Military Counterintelligence sat quietly with him waiting for the others to clear away their clutter and move back to their respective work areas and lunch.

When they were by themselves, Colonel George, who was genuinely concerned, was the first to speak.

'My God, Rodney how the hell do you expect to find, and overturn years of embedded malpractice in a few weeks? It's madness.'

'Rodney, I had no idea how complex and wide-ranging this was going to be. Do you want me to close this down with Sir Geoffrey and the PM?'Brigadier Robinson was concerned for his deputy.

Rodney put his hands behind his head and looked at the ceiling. He closed his eyes for a few seconds, then he propelled himself forwards, both hands flat on the table. He had his old grin, broad as ever.

'Not yet, sir. I have three, maybe four things going for us that they don't. First, we bought ourselves nearly a week's grace to research and gain intelligence and analyse it. I have total belief that by the end of the week I will have more than enough leads to strike at. Second, I have Mr. Reid and our Ghost is still in play. Third, we have your support and I know you will rein us in if we go off mission. Finally, we owe it to the team to give them a chance.'

'Hmm. What do you think, Colonel George?'

'Think that you should let Rodney have a go. Review the situation after the week. I'd be happy to attend then; good bet that the team comes up with something. They haven't failed you yet, Brigadier.' Colonel George stood up and put a hand on Rodney's shoulder. 'I know where my money is going on.'

'Thank you.' Rodney looked up at the Colonel.

'Don't thank me yet, Rodney. I have to get Sergeant George released, and God knows which part of the world he's in. And of course, Major James, although I expect that he'll jump at the chance of an adventure.'

'Come on then, let's get some food if the team haven't cleared the decks.' The Brigadier led them off. Even so, they stopped and looked at Rodney's organisation chart as they passed.

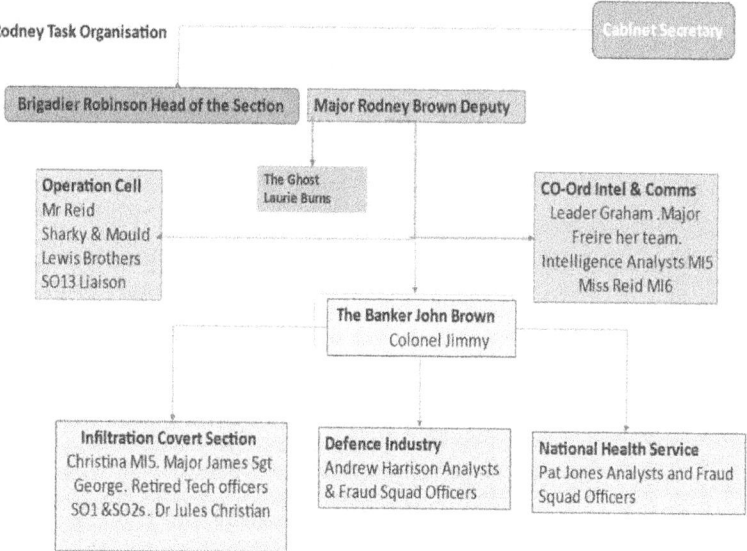

Chapter Forty-Six

Reid's Magic

Rodney was thinking of his man in Moscow. He wasn't overly concerned but he would have preferred if Laurie had contacted him. Laurie was the most unlikely character to be a spy. Although Rodney didn't think of himself and the rest of the team as spies, more like troubleshooters – your compliance and corrective team, but with teeth! He turned the thought around in his mind. Rodney had written up his notes and was winding himself up to interview the 'Brothers Grimm' they had lifted last night. He had his feet up on his desk and his hands clasped behind his head, eyes closed. He could feel himself nodding off.

'Rodney!'

Rodney came alert instantly, put his feet down and stood up quickly. Mr. Reid stood in front of his desk with a half grin, half scowl on his face on his face.

'Not keeping you up are we, sir?' Mr. Reid's question was cutting.

'Not at all. I was just thinking about stuff.'

'Harrumph. Come on, Major, let's grill the Brothers Grimm.'

'Which one first? Dimitri or Leonid?'

'Don't think it matters much, they're both professionals.'

'So are we, Mr. Reid. Come on, let's have some fun. I could do with a diversion.' He paused. 'You do have the doctored pictures?'

'Oh yes.'

The first brother was as Rodney had left him in the early hours of the morning, still chained to give him access to the bathroom, his bed and one side of the table. But he had been given a paper suit to wear and he sat miserably at the table with a blanket over his shoulders.

'Leonid, can I introduce Mr. Reid. He is here to debrief you.'

'What do you mean?' he was suspicious and eyed Mr. Reid up and down. 'You have no right to keep me here.'

'When and if you are released is up to you,' Rodney snapped back.

'Dimitri is already free.' Mr. Reid smiled.

'I don't believe you.'Leonid shouted.

Mr. Reid pulled a picture from an envelope and placed it face down on the table. 'When I said Dimitri was free, well sort of. Let's say he's now a free spirit.'Mr. Reid flipped over the picture. It showed Dimitri, pale-faced, eyes closed with a neat red hole in the centre of his forehead.

Leonid snatched up the picture and studied it carefully. Satisfied that it wasn't a fake, he let out a roar and threw himself at the two British Secret Service men. The chain held him back. He thrashed in frustration for a few minutes while Rodney and Reid looked on, before collapsing in the chair on his side of the table. 'You bastards.' was his heartfelt outburst, and then he put his head down, weeping silently.

They gave him a full minute to compose himself. Reid poked him hard on the top of his head several times. Leonid, surprised and angry, stood up quickly and lunged at Reid. The chain whipped him back by the wrist as it got to the end of its travel. Leonid slumped back into his chair and glared at Reid.

'When I can, I will kill you!'He snarled.

'Don't think so, old son. Unless you give us the information that we want you'll be joining your brother. 'He paused. 'And in a few hours…, ' he paused – 'he'll be ashes.'

'No, stop. I need to take his body back to our village to be buried with our family.'

'You're not listening, Leonid. Unless you start telling me what I want, you'll be burning with him.'

'Ah! You will let me go. You will stop the cremation?'

'Stop the cremation, yes. Free, no promises but possibly, depending on your willingness to help us.'

'Where to start?'

'We know about Mr. Ashchurch and others but we want off you the whole network leading into the main fraud in areas of say the National Health Service, the defence industry and the construction industry etc. The laundering of money. Using the money to bribe officials. That will be a start.'Rodney looked up at the ceiling to indicate to the watchers that they needed to start recording. He also put his hand into his jacket and started his personal tape recorder as a backup.

The floodgates opened and the intelligence they needed came pouring out. Rodney let Mr. Reid have his head. He made the excuse of stopping the cremation to leave the room and replaced himself with Andrew. He palmed the recording machine to him as he relieved Rodney in the room. Rodney could tell that the debrief as it now was would go on for many hours. Before leaving the holding level he ordered food and drinks for Reid, Andrew and Leonid. He also went to check on the two gunmen who were still stewing over their fate. He made a mental note that these two particular low-level villains could be better served and processed by Special Branch. He had what he wanted with the two Brothers Grimm. Tomorrow Mr. Reid and Andrew could begin the process with the other brother. His last action was to go to the room which housed the audio-visual recording equipment and to speak with the two techs that ran the suite.

He was surprised by the room, which was much larger than he remembered and it was crammed with hi-tech equipment.

'Hi, team. Going well?'

'A dream, Major.'The older tech, who Rodney knew as Danial, answered. 'Mr. Reid can really draw people out, can't he?'He pointed at the screen showing the room and the prisoner giving forth. He switched on the audio briefly. 'Everything being recorded to your satisfaction.'He waved his hand at the screen and the speakers. He didn't expect an answer but did get a nod from Rodney. It was enough.

'He does it so well, I'm impressed.'Jan, the other tech, said eyeing Rodney.

'He's a one off.'Rodney agreed with them both, he rubbed his chin. He listened to Leonid still giving forth for a moment before asking them for what he wanted. 'How can we arrange for my team to get the recording in quick time so that they get the transcripts done quickly?'

'No problem. We are recording on two machines, but we can easily record on three so that you can have copies of the recording as and when and we'll still have two master copies from now on. Send someone down and we'll run off what we have so far. Give us a half hour to sort it.'

'That's just great. Thank you.'Rodney wished them well with a sloppy salute and left them working their magic for him.

Back in the operations centre Rodney briefed Graham and gave him a heads up on the need to get an analyst down to the recording room and get the voice into text asap.

'Sure, Rodney. I've got a computer program that translates voice into text automatically. It's not perfect so we check it as we go along, but it's faster than steam typing and takes 99.9 percent of the hard work out of it. Just leave it to me and I'll sort it.'

'Thank you. By the way, I am going to give the two assassins back to Special Branch. They are low level and no use to us. I'll be in my office but I'd like to see the results so far before I leave this afternoon.

I'm leaving around six for the flat. I simply must get some personal admin jobs done at home.' He then asked Graham if he had had anything from Burns.

'Nothing yet, Boss.'

'Hmm, just beginning to wonder what he is up to.' Rodney shook his head and wandered off.

Chapter Forty-Seven

Laurie Burns Takes a Day Off.

Burns gently put his bags into the boot and climbed in the front passenger seat. He turned to the taxi driver.

'Sergei, I want to get lost for twenty-four hours. Can you do that?'

'I can do that, but you must have an idea what you would like to do?'

'Truth is Sergei I've been working so hard recently and I just want to get lost without my phone going off all the time. Somewhere just to relax without people wanting to get hold of me and to do something for them. What do you think?'

' Well, despite my appearance, my family and I were once relatively well off. One thing that I did inherit from my father, God bless him, years ago, was a small dacha, a garden house really, with a little land and not too far out of Moscow. I haven't been there for a few months, too busy trying to make a living. Yes, that would be possible. Need to get some provisions, food and drink but it's got water and electricity. Bit primitive by your hotel standards but it's out of the way and if you want to get lost for a day it's ideal. And the truth is that I need to do a little clearing up in the garden or my neighbours will get fed up with me.'He chuckled.

'Ideal, Sergei. I like a bit of gardening myself and I'll pay you for overnight accommodation at the same rate as the hotel. Now, let's go shopping for the provisions we'll need to eat like a prince – my gift to you for your hospitality.' Laurie was relieved; Sergei had come up with the perfect solution. If Sergei was suspicious of Laurie's motives, he neither probed nor showed it. That was appreciated by Laurie as he didn't really have a good excuse apart from the one that he'd given.

They spent the next hour shopping in the small shops in Moscow's backstreets. They topped up the ageing taxi at a petrol station and headed out of town into the countryside. Laurie relaxed into the passenger seat. There was a family photograph dangling on a plastic fob suspended from the rear-view window. The photo showed a woman and two children.

'You have a family, Sergei?'

'Yes and no. Sadly, my two sons are grown up, in the army now. Yes, it is good that they are no longer in Afghanistan since we began to withdraw. But they are now stationed on the Sino-Russian border, a long way from here. After nearly three years in Afghanistan, with no leave, I would add, they went direct from there to their new posting. I haven't seen them for four years now. On the plus side they are doing well, both now senior Captains in the Artillery. They do write occasionally and send me the odd parcel but I miss them. Their mother, a lovely lady, unfortunately passed away when they were very young. So, I brought them up the best I could.' There was a sadness in him now.

'I am so sorry, Sergei. It must have been difficult for you.'

'It was, but I would not wish a day of my life away. There were many happy times. You remind me of my boys in some ways. Quiet and deep. What about your life, my friend?'

'I was a soldier for many years. Never made more than Sergeant though. Now I'm a businessman. Recently married for the first time and a long way from home.'

'There you are, soldiers; you can always tell them apart from us civilians. Maybe that's what I sensed.' Sergei seemed happy with that.

Ten minutes later they were bouncing down a metalled road between what seemed to be well-kept small holiday and residential homes. Each house had a large, elongated plot of land to the front. The plots of most were well-tended and growing food for the table. All without exception had a half dozen or more fruit trees. There seemed to be chickens everywhere. Laurie could make out tables, chairs and awnings in front of the houses and not a few had a barbecue fired up on outside kitchens of various standards and construction.

Towards the end of the track was a larger single-storey dacha in a double plot with a dovecot and brick outside kitchen. The grounds were a little untidy and the grass long but, on the whole, a very attractive property and Laurie told Sergei that he was impressed.

'As you can see, my friend, the family was not always poor and I keep it on for my sons. I could sell it and I would be comparatively rich. It is all I have to leave them except the small flat in Moscow which I rented but now own outright. As you see, I am a capitalist just like you!' Sergei laughed. 'Come, Laurie, let's get inside and have a coffee before we tackle the garden.'

Laurie carried the supplies while Sergei fiddled with his bunch of keys. Once inside, Sergei opened the shutters, allowing sunlight to stream in. He tinkered with the stove and soon had the coffee pot on; the aroma of the strong coffee dispelled any mustiness from the house being shut up for a while. Laurie had a good look around. Apart from the large lounge diner there were two bedrooms, one with a double bed and the other with twin singles. A separate toilet and shower and bathroom. All the rooms were well decorated and family treasures and history were on display. These included a picture of his two sons in the uniform of Captains in the Artillery. Laurie, ever suspicious by nature, was happy that Sergei was who he purported to be, a simple if lonely man. While the coffee came to the boil Laurie helped to put the provisions away.

Sergei declared the coffee ready and they sat in quiet companionship at the dining table, drinking and looking out of the French windows at the garden. Laurie broke the silence that had descended on the two men.

'I can see why you would want to keep this place, it's quite something. Think I would rather live here than in a flat in Moscow.'

'One day, I hope. Almost there but I need another year with the taxi and then I can sell up in Moscow and live here. With my double plot I can grow what I need and even have a pig, rabbits and chickens of course. Behind the house is common land, a lake and forests where I will shoot the odd fowl and fish.'

'Sounds like you should come and live here sooner than later while you still have your health.'

'I have my target. Another year, I will be there.'

'What's the amount you need to earn to realise your dream?'

Sergei told him and Laurie did a quick calculation – it was a little over £10K. *Peanuts; almost an expense item with a good story.* He had his credit card, courtesy of HMG, and they would never question an emergency payment for a service. He decided to engineer it. Now he had an idea and he would work on it.

'I have a question. Are you restricted in your movements? For example, can you drive as far as say the Polish border or are you restricted to the Moscow area?'

'No, I am permitted to go where I want. Can't cross a border officially out of the Union of course but apart from that I am a free agent.'

'Interesting. Now, let's get to the garden for a few hours and then have a feast, what do you say?'

Sergei brightened. 'Come on then, let's raid the tool shed.'

They worked hard for several hours, stopping now and again for a cup of tea on the run. Both enjoyed each other's company and neighbours stopped by from time to time to see Sergei and ask him how he was. Some even stopped for a while to help tackle some of the jobs. It was a close-knit community, released and away from the strictures of the State. Laurie got the impression that what went on in the community stayed in the community. They had created quite a lot of cuttings which they heaped on the barbecue in the outside kitchen and lit it, adding a few logs from the log store.

'We will let that burn down and then we will cook those steaks you bought on the barbecue along with the potatoes and vegetables. I'll get the vodka; we have earned a drink.'

On Laurie's mind as he stared at the fire consuming the logs were two important worries niggling at the back of his mind. True to form, as ever he was enjoying himself, but he did worry about Servo and Carla getting the intelligence he needed and at what cost to them both. He was savvy enough to know that the information they were going to rob from the KGB database not only might be flagged but there might be an alert automatically sent to internal security if they didn't have the right clearances. They were taking a big risk and he just hoped that they would be able to transmit the information to Rodney as they had claimed. Even if they got clean away with the information, when the team began to roll up the villains the KGB would know that the information had leaked and they would audit and carry out a witch hunt. There was nothing he could do about it. They were both old enough and ugly enough to know the risks and if their robbery could be traced to them. He would be happier if he knew that they were going on the run with him tomorrow. The other matter was that he should really let the boss know that he was ok so far. He knew that Rodney would be concerned, but he was justifiably worried that any call would be traced.

'You look troubled, Laurie.' Sergei had come up to him with the food ready to cook, vodka glasses and a bottle all crammed on a tray.

'No, not really. I was thinking about tomorrow. Back to the rat race.' He smiled, reached for the bottle and the glasses and set them on the garden table. 'Let's drink to your boys.' He pulled the stopper from the vodka and poured two brimming tumblers. He held a glass out to Sergei. They clinked glasses 'To the boys.'

'To my boys,' Sergei repeated and they drained their glasses. Sergei went and started the food while Laurie refilled the glasses and sipped at his as he watched Sergei expertly first cook off the vegetables and potatoes, then when they were cooked, he added them all together in an iron pan and roughly mashed the mix before adding olive oil, then garlic, spices, salt and pepper. A quick stir before putting the pan back on a cool part of the fire.

The sun was still up but the chill of the late afternoon was now noticeable. Sergei shivered.

'Think that we should eat inside and watch the sunset through the windows.'

'Good idea.I'll set up inside while you finish off the steaks.'He grabbed the bottle and glasses. Inside he found the cutlery, mats and plates, set the table and then went back to collect the vegetable and potato pot off the fire grill. Sergei finished off the steaks and headed after Laurie.

It was a memorable meal that stretched into the late evening. Sergei, Laurie discovered, had had a successful career as an engineer on the rail network for many years. A civil and mechanical engineer by charter, he had held a senior position. The problem was that he had crossed the local bigwig party member. He was accused of smuggling people in a special compartment built in the train's coal tender and smuggling people into the west. His career was finished but he didn't regret it; he'd still got his pension and redundancy and the taxi had meant freedom. The accusation, he admitted now that the vodka had taken its toll, was to a degree true.

'There were some people, I can't say more than that,'he slurred and raised his glass. 'They were in real trouble with the KGB. My foreman and I created a special compartment in the place where we kept the coal for the engine. It could hold four people comfortably with some luggage. In this way, over the time we were operating we sent a hundred or more people over the border to Poland. It was discovered when the engine came into the workshops for a major overhaul. I admitted that I had a responsibility to inspect trains so I was disciplined and then gently dismissed with no stain on my character. Why? There was an acknowledgement I found out later that many in the KGB and my bosses at national level felt that the local KGB security team was lazy and was responsible for not discovering the smuggling at the outset. Unfortunately, they were protected and they didn't want any embarrassment sticking to them too. So, I was let go as an example. The best thing was that they gave me a redundancy pot, enough to pay off the flat in town, not that there was much left on the mortgage. And money left over to buy and licence the taxi. That was almost ten years ago now, no regrets.'Sergei laughed, head lolling, before finally falling gently into a drunken sleep. Laurie maneuvered him over to the bed, checked all was well in the outside kitchen and locked up for the night. In the morning he would get his flight back to London. He just hoped that Servo and his lovely lady could get the information they needed or his trip would have been in vain. He wasn't sure why he had decided to spend another day – he rationalised that it was because he hoped that Servo and Carla would be on the same flight tomorrow. Laurie took off his shoes before he collapsed onto one of the single beds. He slept soundly till first light. Sergei slept on.

Laurie struggled out of bed, washed and dressed and set the coffee pot on the oven and set the gas to boil it. He cleared up the debris from the evening meal and washed up the crockery. He found the cooking oil, bread, bacon, mushrooms, tomatoes and eggs they had bought the day before. He set a large pan over the main gas ring and threw the tomatoes into the pan with oil. He quickly set the table. Then he added the bacon to the pan and then the mushrooms. As the bacon crisped, he added bread soaked in oil and seasoned the pan with pepper. Sergei stirred at last, woken by the smell of coffee and the breakfast.

'Good morning, Sergei. Time to eat.'

Sergei rubbed his eyes and complained of a hangover. He shook himself and straightened his clothes, went over to the sink and washed his face with water to refresh himself.

'Breakfast will sort you out. Take a seat. Two minutes to an English breakfast.' Laurie called and brought the coffee pot over to the table.

Laurie added the eggs and the aroma of cooking breakfast became overpowering. Once the eggs were cooked, he brought the pan over to the table and served.

Sergei wolfed down the food, his body soaking up the calories. 'Wow, excellent. I am converted. Do you have a breakfast like that every day in England?'

'No, not every day, but few days go by without an egg and bacon sandwich.'

'That sounds interesting. Perhaps we should prepare a few for our trip to the airport?'

'Certainly, Sergei. I'll make you a couple of sandwiches. I'll clear up and you can check and lock up the house.'

As they left Sergei called out to the neighbours that they were leaving but that he would be back later that day. He asked if they needed anything and soon had half a dozen of the older residents asking him to bring them the items that they wanted. Orders came thick and fast and

Sergei had to resort to pen and paper to record everything. He winked at Laurie.

'Got to do this as we will be old ourselves one day.'

Laurie slapped him on the back.

The trip back to the airport was trouble-free. They stopped at a big Svetofor supermarket outside Moscow. Laurie helped Sergei fulfil the neighbours' lists and topped him up with some luxuries that he wouldn't normally buy for himself. There was a bank next door and Laurie drew out enough to pay Sergei and some for a gratuity that would help towards the retirement target Sergei had set himself. He crossed his fingers that Rodney would not kick up a fuss.

They drove to the airport in a companionable mood, talking of nothing much but both just enjoyed the company.

At the airport Laurie gave the envelope containing the money to Sergei. Sergei was overwhelmed and protested. 'Listen Sergei, I or my friend may need a honest man in the future and I just want you to know that I owe you, not the other way round. I had a great time with you. I'll remember your generosity for a long time.' Laurie held out his hand and Sergei took it and shook it hard.

Sergei was moved. 'Welcome anytime. Stay safe.' He put a finger to the side of his eye and pulled the skin down. 'If you have friends here in trouble, I still have a few tricks up my sleeve for,' he paused, 'a border crossing or two.'

Laurie could only smile. 'Be careful what you wish for, I may take you up on that offer at some time.'

Sergei took out his card, a new and clean one, passed it to Laurie and with a wave was gone.

Chapter Forty-Eight

Sheremetyevo

Laurie entered the hustle and bustle of Sheremetyevo Airport. As ever, he was struck by the people, rich and not so rich. He had been to the other side of the airport, for domestic internal flights. The domestic side was almost an airport in its own right. The not so rich he figured were transiting through Sheremetyevo to get the transport over to the domestic side. As ever he was struck by the Russian disregard of the 'politically-correct'and admired the ladies in their great fur coats and both them and the men smoking away as though there was no tomorrow. A few had been at the vodka early and slumped around the terminal. He noted again that he found the Russian were never the 'shrinking violets' that he often encountered elsewhere. He had dressed to blend into the Russian diaspora and felt comfortable in himself. All he had with him now was his carry-on and briefcase.

He checked in at the British Airways desk, so all that was left to do now was get through the passport and security checks. With time to spare he sought out one of the two main airport restaurants. He decided on the 'Altitude Restaurant'based on the 11th floor of the airport terminal with its panoramic views of the airport's runways and surrounding areas. A great place to wind down after the underlying if unacknowledged stress of the last few days. He had eaten there before and liked the menu with the Russian-influenced cuisine; good ingredients and well served. The great thing was that there was no rush. The fact that he could take his time suited him as he wanted to leave it to the last moment before he went through the security gate in the hope that he would be waved through without any hassle; one thing was sure, he could never take that as a given.

In the Altitude restaurant he was welcomed and shown to a window seat. The waiter gave him a menu to study and asked Laurie in Russian if he would like something to drink. Laurie thought for a moment and then asked for a heavy Russian red wine from the Rostov region if they had one. He got a nod and the waiter disappeared.

When the waiter returned with a bottle from a Rostov vineyard, he showed Laurie the label. It was one he knew. He studied the menu while the waiter uncorked the bottle. The waiter held out the cork to him to smell. It was fine. He nodded and the waiter poured him a half glass. He smelled it and then swirled it, looking at the glass for the tears which slid down the glass. A last smell to test the aromas. It was fine, so Laurie indicated to the waiter to fill the rest of the glass.

Once done, Laurie smiled. 'Please –Pozhalusta, I'm hungry – Ya golodniy. Let me start with an Olivier salad. Then Kotleti and finally Medovik to finish and coffee. Thank you —Spasibo.'

At the end of the meal the same waiter asked Laurie if he would like anything else. 'I'm full, delicious —Ya nayelsa, vkusn! Just the bill please.'

Looking at his wristwatch Laurie judged that it was time to go and face security. He was not too worried. Not as worried as if he had been carrying any contraband. He would, as an afterthought, buy a bottle or two of good vodka in Duty Free to take back to the office. Just might mollify Mr. Reid when he had to sign off the money he'd spent on the trip, at least he hoped so!

The first thing that Laurie did was to walk quickly down the steps to the departure level, avoiding the lift so that he got his heart pumping and generated a little sweat. He would appear at Security looking as though he had rushed to catch his plane. There was a queue but not much. Security airport police stood around and Laurie made sure not to make eye contact.

He shuffled his way to the front of the queue. He stood patiently until called forward. At the desk he gave the officer a smile which was not reciprocated. *Miserable. They never smile or acknowledge you.* It was just their way of doing things. He presented his passport and ticket to the security officer and looked hot and bothered.

The officer studied his passport and visa in detail. He held the passport in one hand and called a policeman over to his booth. Laurie's heart rate rose alarmingly. It took all his will to calm down and look innocent. His rising fear was wiped out when he heard the security officer ask the policeman if he would get a temporary relief for him so he could have a quick toilet break. The security officer stamped the document, slapped Laurie's passport and ticket down on the counter and with a rude, dismissive wave sent Laurie on his way.

Laurie breathed a sigh of relief. It was not completely over yet but he was airside and that was a big win in his mind. Next stop Duty Free and he took his time choosing two great bottles of Beluga Gold Line vodka. Expensive even at duty free prices, but one of the best you could buy. He waited at the kiosk to pay and noticed a man studying him. He didn't look like an official, but then again... He was well dressed in a dark business suit and plain blue tie. A receding hair line emphasised a thin grey face with an aquiline nose. He carried an expensive calf briefcase. The case the man held, to Laurie's mind, marked him out as an American. He was slightly familiar, but Laurie could not place him. He paid for the vodka, dismissed the man from his mind and made his way to the gate. The gate was open and calling for passengers to present themselves.

By the gate he sensed rather than felt a 'brush past'as the man he had pinged earlier had moved in close to him and then moved up to the gate and turned to work with the British Airways team checking tickets before they entered the air ramp to the aircraft. The man manoeuvred himself so that he was in a position to take the ticket that Laurie presented. The man smiled, checked the ticket against the passport, closed it and passed it to Laurie with a 'Have a good flight sir.'The man looked away and took the next passenger's ticket.

Laurie grasped the passport and ticket and felt something hard in the pack. He continued to the aircraft, holding his documents tight in his fist. As he walked into the aircraft doorway to be welcomed by the hostess, he palmed the item that he had been passed. He realised it was a flash-stick. His grin for the hostess was doubled – Servo and Carla had done the business. He hoped that they would be safe. For some reason he was really worried about them. He put his carry-on bag, duty free and briefcase into the overhead bin and settled himself into his seat in business class.

He shut his eyes, listening to the aircraft engines run up. He heard the captain order the aircraft doors closed over the speakers. Only when the aircraft was roaring down the runway did he open his eyes.

The fear of a tap of the shoulder even at this late stage was real. As the aircraft left the runway and climbed away, the fear faded and he let out a long breath. Safe now and going home. Laurie thought to himself, *I'm getting too old for all this excitement.*

Chapter Forty-Nine

The Ghost Turns Up

In the evening Rodney arrived at his apartment building around eight. He was relaxed. He felt that the team were focused on the task in hand and he had a breathing space. Whilst he was not worried about Laurie, he was a little concerned that he hadn't phoned him.

He had a few words with the concierge Joe, the old soldier who was always good for information on the other tenants and owners in the block. Rodney liked to think that it was an old soldier to soldier thing. All was stable; no more new incomers and Galena Vorakova, the beautiful now official Russian Cultural Attaché, was at home.

He thought about calling on her but decided that it was a bad idea. He stroked the scar on his face running down from his eye to chin. It was in the same position as Galena's, almost identical. He smiled at the thought; perhaps they had something in common after all. OK, she was a little older but so was Jane. He moved his head slowly left and right a few times. He was getting into dangerous ground. *Don't go there*, he promised himself.

He took the stairs two at a time instead of the lift to the second floor, jogging up them effortlessly. He needed, he thought, to maintain his fitness as best he could. It would be all too easy to become idle whilst stuck at the office on this mission. He didn't see himself getting out into the field; he would engineer it was his thought.

Inside his apartment he took off his jacket and hung it up on the hall clothes-hook. Then he removed his pistol from his shoulder holster and made it safe. He carried the gun into his bedroom, threw it onto his bed and got undressed. After a day working in London, he always felt grimy. He hung up his trousers and stuffed the rest of his clothes into the laundry basket. He had got Joe to rehire the three-times-a week-cleaner he had previously employed and a routine for her was to run anything in the wash basket through the machine and iron it. There wasn't a lot for his cleaner to do as Rodney's military training to keep a clean, tidy billet still held sway. The cleaner was happy to fill her hours any way she could.

After a shower he put on his old favourite sea-washed jeans, black sports shirt, and loafers. *Time*, he thought, *to raid the cupboards, fridge and freezer*.

Rodney selected a series of ready meals. Chicken Masala for two. A portion of rice and a punnet of Chinese stir fry vegetables. He took out a packet of precooked prawn crackers, which he would blow up to size with a short burst in the microwave.

He spread his feast out before him and read each label to compute which to microwave first in the hope that the whole meal would be hot at the time the last one was cooked. He had just got the order of things sorted, crackers, rice, veg and lastly the masala, when the doorbell rang. He hung his head and pressed both hands down on the kitchen counter. *Aar, fishhooks*. He could see his quiet, restful evening fading into oblivion. It meant that the caller was known or the front desk would have called up, or at a stretch it could be a neighbour. He grunted again and headed for the door. Looking through the spy-hole he saw Laurie standing there. He was surprised and suddenly delighted.

Rodney threw open the door.

'Hi, Boss. Got any food?' Laurie waved the bottle of vodka. 'I've got the drink.'

'Welcome back. Good to see you in one piece and your normal happy self.'Rodney drew Laurie into the room and silenced him with a finger to his lips. He found a pad and scribbled on it. 'I may be bugged.'Laurie read it and shrugged.

'On second thoughts Boss, let me take you out for a meal.' He glanced at Rodney's selection of fast food spread out on the kitchen bar. 'Think that we can do better than that junk food you were about to eat, don't you?' He laughed, 'Stuff that rubbish back in the stores and let's go.'Laurie left the bottle of vodka on the bar.

'OK, give me a minute.'He quickly put the food away and went to get his gun and a jacket to hide it. 'OK let's go, I know just the place.'

As they left the flats Rodney spoke quietly to the old soldier on reception. 'If I'm followed, let me know later.' The man winked.

Rodney led Laurie down the South Bank and into Borough High Street. They turned into a dark narrow lane leading to the Boot and Flogger. Neither man had said a word during the short walk, they were too busy concentrating on the people out and about to see if they could pick up a tail. If there was one, he or she or even they, were good. Neither man picked up anyone following them.

Once in the pub Laurie looked around before asking Rodney 'What's this bugging all about?'

Rodney reminded him about Galena and his suspicions. True, Graham had had his place swept for surveillance bugs and cameras, but he wasn't taking any chances that Galena's KGB technical men didn't pop in when he was at the office.

'Can you imagine, if they have bugged me it would make their eyes pop if you were telling me all about your recent adventures.' Rodney laughed. 'Mind you, we might, if they have or do bug me; we could use it to our advantage.'

'With you, Boss. To deceive is every spy's aspiration. To screw the opposition is better!'

Both men laughed.

'Well, leave that to me, Boss, I will get the flat swept for bugs in the morning. Now, let's get some grub and a drink and I'll tell you about my trip. Cost you a bit, but that's the price of doing business.'

They both had the special of the day, beef, specialty of the pub and of course a bottle of very good house red. While they ate, Laurie told Rodney the details of the trip and the flashstick palmed to him at the airport. He told Rodney that he had given the stick to Graham and it was in the evidence log. Graham would make a copy for Colonel Jimmy, who was going to work on it overnight with a couple of translators and that he would be going to help later.

'Well done, Laurie. Well done. So, how were our friends Servo and Carla?'

'Good. God, our Servo scared me. I just hope that you've got something to keep him out of trouble when he arrives looking for a job for him and Carla.'

'Sorted, no need to worry about that. That is if they do come over? New identities, pension, jobs etc, etc.' Rodney took a drink of his wine, he was thinking about Laurie and the taxi driver. 'Think that you'd better tell me about this taxi driver and why I'm going to approve the 10K you gave him. I'm going to have to get it through finance somehow.'

'I think that I can convince you that to have an asset that can get people out of Russia into Poland is cheap at the price. I can handle him until we can hand him over to a Security Services agent handler. Might save a few lives and help get people we want out of Russia.'

'Put like that,'Rodney conceded, rubbing the side of his nose, 'Seems cheap at the price. I back-charge MI6.'

'Good. Settled then.'

Rodney waved over Fred the manager. 'Can we have another bottle and is Richard in the back room tonight?'

'Yes, to both.'Fred laughed.

'Come on Laurie, think it's time to reacquaint ourselves with Richard Heard. Whatever you do, do not cut cards with him or you will lose.'

'We'll see.'

Richard and his two cronies looked up as the two Secret Service men entered. They were playing a hand. Poker, five card draw. Rodney and Laurie waited patiently, leaning their backs against the door. They watched the raises and play. It was interesting. Finally at the end of play Richard scooped the pot.

'Well, well, Rodney and Laurie. Good to see you. Take a seat. What brings you two here tonight?'Richard shuffled the cards and cut them three times. 'Care to cut for a fiver? Aces high.'

'No thanks, Richard. I don't want to lose another fiver.' Rodney grinned, 'but maybe Laurie might want to chance his arm.'

Laurie leaned over and cut the King of Hearts. 'Beat that.'

Richard calmly studied his pack and cut an Ace.

Laurie threw his card on the table. 'Rodney warned me about betting against you. Now I know it's true. How do you do that?'

'No idea and if I did, I wouldn't tell you. I just wish for a card and there you are.'

The room laughed while Laurie sourced a fiver from his wallet.

'So, gentlemen, is this a social call or business?'Richard was curious. The other two men sat silently watching the interplay. They knew about Richard's time with Rodney's outfit last year and were wondering if Richard was on for another job. They had known Richard since school and were a team of three and had been inseparable friends since then.

'Could be business, Richard, if you're up for it. A bit part in a larger game.'

'Happy to help. Need to talk to the boss of course. How long?'

'A fortnight, maybe three weeks max, start as soon as you can.' Rodney thought that should be enough for the part he'd planned for the oil man. 'What do you two do for a living?'

Richard introduced them. 'This is Greg Masters, guru of international banking. Specialises in money and currency transfers, securities, offshore stuff. A disciple of your Banker John Brown. Peter Cosworth, guru in corporate and contract compliance; due diligence, risk and, without embarrassing him, he can home in on a fiddle better than anyone I know. Peter is also ex-Army, some minor Guards Regiment.'

They spent a time getting to know each other. Richard's friends were certainly bright and knowledgeable. What Rodney liked about them was that they had an energy and zest for life.

At the back of his mind Rodney was computing if Richard's friends could help him. The right talent was always welcome.

He would speak to Richard tomorrow. Laurie and Rodney watched the men play a few hands. They finished their drinks, said their goodbyes and made their way into the street. The temperature had dropped a few degrees and they wrapped their coats around them.

'I'll walk back with you to the flat and then get a taxi to my hotel.'

'If you're sure. I'd enjoy the company and it's another chance to see if we have a tail. By the way, what did you think of Richard's two mates?'

'Same as you, they could be of help to the team.'

'Nothing gets past you, old son, does it?'

' I'm still here, Rodney.'

They walked on. They picked up a tail as they went through the pedestrian tunnel at Southwark bridge and on to the Thames path. There were a few people about but they knew that the man following them was a professional by the way he kept his distance as they varied their pace.

'Think that it's a nightcap in the Founders Arms and let's see if he joins us?'

'Good idea, Laurie. From the little I glimpsed thick set, hat, dark overcoat. Polished shoes. Hands in pockets, collar up. five feet ten or thereabouts.'

Laurie shook his head, puzzled. 'Don't think that he's Russian or Eastern European from the loose stride and the easy way he walks. Hmm. His hat's a dead giveaway, I'd put money on it that he's a Yank. Foe or friend, CIA or FBI.'

They were passing Tate Modern now and the pub soon loomed ahead. 'Could be one of Carol Windsor's men if she is still head of station liaison here. We'll see soon enough.'

They climbed the few steps into the Foundry Inn. Rodney went to the bar to order drinks and Laurie peeled off into the shadows. The Inn was not busy, only a few late-night diners and a couple of groups of friends. The Inn was large enough to absorb all the night's punters without looking busy or untidy.

Rodney paid for the drinks and carried them to a table where he could see the whole of the Inn but was not necessarily that obvious in his choice of table. The man who had been following them didn't make it obvious either when he entered the Inn. He simply entered and headed for the bar, ordering a Bourbon. Rodney turned away so that his eyes wouldn't meet with the man's. He looked over at the lights of the Thames and the river traffic ploughing up and down the waterway. In the reflection of the panoramic Inn windows, he saw the man take a seat near the entrance. *Cautious man,* Rodney thought. He waited for a few minutes until Laurie walked straight to the man's table and sat down. Rodney picked up his drinks and joined them.

The three men looked at each other and toasted, clinking glasses. 'Guess you guys pinged me. Must be getting old.' He was, as Laurie had predicted, an American. Around their age and showing a few life scars and a broken nose set with an obvious twist to the left. 'Major Rodney and Laurie Burns, right?'

'And you are?'

The man carefully put his hand into his coat and withdrew a wallet. Flipping it open, it showed the Homeland Security details of an FBI badge. He handed it over to Rodney, who studied it and read the name. He decided that it was genuine.

Rodney passed the warrant card back. 'Well, Special Agent William Murphy, this is a surprise. We were expecting a Russian perhaps, not an American. That was the last thing we expected. So, what's this all about?

'My Chief, as you know, is Carol Windsor. She was, as we all were, interested in your comeback and why during your absence the lovely Galena Vorakova KGB had moved into your apartments. That alone was a trigger to open your file. Look at it from our perspective; we were simply curious, that's all. We couldn't rationalise why she would move in a floor below you.' He took a drink. 'But as for what it is all about? Well, Rodney, can I call you that?'His voice was pure New York, a bit nasal and gravelly. He got a nod from Rodney and continued, 'Well, you and your boys can't stiff one of the biggest international construction companies, albeit British, for more money than you or I will ever see in several lifetimes, at least that's what I have been told, without attracting attention.'He took a drink. 'I know that you can understand that the construction company does business in the US and parts of the world where we have an interest, even collaborations with the Brits. So, we're curious.'

Rodney grunted. 'Hmm. That word "curious" again. I can understand why. I think that it's fair to say to you that my team is still active. If we find the US is compromised in any way, I sure that my boss would want to share it with your people.'

Murphy looked down at his glass and swirled the oily amber liquid. 'Good to hear. Probably more than we deserve. Your people, I take it, will be OK with the FBI and not the CIA? I know you always think that we ourselves have a down on the CIA and there is good reason. That's why our Homeland Security boss in the UK is FBI, not CIA.'

'Why's that?' Laurie had been following the interchange between the two men and was interested in why the FBI, whom he thought of as domestic and CIA as international, were in the UK instead of the CIA.

Murphy looked at Laurie. 'Story goes that it's down to your Burgess and McClain et al. and their interaction with the CIA in the States. So, it was felt that the FBI was a better bet than them for the UK. The CIA simply are carrying too much baggage. Hell, I love it here, long may that be the case. London is a great place for a city boy like me.' He looked sideways at Laurie summing him up and wondering if he could ask the question on his mind, 'Is it true they call you the Ghost?'

Rodney and Laurie laughed at the serious expression on the FBI man's face. 'I gave him the title or rather my deputy Mr. Reid did. We reckon that Laurie can disappear and carry out a job before you've buckled on your belt. True, but I've noticed lately that he's slowing up a bit. But he's still the original invisible man.' Rodney grinned at Laurie.

Laurie was not really embarrassed and enjoyed the title but shrugged the remarks off. 'Refill the glasses. Same again?' He got the thumbs up.

Murphy was not finished with Galena. 'Must be worrisome with Galena living below you, Rodney? Can't touch her, I suppose, as she is an official at the Embassy now.'

'You know what they say, William, keep your friends close and the enemy closer. But yeah, it's a puzzle that I haven't got my head around completely yet. It's certainly inconvenient. Is it dangerous to me on a personal level? Probably, maybe, could be in time. I am pretty sure that I'm targeted by them. Is it dangerous to both our organisations? I don't think so, this is personal.'

'Wow, that's not good, Rodney. What are you going to do?'

'Not sure yet. Thought about inviting the lady up to my place for tea, but I think that's simply too dangerous. On the other hand, could be that it would at least give me some idea of what they were planning.'

' My advice, Rodney, is to stay away from her. She has a wide circle of protectors; some scare the hell out of me. She's a very dangerous lady.'

'I appreciate your advice and will continue to ponder the conundrum.' Rodney thought for a moment before looking directly at Murphy. 'I don't suppose that you could give me a run list of Galena's circle of friends? Could be useful to us, me personally.'

Murphy nodded his head for a moment. 'Yeah, why not? No strings. I'll talk to Carol in the morning. You're lucky, you're a favourite of hers, by the way. I'll get the names over to you in the morning, say around lunchtime. You can buy me lunch in that awful canteen of yours. Shame that you don't have a high terrace to take in the smells of the Thames and the sounds of London like the other half of the Secret Service on the south of the Thames.' Murphy laughed.

Rodney gave a crooked smile. 'Got to admit our canteen could do with a facelift compared to the other place. But it's honest food and they serve a great red wine. Get me the list and I'll pay.'

'Deal.'

Laurie joined them, putting the drinks on the table, but continued to stand. He raised his glass. 'Drink up lads, they want to close and we all need our beauty sleep.'

Outside they said goodbye to Murphy, who wandered away to the west on the South Thameside promenade. Rodney and Laurie watched him until he was out of sight.

'Interesting development. I think that he was worried about something. Can't put my finger on it,' Laurie mused. 'Think he was fishing about the construction company.'

'You may be right. I might get more from him tomorrow when he brings me the list of Galena's people. What are you going to do now? Want to crash at my place?'

'No thanks, appreciate the offer. I am going back to the office. They may need the odd help with the Russian translation. They were running it through the translating program when I left them earlier, with help from a couple of Russian speakers from MI5., but I know using the program and hired-in people alone can miss things no matter how good they are. Things can get corrupted or misinterpreted. Thought that I'd cast my eye over what they have so far. Be good to have something for you and the Boss in the morning. Plus, if it shows that other countries are compromised, the USA would be a 100% bet. Might give you some bargaining chips when Murphy calls tomorrow.'

'You sure? It's late.'

'Absolutely. I can get a taxi or walk.'

They shook hands. 'Until tomorrow.'Laurie waved and headed for the bridge to cross the Thames and find his cab.

Chapter Fifty

Revelations

Rodney found it hard to get to sleep; the day's activities and the return of Laurie, not to mention the sudden appearance of Murphy of the FBI, churned in his mind. He finally crashed into a deep sleep around 2 o'clock and woke at 6 o'clock like the morning before, surprisingly refreshed. He made it to the office just before seven. He went to Graham to get a quick update.

'What have you got?'

'Morning, Major. A lot. And a few tired bunnies, but they're more than happy and running on adrenaline.' He waved at the crew who had worked overnight. 'Boss is here for you to download on him before you get some sleep – yes, sleep.'

Rodney walked over to the team members working round the conference table. There was Colonel Jimmy, Laurie and four of the Colonel's analysts. The two Russian speakers and another two, one from the NHS team and the other one from the Defence contractor team. Drooping with the rest were Ms. Reid, Doug Reid's daughter from MI6, Christine from MI5 and Mr. Reid himself.

'Good morning everyone. What do we have?' Rodney was upbeat in his approach, trying to rouse the team who did indeed look as though they'd been up all night.

Mr. Reid put his hands on a thick file. 'It's all in here, Major. But I'm going to give you a quick brief and then you can study the evidence that Laurie brought with him. The two main findings from the evidence are that firstly other countries in Europe and the States are under attack. The second thing is that there is a systemic KGB-backed campaign to infiltrate the trade unions and work towards orchestrated general strikes to cripple the country. All this activity has one aim, undermine the economy of a country. Weaken it, deter investment etc. All yours, Boss.'

'Got it. Now, all bar Laurie, off you go and get some rest. Come back when you're rested and ready to work. Thank you all for the effort overnight, I can't thank you enough.' Rodney picked up the thick file, weighed it in his hands then flicked the pages, 'Right, off you go.' He would have liked them to stay but by the look of them they were completely spent. It would take them twenty-four hours to be of any use to anybody. 'See you at 0900hrs tomorrow and not a minute before.'

They all left except Mr. Reid and Laurie.

'I want to stay a little longer, Major. Give me an hour and then I'll go.' Mr. Reid had earned the right to ask time and time again.

'OK, here is the deal. You stay for an hour and I get the driver to drive you home.'

'Deal.' Mr. Reid had his second wind. 'Laurie, get Andrew and Pat, the Banker if he's in. Get Graham to organise egg and bacon sandwiches and tea for all in quick time, then he can join us. Ten minutes, no more. Go.' Mr. Reid fell into a chair and motioned Rodney to join him.

Rodney took a chair next to Doug Reid. 'What a night, Rodney. The intelligence on that stick was like peeling an onion. Level after level of deception, it's astounding. But we have names. What they do, where and how. Companies and organisations involved. Methods they use in money laundering, places a group of banks used to hide money. Staggering what files are on the flash stick, it's the lot. Just shows that what Polyakov brought over was just the tip of a giant iceberg.' Mr. Reid, despite his tiredness, was enthused. 'Got to say Rodney, this is too big for us to handle.'

'Hm, thought it might be, but I have a solution. What countries are involved?'

'The States and Canada. France. Spain. Germany. Italy, Holland and Belgium. But there is also reference to Poland, Sweden, and Denmark as future targets. What really got my goat is the unions. How could they be so stupid to be taken in? The losers are the men and women members who are risking their livelihood by being led by the nose into oblivion. There's no other word for it but economic terrorists bent on doing our country harm. We have to stop them, Rodney, expose them and rid our country of them. 'Reid's passion was evident.

'Just so you know Doug, my plan is to focus on our country. If I can persuade the powers to be then I am going to get the Americans to handle the rest.' Rodney was serious. ' Got to be a little bit careful that we don't expose ourselves to the rest of the other countries to our disadvantage.'

'I believe that we can do that. Laurie can filter our stuff from the rest and identify where there is a cross-channel link. From what I've seen, most countries operated in a vacuum. Where there's a link it's in the products, money flow and banks. This we can isolate. I'll get Laurie on it, he can sleep after that. With the help of Andrew and Pat it shouldn't take too long.'

The food and drinks arrived on time with Laurie and the table swelled with Andrew, Pat, the Banker John Brown and Graham. Graham had brought Major Freire to the meeting as he felt she was going to be busy and needed to be there. Rodney looked up as she arrived but nodded to Graham, indicating that he had made a good call.

They all tucked into the massive pile of egg and bacon sandwiches and the mugs of tea. Rodney spoke over the munching.

'Listen in, everyone. We now have a source of intelligence. It does confirm that the fraud involves other countries. Time is very short. I want our country ring-fenced from the others. The Banker, Graham. Freire need to make it happen. I need to talk to the Brigadier and get permission to hand over the other countries to the Americans who have much larger resources than ours, and he will need to get permission from our masters. Your task this morning to the exclusion of everything else until it complete is to separate out the UK and package the other countries in another file. OK. You have Laurie for a little longer but he's been up all night so as soon as he's gone through the architecture of the file and you know what's what, make him rest. I'm meeting a third party at noon where I want to hand over the other countries. I need permissions before that so I need to get going. I'll try to get back for midmorning but now got to go.'Rodney stood. 'Wait, sorry. Freire and John, five minutes please.'

Rodney took the two to one side. 'Sorry to land this on you but it's so important to our mission that I need to ask.' He slapped the folder. 'This is my copy of the data on the flash stick. In the folder are the four principal banks used to store and launder the money from their crimes. I looked at the section and it gives details of the banks in Jersey, the Caymans and Switzerland. It gives bank account details and what appear to be encoded passwords which would enable anyone to manage the accounts. From the little I know of overseas accounts there appears to be the right number of numbers but I suspect that it may or may not be scrambled. Freire, can you get it decoded if it is? Use all resources – GCHQ, SIS analysts etc. And together with John Brown when the decode looks like it should, let's rip out all the money from these four accounts at the same time, get it transferred around the world to lose the trail and finally deposit it all in the Bank of England. Again, it's the timing to get this done before the hoped for third party, yes, the Americans, takes over. OK with that?'

'Big ask, Major.'John Brown said. 'What do you think, Freire?'

'Let us have a look at the data and see what we can do. No promises, no disappointments.'Freire put out her hand for Rodney's folder.

Rodney passed it over to her. 'John, I met a friend of Richard Heard last night, Greg Masters, who Richard claimed is the acknowledged guru of international banking. Specialises in money and currency transfers, securities, offshore stuff. Greg said that he knew you and thought that you might remember him?'

'Indeed I know him; worked with him, a good man. Discreet. Could do with him right now!'

'John, please call Richard. Graham has Richard's number if you don't have it. Tell him from me to get Greg to drop everything and get himself here.'

'Good find Rodney; I would feel much better having Greg with me.'

'Whatever you need John, just get it. Now, I need to brief the Brigadier or he will be wandering in and distracting the team, which is his right and welcome too, but let me try to get a clear window this morning for the team to concentrate on the mission. Freire, better brief Graham so he can get Greg processed. Official Secrets and all that stuff.'He got a nod from her. 'See you both later. Good luck.'

Chapter Fifty-One

Brigadier Robinson and Rodney

He got a shout from the Brigadier to come in when he knocked the door to the Brigadier's office.

'Rodney, good morning. Exciting times, I hear. I was wondering when you would show. I caught sight of Mr. Reid on his way home. He tells me that you have much to tell me and that part of the team worked overnight. Good timing on your part though as you are just in time for a cup of tea or coffee. Tell me all.'

On cue, the lady with the early morning trolley of refreshments knocked at the door and entered. She was an elderly lady in her habitual uniform of a much-washed blue pinafore. Her faced creased into a smile as she took the orders from the two men. She was always on time and a great source of in-house gossip.

'What's today's news from the floor, Freda?' Robinson asked kindly as Freda poured the drinks and carefully placed a biscuit on each saucer. For an elderly lady she had a surprisingly steady hand, something Rodney noticed as she passed the drinks over.

'Same old, same old.' She ran through the latest about who was seeing who and who was doing what, 'There's a fund raising for young Mr. Breakstone's trip to Everest.'

' Oh, I didn't know but I'll make sure that I put something in the pot. Any gossip about us?' Robinson asked cheerily.

'Not a peep, except that they believe that the Major is up to his tricks again. With all the comings and goings.' She gave a chuckle. Without waiting for a comment, she whirled her trolley round and headed for the door. 'Got to get on, good day gentlemen.'

When she was gone, closing the door behind her, Robinson waited for Rodney to begin.

'It's a great jigsaw but I'll do my best to keep it simple. Laurie is back and brought with him a huge amount of data that Servo and Carla had cobbled together on a flash stick. It's a gold mine in more ways than one. The team worked overnight to download the data and translate it. You will be able to view the data at your leisure today, but for now there are major developments that we need to discuss urgently.'

'Go on. Do we need the Cabinet Secretary with us?'

'I'm hoping that after this meeting you would go to see him while I get on; I'm hoping that you and he can agree on my way forward. Let me tell you quickly about the first development. From analysis of the data, we have the four private banks used to store the money generated from this fraud and presumably fund operations. By the way, the code word for this activity is "Midas." We have a whole string of banking data and codes. We will know what a code for the banks looks like when we de-code what we have. The Banker, Freire and her GCHQ friends are working on this. We called in a friend of Richard Heard's, a specialist, to help John. John knows him and Graham will do the admin etc., for him to be able to work with us. I really need them to crack this by midday, early afternoon latest. I will come to the reason momentarily.

'I've instructed them that as soon as they have access to the accounts, God willing, to empty the bank accounts and transfer the funds around the world until the trail is lost and then credit the lot to the Bank of England.'He heard the Brigadier's intake of breath, but he allowed Rodney to carry on while he made a few notes. 'The second matter is that the data shows not only the details of all our villains but for the States, Germany, France, Holland, Spain and Italy. There are a few small operations in other countries. It's a long story but I'm meeting Special Agent Murphy, one of Windsor's men, here for lunch on another matter but it's probably related.'Rodney paused for the Brigadier to take in the enormity of the scams. 'My suggestion, because with the mass of data we have we'll be able to sort out our own criminals but not the rest of the other countries. We simply don't have the manpower. What we do is give the data on the other countries to the Americans. With their vast FBI resources there's a chance if they move quickly to roll up the whole of MIDAS. Part of the deal should be that the Americans give us the credit vis-à-vis the other States.'

Robinson sat quite still for several minutes. He had swung his high-backed leather chair sideways and was looking up at the portrait of the Duke of Wellington that hung over his fireplace. Hoping, Rodney thought, for divine intervention perhaps. When he eventually spoke it was with uncharacteristic emotion.

'Wow, Rodney, what have we got ourselves into now?'

'A very typical KGB operation but the largest we have seen. A far-reaching operation to attack and weaken the fabric of those States targeted.'

'They really are scoundrels, are they not?' The Brigadier was angry. But he suddenly smiled, and it lit up his face. 'And we are doing exactly what we were created for, countering them. Now, let me outguess your thought process. The reason we are scrambling for the money is to get control of it before the FBI swallow the lot and spend years wrangling between countries for their share. Am I right?'

'Spot on, sir.'

'And you will not be passing the bank details to the FBI?'

'Correct. At this stage they get everything else.'

'Good. I'll go and see Sir Geoffrey and probably the PM if she is in. I had better let you get back to your team. As for Murphy, tell him that we want to see him and Ms. Windsor tomorrow for a meeting here in my office. You can tell him that it's related to our issue with the construction company and American and her allies'interests. Pretty sure that will hook him, don't you think?'Robinson chuckled and stood up, ready to go. Rodney remained seated. With a sigh Robinson sat down again. 'Something else?'

Rodney grinned. 'There are two other small points. We don't know yet how the cross-border or cross-organisation links work but we will get there. The other is that it's time for us to take out Ashchurch. In my opinion the timing is right to prevent him running and alerting others.' Rodney looked expectantly at his boss.

Robinson grunted and stood again ready to go and see the Cabinet Secretary.

'Your call, Rodney and I'll back you up.'

'Thank you, Brigadier. One other matter that has really upset Mr. Reid is that they have been infiltrating the unions and making mischief with the aim of upsetting the industrial base.'

'Let's to it then, Major. As to the unions, I know a man. You can forget about that problem. I'll get the information from Graham and my man will sort out any people that are bringing the unions into dispute and undermining us. Best we let them clear out their house, don't you think? Now, Major, "Let loose the dogs of war!"

Chapter Fifty-Two

The Banks and The Banker

When Rodney got back to the operations rooms he went straight to see John Brown the Banker. He found John working alongside Freire, swamped in fistfuls of paper. He watched them for a moment until they saw him hovering.

'Ah, Rodney, there you are. Grab a chair and sit in.'

Rodney pulled over a chair and sat between them. 'What have we got?' He looked at his watch, which showed 1115hrs. Only a little under the hour before he had to meet Special Agent Murphy for lunch.

'Busy?' The Banker missed nothing.

'Very and got a meet with the FBI at around noon.' Rodney ran his hand through his unruly hair.

The Banker smiled. 'Heavy holds the Crown, my son.' Rodney laughed, he always liked John's Irish-accented asides. Beside him Freire looked up and smiled. John continued. 'Thanks to our lady Major and her friend at GCHQ we have three of the four banks' details and access to the funds. The last one is a hard nut to crack, we thought we had it a few times but each time we thought we were there our data evaporated like smoke. We have a few ideas and we'll get there. Just need more time.'

'Which bank is it?'

'Guess.'

Rodney sucked his teeth, pursing his lips. 'Jersey Royal.'

'Spot on, Rodney.'

'What's next? Move on the three we have?'

'As we speak Greg Masters is signing his life away with Graham, Official Secrets Act and all that, so we're expecting him any minute. Then, in the next few hours together we'll move out the money in the three banks we have identified at least. I'd like to get the other bank cracked first.'

Rodney was more than pleased. He hadn't expected such a quick result.

'What sort of money are we talking about?'

'A great deal, Rodney. We didn't want to access the accounts properly in case it triggered an alert in Moscow, but I can say as a preview it looks like many billions.' The Banker smiled.

'A lot then?' Rodney was astonished but tried to hide his delight.'

'A lot more than enough for the owners to come for us with an army, unless Greg and I can work out a scheme which will hide the transfer.' The Banker hesitated. 'The truth is, Rodney, that we must attack all three banks at the same time, preferably all four. We must make sure that we leave no footprints when we do. Freire here and her team are the key. They will make sure the money is flying from one ISPN to another around the world. There's no chance that they'll trace us, I can assure you. The only thing that I am muddling about is that when we empty the three accounts from the banks it may or not trigger a flag in the Jersey Royal Bank if we don't have their access code by then.'

' Just keep thinking, Mr. Brown. Three birds in the hand are better than one in the bush. Let's be bullish and go for it. We can worry about the Jersey Bank later. So, what's the plan?'

'As I said. Rodney, as soon as we have Greg, he and I will, with Freire and her team, go for the money. Freire will also continue to work with GCHQ to crack the account in the Jersey Royal. I have a Bank of England account set up to receive the money. The bulk of the money is going into an escrow account. The only people that will be able to access the account are you, the Brigadier and myself. All three of us must to be present at the Bank at the same time. We'll put some money into another account for, shall we say, expenses which we can access more easily. Friere holds the passwords and the account number which she'll issue when we're ready.'

'It all seems to be going in the right way; all good, and now we have the names of the conspirators in the UK we at last know who we can trust in the Treasury, the Paymaster General and Her Majesty's Customs and Excise.' Rodney was thinking of what else he could do to help the Banker. There was really nothing, the technicalities were beyond him and he knew it. Instead, he simply asked. 'You will let me know when you transfer the money?'

'Sure, come back in an hour anyway and see us at work. It will be an education.'The Banker clasped Rodney on the shoulder. 'This wouldn't have been possible without you.'

Rodney turned away, embarrassed. 'Thanks, John. Got to go.'

Rodney found Mould and Sharky with the Jones brothers working on a plan that Mr. Reid had left them. Mould saw Rodney heading their way.

'Look sharp lads, Boss is here.'

'What are you up to, guys?'Rodney nodded to them all and the SO13 liaison officer attached to the team.

Sharky answered. 'All good so far. Working through all the names that Mr. Reid left for us this morning. We need to tie up some final details as to locations, and then we'll pick up the remnants of the construction companies' people who we need to.'

'Good, I 've got a quick job for you. I want Ashchurch picked up and brought here. Stick him in the cells for me to interview later. When do we expect that Mr. Reid will be back?'

'We don't expect Mr. Reid for a few hours at least. Do you want us to get hold of Ashchurch sooner rather than later?'

'Yes, immediately and do it quietly. There must be no fuss.'Rodney locked eyes with each member of the team. He got a nod from them all. It was enough.

He left them to get the job done that he had set them; the time to meet the FBI was getting close. He had one more call to make. He spoke to the Brigadier; Rodney had had a rethink. With the imminent raid on the banks, he had a concern that the knowledge of the raid would be found out by the Americans; with their vast intelligence gathering networks, it was a real possibility. They needed to meet the Americans tonight and tell them what the situation was. There was no pushback, the Brigadier immediately grasped the situation as Rodney knew he would.

Chapter Fifty-Three

Special Agent William Murphy FBI

When Rodney got down into reception Special Agent Murphy was waiting for him.

'Good day William, I hope you haven't been waiting too long; busy day, forgive me.'

'Nothing to forgive, I just got here. Let's go eat.'

Murphy unloaded the belongings that he had on his person into a tray which was taken by security. They retained his mobile phone and passed him a ticket to retrieve it when he left. He had a briefcase with him which the security first ran a metal detector wand over before asking him to open the case. They gave the case a good going over and removed a camera. He was given a ticket for this item too. The security moved his bag and tray of belongings through an X-ray machine and then had Murphy take off his belt and shoes and asked him to step through the personal X-ray.

Safely through, Murphy remarked, 'Hell of a way to treat a friend.' Rodney smiled wryly for he knew that getting into the American Embassy workings was even tougher.

'Nothing that our chef can't compensate for for the inconvenience – let's go and eat. A small price to pay.'

Rodney had Murphy signed in and they went up to the restaurant. Rodney pushed through the door into the wood-panelled room of the canteen. Many of the tables were occupied but Rodney had booked a corner table away from the hubbub of the diners. In fact, although they had joked about the eating place in the Westminster MI5 building compared to the MI6 facilities last night, it was really very good. There was a lively staff programme of events which Murphy commented on as they passed the room's notice board.

Murphy looked round the room and at the people; he recognised a few of the more senior men and nodded to them when they caught his eye.

'I take it all back, Rodney, much friendlier and cosier than Greyfriars.'

'Thanks, William. Time to choose today's special or another of today's offerings. Special for me, but soup to start. Always think you can count on the house soup like you can on the wine being half decent.'

The waiter arrived to take their order and Rodney ordered the house red as well.

'As I am host, let me set the agenda; business first and then the wine. I bring an offer for our American allies. My boss would like yourself and Ms. Windsor to come to a meeting here tonight. We did think tomorrow to give you more notice for a meeting, but the rate of the developments we are having to handle means we need to give you a heads-up sooner. It's in part to do with the construction company and other similar revelations. How does that sit with you?'

'Well, my boss is in residence this week and I don't think that she has anything major on her calendar that can't be moved. I know; it's my job to get the calendar sorted for her and I feel like a damned secretary at times.'

Rodney laughed. 'There you and I differ, I don't think the Brigadier would take kindly to me trying to organise his life outside of operational necessity.'

Murphy smiled wryly, reached inside his briefcase and brought out a slim file. The file was plain apart from the FBI icon embossed on its cover.

'As promised, Major. In this file are the details of the contacts and connections your lovely lady KGB declared cultural attaché either works with or she has links to.'He paused. 'You may well find a few names you will know and be surprised by. There's an annex showing the names and address of all the Russian agents in the UK that we're aware of. This is my personal gift to you and I will get my balls chewed by my boss when she knows. The reason is that we are picking up vibes, no more than that, that indicate you're on a hit list and you may not be alone. And it could be soon, old son, if not imminent. So be careful; stay alert. For the record, two sources have confirmed the evidence in the files. Where there's an issue, there are notes. I know that you will treat the file with care and circumspection. With a photo against each name, we would say that it's gold dust for you and your team.'

Rodney weighed this up for a moment and considered his counterpart's words. His gut feeling was that he could trust this senior FBI Agent but he also was aware of the duplicity and fragility of the special relationship where the American preference and national interests would coerce the UK to follow American dictates.

'I'm still sort of wondering why you and the boss decided to give me this intelligence which has a value?'

'Rest easy, Rodney, the Boss likes you. Plus, quite apart from the probability you may or may not succeed the Brigadier when he retires, you are an important part of the Service, and we want you to stay alive and well.'He laughed.

'You flatter me William, but I'll take what you say on face value. I'm grateful for the file and the heads up. Now, back to the meeting tonight. It's very important. I don't want to expand on the meeting currently as my team are still working on the briefing notes. I can say to you and for your bosses' ears only, it involves corruption and to my mind economic terrorism perpetrated against your country and several of America's allies. We would want America to take a lead role in sorting this problem out. Having said that, we will take care of our end in the UK but will work with you where borders may blur.'

Murphy sat back in his chair, staring at Rodney. 'How big is this corruption you're talking about?'

Rodney looked Murphy straight in the eye. 'We are talking billions and all the misery, strife and devastation to countless lives.'

'Good God! You mean it, don't you?'Murphy was unprepared for the news.

'I mean it and we can prove it. It's the brainchild of the KGB, who run it like a rabid cancer in our countries .'

'You sound bitter.'

'I've seen just a small part of this insidious operation and its effects on the otherwise good people who are drawn in. I want you to remember that many participants who on the one hand perpetuate the frauds are also themselves unwittingly unwilling participants and victims of the fraudsters.'Rodney thought that Murphy needed more. 'You can use whatever adjective you want. Blackmail, threats, coercion, fear of reprisals, fear for self or family, it's all there. I am not excepting that many are evil and need to be dealt with. I am saying tread lightly, my friend William. Going in guns drawn is not the only way to get the best outcome.'

Murphy put his head down and finished his meal. 'Well, Major, I didn't see any of that coming. Would it be overkill if the Ambassador attended the meeting?'

'My personal opinion is that it would save you and the boss having to brief the Ambassador on a difficult situation and convoluted matter and one that he will need to take up with the authorities back home. I must caution you, and it is only fair as far as the UK is concerned, that we are moving as fast as we can to roll up our villains and where we can, to recoup what has been stolen from us.'Rodney paused. 'But because we are confined to the UK frauds for now, we don't think that we will trigger a panic in other countries.'

'Thank goodness for small mercies. One question that I'll be asked is why the hell didn't the Brits tell us sooner?'

'Good question. We only knew for sure when our man got back from a mission last night and he confirmed that other countries were involved. We suspected we weren't the only country targeted but we had no evidence. Now we know. Our analysts are still working on the intelligence as you might expect. We were confident enough with what we have to ask for the meeting within twenty-four hours. So, timeline wise I think we are bulletproof. What do you think, William?'

'Good enough.'Murphy laughed. 'Now, better get back and sort my end. See you tonight. Keep the file to yourself and the Brigadier and I suppose Mr. Reid.'

Chapter Fifty-Four

Banker

Rodney returned to the operations room and sought out the Banker. He had found it hard to concentrate during lunch, worrying about the Banker and how he was getting on. He was surprised to find his boss with John Brown and Richard's banker friend Greg, sitting laughing and drinking tea. The rest of the room was head down and working.

'Rodney, good timing. We have emptied the banks' accounts and her Majesty's Treasury is all the richer for it.' Brigadier Robinson was delighted, and it showed. 'How much did we get, do you think?'

'I have no idea but I expect a lot. I hope.'

'£300 billion so far and counting.'

Rodney was shocked at the sum involved.

'My God, how is that possible? What about the Royal Jersey Bank?'

John grinned. 'Jersey fell to us just after you left and as for the yield, remember that this money is not just ours but belongs to many other countries as well. We've downloaded the statements from the accounts which go back some twelve years. For the most part, they show us at least which country the money came from. Some money is untraceable, however, so that's ours, I think. Still a lot of work to do on them yet.'

'I simply can't comprehend the amount, it's staggering.' Rodney was still rocking but there were concerns building in his mind and he needed to talk about them. 'It poses two main problems as I see it. For the operational cell, this action now makes it time-critical that we roll up the fraudsters. As soon as they know that their money has gone, they are going to come after it and I expect that a red flag is already flashing on someone's screen in Moscow. They will, I'm sure, in respect to the international frauds begin to close them down and eradicate any links to them. On the other hand, they may have a resilience plan and just carry on. The loss of the money must signal to them that we have got hold of the database somehow, so I need to get friends out of Russia. It means, as I say, that we need to pull out all the stops to roll up their UK operations.'

Robinson could see that his deputy was more worried than he was displaying and felt that support was appropriate.

'I would suggest, Rodney, that you focus on the operations with Mr. Reid and myself, while John and his team will focus on the money and the intelligence you need to begin the rollup of the UK fraudsters. What do you think?'

The three men looked at Rodney whilst he thought through the Brigadier's plan. 'That's a generous offer; let's give it a go. I'm glad that the planned meeting with the Americans, which seemed acceptable at the time, has been brought forward to later tonight. The sooner we have a briefing dossier together the better. I need to check with Graham to make sure the dossiers we'll need to hand over will be ready in time for seven tonight. Sir, I was wondering if you would use your magic to get them here any time after seven pm. I also think that the Ambassador should attend as well, if possible.'

'I'd better get on it, Rodney. Come and see me after you've sorted Graham and his team. To all of you, my thanks. Very well done. No matter how busy we are, keep a little time for thinking – we have to have something in reserve. Above all, we must ensure that this mission doesn't lose its shape and get out of hand.'

The Brigadier stood and walked away. He shared his deputy's concerns about time, space and resources.

'Well, Rodney, this is one hell of task that you have us involved in. We'll do all that we can to support the operation; and I thought I was retired, so I did.' John Brown laughed out loud, causing heads to turn.

'Good job, John. Now, to speak with Graham. I'll see you later and I'd ask you to hang on tonight for an hour or so until we've spoken to the Americans.'

'We'll be here.' He nodded to his companions, the rest of his team.

Rodney waved and moved to the main ops room where he found Graham, head down and papers scattered everywhere on his desk. Major Freire was by his side.

Chapter Fifty-Five

General Polyakov

The General sat at his desk staring out of the window. Inside he was angry but it was his way not to show emotion to the staff. He had put a few polite questions to Colonel Pushkin when the Colonel had brought him the news of the disappearing funds from the banks and the downloading of the fraud files. He may have reddened a little, but only for a moment. It was not noticed. He had found over the years that losing your temper did nothing to resolve a problem. He nevertheless wished that his old friend Brigadier Carl Tsygankov was still with him. He missed Carl's good counsel and the companionship they had shared as old soldiers.

The report on his desk clearly showed that four bank accounts had been emptied. The investigation showed the database with the details of the international fraud had been copied and downloaded in its entirety by someone in his directorate, in Pushkin's department.

Few personnel had access to the files and the names of those privileged came to ten people – not including himself, thank goodness. Colonel Pushkin was one of them. That left nine suspects. All denied copying and downloading any data. They had all been interviewed. All denied any wrongdoing and anyway, five of the nine had been out on assignment when the breach was made. He knew that he hadn't been into the files – he didn't have access and he'd ruled out the fanatic Pushkin. But you never know, he could see where Pushkin with some 41 billion dollars could make a lot of friends. Still, fortunately both he and Pushkin had been away at the time of the robbery. That left the four possible suspects and that didn't allow for the fact that they could have been hacked by anyone with the right skills. But as it was on the section intranet, no one could have accessed the files from outside the section rooms. It was not impossible that a thief could have broken into the section's rooms and hacked the system. Whoever carried out the deed, it meant that they had access to the team's intranet, one way or another.

He allowed himself a smile. Carl Tsygankov would be amused and not put out at losing his mega pension from the scheme. To be fair, Carl had warned him that it was time to roll up the scheme and bank the money. The money was the main issue as far as Polyakov was concerned; he was going to have to explain to the Chairman as the department had lost it.

The potential of the files being hacked gave him an idea. The cyber division of the KGB was, whilst not new, working hard to establish itself as a weapon in a covert war born out of the old codebreakers division. He would set the dogs on the four internal suspects and the possibilities of a thief. If they failed to find the culprit, he could always blame them and Pushkin as head of section.

He swung his chair to face the desk, lifted the phone and dialed. The phone was answered immediately.

'Colonel Pushkin, this is what I want you to do.'

Chapter Fifty-Six

The Americans

After he left the Banker, Rodney talked to Graham and his cell. They were busy, that was for sure, passing papers from the copiers and shuffling the copies of data into organised piles. Each page coming off the copier was first stamped 'secret'. It looked to Rodney that the team were compiling fifteen copies.

Freire was the first to notice Rodney hovering in the background.

'Hi Boss, come to see where the real work is going on? Excepting of course yourself and John Brown's coup?'

The comments drew a wry smile. 'Well, yes actually. I need to know how far we are away from completing the documents with all the data?'

'We're about there. I'm just putting the contents list together. I can give you a draft now?' Graham said over his shoulder.

'Thank you, that would be very helpful. The issue that I've got is that because our Banker has been so successful, we need to bring the Americans in tonight. We need them on board.' He got a quizzical look from Graham and Freire. Rodney smiled at them to reassure them. 'I'll explain to you both later why we need our American friends. But for now, the contents list would enable me to manipulate the sections I show to them. For example, whilst we will do want to be open with the Americans, I don't want to show any finance information. We don't want to get into a bun fight for the money recovered, that will cloud the issue and dilute the resources.' He carefully studied the contents list which Graham handed over. 'Good; can you do me three copies stamped up Secret for UK and USA eyes only? Leave out the section on finance and the annexes showing the money recovered so far. Can you do that?'

'Sure. I understand where you're coming from. Give me say an hour and I'll have the documents prepared.' Graham looked at his watch. 'Let's say four o'clock.'

'Deal,' Rodney responded.

Chapter Fifty-Seven

Operations and the Files

The lifting of Neil Ashchurch, the senior Treasury civil servant, was a classically finessed operation. Fred Jones was waiting at the kerb of Number 11 in a ministerial car with heavily tinted windows. Fred sat in the driver's seat wearing a chauffeur's cap, staring straight ahead. Lewis Jones had gone to see the 'Sergeant at Arms' in the reception of Number 11. He had a few words with the sergeant and they agreed between them that the sergeant would go and speak to Ashchurch and tell him that the Minister was waiting in the ministerial car to see him urgently.

The simple plan worked flawlessly. A flustered Ashchurch appeared in the reception area and Lewis steered him out of the building, encouraging him down the steps. Lewis overtook the civil servant just before they got to the car and opened the door. At the last moment he reached back and grabbed Ashchurch. As soon as Ashchurch realized the rear of the car was empty, no minister waiting for him, he bent and tried to turn but Lewis pushed the civil servant and threw him into the back and locked the door so that Ashchurch was unable to escape. Inside the car Ashchurch hauled himself upright in the seat and his immediate reaction was to protest. His protest turned to alarm when Lewis pressed a pistol into his side and told him to be quiet and relax.

By the time Rodney took his leave of Graham, the Jones brothers had Ashchurch in a cell in the basement of the building. Rodney made his way over to Mr. Reid's team on the far side of the operations center. Lewis stood as Rodney approached.

'We put Ashchurch in the cell next to the brothers.'

'Any issues that we'll need to sort?'

The other men in Reid's team had all risen to their feet out of respect. 'No Boss, all good. No fuss at all until we put him in a cell and he made a fuss about his civil rights.' Lewis paused 'Do you want to see him? I'll take you down.'

Rodney smiled. 'No, not yet. I'll wait for Mr. Reid. I don't think he'd thank me if I denied him his pound of flesh, do you?'This raised a laugh from the team. 'Come to think of it, I've got a few minutes and I'd very much like to know where we've got to?'

Fred said, 'Take my chair.'He pulled it out. 'I'll get you a cup of tea and whatever is left that looks edible. I just hope that Laurie gets back here soon. We're all starving.'

Rodney looked round at his staff; they were all big men. 'Humm, I don't think that any of you are going to fade away. In fact, you all seem to have put on a few pounds while I have been away so I am thinking of introducing a get-fit regime undertaken by Mr. Reid and a healthy eating menu designed by Dr Christian.'There were groans. 'OK, maybe not. Right, tell me all.'

In the end, Rodney spent almost an hour going through the records and plans that the team were developing against the lists of fraud members detailed in the intelligence brought back by Laurie. The construction company men in the scheme to defraud were all in custody, being debriefed and charged as necessary by the Fraud Squad. He was pleased that the team were grabbing the initiative and planning for future operations against those named in the data. He really needed to talk to Mr. Reid now; he needed his input and good counsel. The data was a double-edged sword. It was all very well being given the names on a plate but it meant that he needed to change his approach and methodology. He had had a simple plan and now it was no longer relevant. He decided to park his angst and concentrate on something else. Rodney looked at his watch; time to go and see if Graham had worked his magic.

He had a question forming and he said it out loud.

'Have we heard from Mr. Reid and the rest yet?'

Lewis answered for the team. 'Nothing yet, but when he left he told everyone that he wanted the full team on parade before five tonight, so you can count on that.'

Rodney addressed them all. 'Good stuff, team. Can I ask you go one step further and work with Mr. Reid when he arrives, as follows.'He waited for the men to get their notebooks ready. 'The point is that I was going to infiltrate the two organisations and move on from there once we had identified the heads of sheds and some of the soldiers. Now that we have had the intelligence handed to us on a plate so to speak, it's almost too easy and that worries me. Please get Christine and her team and Sgt George when he arrives from wherever he is serving to link up with Mr. Reid and yourselves. What I want from you now is to start to draft a series of options for Mr. Reid on how we roll up the villains. Top to bottom. With, I would add, as little collateral damage to civilians as possible. I would appreciate the team presentation tomorrow at 1400hrs to myself and the Brigadier. Don't forget the resource listing of men and materials. That is, who does what, how and when and with what. Don't also forget that the villains we lift need to fit into Shepton Mallet prison, so check the prison capacity. All that sort of stuff needs to be in the plan. Can you do it?'

Lewis, looking round at the depleted operations team for support, said, 'We can certainly make a good start and with Mr. Reid and Christine's teams. Add to that Mould and Sharky back later this afternoon, all things are possible. I can't see how the team shouldn't be able to give you what you want. Together we'll make a start now with what we have on building the framework of the plan until the Boss arrives. He may have ideas of his own, but we'll try to outguess him. We need to overlay any plan with the SO13 input from our liaison officers.'

'Good.'Rodney turned to leave but turned back. 'I have had a whisper that we need to watch our backs. Given the source, we need to address the threat in full tomorrow. Feel free to consult me if you need to. Good luck.'

The men watched him walk back to Graham before Lewis broke up the moment.

'We'd better get on. Let's split the team. Half on the Health Service and half on the Defence contractors. What do you think?'

They all nodded. The attached Special Branch Inspector Jim Broughton spoke up.

'Let's to it. Despite your Boss's laidback manner, I don't think that I'd like to be the man that let him down.'

'You're right there. And even worse is Mr. R. He'll eat you soon as look at you if you cross him.'He had an afterthought. 'One of us had better get the security alert out to everyone. I'll sort our lot. Jim, you'd better tell the Commander.'

The Files

Rodney found Graham slumped in his chair and unusually for him, jacket off and an open collar. His tie was rolled on the desk in front of him. His head was back and his eyes closed. His arms were up, clasped together behind his head, taking its weight.

'Hard day at the office?'Rodney commented, coming up behind him.

Graham jerked upright in his chair and swung it round to face Rodney. 'Sorry; just taking a power outage.'He shook himself. 'OK now.'he said and stood. Graham reached forward and picked up three two-inch thick files from the desk. He proffered them to the Major. 'The Americans' files; and these,'Graham patted five files each three inches thick, 'are the ones with the financial data.'He smiled. 'Our Banker and Colonel Jimmy have a copy each, which they've signed for. Now I need you to do the same. I've made out a chit for the Americans to sign for their copies off you when you hand them over. Please bring the chit back signed and dated. I need to get it to Registry for our lovely Julia Wingate to book in. I suggest that you take the Americans copies and three of the full files for yourself, the Cabinet Secretary and the Brigadier to study. Please make sure that they sign for them too or life will become complicated.' He allowed himself to laugh. 'Don't think that we need any more complications at the moment, do you? I'll secure the remaining files in Registry.'He paused. 'I assume that you and Mr. Reid will share your copy?'

'We'll share my file. Have to say, bloody good job, Graham.'

Graham hid his pleasure at Rodney's praise well, as he responded.

'It was a team effort, Rodney. I couldn't have done it without their help.'Graham waved his hand at the men and women around him. 'There will be a second and third volume of course, which John and Colonel Jimmy are compiling. This is the finite document covering the construction companies' operations and monies. They'll begin to prepare two more volumes, for the Defence Industry and the Health Service. Anything else for the moment, Boss?'

'Well, actually there is.'

Graham groaned. 'Today?'

It was Rodney's turn to laugh. 'Yes and no.'He handed over the file given to him by the FBI man, Murphy. 'In this file is a list of all the men and women associated either with the KGB or with KGB agents and covert operators posing as attachés etc. in this country. Clearly there are two imperatives; one is any correlation with our mission and the other is who on the list are likely heavies and who do they report to? It may be obvious as they included a helpful organogram.'Rodney flicked through the file until he came to the organogram; he studied it for moment. 'Does seem that my neighbour Galena is near the middle of the spider's web. I'd be surprised if the list is completely 100% and up to date, but it may be close. So, can we get Ms. Reid our MI6 liaison officer and our Christine from MI5 to work some magic with their mates?'Rodney handed over the file. 'It's personal too. I think that I'm a target and the more we get into this mission the more will be the enemies desire to get at me. I know that I'm a thorn in their side at the best of times, but this is of a different magnitude. The more that I know about the enemy, the better. I don't want you to bother Mr. Reid, he has enough on his plate, as do the rest of the team.'

'Do you think that's wise Rodney? I know your reasons to think that, but you may not be the only target. Consider that any known member of our team that the KGB are aware of may also be a target. I really think you need to alert the Brigadier and Mr. Reid; the Jones brothers, Mould and Sharky, Pat and Andrew and Laurie at the very least.'

Rodney walked around in a tight circle twice, thinking hard. Graham could hear the gears whirling in the Major's brain. Graham knew that Rodney wanted to do his best to relieve pressure on the team, but now was not the time to compromise the personal security of the team members.

'Hell, dammit. You may be right of course, and Murphy has warned me. Whilst because of my neighbour I still think that I'm the main target, I'll do as you say. I agree that I need to tell the others to be on the alert. Thank you for your good counsel, Graham. Unforgivable, selfish even, of me to not to acknowledge that others could be or even are in imminent danger. What is really pissing me off is why haven't our own Security Services warned us instead of the Americans? Can you ask Christine and Miss Reid to investigate why not and get back to me ASAP? All right, got to go, I'll go and take the files to the Brigadier. You'd better give me those Registry sign-out sheets to sign and I'll get the Brigadier to sign again when I hand over the files to him. I'm expecting Mr. Reid and the others who worked through the night to reappear soon. Could you ask them to be available for a briefing on the threats to them, let us say around 5 pm?'

'OK, no issue Boss. You'd better get going Rodney and sort out the Brigadier. The clock's running.' Graham handed over the files and forms.'Just sign here for me.'He handed a pen to Rodney and directed him to the release form.

Chapter Fifty-Eight

The Brigadier and the Major meet before the Security Meeting

Rodney looked at his watch, it was almost 4 o'clock. Time was short. He knocked and entered the Brigadier's office.

'Rodney, come in.'Robinson got up from his desk and walked over to the easy chairs, flopping down in one and waving Rodney to the other. 'Just so you know, the Americans, including the Ambassador, have confirmed that they'll be here at seven tonight. Our side is you, me and the Cabinet Secretary; Mr. Reid if you like. Got a few more chairs coming in plus light supper etc. Just as well this office is big enough. The Secretary and I will brief the directors of MI5 and the SIS later tonight after our meeting.'

Rodney nodded and fiddled with the files. Robinson picked up the vibes that his deputy was under time pressure. 'Rodney, I can see that you're busy, so fire away.'

'You could say that. I'm hoping that it will calm down shortly, just got to get a lot done in the next few hours. Right, here are three files for the Americans, without the finance details. Two other files, one for you and the Cabinet Secretary with the finance detail as we know it at this moment in time. This will build up, I'm sure, as we move further into this mission.'He handed over the files. 'I need you to sign for the files or my name will be mud with Graham and I'll get locked up.' Balancing the bundle on his knee he signed for his five files. He looked at the sheet that he would need to get the Americans to sign and nodded. 'OK, what's next?'

'Personal security for you and the rest of the team.'

'Go on, I'm listening.'

'I'm convinced from the conversation that I had with Murphy that we are targets. We're rocking the Russians' boat. I did want to think that I might be the only one, but I believe that the team maybe or rather could be targets. I was happy to handle that scenario but Graham convinced me that there could well be other key members of the team who are known to the KGB and so who could also be targets.'

'Go on; I'm with you and I don't disagree that there could be an issue.'

' I'm calling a meeting at five tonight and this is my outline plan, but in brief, going to get you a minder, going to send the wives and any offspring on a holiday for a couple of weeks. Thinking of getting the key team members to live together in clusters. Other precautions will be added.'

'So, who is my minder to be?' asked Robinson.

'Sgt George, as soon as he turns up.'

'Fine with that.'

'If and when we identify any targets that would do us harm, I'm thinking of setting up a surveillance group using Simon's men. Everyone else who could help us is stretched.'

'I don't have a budget for that, even if I think that it's a good idea.'

'Think that John may help me on that score.'

'If he can, I wouldn't object.'

'Thank you. Better get off to sort the money and get ready for the meeting.'

The Security Meeting.

Rodney returned to the main operations room and gave Graham the sheet signed by the Brigadier for the files. Graham thanked Rodney and asked if the Boss had been happy to sign away his life.

'No issue at all; I left him doing a page check and reading himself into the data in preparation for the Americans at seven tonight. I've got half an hour before the security meeting and I need to prepare.'

'OK. Just so you know, everyone is back in and I'll get them at the conference table for five.'

'Thanks. If Laurie is back in, please make sure that he floods the table with snacks, sandwiches and tea, coffee etc.'

Rodney left Graham and sought out the Banker and drew him to one side.

'John, I need some funding, off the books, to pay some people for services unspecified. Can you do anything for us?'

'Well now, son, that depends so it does.' His Irish accent was broad in the humour that he found in Rodney's request. 'How unofficial is this?'

'Well, it's a plan that I agreed with the Brigadier and the only way that I can make it happen is to fund some off-the-books security and surveillance.'

'OK. I don't see why it can't be engineered. How much are we talking about? When and for how long?'

'Soon, in a few days. One or two individuals off the books and a team of say twenty to forty of Simon's Somalis. Could be for a fortnight. Basic expenses. Nothing's confirmed yet. Can we move quickly if we have to?'

'Let me think for a moment. Hmm. Let's see. Say £250 a day including expenses all up a man. Let's say £5 to say £10k a day. Call it twenty days for ease, that's roughly £200K. I'll double that for unforeseen contingencies. No issue, Rodney, I'll put the money in a current account and you can come to me and ask me to pay out as needs be. I'll probably get Pat to run the account, I've noticed that he has a good head for that sort of thing.'

'Thanks, John. They say that money makes the world go round but it's more fundamental than that, isn't it? Without money, nothing can get done.'

The Banker laughed. 'I do believe, Major, that you're becoming an establishment man. Shame, so it is.'

'I'm due for a security meeting with the team at five. You're welcome to attend.'

When Rodney got back to the conference table the team was already assembling, tucking into the drinks and food. He waved to them and took the chair. Mr. Reid, looking remarkably refreshed, sat next to him. Rodney shook Mr. Reid's hand and held up his hand displaying five fingers. Then Rodney made the sign for food and a drink. He wanted five minutes to get his notes and plan in order. Mr. Reid nodded and moved off to get the Major some food and a tea.

The table settled whilst Rodney readied himself.

Then he got down to business. At the table were his core team, Mr. Reid and Graham, Andrew and Pat, Mould and Sharky with Laurie, the Jones brothers, and the Banker. Others were Christine from MI5 and Ms. Reid from the SIS. Sgt George SAS had just arrived and looked expectant. The last to the table, as guests, were the liaison officer from Special Branch and the Fraud Squad and Commander Bob Coveney SO13.

'We meet again – Bob, thank you for responding to my request to attend. Sgt George, glad to have you back on board.' Rodney consulted his notes. 'Also, I want to thank the team for the amazing job that you've done and your contribution so far. Now, there are two parts to this meeting and I will be as brief as possible. But first I want to say that the last few days have been frantic and we need to begin to slow the pace or we'll begin to make mistakes. So, check and check again and look before you leap. That's from a direct quote from David Crockett; the only time he forgot to follow his words he ended up dead at the Alamo. So saying, we are now in possession of a list of KGB operatives and their enforcers in this country. This list is pretty comprehensive but may not be complete in every detail in the context of those on it. The list is being analysed and will be shared, both it and findings, with interested parties.'Rodney nodded to the Commander. 'Add to this the intelligence we are now in possession of, we have already and will have in the next few days stirred another hornets' nest so we must look to our own security.'He paused. 'I am declaring a red alert for those members of the team that the KGB know well.'

The room was suddenly silent. The team members looked at each other, not in surprise but in the realisation that they were potential targets.

'I hope that I'm wrong but my immediate plan for the next few days is as follows. Sgt George, for the next few days I want you to protect the Brigadier. I am sorry that my request for your help wasn't to do that task, but for the immediate I need your help.'

'It's a given. A pleasure to help.'Sgt George affirmed his willingness to act as bodyguard for Robinson.

'Thank you.'Rodney turned to his team. 'I want you to buddy up. I have some contingency money.'He eyed the Banker, who nodded.'If you want to send your wives and children on holiday for a fortnight or so, we'll foot the bill. Suggested buddy groups are Mr. Reid, Mould and Sharky. Group Two: Graham and the Jones brothers. Three: Banker, Andrew, and Pat. Laurie, you're confined to this building unless out with a buddy group, so book yourself the guest suite downstairs for little longer. Colonel Jimmy is confined to this building. OK so far?'

'What about you, Boss?'

'Sgt George, I need an off-the-books recommended K man.'

George thought for a moment. 'Ex-Sgt Armand. I will get him here in the next two hours. We've worked together and he's had my back more than once.'

'Good, sorted. In addition, once we've identified the most dangerous men on the list who are likely to be the ones to come after us, they'll be shadowed by a team of twenty, more, if necessary, of Simon's cousins in this country. Nobody knows them or who they are. They will be led by one of our own who's below the radar.' Mr. Reid mouthed to Rodney, 'Saied?' He got a nod from Rodney. 'The leader will report direct in to Mr. Reid. SOP, flak-jackets and side arms for all until we are stood down. Anything to add, Mr. Reid?'

'Not at this stage, but we could add the Taser to our personal armoury. I take it that the attached personnel'–he meant the Special Branch and Fraud Squad – 'will take care of their own?'

The Commander responded. 'I'll sort that.'

'Thank you.' Rodney was relieved but didn't show it. 'Right, and so on to the final item for this meeting. No plan survives contact with the enemy. Well, since we now have a welter of new intelligence on the targets in the next two groups of frauds that we want to sort out, that is the Health Service and the Defence Industry, we need to re-visit my plan.' He passed enough copies of his organisation chart along the meeting table. 'The need for the covert group to find the villains has, to a degree, been overtaken by events. Study the chart for a moment. A bonus is that with the new intelligence that would have been sought by the covert team we can release that manpower into other areas. Look at the organisation chart.'

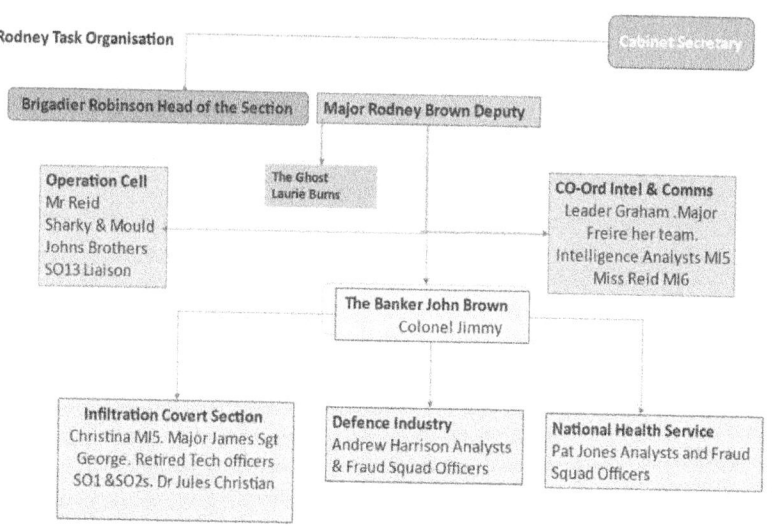

'This is the opportunity to release more manpower from the covert infiltration section, which means that we can bolster Mr. Reid's group.

Mr. Reid and Christine, get hold of Major James and stand him down unless you have a job for him. Mr. Reid may like you to come up with a new plan to take out and hold the villains for interrogation when identified or some other ideas, open to suggestions. I still think that Andrew and Pat need to stay with their roles under the Banker and Colonel Jimmy. OK so far?'

Mr. Reid took up the story. 'We'll see how the redeployment pans out. We'll come up with an outline plan with options should we need to get hold of any targets who would do us harm. Who to lift them, when and how and resources not limited to the holding prison etc. Shall we say 1400hrs tomorrow?'

'That will be fine. Now, anyone got any questions before we get back to work?'

There were none. The team knew what they had to do.

The team dispersed, leaving Rodney and Mr. Reid alone at the conference table. Rodney put his head in his hands, elbows on the table and breathed out slowly.

'Knackered, Major?'Reid was unusually sympathetic. It was not his way.

Rodney sat up, rocked his head back then got a grip of himself.

'I confess to you, Doug, I'm a little wrecked. Life used to be so simple.'

'Well, you got that wrong.'Reid waved Neil Ashchurch's file. 'It's time, Rodney, that we had a chat with him,'he said gently.

'Oh, bugger; forgot about him.'Rodney gathered his paperwork. 'Got an hour before the Americans arrive. Do you want to sit in when they get here?'

Doug Reid shook his head. 'I don't think so, but thanks for asking, I have a mountain of work to get through. Can we talk after they leave? Graham told me about their visit and the list etc. I have my own copy. I am with you on one point, it all seems too pat, too easy. There has to be a catch somewhere. What that catch is I can't see at the moment, but it makes me cautious. Maybe worrying about nothing. Come on Boss, fun time, let's stuff Neil bloody Ashchurch'.

Chapter Fifty-Nine

Neil Ashchurch

They found Ashchurch completely calm and ready to be cooperative, much to Mr. Reid's disappointment and Rodney's relief. Cooperative to a point at least.

When they entered the holding cell deep in the bowels of the MI5 cellars, they found Ashchurch lying on his bunk, staring at the ceiling. He looked up at the two men as they entered his cell and smiled. He pulled himself up and crossed to the cell's chair. He had his jacket off and was otherwise dressed in the clothes he had had on when he was arrested. He didn't look like a man who'd spent the last how many hours in jail, he was immaculate. He slid into the chair and looked up expectantly. Rodney and Reid took the two chairs opposite Ashchurch. They looked at him, waiting for him to speak first.

He began. His voice was a lazy upper class one, his diction clear and his voice cut through the air like a laser.

'I've been thinking. I'm grateful that you gave me time to do just that. Of course, naturally I was initially angry. Angry at being found out, probably. Disappointed that all that work and the many years of deception was for nothing. Shamed now too. I admit that I am probably in your language a traitor.'

'You sound as though you've come to a life-changing decision?' Reid was perceptive as ever.

'Yes, I have. Who am I talking to, by the way?'

'Does it matter?'

'It matters to me as I need to know if you have the power to deal.'

'I am Major Brown, SIS, and this is my partner. My boss is Brigadier Robinson.'

'Ah, the deceivers. Majorette's special men. I hear that you can work magic when you want to. Fair enough.'

'And your decision?' Reid was surprisingly upbeat.

'It seemed to me that I could simply stay silent and wait for the Russians to exchange me at some time in the future for one of you.' He cocked his head to one side. 'But I don't want to end up in some featureless 1960s block of flats on the outskirts of Moscow, talking to myself and drinking myself to death on cheap vodka with other miscreants like me. Not the expat retirement I envisaged. Then there's the chance that as an embarrassment to them I would be "disappeared."'

'So?' Rodney wanted to know; his voice hardened. He really didn't like Ashchurch.

'I'll give you everything and more in exchange that I go free, with my family, my UK bank account contents. My UK assets which I would liquidate and disappear.'

Rodney grinned. 'An interesting proposition, but what makes you think that you can give us anything that we don't already have? Do you really think that your Russian masters would let you do that and simply disappear? They have a long reach.'

'I don't see that they'd be too upset after they think about it. They would acknowledge I had done my bit for years and I'd be saving them money and embarrassment if I disappeared. No, I don't see them being too fussed.'

Rodney thought, *better you than me mate, they will be after your hide, I would.*

Ashchurch went on, 'Well, Major, I am prepared to admit you may have a lot, but what about the shadow team and collaborators in various government departments? I doubt that you have it all. I purposely kept some of my key people in the Civil Service and other organisations separate from the Russians. Many don't know that what they're doing is not part of their normal job; others were bribed, threatened, coerced etc. A few may even have been of an ideological persuasion. But it didn't seem right to expose them to my greedy paymasters.' He smiled. 'And it was a source of extra money for me from various companies. That won't be on your radar. Must say that I rue the day that I employed that compliance man.'

'You mean Colonel Jimmy?' Reid put in.

'As you say, Colonel Jimmy, bloody man!'

Rodney was astounded by Ashchurch's outburst, but it did give him an insight to the character of the man. He could be rattled. Rodney was driven by the need to get all the skeletons on the table and he didn't want that to cloud his judgement. He balanced having the whole picture in the context of the fraud with wrapping up this mission as quickly as possible. It still rankled that this task wasn't what he would have considered a core task. At the same time, he admitted to himself that he was proud of his team and the progress that they had made.

'Mr. Ashchurch, I know that General Polyakov is head of shed, but who are his other key players?' Rodney wanted to know. He changed the subject to get the interview moving forward.

'I can tell you that, no reason why not. He's supported by a very able Colonel called Pushkin and a small team, a dozen or so. I did report to Brigadier Tsygankov, but he's retired, more's the pity. I believe that your team knows him well?'

Rodney wouldn't be drawn; instead, he said calmly, 'I'll consider your offer seriously. But I need to have something to convince me that you can deliver your side of the bargain. So, I am going to give you a couple of reams of paper and you can draft out your story. Sure, leave blank spaces which you can fill in later with those people and any matters that you consider would make my agreement to your offer a no-brainer. Do that over the next twenty-four, forty-eight hours and we can talk again.' He smiled. 'Does that proposal sound about right to you?'

'Well, it's certainly a way forward. OK, don't forget the pens.' He thought that he had Rodney in his pocket at that moment. That was the last thing Rodney would have agreed with, and it was as far from the truth as you could get. There was a silence in the room until it was broken by Mr. Reid.

'Hmm. Tell me, what is the role of Galena Vorakova in all this?' Rodney was surprised by Mr. Reid's question as it was one that had been forming in his own mind too.

Ashchurch turned his attention to Mr. Reid and studied him for a time.

'You know that she holds an officially declared diplomatic cultural post in the Russian Embassy. She's bombproof unless you declare her as an unfit person and send her home. Will my evidence give you the justification to do just that? It will.'

'You didn't quite answer my question. What part does she play in the scheme?'

'I didn't, did I? Galena is the font through which all matters, opportunities, progress, difficulties that I would feed back to Colonel Pushkin and Polyakov. In the past it would have been Tsygankov, but there you go, life moves on.'

'It does,' Rodney looked at his watch, 'and sadly so does time. Got to go. We'll arrange for the paper and pens so you can begin to flesh out your, shall we say, story.'

'I prefer "report."' Ashchurch stood and held out his hand. 'You won't be disappointed, I assure you.' Rodney took the proffered hand.

Chapter Sixty

The Deal

The parties to the meeting had just arrived as Rodney and Mr. Reid joined the others in the Brigadier's office. Mr. Reid wasn't staying but he wanted to welcome the FBI chief Carol Windsor, who headed the FBI in London and knew him and he gave her a warm welcome. Rodney introduced Reid to Murphy. The two men eyed each other for a second and decided that they could do business. Having said his welcome to Carol, Mr. Reid made his excuses and left the room.

The Brigadier and the Cabinet Secretary were talking to the Ambassador. The Ambassador was a political appointment but he was experienced and, Rodney had heard, highly intelligent and clever with it. After introductions the room settled. People filled their plates and glasses and sat around talking. The Brigadier nodded to Rodney who got the meeting started.

'Lady and gentlemen. We have a story to tell you and an offer you won't want, we hope, to refuse.' Rodney began and continued for more than an hour, directing the meeting to various pages in the documents that they had been issued with. He concluded with the offer to the incredulous American audience. 'The fact is, with our resources we can really only just about handle the UK end of the fraud, so we are asking that, although of course you will want to follow up on the evidence of fraud in the USA, that you also take the lead in alerting and supporting the other European states that are affected.'

The Americans put their heads together. Eventually the Ambassador looked up. He wore those rimless glasses and he removed them and looked directly at Rodney.

'Well, Major, what a story. What a revelation. So, where's the money?'

'Safe.'

'What do you mean, safe?'

'We emptied their banks.' The Brigadier answered the Ambassador.

'All of it? Our money too?!'

'Now, that's a moot point Mr. Ambassador. However, the team is working hard to separate out as best they can any refund due to those countries that they can identify have had money taken.'

'How much money are we talking about?'

'The pot is around 41 billion pounds, give or take,'the Cabinet Secretary stated.

The Ambassador's eyebrows shot up. 'Wow. And the American share?'

'Well, that's what we are working on. From the little that I've seen in the document the sum vis-à-vis yourselves it is likely to be substantial,'the Brigadier confirmed.

'Do you have a time frame?'Carol wanted to know. She knew that as soon as Washington was alerted, they would want the money.

The Brigadier looked at Carol; he knew what she was thinking.

'Remember that we have only been aware of this fraud for less than a week, the international nature of it for less than twenty-four hours, and also that the money owed to third parties still even existed. I think that a week's grace for the team to check the numbers would not be unreasonable.. 'He paused. 'And I think that you and the other third parties would want to at least to find out what the pots of money relate to.'

If the Ambassador picked up a hint of censure in Robinson's reply, he let it go. 'I have to say, this is a bombshell of the first order. We need some time to work this through.' The Ambassador was noticeably shaken. 'Let's meet again at this time tomorrow. I need to talk to the White House and Carol and Murphy need to get their head around this. Any chance that they could spend some time tomorrow morning with your team, Major, so they can get up to speed quickly? It would be a great help and a personal favour to me.'The Americans stood on cue.

Rodney looked over to the Brigadier and the Cabinet Secretary and got a nod and smile from both men.

'Of course, Mr. Ambassador. Shall we say 10 o'clock tomorrow?'He turned to Carol and Murphy. 'I look forward to hosting you myself.'Rodney shook hands with the visitors.

After the Americans had gone Robinson did the honours and poured them all a whisky.

'I think that went rather well, Rodney, don't you Sir Geoffrey?

'Hmm. The Major, it seems, could sell fridges to Eskimos.' His face was impassive. 'I don't think that we should underestimate the Americans. They will want their share and more, you can bet on it.'

'Quite right, an astute observation.'

'Well, I must go and brief the PM. She'll be delighted.' The Secretary left the two men who soon collapsed in the easy chairs and looked at each other.

'OK, let's recap and then get some rest. Tomorrow is another big day. By the way, Sgt George has been in and made it quite clear that I am to be looked after no matter what I say, and by the way there appears to be an ex-Para French Sgt called Armand waiting to escort you home, Rodney.'

'Better go and meet him, then.'Rodney headed for the operations centre. He needed to sign in his files for the night. In the meantime, Graham had seen to Armand's paperwork and Rodney found them waiting for him. Rodney apologised for his lateness which was accepted by Armand with a wave of the hand, a 'not a problem' gesture. Armand was the same height as Rodney, but slightly lighter with dark hair. The French man had dark, intelligent eyes which scanned his new charge. Rodney did the same. Good eye contact between them. Instantaneous rapport, as was often the case between military men. They would get by with a little of each other's language. Armand's language skills were the better of the two, much to Rodney's relief.

Chapter Sixty-One

The Attack

Rodney checked the time; it was going on nine thirty when he checked his key into his flat door. It always amazed him that when a potential threat was identified how his whole being went into a different mode.

Heightened alertness and adrenaline ready to pump, he drew his weapon and slipped off the safety catch. Holding the gun at the high port in his right hand he gently pushed open the door with his left foot. There was just enough energy in his push to swing the door fully open. The flat was dark and silent. Weapons ready. Both men breathed easily, mouths open, the open mouth enhanced the hearing. There was nothing discernible.

Rodney led the way. By the light of the hall and the street Rodney moved quickly, closing the curtains. Once done he switched on the lights. Both men searched the flat room by room. The flat was clear.

'Welcome, Armand. Think that we need a drink and some food.'Rodney chose a bottle of wine from the rack.

'I'll cook.'Armand searched the fridge and cupboards. The flat was well stocked. Armand chose his ingredients well and in twenty minutes had produced a fortified chicken stew with vegetables and spices.

The men ate, swopping experiences. As soldiers do, they sought to find a common ground and where they may have served in similar theatres of operations. They had a few hits as they trolled through their soldiers' experiences and relaxed in each other's company, both now confident and trusting in each other's abilities.

'Think, Major, that you should get some sleep. I will take the night shift. I can sleep tomorrow, while you must work.'

Rodney grunted then laughed. 'You're right of course. If you're sure, then watching my back overnight would be welcome.'

He was weary and dragged himself off to the bedroom. He slipped his shoes off and crashed onto his bed. He put his pistol in easy reach, after that he closed his eyes. He was asleep in seconds.

Armand cleared up the meal and drinks then moved one of the easy chairs to the entrance to the hall and angled it so that he could see if anyone entered by the flat door. They wouldn't immediately see him because of the angle of the chair. He switched off the lights and settled in for a long night, gun ready, safety catch on, resting the gun on the arm of the chair.

Around three in the morning he became alert. Something had changed. The blackness in the flat deepened. It was like a creeping cloak. He had been watching the light from the hall which had been leaking under the door and a pencil shaft of light shone through the keyhole. The light in the hall had disappeared. He readied himself for whatever may come. He thought about waking Rodney but on balance thought that if anything kicked off then Rodney would wake.

Armand raised his gun and as quietly as possible slipped off the safety catch. The 9mm Browning was the British Army standard side arm that he'd been issued with earlier by Sgt George. He listened, mouth open and ears cocked, hardly breathing.

He sensed rather than heard a key being inserted into the lock. Armand stood silently, then crouching he placed himself to one side of the lounge wall. Whoever they were they wouldn't see him until they were fully committed to the hall.

His night vision was completely developed. He saw one man armed with his gun, arm extended, slip through the flat doorway. Another man was following him, gun arm down.

Armand brought his gun up and shot the first man in the head. The man dropped like a suddenly liquified jelly. Very dead. Several things happened at the same time. Rodney woke and leapt off the bed, grabbing his gun, struggled into his shoes as he was up and running for his main room. Armand flicked the lights on as the second attacker disappeared down the corridor, heading for the stairs.

'Major, take care of him.' Armand pointed to the dead man sprawled in his hallway. 'I want the other one.' Armand was out of the door chasing the second man.

Rodney checked the fallen man and surged after Armand. The dead man could wait.

Racing after Armand, Rodney leapt down the stairs two and then three at a time. Almost in freefall, he caught up with Armand leaving through the entrance door in the reception area. Rodney followed immediately after him.

In the street Armand and Rodney saw their prey sprinting to the left for a car twenty metres away, engine running. Rodney raced after the man whilst Armand knelt. Armand took aim and fired at the tyres of the car. He hit the rear and front tyres that he could see, then he was up and following Rodney.

'Stop or I fire.'Rodney called. The man still raced on. The driver put the car in gear and tried to take off but with two tyres out he found the car steering too heavy and made a move to clamber out of the car. Armand put more bullets into the engine compartment. The engine choked to a stop.

The second attacker from the flat reached the car and hesitated as Rodney called out again, 'Stop! Stop! Stop or I'll shoot!' The attacker turned quickly, crouched, gun out. The man was blocked from escape by the car. The man's brain raced. There was no escape. He brought his gun up. Rodney and Armand knew that he was going to fire. Armand was now only three steps away from him. With a split-second decision, Armand, almost on top of the quarry, fired twice, shredding the arm and shoulder holding the gun. A third shell hit the man's gun and it flew out of his hand and skittered onto the pavement towards Rodney. Rodney kicked it away. The man wrapped his shattered arm and shoulder around himself in an automatic gesture and toppled over grunting and grimacing with pain.

The driver gave up his to plan to escape down the embankment. He put both hands on the steering wheel in surrender. Rodney raced round the car leaving Armand covering the fallen assassin, opened the driver's door, put his gun to the head of the driver, reached over and removed the keys. 'Out, now!'he ordered. He kept the gun touching the head of the driver. He moved him around the car and forced him to lie face down two yards from the other man. Close enough to keep an eye on, not too close that they could raise any trouble.

Rodney stood up then stepped back. 'Armand, give me your gun. I'll cover you while you search them.'

Armand searched them, walking round the bodies so that he wouldn't block Rodney's line of sight if he needed to fire. Whilst Armand worked on them, Rodney studied them. Well dressed, short military-style haircuts, middle thirties. Almost certainly Russian from the curses coming from the wounded man.

The street was well lit and by now there were lights on in many of the windows, all adding to the illumination of the area. People were beginning to spill onto the street. They were going to be a problem sometime soon. 'Stay back. 'Rodney, turning to confront them, called out in a voice that stilled them. The neighbours from the street shuffled back, craning their necks. As Rodney turned back, out of the periphery of his vision he thought that he saw Galena, his KGB neighbour, scuttle back into the flats. Joe the concierge appeared, roughly dressed, holding some rope and electrical ties. Rodney asked for the ties and Joe handed them over.

'Get back in the flat now, Joe. Stay there and call the police and an ambulance'.

He passed the ties to Armand who secured the driver's hands and feet, then the wounded man's legs.

Rodney took stock of the men in front of him. The attackers were in dark suits, white shirts and ties; they could have been mistaken for businessmen. This puzzled Rodney, he would have thought that they'd be in dark tracksuits and balaclavas. Clearly not your run of the mill hit team. They were both well-built with short haircuts. The wounded one keened quietly to himself now, swearing from time to time in Russian. Cool customers indeed, Rodney thought, guessing them to be ex-military. Not British, that was for sure.

Sirens were blasting the night and blue flashing lights were close now. Rodney held the men in the aim. His preference would have been three dead men. He knew it was too late now that the residents had seen them breathing.

Armand pulled out some identity paperwork, recovered a gun from the driver and a knife from each of the men. 'Russian, 'Armand said, holding up the two knives. Both knives had been retrieved from a wrist knife holder that could be used to project the life some yards. 'Spetsnaz.'

Rodney was puzzled; the Russians normally used third parties from other Eastern European countries. This would be a messy affair now and he needed to mitigate the fallout. He hadn't fired his gun so he would swop his pistol for Armand's. Better he claim that he'd done the shooting rather than Armand, who as a third-party minder would draw flak. He handed Armand his own gun. The unsaid message was clear and Armand simply nodded.

He needed to let the boss know and Bob too. They could sort this out with the Metropolitan Police better than he could. He got Armand to call Sgt George to warn him that there had been an attack and he sent a text to the members of his team on a team members' 'Charlie-Charlie 'call.

The arriving police officers were met by Rodney with his SIS identity held high.

Fortunately, one of the officers knew the Major but it still took Rodney an hour or more to extract himself and Armand. There would be questions and the clean-up of the flat would take a day or two. Rodney excused himself with difficulty from the police Inspector who had arrived and was intent on holding him up all night with his facile questions. Rodney collected some kit and he and Armand headed for a local hotel for a couple of nights.

The organisation had a very efficient clean-up and redecorating crew. Rodney was confident that he would be returning to a pristine flat with all traces of the shooting eradicated and that his hallway would be freshly decorated. That at least was a plus. For now, all he wanted was a bed.

Chapter Sixty-Two

The Operations Centre

After a disturbed night, Rodney and Armand got in around nine.

Rodney had spent some time on the phone with the Brigadier the previous night and they had come to some agreement on the way forward. Robinson had agreed to speak to the Cabinet Secretary and Home Secretary and revert to Rodney later in the morning.

For his part, Mr. Reid had had all the team full on since seven that morning, including the Banker's team as well as his own. The attack had focused minds. He was putting the final points to his plan so that he could lead the briefing later. Rodney collapsed in a chair next to Mr. Reid. Mr. Reid looked up.

'Had a night of it?'

'His Scots accent was harsh. It always was when he was annoyed, or in this instance concerned, not that he would let Rodney know that.

Rodney could read his 2IC and just smiled.

'Could say that. One dead, one wounded and not likely to be using his left arm or shoulder for anything for a long time. One captured.' He put the spring-loaded, knife-firing, wrist-mounted device on Mr. Reid's desk and placed the knife alongside it. 'Armand lifted three of these from them. Spetsnaz, working for the Moscow KGB is my guess. If it had been local they would have used Eastern European thugs like the two brothers we have downstairs. Looks like our activities have reached the higher echelons of the First Directorate.'

Reid studied the device and knife. He held the knife up to the light. He tested its balance. Flipped it and spun it to a wooden board a few metres away. It stuck in, quivering. Heads turned and there were a few smiles but it was just Mr. Reid having a moment. Rodney retrieved the knife.

'Souvenir for you, Mr. R.'

'Thank you, Major; much appreciated. I will add it to my collection. Mrs. Reid doesn't always approve, but she dusts it every week.'

'Lucky man. Hope that she's not too pissed off with me, having to move out for a while.'

'No, laddie, you've got a lot of Brownie points out of it.'

'Really?'

'Oh yes; our ladies have gone, all of them. Taking all the kids and grandkids to a sun-dome for a fortnight with an option for further weeks. Going to cost you a fortune.'

'That's fine; cost of doing business.'

'Then there's the cost of transport; a private coachload by car ferry then direct to the site in De Haan in Belgium. The coach is on hire for the duration so that the ladies can go shopping.'

'Wow, that's just amazing; I hear it's a cracking complex, something for everyone.'

'Glad you approve. Now, let's close out last night. Any fallout?'

'No, it's being handled by the Brigadier and Bob.'

'What about Armand?'

'All good. Top man, we need to get him in the team.' Rodney told Mr. Reid what had happened. 'As far as anyone is concerned, I did the shooting, only Bob and the Brigadier know the truth. He was quite brilliant, cool as a cucumber. And fast, very fast. Anyone would have thought that you had trained him.'

He got a rare smile from Mr. Reid. 'Thank you for that. Now fuck off, Major, and let me get this briefing finalised.'

Rodney patted Mr. Reid on the back and got a growl in return.

Laurie was his next call. Laurie was fussing around his 'food bar' as they now thought of it.

'Morning Laurie, all well?'

'Good, waiting for another task. Want some breakfast?'

'Yep, and your new task we'll discuss at the breakfast table.' He went to the conference table and waited for Laurie to bring him breakfast. He opened his logbook and scribbled.

Laurie put down the bacon and egg sandwich and tea in front of Rodney and sat down.

'Major, let's have the task.'

'Listen in: the Banker has the funds. Get hold of Simon in Somalia. I want twenty, plus twenty more on standby of his brothers to do surveillance for us on the thugs, plus any dangerous men in the list Graham is holding that we deem may want to do us harm. I want you to get hold of Saied, he is to run the field team of twenty or more men. You are the liaison officer between him and Mr. Reid, or me if he is not around. Murphy gave me a list of KGB men and women and various agents. I want you and Saied to concentrate on any people on the list that are what we would define as armed and dangerous. Liaise with Graham, Christine and Ms. Reid. They are supposed to be identifying the men who are the most likely threat. Keep Mr. Reid up to speed.'He took a large bite of his sandwich. 'If you need more men, talk to me.'

'Got it. Heard about your bust-up this morning.'

'Hmm, it was a wake-up call for us all. So, stay safe. Get the list sorted, Simon and Saied and get the men on the street ASAP as soon as you have identifiable targets. Finally, talk to Freire about communication and Christine about tracking devices for target cars etc. You know the drill as well as I do. Now, I'm expecting the Americans, so make yourself scarce.'

Laurie got up to leave. 'Feeling a little claustrophobic confined to this building 24/7. Any chance that I could get out on Ops now and again?'

'Sorry Laurie, I need you here as my anchor. You and Graham need to keep this place ticking over while this mayhem runs its course. Sorry, mate.'

'Ok Boss, I understand.'Laurie disappeared as the Americans arrived with the Brigadier.

Rodney sighed; he really would have liked more time to get round the team. Now he'd be tied up with the Americans till lunch. He frantically finished his notes on the orders he had just given Laurie when the Brigadier caught his eye. He closed his book. Time to do his duty.

He joined the Brigadier and the two Americans and welcomed them.

'Carol, Murphy, welcome to the engine room.'

'Thanks, Rodney. Quite a set-up.' Carol was impressed.

'Hear you had visitors last night?'Murphy nodded to Brigadier Robinson, who had obviously told the Americans.

'Yes, we had some excitement. One dead, one wounded and one captured. I owe you, Murphy, for the warning, but the three men that I encountered weren't on your list. They were Spetsnaz, all three of them, we're sure. I think that it was a crew drafted in, probably last night. The reason that I think that is that they were all dressed in smart suits as though they'd just got off the plane. Special Branch are checking it for me.'He paused, smiling. 'Guess that Moscow Central is really upset with us for nicking all our money back, with interest of course.' He got a laugh from Murphy and a smile from Carol. 'So, saying that let's start your tour in the adjoining room with the Banker and his team.'

John Brown had his head down with Colonel Jimmy working on financial spreadsheets spread over the working tables in the room next to the operations centre, which was now fully dedicated to the finance team.

'John, I have some guests for you.' Rodney introduced the Americans.

'Happy to meet you both. Welcome. Have you come to take on your and other third parties' round-up of the miscreants?'

'Well John, that's the question. Rodney laid this bombshell on us last night,' Carol said, nodding round at the paperwork charts and computers littering the room, 'and we need your help to get our heads around all this. The big question that my boss will ask is what do you think our recovery pot will look like?'

'I would think that there would be a payback into the USA in excess of 50 billion. Tempted? There will be a little shrinkage. We need to fund a few extras to get this sorted.'

Carol eyed John. 'That's not Irish blarney for skimming the pack?'

'Heavens, no. It will all be shown in the accounts. Don't forget that every second of every day you're being ripped off and will continue to be until this fraud is stopped. Reason enough, I would have thought. Not least the kudos the USA will earn from your European allies, not something your President could or should turn down. I expect that you'll want a Treasury man to join your team once you're underway?' John said defensively. 'Now, I'm going to introduce you to the team here and then they'll take you both through the logic and accounts in a brief way, but not too brief that you miss the important points.'

Rodney chipped in. 'Thanks, John. How long will this take do you think?'

'An hour or two. When we're done, I'll bring our guests back to you.'

'That sounds fine,' Rodney commented. 'When you and Carol are ready, Murphy, I'll give you a brief on the field operations headed by Mr. Reid.'

Rodney left them to it; he needed to talk to Major Freire and Graham. He found them together working through a pile of signals that had come in that morning, separating them into piles for the various members of team.

'Hi you two. Got a minute?'

If they were annoyed at the interruption it didn't show. 'Sure, we are just about done here.'

'Anything interesting?' Rodney wanted to know.

'Yes and no,' Freire answered, 'yes, the intelligence we see before us confirms the involvement of the fraudsters definitively, but interesting, no. There are no surprises so far.'

'We'll pass this on to operations and the finance team as appropriate.' Graham was squaring up the piles of signals and posting them into trays where the team would pick them up and deal with them. He finished off and gave Rodney his full attention. 'What's on your mind?'

'Well, it's complicated. But I need to discuss it with you both.'

'Sounds expensive.' Freire remarked, smiling.

'Could be. In principle, Mr. Reid is putting together the plan to lift the principal players of the fraud in Defence and the Health Service in just the same way that we did for construction, with the aid of MI5 and Special Branch etc. Once this is done and we've had our pound of flesh we hand over to Fraud Branch in its entirety, leaving us free to concentrate on the Russians and their agents.'

'Is this because of the attack on you last night?'

'Partly, but the plan if that's what it is, has been forming in my mind for a day or two. I believe that we've fulfilled the main tenets of our mission. A mission so far away from our normal work that it's time we got back on track.'

'Hear, hear,' Graham said.

'Let me guess; you want to reset the priorities and the team? My team and Graham's too?'

'Spot on, Freire.'

Graham groaned. 'Hit me with your thoughts.'

'Put simply, from the list we got from our FBI friend Murphy I want in-depth intelligence on each man. Get Ms. Reid from 6 and Christine our lovely MI5 attachment to join you. I've some extra legs coming in the next few days. Twenty or more of Simon's Somali men led by Saied who will work through Laurie to Mr. Reid and you. Priority is those elements of the Russians and their agents that are likely to do us physical harm, we'll deal with the remainder another way. I've already talked to Laurie, so expect him to appear anytime now.'

'Er, what are you going to do with the ones that could harm us?' Graham had forebodings.

'Neutralise them, one way or another.'

'Thought that you'd say that.' Graham folded his arms over his chest. 'Within the law, I hope?'

'Possibly,' Rodney grinned, 'or not. We'll see.'

'Does Mr. Reid know about this?'

'He will, in about five minutes.'

'Good. He's been working on a plan you asked him for, over at his desk for the last three hours.'

'That's fine. I don't think that my way forward will affect his plan in the immediate future. His plan only went as far as lifting the villains. So, no harm done.'

'Hope that you're right, Rodney. We'll reorganise ourselves in the expectation that you'll want us up and running in the context of villains as soon as possible, whilst still processing information on the Defence and Health Services, and in a position to give you our first run at identifying targets to go for after yesterday.'

'That should do it. Now, as you say, I need to get Mr. Reid on board.' Rodney was not really looking forward to finessing Mr. Reid to come along with his plan.

Mr. Reid had his head back, leaning back on his chair, eyes closed.

'Hi, Doug. Finished?'

Doug Reid opened his eyes and sat forward on his chair. He reached out, grabbed a folder and passed it to his boss.

'Read and digest.' The other men of the operations team stood around in expectation. 'All of the team have had input and they're keen to hear your thoughts, Major.'

Rodney opened the file. 'Any tea and buns? I need a sugar rush.' Mr. Reid nodded to one of the team who disappeared to get the necessary. Rodney read on. Mr. Reid had followed the tried and tested military mantra of getting things on paper in a formal way. Starting with the Mission, then the Aim, and then any limitations to the aim. Followed by enemy forces, friendly forces in direct and indirect support, then courses open and then course chosen. The plan. Then it went into the plan – who did what, when and with what. Communications, resources needed and finally, administration. It was a classic military planning example.

A cup of tea and biscuits was placed before Rodney. 'Thanks. Good job, Mr. Reid. I don't have any observations. It's exactly what I wanted.'

He turned to the team. 'Good job, team. Now, I need a little time with Mr. Reid to talk about future ops.'

When they were alone Rodney told Mr. Reid about what he wanted when Doug and his ops team had sorted the immediate mission.

'How long, Doug, do you think it will take to extricate ourselves from this current mission?' Rodney placed the file on the table and tapped it.

'It's all a question of resources, Rodney. As you read, from "go" to picking the targets up and locking them up is two days. One day for the Defence targets and one for the Health Service. That's the best that I can do.'

'OK. Let's accept that. You have the addresses and locations of all the targets?' He got a nod from Mr. Reid. 'Can the support, police, Special Branch, MI5 be ready for first light tomorrow?'

'Already sorted. We go first light. Defence first. Following day, Health.'

'As ever Doug, classic, thanks.

'I have a full briefing of our boys and the supporting agencies and staff a bit later than originally planned, it's now at 1500hrs. I needed to give our friends time to get their reps here and to ensure that they'll still have enough time to brief their own masters and their men before we attack in the morning.'

'Will you give the briefing or do you want me to do it?'

'I'll do it. I've put it together so I know it back to front. And it will give you two days to work on the new mission, which I think is even more important than this one.' He patted the file. 'I'll handle this file, you sort the other. The sooner that we are in a position to take out these killers the better.'

'That's my aim. But as a second priority I also need to give MI5 whatever we can on the rest of the people involved with the KGB. Having Christine on attachment should help there.'

'What about Galena, your neighbour?'

'Hmm, I need to speak to your daughter, Ms. Reid. Because Galena is a declared Attaché, she's a political hot potato, but I did catch her out of the corner of my eye last night with the neighbours who piled on to the street after the incident. I noticed that she was the only one fully dressed. I think that's significant, don't you?'

'Politics never bothered you before.'

'Happen. I might just knock her door tonight. Can't help, just friendly. Could ask a few questions.' Rodney looked at his watch; it was lunchtime. 'Think that I'd better collect our American guests and take them to lunch. How do you feel about them sitting in on your briefing?'

'No issue, providing that you get a commitment from them that they keep what they hear today to themselves. I don't think for a moment that Windsor is a problem, but we don't really know Murphy yet.'

'Thanks, point taken.' Rodney thought about Murphy; true, he had given Rodney some good intelligence but that could have been a sweetener for something bigger in return. He would think on it.

Chapter Sixty-Three

Moscow Centre

'Well, Colonel, what have you got to tell me?' The Director of the Division, General Polyakov, sat behind his desk looking at the officer standing in front of him.

'There was an unfortunate incident in London with a team of our men.' Colonel Pushkin was outwardly relaxed. Inside he was concerned.

'Would this be the incident that left one dead Spetsnaz soldier, one wounded and him and another of ours arrested? The damage to our men carried out by one Major Rodney Brown and another man? Would that be a fair summary, Colonel?'

'Yes sir, it would.'

'Thank you. Now I know that the motto of our Spetsnaz is roughly any target, anywhere, anytime. But don't you think that in this case that might apply to Major Brown instead? I asked you to incapacitate Major. Brown and clearly you didn't. For my peace of mind, what was your plan?'

'They were supposed to make entry to the Major's home, restrain him and inject him with a life-limiting concentration of potassium chloride. It is rarely if ever picked up on an autopsy even if there is one.'

'I think that we can be certain that the sudden death of Major Brown would have attracted a postmortem. Well, we failed big time. So, tell me, what is your next plan?'

'I am planning to use assets that are already in the UK.' He smiled his disarming smile that seemed to serve him well. 'I did speak to Colonel Galena this morning. It appears that the Major had a minder with him. I will make sure that we get him this time.'

'Two points; the first is that it must be nowhere near his flat, for that read Galena. The second, what did you not understand when I said that I wanted him incapacitated? That means not permanently. In fact, I wanted him whole and healthy. Here is the thing, as you screwed up I want you to arrange for him to be held for a time. I would like him questioned and the only answer I want from him is where my money is.' He stood. 'You may use mindbending drugs to get him to talk. No permanent damage, physical or psychological until you have the information. Do you understand, Colonel?'

'Perfectly, General.'

'Good.' He smiled, 'and when you have the information, we'll decide together what we'll do next, about the money and the Major.'

Chapter Sixty-Four

Lunch

'Think that I might need a season ticket if I eat here again,' Murphy said as they sat down.

Carol said dryly, 'Don't think that they could afford you Murph.' Rodney and Murphy chuckled.

'Welcome both, have a look at the menus. They'll come and take your order when you're ready.'

The two Americans scanned the menu and both chose the restaurant special, fish and chips. Rodney followed suit. He called over the waiter, ordered the food and added a bottle of house white.

The table settled into a short silence before Carol opened the conversation.

'I just wanted to check, Rodney, that you are recovered after your experience last night?' Rodney waved dismissively. 'Even so, got to be a shock.'

'No issue; we were prepared. More pity them, sent on a mission without adequate preparation. Unforgivable really, whoever sent them should be shot.'

'Generous of you Rodney, and by contrast Murphy and I were totally blown away by your team in what you call the finance cell. Amazing what they've achieved in such a short time. But listening and talking to John Brown and the others I can see that the organisational genius behind it is something I envy. Where did you learn how to do that?'

'Well thank you for that, but the real praise should go to my Army training. I was so lucky to have had that. The training taught you to plan and visualise a situation as a whole. We have a crib, a template really, or templates for every phase of a conflict. Infinitely adaptable to any circumstance. I expect that the US Army has a similar system.'

'Even so, it's all in the execution. Not many people could make 300 billion plus in a week and destroy an enemy that has built up a criminal organisation over years. No wonder that you're not popular.'

'Well, as you saw this morning, we're blessed with a team of hard-working experts who just instinctively know what to do when given the scent. After lunch you might like to sit in on Mr. Reid's briefing for the next phase.' Rodney moved to close the subject as their food arrived.

They fell silent for a while, as the waiter placed the food in front of them and poured the wine.

They toasted each other and tucked in.

Murphy took up the conversation. 'We agreed with the Brigadier and John that we could send over a Treasury man to work with the team. The aim of this will be to get the detail of our and the other countries affected in order to carry on what you have achieved.'

'Does that mean that you have the go ahead to take on our neighbours problems?'

'The authority came in the early hours of the morning to take on the task. Must say, Carol and I were surprised that we got the authority so quickly. Think they may be as concerned about the fraud being leaked as they are about the issue itself.'

Carol pulled a face. She clearly thought that Murphy had spoken out of turn and changed the subject.

'My understanding is that you have four areas of activity. The Banker's team, communications and intelligence, administration coordination which works closely with Comms and finally the operations who execute the physical stuff. Is that right?'

'That's correct. I lead the four teams and work to the Brigadier who facilitates us when we need more resources and anything else you can think of and of course, he fights our battles, political and otherwise, in-house and outside of that bubble.'

'Your system clearly works. I am thinking that we might, with a little tweaking, be able to mirror that when we move on our perpetrators. I am thinking that we need to do something similar and also set up the other countries in a similar way if they don't have a team like yours. Why reinvent the wheel, even if it's not the American way?' She gave an open and friendly chuckle. Her face lit up.

'That sounds a good way forward.'

'We may need to ask for some guidance; is that going to be a problem?' Murphy put in.

'I am sure that Brigadier Robinson will be only too pleased to support you.'

'Is that a yes?' Carol persisted.

'Yes.' Rodney knew that it would be a feather in the PM's hat and one she would make good use of at the right time. Not only for her party, Parliament writ large but allies, especially the President.

'Good; now, what about this afternoon?' Carol seemed relieved that she could count on Rodney and his boss. It did not go unnoticed by Rodney and he was secretly pleased for the team.

Rodney poured wine for everyone while they continued to fight their way through an overlarge plate of fish and chips. 'After lunch we'll visit Graham and Major Freire and see how both of those teams work and how they meld together to feed Finance and Operations. After that, at three o'clock, Mr. Reid, who leads the operations cell for me will give the orders for lifting the perpetrators as you would say in Defence and the Health Service. I have to ask you to keep anything you hear to yourselves and not to share it with anyone else for the two-day duration of our attack. That's the bargain for your attendance.' Rodney had eye contact with them both. They both nodded. 'This is really important; lives may be at risk if our plan gets out. I've been through the plan with Mr. Reid and it's a good one. If you can keep your side of the bargain, I'll give you a copy of the briefing and orders document. Deal?'

'Deal,' said Carol.

Deal,' said Murphy enthusiastically. He was thinking that if he had to replicate the document for his people, he would find it difficult to do so from a blank canvas.

'Good, so be it.'

'And after the two days, what happens to your team then?' Murphy was curious.

'We sign over the bulk of the mission to the Fraud Squad, supported by the serious crime law enforcement agencies. I'll keep John's team mainly intact as they'll be needed for continuity between ourselves and yourselves and others. They'll still have a lot of work sorting out the finances and which money needs to go back to whom. The intelligence and admin cell will still need to support them as arisings will almost certainly continue for a period. As a team, apart from what we need to do to support others like the Banker, we'll revert to what we do best. We all go hunting.'

'What do you mean?' Carol was serious.

'We'll seek out and destroy any KGB agents, third parties and associates who wish to do us harm so fast that it's going to make their eyes water.' Rodney grinned.

277

'Good luck with that, Rodney.' Carol meant it. 'Did Murphy's list help? He told me that he gave you some assistance.'

He looked at Murphy who ignored him as he finished his food then grunted.

'Told the boss that I was supporting you with the unedited file. No redactions in sight.'

'In that case, just as well. I thought that I was a target but even if the rest of the team were, shall we say, not high on the list, they may still be targeted. But the file made me re-evaluate and now, thanks to you both, we're all, as they say, on a war footing and out for revenge.'

'Revenge is always best taken cold, Rodney,' Carol cautioned.

'I can promise you just that, Carol. Anyone for a dessert?'

'After having eaten a Moby Dick of a fish and half an acre of chips – there you are, been over here too long, should say fries; I think that a cup of tea with Graham and Major Freire would be just fine, thank you.'

'Agreed,' said Murphy. 'Let's get back to work.'

Chapter Sixty-Five

Mr. Reid

Murphy and Carol Windsor continued to be staggered at the organisation and the lack of any friction between the people who were under such pressure to perform. As for the organisation, they could not fault it and even Murphy, a 'dyed- in-the-wool' FBI establishment man, was full of admiration.

Both felt that the straightforward lines of communication, the battle boards and the handling of intelligence and information was something that they might replicate. They particularly liked the log sheets and books the principals kept and shared as a great idea for future reference purposes.

Time slipped by and it was with some regret that they were dragged away from Graham. He took them to join the gathering orders groups and showed them to their seats at the end of the table next to the Brigadier and the Principal Private Secretary, Sir Geoffrey. Murphy made to take out his small notebook but the Brigadier put his hand over the notebook and patted his arm.

'Sorry Murphy; no notes. I can assure you that after two days you'll have all you need.'

Murphy shrugged. 'Sorry sir, force of habit.'

'And a very good one it is, but just not today.' Both men chuckled.

Rodney, sitting to the right of Mr. Reid, brought the table to order. 'Welcome. We all know each other but for good order and for our guests Murphy and Carol from the FBI let me just run through appointments and identify yourselves – hold hands up or something.

'Representatives from Special Forces, Special Branch, Fraud Squad, HQ Metropolitan police who will coordinate other police forces, MI5, the SIS liaison officers and of course the in-house team, not excepting our communications hub. Right, people, this our last push before we hand the issue over to the normal authorities and I'm sure that the police and MI5 will be relieved.'

There was a polite laugh that ran round the table, 'The back-room team, Graham et al, will have all relevant files and data ready for you to sign for as we hand over to the Fraud Squad, Special Branch and MI5 forty-eight hours from now.'

There was an audible shuffling in the room. Many had not expected Rodney to be withdrawing so soon.

He picked up what he interpreted as disquiet. 'Fear not, after the next forty-eight hours we will have broken the back of this fraud, and quite rightly, it's for law and order to reinsert itself into the game without us forcing the pace or anything else for that matter. Of course, we'll be available for any member of this table that needs our help. We're outrunning our usefulness and the team here have to move on to counter a very real and immediate threat to some members of this organisation's staff. You will all know that I was attacked last night, and the ongoing threat has to be neutralised. On that note, I'll hand over to Mr. Reid.'

Mr. Reid rose and moved over to the lectern.

He smacked the lectern hard with a stick for quiet, which was an old instructor's trick. The room fell silent and refocused their attention in expectation.

'Listen in. First health warning. You keep stum about what's said here today, any leak will be career limiting, possibly with an adverse health outcome.'

Having given his warning, he began.

'The mission is to neutralise the fraudsters' operations by arresting the targets that we've identified.'

He let that sink in. 'The aim: Destroy the enemy's ability to defraud this country.' He repeated the mission and the aim as was the custom and to leave those listening in no doubt what was expected of them. 'Limitation to the aim. We are to execute the mission within forty-eight hours. We are to destroy the enemy ability to defraud the Defence industry for those three companies and organisations we have identified within the first twenty-four. We'll then move immediately to destroy the enemy ability that we have identified in sectors of the Health Service.'

The room held its breath and Rodney glanced around the table before focusing on the Americans, who were open- mouthed. Rodney didn't think that they'd ever been subject to a military orders group of this intensity. He allowed himself a small smile. There was a lot more to come.

Mr. Reid continued. 'General outline. We have a list of names in both the target industries that we are going to hit. Be aware that whilst we have already detained the individual who we believe is the head of the fraud in the United Kingdom, he will have deputies. He is being cooperative and more intelligence is expected. Be aware we are confident of neutralising the target businesses by taking out the principals and known subordinates. There will be stragglers on the periphery which law and order can pick up at a later date. We expect that some of these enemies will have developed their own circles of fraud and this may be linked to serious crime. These targets are serious people and dangerous. Taking nothing away from the professionalism of our police, with each police snatch squad will be two Special Forces soldiers to advise and take executive action if life is threatened.' He paused and looked round. 'We are going to form snatch squads and then lift the enemy all at the same time so no one can warn another.'

Mr. Reid went to the first of the flipchart boards. He turned over the first sheet revealing the headings – mission, aim and limitation; under each heading was written the statements for each. 'Absorb and retain these cardinal orders for the remainder of this orders group. Burn them into your hearts.'

He then went to the second flipchart and turned the first page. Underneath the chart showed 'Defence Industries' in large lettering.

'Your actions are going to save the country billions and get the arms to the soldiers quicker and save lives in the Health Service. Motivated? Good. The scams that these people are perpetrating are listed in the annexes of your pack. Substandard materials, reworks, delays, you name it.'

He paused and flipped the chart again. 'The Plan.' He stroked the sheet; on it were seventy names; against each name was where they worked and where they lived. The list was broken down into geographic areas. 'The teams will deploy overnight and lift the targets at first light at 0500hrs. The targets will be taken to Shepton Mallet Prison and signed over to the Fraud Squad. Detailed plans...'For the next half hour Mr. Reid was animated and allocated men and resources to each of the targets.

At the end of the detailed plans Mr. Reid called a ten-minute break. 'Get yourself some tea or coffee. Be back here in ten. Don't be late!' His harsh Scots voice would be enough to get them back.

Rodney nodded to Laurie to get coffee for the Brigadier and his three guests. He got a nod back. Reid sidled up to Rodney.

'OK so far, Boss?'

'Spot on Doug, said Rodney, 'it's going so well that nobody has nodded off. They are all alert and wanting more.'

'They'll get it shortly.' Reid was fired up. 'What are you going to do while we sort this?'

Laurie arrived, fed the Brigadier and his guests and brought Rodney and Reid tea and a bun.

'Thanks, mate. What I am going to do if I don't have to get too involved in this operation is to plan our next hit on the enemy who are after us. I have an idea but it will depend on the Brigadier. I'll discuss it with you first after this meeting, OK?'

'Happy with that. Now, I need to get back and sort this lot.'

'Right. All back?' Reid scanned the table. Satisfied, he began again. 'Command and control; Major Brown is in overall control of this Mission. I am the Tactical Commander. All reports will come to me via Major Freire's signals team. Your callsigns, contact numbers, are in your briefing packs. We will beef up our communications to cater for seventy teams out in the field but it goes without saying brevity is essential. Your call in will also be automatically copied and relayed to the Metropolitan Command Centre. What I want to know are two things. First, you have arrested your target. Two, you have handed him with any incriminating evidence over to the Fraud Squad. When I'm satisfied that we've done all we can I'll initiate an all Charlie Charlie callsigns call. That will signal the end of the Defence phase.'

Mr. Reid moved back to his flip chart. 'Administration...'

He finished with a few remarks and then asked for questions. There were only a few about what if a team's target was not at home.

'Find out where he is. Chase the target down. Innovate, improvise, overcome any hold up.'

'For the far-flung units, would they be able to get back for the next phase?'

Mr. Reid responded. 'They're not tasked for the Health Service.'

'Do we enter the targets' premises and seize phones, pcs, laptops, files etc.?'

Mr. Reid passed the question to the Deputy Commissioner. The Commissioner stood and addressed the meeting.

'The local policeman with each team will have a search warrant and once you have your man will call for a search. Anything seized will follow on at best speed to the Fraud teams at Shepton. This will free the snatch teams for the next phase. Mr. Reid has detailed this in your briefing document.' The Deputy sat down.

Mr. Reid stood up and thanked the Deputy.

'Listen in; you've had an ear bashing for nearly two hours. Stretch your legs. Grab food and drink from our in-house canteen in the other room and get back here with your fodder in ten. We've broken the back and the Health Service briefing should only take an hour. You have a lot to do tonight, so go!'

Rodney went to see the Americans.

'OK so far for you?' Carol and Murphy both wanted to ask Rodney if this was how it was always done.

'It's our way; sometimes more formal, sometimes less, but it works.'

'Any chance that one of us can be here when it all kicks off tomorrow to see the plan in action? It would be so helpful to use when we have to replicate the exercise in the States.' It was a genuine plea by Carol. Rodney realised for the first time that the Americans might be nervous of their ability to manage the situation. Perhaps nervous was the wrong word, more like apprehensive.

Rodney looked at the Brigadier and Sir Geoffrey, and both inclined their heads.

'No problem, but please try to stay in the background as we will be busy.'

'Of course, Rodney and thank you, Brigadier.' Carol was genuinely grateful to the British.

Rodney turned to the Brigadier. 'Are you around tomorrow, sir? If you are, I could do with some time with you.'

'I'll be around all day. Probably getting under everyone's feet.'

'Great.' Rodney left them as plates of food piled high appeared on the table followed by drinks.

Refreshed and still eating, the table had an expectation of more as Mr. Reid began to take the attendees through the Health Service frauds. There were only twenty-six fraudsters to pick up. The Health Service was different, being a national asset. It would be treated differently but the worst of the perpetrators still had to be arrested to stop major frauds. The same sequence of orders was followed and Mr. Reid finished in under an hour. There were no questions and the meeting broke up after the Brigadier thanked everyone and wished them 'good hunting'.

Rodney watched the room empty. He had been in their shoes over the years and in a way still was, but he didn't envy them the task ahead; it would be a race to meet Mr. Reid's targets. *No sleep for them tonight.* He smiled to himself.

Chapter Sixty-Six

Moscow

General Polyakov was in a reflective mood as he viewed his office. By many standards it was plush. It was certainly big with his large desk and to one side a well-polished oak meeting table for ten to sit comfortably. To the other side of the room leather club chairs were arranged around a log-fed open fireplace. He was remembering when Brigadier Tsygankov had visited him and fallen asleep in an easy chair while he had waited for the Polyakov to return from a meeting.

He envied his old friend in his dacha, making his wine, keeping his pigs etc. He wished him a long life. The General was worried about the loss of the money. It was increasingly obvious that the networks associated with the money-making fraud had been busted.

The loss of the data from his department meant that he was not in a good place with the Chairman of the KGB. On the other hand, he had a lot of credit with the old Chairman. In his tenure he had reorganised the Directorate and built strong communication channels with the others. It was recognised that his changes had meant a reduction in duplication of work, which was a perennial problem in the KGB.

He wondered if he could fall on his sword and resign. Somehow, he didn't think that a simple request would be good enough, but it might be worth a try. His deputy, a Brigadier, was more than capable of taking on the Division.

Assuming that they allowed him to resign, he wondered what he would do with himself. True, he was well set up with a house and lands in the hills southwest of St Petersburg. Very different from Tsygankov's estate but enough land and livestock to make him self-sufficient. Plus, he thought, with his medium-sized lake fed from the river he could sustainably farm perhaps trout and more. The more he reflected on it, the more he liked the idea.

The General buzzed for his Deputy and Colonel Pushkin. He called his secretary and part-time lover to get coffee for three.

The coffee was served as his two officers arrived.

He moved to the meeting table and asked the officers to sit.

'Brigadier, Colonel, I have been thinking about the trouble caused by Brigadier Robinson and his team, not to mention Major bloody Brown and his sidekick Mr. Reid. As I see it, although the Brits could replace them...' He paused, 'eventually, whoever replaced them would take some time to get up to speed, if ever. So, my decision is that they should be eliminated so they cannot cause this Directorate any further trouble.'

His officers looked at one another. The message that went silently between them was that it was about time.

His deputy was the first to speak. 'What about the money? I have to say, I think that we should consider it as gone forever. If anyone can hide money it's the Brits.'

Polyakov grunted. 'True.'

Colonel Pushkin wanted to know if the General had had any thoughts about how to achieve the eradication of Brown's team.

'Not really, Colonel Pushkin, but I expect that you will have been thinking about it.' Polyakov knew he was distancing himself from the issue but if something went wrong, he needed to be on the sidelines.

'Let's see, General.' Colonel Pushkin began. 'I have indeed given some thought, as you might expect, to how to level the playing field. We do have a few assets in the UK that could achieve the elimination of these three men. But they are not KGB, they're Chechens. Six of them and they do the majority of that sort of work for us in the UK. I would be reluctant to use our KGB assets already in the UK; they are either declared and official like Colonel Galena or undercover and not the sort who could handle this task anyway, but they can support.'

'Hmm. Do you think that we should back these Chechens from here with a few of our people to keep the hired help focused?' The Brigadier was thoughtful. 'What about Major Servo? He must be going stir crazy with that research project we have him on.'

'Could do that. Colonel Pushkin, anyone he normally works with?'

'Well, there is Carla. Together they are a good team and resourceful. Don't you agree, General?'

Polyakov avoided the question. 'They are an item according to my secretary, so you would expect them to cover each other's back. They have been to the UK and know their way about. Think that may be an advantage, unlike the three who failed who were sent into the lion's den. Do you think that you should add a couple of extra hands for them?'

'Could do. I know a few men in the service who could support Servo. English speakers. Knowing Servo he may want to pick his old cronies, but I think that the men that I'm thinking of knew Servo from his time in Afghanistan so he may know them anyway. We'll see.' The Brigadier was thoughtful again. 'Of course, they weren't in his Company but nevertheless they are blooded KGB and resourceful.'

The General thought that he'd got them directed where he wanted them and he further removed himself from the responsibility with his closing remark.

'Hmm. Well, I leave it to you, gentlemen. Just let me know the outcome. And now I really must go and see the Chairman, he has asked to see me today. Thank you for your counsel etc.' With his customary wave he stood and went to his desk to collect his high peaked hat. The men left his office, discussing the way that they would set up the attack.

Chapter Sixty-Seven

The Lifting

Mr. Reid and Major Freire manned the operations desk from five in the morning. Mr. Reid was his normal dour self as he supped his first steaming coffee of the day. He placed his cup on the desk and stared grumpily at the signals team screens. The signal screens were flashing messages which were unintelligible to him.

He felt that technology was leaving him behind, and it hurt. He turned away from the screens and searched the room for something that he could relate to, brightening as Freire offered him a double egg and bacon sandwich. He rubbed his hands together then took the offering.

'You certainly know how to make an old man's day.' His mood lifted.

Freire reported, 'OK, we're good to go. We tested the links with all the teams and they're all good. We log and record all communications digitally so that we can get to any conversation quickly. Analog is out, digital is in.'

'Sounds complicated.' He felt lost again.

'Just sit and watch and listen.'

Reid grunted; looking over his shoulder he could see Mould, Sharky and the attached officers from the Fraud Squad, the Met and Special Forces. They constituted his in-house Ops team. He knew that they would rather be out with the snatch teams, but somebody had to watch the shop. Their time would come again. The team had rearranged their operations cell so it looked like a call centre, arranged in a half circle with the desks and chairs facing the battle boards that would be progressively filled in as the operation progressed.

They would take the calls as they came in and mark up the battle boards. Battle boards that at least Mr. Reid could understand and touch. The calls would also be monitored and actioned by the Metropolitan Control Centre (MCC) and Freire's team. The MCC then had the task of calling in the local police specialists to seize, bag and log material and assets needed for evidence and for the Fraud Squad to build its case. It was Freire's task to join the two centers together and hold the master record of all actions. The records and subsequent file once compiled by Graham and his Admin cell would be copied and issued to the parties that needed it to prosecute any necessary actions.

Major Freire's staff's job was going to get frenetic in no time flat and she wanted to clear their desks. She looked at Mr. Reid.

'Where are you going to base yourself Mr. Reid?' He was in her chair. 'I can get you another chair if you are staying?'

He picked up the signal to fuck off, even though it was delivered gently.

'Much as I would like to stay here, Freire, I think that I'd better join the boys, they may need my input when they get busy and start to feel unloved.' He glanced over. 'The Americans are arriving and it's my task to look after them as well.'

Freire laughed. She was tall for a woman, clearly fit and attractive in a way that no one would take offence, neither man nor woman. As a woman in what was still primarily a man's world, she was lucky. She neither gave nor attracted offence. A classic beauty, was Mr. Reid's take. The fact that Graham, a 'dyed-in the wool bachelor', couldn't do enough for her and enjoyed her company was testament to that.

As it was, Graham arrived as Mr Reid was moving on to his team.

'Morning, Graham. Ready?'

'Ready as I'll ever be,' Graham said.

'Good, it's going to get busy any time now.'

'Don't worry, my people will be here any minute and we'll both serve and support you, as is our mission.'

'Good man.'

Reid sauntered over to his Ops team, checked in with each of the men and then sat facing them. Battle boards to his rear, he sat calmly waiting for the first call.

When the first call came in it was notification that callsign twenty-four had their man. After that the phones rang nonstop for the next two hours. They discovered only three of the targets were missing from home. One was the operations director of one of the key defence companies. He was later found to be in Saudi troubleshooting a problem in a missile system. He was being recalled and would be picked up at the airport on his return later that night. The other two were low-level salesmen and they were picked up waiting for a flight. All in all, a good result.

Reid was delighted but didn't show it. He rasped in his best Scots, clear and decisive. 'You lot, reset, more battle boards for tomorrow. I want half of you getting ready for the lifting tomorrow; Mould and Sharky and the rest of you I want you to get on to the local boys and make sure evidence has been seized from all the targets and then update the logs and get the lists of seized evidence to Freire. I want it to put to bed and the new battle boards reset for tomorrow ready for the Brigadier and the Major to inspect by 1600hrs. Any questions?' There were none.

Reid left them to do their jobs and went through the operations room to the finance team's domain to join Rodney. Rodney was with the Banker checking the arrangements. Whilst they could not sweat money out of the Health Service it was not the same case with the three Defence companies.

'Morning all, all done bar the shouting. Lost one but they will pick him up on his return to the UK.' Reid reported.

'Good job, Doug; fingers crossed for tomorrow. We are just getting ready for the three Chairmen and their CEOs of our target companies. Do you want to stay and see them cough up the pennies?'

Reid gave a rare laugh. 'Don't think I will, I hate to see grown men cry.' He pointed over his shoulder to Colonel Jimmy and Andrew and Pat. The three men were preparing the presentations showing how much money was to be recovered. Unlike the construction company they had to approach it differently. 'Do you think you can convince the companies to pay?'

John said, 'I think that we have a good chance. We don't have the detail we had for the construction company but we do have financial transactions into the KGB banks. I think that will be enough. The way the fraud was carried out will come to light with the evidence and from the interrogation of the men you picked up today, as we have recovered the money. They don't know that. I am making the companies pay again. Call it a fine for incompetence and defrauding of shareholders and the British taxpayer. And if they want to continue with lucrative defence contracts and permissions to sell overseas, I don't see they have much option.'

'You are a hard man, John. Good luck.' Reid was impressed.

'Hard man, you say. Learnt it all from a master. That is you Doug my old friend.' The Banker smiled.

'Irish charm will get you nowhere.' Reid grinned.

Ms. Reid, Mr. Reid's daughter who worked for the SIS arrived with Christine from MI5 and joined the three men.

'Reporting for duty, Major. Rodney, where do you want us today?'

'Initially with me. We need to sort out a problem that the team has to overcome. Get yourself a drink and wait for me at the conference table. I'll be over in five.'

Chapter Sixty-Eight

Feedback

Rodney grabbed the original FBI names file and the working file of investigations and information into the various named individuals. The working file was growing in thickness but still had a long way to go. It was well-constructed, colour-coded from thugs to agents.

Miss Reid and Christine were chatting together when Rodney arrived. A cup of tea and a breakfast sandwich appeared as if by magic in front of him. Rodney looked over his shoulder at Laurie grinning. 'Join us.'

The four members sat in a tight group at one end of the table so they could share the files. Rodney flipped open his logbook.

'The purpose of the gathering is to review and share the intelligence on the Russian efforts to do us harm. The other purpose is, simply put, that we want to identify their enforcers and hitmen. We'll come to Laurie later, who I hope has sorted a select team to shadow those we identify. Now, it's not the definitive list, we know that, but pretty close. And it may be Moscow will send another team of jokers like those that tried it on last night.' He paused. 'OK, who wants to start?' He peered at the two women.

Christine took first go. 'Graham asked us to run the names in the file and sort them in threat order.' She pulled out a thick file from her laptop bag. 'We identified six potential hitmen from the list of names. Why they are still at large and not been deported is a mystery to me. All six have been pulled for violence but nothing ever seems to stick. They have the same lawyer; he's good and very expensive. So, we deduce that they're being protected.'

'I think that you need to visit the lawyer and have a word. It would be a win if you could get out of him who employs him,' Rodney observed.

'Done that; called the brief's chambers. A little subterfuge but I got out of the clerk that a Mr. Neil Ashchurch paid any bills. Surprised or what?' Christine was pleased with herself.

Rodney smiled. 'Good work, Christine. Ms. Reid, what have you got for us?'

Unlike her father, she had long ago lost any Scots accent that she may have had. Like Freire, she had served in the Royal Signals before she joined MI6 or as some preferred to call it the SIS and her accent was neutral BBC English. Ms. Reid had compared her names with Christine's six.

'We have the same six names as Christine and two others of interest. The two others we see as prime targets for a deeper investigation. The first is an Irishman by birth; a Thomas Reilly and the other is a peer of the realm. The right Honorable Peter Bromhead. Nasty bits of work, both of them. I have a full breakdown on them and their activities as far as we know them. They operate sometimes solo, sometimes together, here and abroad and that's why we know them. Both have been seen with KGB assets in other European countries. The others we do have files on because they are Chetnik and they link to KGB assets in this country. I've exchanged file info with Christine and vice versa.'

'Right, let us have at the eight men named. Do we have photographs of them?' Rodney got a nod from both the women. 'Good, I need copies for Laurie. Dozen copies of each should be a start.'

'If I need to keep an eye on eight men then I'm going to need extra men.' Laurie looked at Rodney.

Rodney thought for a moment. 'I authorised twenty watchers. How do you think that another twenty would look?'

'It would look better. Let's say I put four-man teams on the six 24/7 and that leaves me sixteen men. I will put four men 24/7on the two extra names Ms. Reid came up with. That leaves me eight for QRF, quick reaction force. Plus, of course, our friend.'

'OK. I take it that Simon is up for this?' Rodney queried.

'Oh yes.' Laurie laughed. 'He wanted me to get you to take more men on. So no, it won't be a problem.'

'Good. Is there anything else that you need regarding resources?'

'Transport of one sort or another we can sort. But it would be really helpful if we could draw some cameras and night vision kit.' Laurie looked round the table.

'I'll sort the cameras and NVG and throw in some recording kit. Might be useful.' Christine volunteered. 'Come and see me after lunch and I'll take you up to the stores.'

'Sounds like we have a plan. When can you be operational, Laurie?'

'I'll make a start tonight with the resources I have to hand, I'm waiting for radios to arrive, but the Somalis have cell phones anyway. I do need trackers and I want the teams to wear them too, so Freire tells me she can set up the screens to show our people and maybe targets' cars if we can bug them. So, I'm aiming for tomorrow to get up to operational speed, say by this time tomorrow.'

'You are sure that you can do that?'

'Leave it to me, Boss; you get on with the rest of the show.'

'OK, thank you all. Now, let's get to work,' Rodney said.

He and Laurie spent a little more time going over the task. Rodney wanted to know about Saied and his willingness to take on the task.

'Just try and stop him. He's been away from ops a while and is ready to go. So the plan is that he'll operate the teams out of one of the Somalian houses. We have good communications between us. I'll be here 24/7, got a cot in the back of the room behind the ops desk. Permission of Mr. Reid.'

'Must be going soft in his old age.'

'Wouldn't let him hear you say that, Boss. Think that he's realising that he is not as young as he was. Mind you, he can still motivate the boys and there's nothing wrong with his mind. He has his boys running around at a thousand miles an hour and he's in full control. It's as though he is losing muscle and growing the old grey cells,' Laurie mused.

'That's fine with me. There's plenty of muscle around, I need his brain more these days. Getting back to these lads of Simon's, what are they like?'

'In a word, awesome. Bright and clever and streetwise. They were tickled pink at the idea of shadowing these villains. As one of them said, nobody bothers with them in the daytime and at night they are invisible.' A slow smile appeared on Laurie's face.

'Hmm, very droll. Good to hear though that they are up for it and have a sense of humour.' Rodney sat up, he had had a thought. 'I'll be particularly interested if the targets meet up together and then if there are any new faces that join them. Armand and I, mainly Armand, took out three of their men last night and they must be feeling vengeful. Could be that the Russians will send in another team so I want to be on the front foot this time.'

'Got it, Boss.'

'Good. Now, how about some food and tea and let me get on with my entries into the logbook? I'm so far behind that it'll be a problem if I don't get it up to date.'

Chapter Sixty-Nine

The Chairman and the General

General Polyakov entered the Chairman's suite of rooms. A Major in the KGB who acted as his 'aide de camp' welcomed him. The Major, old for his rank, was an ex-ranker who had been a young soldier in the war, serving in the Chairman's regiment. Polyakov and the Major had themselves known each other for many years and they chatted as old soldiers do for a while, catching up on old times.

The Major was experienced in the world of reading people. He could see that Polyakov was unsettled which was unusual, something on his mind perhaps or he was troubled.

'So, my General, what brings you here today? You can rest easy; the Chairman is in a great mood today. Don't know why but make the best of it.' He patted Polyakov on the back. 'Now, come and let us see the secretary and get you in to see the old man. Let's see the Chairman before his mood reverts to normal.' This throwaway line had them both chuckling.

The secretary guarded the chairman with a zeal normally like that of a guard dog, but she too was in a mood to be reasonable.

'General Polyakov, how nice to see you. The Chairman is expecting you, he has an almost clear diary today. Just let me check that he can see you now.'

Polyakov waited, taking in the antechamber. No frills, but several works of art on the walls and of course a wall full of pictures of past Chairmen, starting from the KGB's formation in March 1954. Polyakov studied the pictures of Felix Dzerzhinsk, the father of the Cheka, with the seat in Lubyanka Building 2 where he found himself too. He moved on to other pictures, that of Ivan Servo and Yuri Andropov, Yuri probably the longest serving. He studied others; some he knew, some he didn't. Some he respected and others he considered out and out thugs.

The door to the inner chamber opened and the secretary stood at the door, beckoning Polyakov forward.

'The Chairman will see you now.' She smiled warmly. A good sign.

The Chairman, Viktor Mikhailovich Chebrikov, was sat behind his desk, eyes screwed up to help him see at distance behind thick pebble glasses.

'Young Polyakov, is it?'

'Yes Chairman, it is. I hope that you are well?'

'Very well as it happens. Cursed as you know by this short sight but I have to get on with it. Come, come and sit in front of me so that I can see you better.' He waved Polyakov forward.

'Thank you.'

'How is Carl Tsygankov? I take it that you are still in touch?'

'He is doing fine, healthy. His vineyard is doing well and he is producing enough now to sell commercially. I envy him his retirement, although he doesn't seem to slow down at all.' Polyakov chuckled.

The Chairman laughed. 'He's an old pirate, you know that. Shame that his last outing wasn't as successful as I'd hoped but there you are. My news is that I am to move on, so I am delighted. It's time to go and I am relieved in many ways. There is a new breed on its way and not for the best. My designate is that civilian Vladimin Kryuchkov.' He spat the words.

Polyakov noted a distaste in the Chairman's remarks. 'You will be missed, that I know, especially by the old soldiers for whom your support over the years has been appreciated. You always had their respect. They'll miss you.'

'Thank you, Polyakov, for your kind words. They mean a lot to me. Things are changing, maybe not for the best and it is time to change the old guard.' The Chairman was reflective for a while. 'What of yourself, what can I do for you?'

'I hesitate to ask, but I have been taking stock and I very much want to retire to my estate and farm while I still have the energy and health to make a go of it.' Polyakov waited. There was a silence but there was the hint of a smile on the Chairman's lips. Polyakov thought that he needed to add to his request. 'I wouldn't be asking if I had any doubt that my deputy, Brigadier General Shabarshin, would make an effective and worthy replacement for me.'

'You have done a lot of good in your post. Certainly, your efforts to modernise the KGB and get the directorates to meld has certainly cut down duplication and encouraged cooperation between Directorates. Still, we are 300 billion of loose change out of pocket.' He laughed out loud, which was not something that Polyakov was used to. 'Not a chance of getting it back, do you think?' He had a sparkle in his eye.

Polyakov realised that the Chairman was de-mob happy. Thank God. 'The reality is that I don't think that we have a cat in hell's chance. Colonel Pushkin has the responsibility of sorting out the mess as he and his team created the problem.'

'Never liked him, too much of a fanatic.' A remark the Chairman would never have made in any other circumstance.

Polyakov pressed his request forward. 'What do you think, Chairman, of my request?'

'What do I think? Great idea. My potential successor is, as I say, not a soldier like you and I. He will, I know, change the whole ethos of my reign, it will all be overturned. So yes, let us retire together immediately.'

The Chairman pressed the bell on his desk and the secretary appeared immediately. Polyakov for himself was amazed, his heart was pounding, he had thought that he would have to fight but he could see the Chairman's clever move. His relief would inherit a new team so that the new man would not have to remove Polyakov. The Chairman knew that Polyakov would never kneel to such a man.

'Chairman, you wanted me?'

'Yes, madam. Get your portable and some paper; we are going to write three letters. And ask the Major to join us.'

While she went for her supplies the Chairman brought three glasses and a bottle of vodka out of his desk drawer.

'Let us make this a social occasion.'

The letters of authorisation were dictated and written while the three men drank to each other's health. The Major would be retiring with the Chairman as was the custom. One letter was Polyakov's letter of resignation which he signed; the Chairman found a stamp and, with relish, stamped the resignation letter and wrote 'effective immediately.' The next was the Chairman's letter of thanks for loyal service. And a third was the appointment of Brigadier General Shabarshin to General of the First Directorate KGB, effective immediately. Finally, he told his secretary to make sure that Polyakov had everything he was due – pension and gratuity, letters of gratitude etc. The Chairman said, 'Please get the pension etc. paid from tomorrow. Any pushback for the paymasters, refer them to me immediately. There my dear Polyakov, done, just like that!' There was merriment in the office for some time.

Job done; they sat together talking of old times for an hour. In the end the Chairman peered at his watch.

'Much as I would like to continue this meeting of old friends, I have my successor coming to view his new empire in a couple of hours and to see me out. Whilst I could put him off, I think that it is prudent to humour him. So, Polyakov, my dear old friend, come and see us when you have time. The Major is coming with me as my, let's say, minder in my retirement. And you need to give your successor his letter and hand in your keys. My strong recommendation is that you do that straight away and be gone before my successor arrives in the First Directorate for a look round. I will give you three hours to clear off.'

Polyakov was quite touched. He couldn't believe his luck; he thanked the Chairman for his support and promised to visit in the not-too-distant future.

'I had planned to see Carl Tsygankov soon and I will ensure I bring a crate of his best wine when I visit you and the Major.'

As Polyakov left he was elated. He had never expected that the Chairman would act so quickly, if at all. He was free of the responsibility that had been getting heavier and heavier over the last few years and the relief was like a millstone being lifted off his shoulders. Would he miss the privileges that came with the post as head of the First Directorate? Not at all, he had had enough and wanted to get back to his estate, but first he intended to lose himself at the Tsygankov dacha for a few weeks. He hoped that his secretary would come with him in his retirement. They had been lovers for many years and now seemed like a good time to repay her devotion.

Chapter Seventy

The Major does his Rounds

Rodney worked on the reports in his logbook for an hour, with an eye on what was going on around him.

Mr. Reid's team was still busy preparing the next day's mission on the Health Service. He heard Mr. Reid raise his voice more than once and Rodney smiled to himself. Rodney guessed that he was motivating a few of his men and women in his unique manner; it wasn't an act for the two Americans who were sitting with his team. They looked suitably shell-shocked. He would need to rescue them sooner than later.

From where he was sitting, he could see into the finance team's room and watched them out of the corner of his eye, moving furniture, preparing for the meeting with the Defence contractors and companies.

Graham's team and Major Freire's were, as ever, in high gear.

He finished his notes and updates and sat back for a while, eyes closed, trying with his tired mind to outguess the KGB response to their failure last night, quite apart from the money and the destruction of their frauds. He knew that he needed to find time to go and see Neil Ashchurch. He needed to see where Ashchurch was up to with his report and revelations on the KGB scams and others he had hinted about. Rodney was weary. He put his head in his hands. 'Need a break. A long one.' He stood, shook himself into action and swung his suit jacket on. He needed to see the Brigadier today about security and brief him on where he felt they were at. But first, he needed to rescue the Americans from the charms of Doug Reid.

'Carol. Murphy. Doug. How's it going?' Rodney had walked over to them and took over. Carol sparked up.

'Amazing what your team is doing, Rodney. I'm going to ask you if we can borrow a few of them? Mr. Reid, of course, when you're over this hump.'

'It wouldn't be the first time that Mr. Reid has worked with the FBI,' he reminded them. Rodney was non-committal, but he saw Mr. Reid spark up and grinned. 'I'm sure that if Mrs. Reid had a ticket too, you'd enjoy a trip to the States.'

Carol nodded. 'That could be possible.' She turned to Reid. 'Think she'd like a holiday on us?'

Mr. Reid was pleased and he showed it. 'I think that she'd be really pleased. She's always wanted to visit.' Then he said ruefully, 'Like as not she'll shop till she drops for the family and I'll probably be broke.' He grinned. 'Happy to help. We Celts have to stick together, eh Murphy?'

'So it is, Mr. Reid.' Murphy's Irish accent was passable.

'Let me take you out of Mr. Reid's way for an hour or two. It's important that you spend time with Graham and Major Freire and then the Banker. I would like you to sit at the back when we tackle the Defence industry. I'm going to disappear for an hour – I need to see one of our star prisoners. I'll be back in time to take you both for a quick lunch.'

Neil Ashchurch was busy when Rodney entered his cell. He was working at the table and it looked to Rodney that he was well on with his confession. A tidy pile of paper filled with Ashchurch's neat handwriting was evident.

'You seem to be getting on, Mr. Ashchurch?'

Ashchurch looked up. 'Yes, cracking through the job. I have to admit, Major, it's cathartic, a relief in many ways. I've been carrying this guilt and the responsibility, if you can call it that, for nearly fifteen years. I'm not going to make any excuses – I did it for money in the beginning. Young family, school bills etc., etc. I was in it right from the start. The architect of the scheme was, you know, Brigadier General Carl Tsygankov. Quite a man, brilliant brain. Wasted on those thugs the KGB. Of course, he's out of it now. We all age, and he is, as you know, very retired.'

Rodney smiled. 'We've bumped into each other over the years, that's true. So, when do you think that you might be reaching the end of your...' Rodney lifted the pile of paper. There were at least a hundred pages already. '...book?'

'Haha, yes, a book, could be. It's a better story than you will find in any thriller. Seriously, I need another two days to complete and check it through. I'm quite happy here. And probably safer.'

'OK. I would like to send an officer down to take what you've already done and copy it. They'll then bring you back the originals immediately afterwards. On second thoughts, I'll get them to bring a scanner and laptop and they can feed it into the machine. I'm uncomfortable only having the one copy of this important document.'

'Good idea, Major. I may need to make revisions for logic and presentation purposes, but I've been putting papers together for my whole career so it should make sense even now.' He cocked his head to one side. 'How is our friend, Colonel Jimmy I think he is called now?'

'Star turn, and tamed.' They both laughed. In another life Rodney could warm to this man. 'You mentioned that apart from the main, let's say, KGB-inspired frauds, you had or know of others?'

'In comparison they were, in the main, small beer but clever. Some of my counterparts in other countries knew that while we were shovelling millions, billions between us into their coffers we would see little of the take, so we did a little creative accounting for ourselves. We weren't greedy. It was invested in trusts overseas for the families. It was to safeguard the families and children. We were under no illusion as time went on, that if things went wrong, we were expendable. No Russian patriotic pension and a comfortable, warm but tiny flat in Moscow for us. I confess that we all agreed we would be disappeared.' He smiled. 'In a way, you and your team have done us all a favour.'

Rodney rubbed his chin, took a deep breath and breathed slowly through an open mouth. 'For fucks sake,' he whispered to himself. He then took a pen and wrote. When he'd finished, he showed it to Ashchurch.

Ashchurch read the paper and looked at Rodney. The paper said to *forget the trusts* in his report.

Rodney mouthed, 'No need for the families to suffer for the sins of the fathers.'

'Thank you, Major.'

Rodney scrunched up the paper and put it into his pocket. 'Just give me the rest and I'll be happy. The names of your counterpart in other countries could swing the deal.' He left Ashchurch and thought that he saw a tear roll down his cheek. *At least*, Rodney thought, *I've done one good deed today.*

Rodney returned to the operations centre. He would talk to Mr. Reid later; he had no secrets from him. He walked over to Graham, who was head down as usual working on some document.

'Where's the shredder, Graham?' Graham pointed and Rodney went and shredded his note to Ashchurch about the trust funds. 'Right, Graham, all good.'

'Yes, Rodney, we're now well up to speed. The only outstanding matter is your logbook. I need it to copy and log.' Graham was slightly exasperated. Rodney didn't blame him being put out.

'I apologise, Graham. Sort of got out of the habit. It shall be done, it's pretty well up to date. If you want it you can have it.'

Rodney grandly handed over his logbook; Graham flipped it open and grinned. 'I see that your handwriting hasn't improved.' He passed it over to one of his ladies.

Chastened, Rodney asked, 'Now, Graham, a favour. Can you send an officer to Ashchurch's cell with a portable scanner and laptop? Ashchurch is writing a massive tome and I need us to capture a copious output a couple of times a day. Can I ask when your officer does an upload each time that you email it to me and the Banker. I need his analysis, helped by you, I hope, to make sense of what he is telling us. Somehow, we need to run what he divulges against what we already know.'

'Interesting, Rodney. Just the sort of thing that I like to get my teeth into. Consider it done.' Graham was beaming, Rodney found his enthusiasm disarming.

'Well, thank goodness for that. Now, where are the Americans and the Brigadier?'

'Ah yes. They've gone up to the canteen. They said to join them when you got back. Sorry, forgot.'

'OK, Graham, no issue; we're all busy.'

'Too true; any chance of a pay rise?'

'You and me both.'

They both laughed. Neither would hold their breath.

Chapter Seventy-One

The Major and the Brigadier

After lunch they both saw the Americans into the finance analysts' room and waited until they had settled in with the Banker. In an hour the Defence contractors and companies would come to get the good news.

Rodney pulled Robinson to one side. 'Got half an hour Brigadier? I'd like to get you up to speed about what we're doing around security for ourselves and some thoughts.'

'Always happy to listen, Rodney. Conference table or my office?'

'Conference table; you, me and Mr. R if he's free.'

'Good enough.'

Rodney found Reid and they joined the Brigadier at the table.

'How's it going Mr. Reid?' was the Brigadier's way of welcoming him.

'Job done for the Defence contractors, they're in the bag. Health Service arrangements for tomorrow all but done. Another half hour should do it.'

'Great, well done. So, Rodney, where are we?'

'We now know, courtesy of SO13, that the three assassins who had a go at me in the early hours of this morning arrived in the UK from Moscow the other night. They hired a car at the airport but we don't know how they got the guns they had on them, or the poison they intended to inject me with. SO13 is working on that and will revert when they have something. I'm not holding my breath; the assassins are professionals and will go to their grave rather than offer information. Unless they let Doug at them.' This brought a grin to both the Brigadier and Mr. Reid. 'Don't think that that's going to happen, their loss. Returning to SO13, they have traffic police trying to pick up the hire car and hopefully the route it took as well as stops and diversions, you never know. We'll see.'

Rodney switched subject. 'What I want to do now is to concentrate on the future, full stop. MI5 and SIS have confirmed six names of interest, possible thugs stroke assassins in this country. I've increased the watcher teams from Simon so we can keep 24/7 surveillance on them all. Field commander is Saied, and the operations room coordinator is Laurie.' Rodney paused for the Brigadier and Mr. Reid to digest that information. Then he continued, 'My premise is that the KGB will send another team and they may or may not link up with one or more of their UK assets. In this context, I'm not keen to get these six men off the street just yet.'

Mr. Reid spoke and commented. 'Understood. If we have eyes on 24/7 the risk to us is not low but I would judge moderate.'

'I agree.' The Brigadier was supportive.

Rodney continued. 'Thank you. My next premise is that the KGB will send another team soon, let's say within the next few days. If we miss them on entry to the UK, just in case I've had a world with Commander Coveney, re Customs and Border Control. In that regard, I'm going to make the assumption that this team will be more cautious and will both settle itself into a safe house and contact a UK asset. After all, they have to find us to harm us.'

'Hmm, I see where you are coming from, Rodney. Is there anything else we can do?'

Mr. Reid said quietly, 'I can think of two things that we might consider. The first is Rodney has a chat with his neighbour. He has a good excuse to do that, even if it's using the ruse of asking her what she saw this morning. I'm happy to go along with you, say this evening?' He took a breath, got a nod. 'The other thing that may be worth a punt is if you, sir, have a chat with the Directors of the SIS and MI5 to see if they would get their teams to keep an eye on the declared assets that might be the sort of individuals that would get mixed up in this. They could be another point of contact for this team coming in. I do agree with the Major, it's a given that the KGB will want another go.'

Rodney grinned. 'Must say I half-intended to see Galena. Didn't know how, but with your support Doug, it's a good idea. But after Armand's performance I will let you off and take him as a minder, keep me under control so to say. Never know, she may let something slip.'

The Brigadier stroked his nose. 'Hmm. Think talking to the two Directors of the Secret Services is a good idea, Mr. Reid. I'll get on it after we have rattled the cages of our Defence industry.' He looked at his two officers. 'Anything else?'

'Just one thing, sir. Moving further down the track, if we can get to the point where we identify the enemy, then I would propose we channel them to a killing ground.'

Both Mr. Reid and the Brigadier stared at Rodney.

'Go on,' The Brigadier directed and added, 'Although I think I know what's coming.' There was a smile appearing on his face.

'Big ask, sir; how about your place?'

Chapter Seventy-Two

The Defence Contractors and Industry Chiefs

There was an air of expectancy in the Banker's room as Rodney and the Brigadier entered. The room was set out and flipcharts and files on desks were neatly arranged for the company. Coffee and snacks were on a side table. The chairs for the bosses of the company were set in three rows with five chairs in each. In the back row four chairs were set to the right for the Minister of Defence, Cabinet Secretary Sir Geoffrey, the Brigadier and Major Rodney Brown. For the American guests two chairs were set at the back of the room.

Some of the analysts sat glued to their computer screens, working away. Andrew and Pat were helping Colonel Jimmy put the finishing touches to the detail on the three flipcharts. The charts on their stands were slightly angled in a curve to face the audience. The whiteboards on the walls were covered in tables of figures, text boxes and circles joined by arrows mapping where there was a linkage. In a word, the whole place looked impressively professional.

The scene was set for what the Brigadier thought was going to be a very interesting afternoon.

'Well, John, are we ready?'

'Yes, I think so. We have really moved on in the last twenty-four to forty-eight hours. Andrew and Pat are lined up to greet and escort our guests in in around ten minutes.'

'Anything that I should know before I welcome them?'

'Well Brigadier, if you would just open the session with words to set the gravitas of their situation, I will then take over and demonstrate just how much money they owe the taxpayer.'

'Are we going to draw in even more money? As we've recovered the money, they're paying twice. Won't they twig that?' Rodney was slightly skeptical.

'Yes and no. We'll never recover 100%. Take for one instance the thousands of man hours these villains have used in the prosecution of the fraud. Hours which in many cases the taxpayer has funded. Whilst we are on the subject of poor practice, I am hoping that our guests will realise that if only their external auditors had drilled down into the accounts, the fraud would have been discovered years ago. Begs a question in itself, why didn't they? In these contexts, Defence Auditors have a case to answer to.'

'I think I get your drift John. I can buy that.' Rodney brightened. 'And I guess it would be immoral not to make the heads of sheds pay something for the way that they ran the businesses; a fine so to speak?'

The Brigadier was amused at the exchange between the two men. Now he felt he needed to get hold of some hooks for his opening address and said so.

'John, we only have a few minutes, can you show Sir Geoffrey and myself something I can hang my hat on when I address them?'

'Sure, come with me.' He led the Brigadier to the flipcharts and pointed out salient points of reference. Then he took him to the whiteboards and traced some of the links between the company men and the contracts etc. Finally, the Brigadier nodded, he had enough. 'Time for a quick drink then.' He called to Andrew and Pat. 'Time you two went to get our guests.'

In the lobby, fifteen men were signing in the visitors' ledger. Bustling, shouldering their way forward. Andrew swept his eyes over the group of men. He quickly mentally put each one into a category. CEO, MD. Technical. Legal. Commercial. He was spot on. He then rated them in terms of threat, who would bully, who would bluster and who would be pragmatic. His analytic skills in respect of reading people were rarely found wanting.

When they were all sorted, Andrew picked up an excitement and expectation. He was not surprised; it was not often that you were ordered without explanation into the heart of one of the Secret Services. Perhaps they thought that they were going to be let into secrets and get fat contracts. They were definitely going to be disappointed. Andrew looked at Pat and grinned. Pat had had the same thoughts. Pat whispered, 'Hope that we have a first aider on hand. Looking at this lot, some are a heartbeat away from a stroke.'

Andrew said with distaste, 'Fat cats to a man.'

When they were ready, Pat said, 'Follow me, please. We'll take the stairs.'

Andrew led the way, with Pat bringing up the rear.

When they got to the operating centre, Andrew opened the door and let the men in. He marched them in as they followed in quick step. No time to take anything in except the noise and busy people working at desks. They got more and more disorientated as they passed through the over-large main room and its hive of activity, then through the arch into the second room with the waiting finance team headed by the tall Brigadier Robinson, shadowed by another man just as tall, John Brown the infamous Banker.

They glanced around at the room and saw the taciturn Minister of Defence glowering at them. This was the first indication that all was not right.

'Please sit, gentlemen.' It was an order. The analysts fell silent, blanked their screens and left the room. Only Colonel Jimmy and Pat, apart from the Brigadier and the Banker, remained on the stage.

The men shuffled into the chairs. Notepads came out and pens were clicked.

The Banker, with his soft, commanding Irish accent, spoke to them. 'No notes, gentlemen.' Colonel Jimmy handed out information packs with a plain cover. 'Keep them closed. We will look at the contents of your packs when we tell you to open them. First, the Brigadier has a few words for you all.'

'Good afternoon. You may have no idea why you are here. Over the next few hours, it will become apparent and it is going to be a shock, so take a deep breath and listen in. You may have noticed a significant proportion of some of your key people didn't turn up for work today.' The men looked at each other, perplexed. 'That is because for up to twelve years fraud has been rife in your companies.' There was an audible gasp from the men and some, blustering about not going to listen to humbug, rose as though to depart. 'Sit down!' the Brigadier snapped. 'Behave yourselves.' Sir Geoffrey and the Minister allowed themselves a smile. 'My team will take you through the fraud, step by step if necessary. At the end of the day, it was taxpayers' money your employees stole. It was your auditors, internal and external, that failed to pick up the shenanigans. It was your systems that allowed these frauds to be prosecuted unchecked. Your company is culpable. It was your company that fed the coffers of the Russians.' He let that bombshell sink in. 'There is, however, a remedy! We will discuss that after the presentation and not before.' He smiled. 'In a moment I want you to grab yourselves tea or coffee, whichever is your poison, and a bun or two. Then settle down for an expensive afternoon and it will take a few hours. For those of you who feel unwell we will get a first aider for you. For those of you who may want to relieve themselves my officers will escort you to the facilities. Those of you who had mobile phones, they were handed in, were they not? If any of you have any Dictaphones or have forgotten to hand in a phone, give it to my officers now. Failure to do so now will constitute a breach of the Security Act and you will go to prison; you have my word on that. You will join the other people from your company who are languishing at Her Majesty's Pleasure as we speak.' The was a shuffling and the odd phone and several Dictaphones were produced, handed in and confiscated. 'Now, that was easy, wasn't it? Let me throw you a lifeline. As companies, you are too important to destroy; you are handling contracts and engineering vital to this country. Contracts are too far advanced to stop. Your companies have technology and skills that we cannot and we will not do without. Get your refreshments now, please.'

Andrew struggled to hold in a laugh, just. Pat scowled at him. The Brigadier had set the scene and he judged from watching the men totter to the refreshments table that they were shaken to the core. Not what they were expecting, that was for sure.

The men returned to their seats, drinks in one hand and balancing a plate of buns on the other. John Brown let them settle and then began.

'Gentlemen, we can cut to the chase and I can simply give you a bill for the money your people stole from the taxpayer over a ten to twelve-year period with supporting bank statements etc. The sums are substantial but they will not break the bank; or we can go through the detail company by company?'

The three CEOs looked at each other and a silent message went between them. The Banker smiled; he knew these 'grey suits' and the way they worked only too well. He got the answer that he expected. The CEO on the front row spoke.

'We would request a copy of the transactions and then a generic explanation from you on the suggested irregularities.'

'The transactions are in the files I gave to each of you. You can open them now. Turn to Annex A. At that annex you will see a simple table. Who paid in, from which contract or operation, the date, how much and the banks' details. That is the banks paying into the Soviets' offshore company banks. Take a look and when you are ready, I will talk about these frauds in a generic manner as requested.'

The groups studied the data and were visibly shaken by the sums involved. They took their time to read the Annex and the rest of the file. It was over half an hour later before they capitulated. The three companies stood and huddled together, then conferred and resumed their seats. The CEO on the front row seemed now to be the spokesman of the others. He stood and said, 'Our files show that a horrendous crime has been perpetrated against us. Undeniably, we as the principal officers of the company, and I speak for all, we have to carry the can, whichever way you cut it.'

'Good decision. Now, let me take you through the methods that your people employed but as importantly why they did it. Few of your team did what they did voluntarily and this will come out in due time. Many were victims just like you. I want you to understand this before you condemn them out of hand. Sure, there will be some that deserve to have the book thrown at them and this will happen, you have the Brigadier's word on that, but the innocents need your protection. Am I making myself clear?'

The Banker took the men through the routes, ways and links the fraud had been perpetrated and managed. Any sceptics that may have been having doubts by the end of the Banker's presentation were reluctant converts. 'There you have it, gentlemen. Do you have any questions?'

The CEO looked round at the others, and all just hung and shook their heads.

'No. What happens now?'

The Banker handed out bankers' drafts to the three CEOs. 'You need to sign these documents and the money you are paying back will be transferred to Customs and Excise today. The banks have been alerted and they are happy to carry out the transactions immediately. I remind you that you and your companies will leave this room without a blemish on your name in the context of current and future contracts with the Government or anyone else.

'Nor will a flag appear against you. If you have a concern about your shareholders, I wouldn't worry. So the dividend may be lower this year due to back taxes etc., and the pension funds may need to dig deep, but they will find nothing and the promise by you of a bumper year next year should do it. I would advise that you change your auditors for one that is known to drill down, not just sign off a presented set of figures and ensure that there is only one set of books in future. Toughen up your financial processes and checks. If you need help I can supply specialists to ensure you are compliant with best practice throughout the business.'

Whether it was the relief of getting off the hook or just an undefinable relief, the men laughed. To know that the business going forward was safe from censure was enough to allow them a feeling of freedom.

After they left, escorted out by Andrew and Pat, Sir Geoffrey wiped his brow with a handkerchief and asked, 'What does today's bag amount to, John?'.

'Well, for the duration of the fraud in the region of 7.5 billion sterling, payable immediately.'

Carol and Murphy were understandably blown away with the way the British had dealt with the companies. Carol said, 'John, Brigadier, Sir Geoffrey, I can't thank you enough for allowing Murphy and myself to sit in. A masterclass. I hope that when we get into this you will allow some of your team to be our guests and help us through?'

Sir Geoffrey replied, 'I am sure that the Prime Minister will want to help you all she can. Although the Brigadier and his team have only a few days more on this mission to tie up loose ends and entertain the Health Service to a presentation tomorrow. The Brigadier and his men are under a real threat from the KGB because of what they did. As you know they have already had one go and will try again at least once, that's their way. I'm sure that once that the threat is neutralized, Brigadier Robinson can have a meaningful conversation over help and support.'

'Thank you, Sir Geoffrey, that would be a great help. I hope that the country will know just what this team has done for them and others, not least the USA. Are we, by the way, any nearer understanding what our Treasury Department could expect from the money you seized off the Russians?'

Sir Jeffrey looked over to the Banker.

'Difficult to be exact. What the team is doing now is identifying the split country by country. I can say that our maths is now projecting a USA windfall of some 60 to 70 billion dollars over the twelve years.'

'Wow.' Murphy was pleased. 'Talk about the special relationship. Guess that's what it's all about!' This brought smiles and few laughs. The Minister had to grin, but underneath was embarrassed that the Americans had been present when a section of industry that he had tacit responsibility for had been caught out.

The Banker continued, 'There will be some deductions of course but I don't think it will dent the headline figure that much, a billion or two perhaps. Current exchange rate, that sort of thing.' He smiled.

Sir Geoffrey looked quizzically at the Banker.

'Really?'

'Oh yes, that's the way it is, but we'll do our best to mitigate any downside. My team have all agreed here that we'll be in a position to hand over in the next twenty-four hours or so a list, country by country, in the same format that we gave to the Defence companies today. That's all they'll need to sort out their end.' He paused. 'With some redaction in the context of UK companies and clearances we want to hand over the whole file over to the Americans, including our data, so they can be confident that they have the whole story.'

Murphy was thoughtful. 'It might also help to take some of the heat off the Brigadier's team if the Russians knew that it wasn't just the Brits that were after them.'

'Generous thought, Murphy. You may be right.' Sir Geoffrey was complimentary. 'If you will excuse me, I need to brief the PM and return to my other duties.' They shook hands with him and returned to discussing the way they would handle the next day. Buzzing in the heads of them all was that with the recovered money from the companies and the funds from the banks where the money had been lodged they were going to recoup some eight to ten billion for the taxpayer. Not, they thought, a bad outcome overall.

The Defence Minister was still there and looked up at the data boards. He was appalled and was going to call in the head of Defence Auditors for a dressing down. He felt Defence Auditors had let him and the country down and he was angry. He turned to the Banker.

'John, can you give me ten minutes? I need to call in the Defence Auditor heads and I need some more help to understand how they missed the obvious.'

'Of course, Minister, come with me. Colonel Jimmy, please join us.'

The Banker steered the Minister to the boards and files.

Chapter Seventy-Three

Galena Vorakova

Rodney decided that he would go and see Galena that evening. He was intrigued as much as wanting to know what Galena saw and what her thoughts were. He had last been in contact with her, apart from the meeting in the Golden Dragon with Polyakov, when he had arrested her when she was a Russian mafia boss running the KGB 'off-book' London operations.

Whilst nothing in life really shook or amazed him, he was still perplexed as to how after being expelled she'd reinvented herself as a declared Russian embassy asset in the form of a cultural attaché.

He grabbed a cup of tea and bun and left the others talking about finance. He called in on Graham and Freire and found Armand talking to them.

'I was just saying to Armand,' explained Graham, 'that I have plenty of room at my place and as Freire and her team were already staying, do you both want a bed for a night or three while your place is being sorted out?'

'Oh, that's a generous offer Graham, one that I would like to accept.' Rodney smiled but thought better of it. 'However, I could never forgive myself if we inadvertently led a KGB killer to your door.'

'If you're sure?'

'Yeah, sure. It's for the best. Another night in the hotel is not a punishment. An additional risk tonight is that I will be paying a visit to our Russian neighbour to see what she knows'.

Freire commented, 'Not impossible for us to bug her phones and rooms?' She looked at Rodney.

'One thing the Russians are very good at is screening their premises for bugs,' Rodney responded.

'Sure, accept that, but we do have a new suite of passive gismos that are not detectable.'

'Hmm, maybe after our visit when I see the lay of the land we can talk again, Freire.'

'OK, Boss.'

'Well, better get going and see Mr. Reid before I disappear.'

Rodney could see Mr. Reid looking over at him and waving him over. Mr. Reid watched Rodney stride towards him.

'Well, Major, how did it go this afternoon?'

'Good. Lots of money recovered for the taxpayer.'

'I don't expect that we'll get a refund,' Mr. Reid said gloomily.

Rodney laughed. 'Don't expect we will. I'm taking Armand with me to see Galena shortly but I wanted to touch base and ask if we were ready for tomorrow and if I could do anything?'

'We're good to go for tomorrow. Today's operation went well and we're close now. It's up to the authorities, police etc., to move the game forward.' He thumbed over his shoulder to Laurie, who was making himself comfortable in the operations area. He had set himself up with a table and on it a computer linked to the room's intranet and above his desk a large-scale map of London and another to the right of the whole UK. 'Once I've sorted this lot, tomorrow I'll help Laurie with some extra analysts and computer power, tracking of our teams and the enemy. I thought that you might want me and our lads here to support him. He has to sleep sometime and he's running the canteen too.'

'Fine with all that,' Rodney confirmed. He and Mr. Reid spent some time together, reviewing and mulling over the next phase in the context of the KGB. Mr. Reid liked the idea of setting a killing zone.

When they'd finished, Reid sent Rodney off. 'Right, Major. You and Armand get off and sort Galena. I'll look after Laurie and get him properly set up. I'll check with Christine and get her to make sure that the immigration boys are on the ball. We simply must get the intelligence on any KGB entering the UK. Don't be late, tomorrow is another big day for us.'

'No problem. Any chance that we could borrow one of the team to drive us over to my flat and get him to take us to the hotel after we see Galena?'

Reid looked round and tasked Lewis Jones.

'Right, off you go.'

Lewis pulled up outside the flat's entrance. Rodney and Armand quickly disembarked and walked to the reception area. Once inside, Rodney fended off the receptionist who like Rodney was an ex-soldier and was concerned. Rodney had to persuade him that all was well. What Rodney did find out was that was that his flat would be ready tomorrow early afternoon and he would be able to move back in.

'I suppose that the neighbours and others will have been trying to find out what happened?'

'You could say that again, Major. It was nonstop this morning with calls and people popping in to see me to find out what happened. They got short shrift, but I had to settle the occupants of our own flats down and they're as happy as they will ever be.'

'Well, thanks for that. Armand will be staying with me for a while; until any threat is over at least. What about the Russian lady in the flat below, how is she?'

'She's been out all day and just returned.'

'Good. I need to see her as she was on the street and I need to ask her a few questions.'

'Good luck with that then; she gave the police short shrift.' He chuckled. 'They held up their hands as soon as she showed her diplomatic credentials, but they weren't happy.'

'Well let's see if I can do any better.'

Rodney led Armand up the stairs and they stood outside Galena's flat door. Armand stood to one side. Rodney rang the bell and stood in front of the door's spy hole. After a few minutes Galena opened the door.

'I wondered when you'd get around to visiting me.' Galena saw Armand out of the corner of her eye. 'Just you, Major. Your minder needs to wait for you.'

Rodney nodded to Armand, who nodded back. Armand would wait outside the door and make sure that Rodney wasn't disturbed.

Galena led Rodney into her flat. It was certainly a model of what money can do with a decent interior decorator. Rodney was slightly disorientated as he had expected the flat to mirror his own, which it didn't.

'So, Rodney, what would you like to drink?' Galena indicated that Rodney should sit in one of the heavily upholstered chairs of the expensive three-piece suite.

'I would really like a strong black coffee. It's been a long day as you can imagine, not a lot of sleep. I really do feel strangely relaxed in your beautiful flat and this comfortable chair could have me asleep in a few minutes if I don't get some coffee down me. And I did want to ask you a few questions.'

Galena laughed. 'Coffee it is and for God's sake don't fall asleep here or I'll get sanctioned, having an English spy asleep in my apartment.' She moved well and Rodney appreciated her as a woman. Maybe it was because he was tired and the warmth of the room, but he found himself fancying her. Mentally he told himself to behave. This brought a smile to his face.

The smile did not go unnoticed by Galena, who set a cup down in front of Rodney and poured coffee from a cafetiera.

'Something amused you, Rodney?'

'Better that you don't know.'

'Come on Rodney, don't hold back.'

'Ha. I was just thinking in my tired head what an attractive woman you are, Galena.' He shook his head. 'I just feel - comfortable here. Crazy really. Sorry.'

'No no, no, I take that as a compliment. Thank you. So, ask your questions and then go and get some sleep.'

'I have only three questions.' Rodney sipped his coffee and felt the caffeine kick in. 'Were you aware of what was going down earlier this morning?'

'In a way, but not actually what was going to happen. Colonel Pushkin was incandescent when he found that you'd emptied his piggy bank. He was responsible for it, as you can imagine. But about his ill-advised attack, no, I knew nothing. I might add that the Ambassador is pretty fed up with him. He himself knew nothing of the hit.'

Rodney looked Galena in the eyes. He believed her.

'In your opinion, do you think that they'll try again? Will they alert you this time? Am I the only target do you think, or other members of my team?'

Galena took a big breath. 'What do you think, Rodney? Sure, they'll try again. Will I know about it this time? I really don't know. As for your team, maybe, but you're the one that's the cause of all the trouble.' She laughed. 'I think that Polyakov and Tsygankov see you as an errant child who is simply troublesome, more than an enemy.' She leant forward and stroked his cheek. 'Such a shame, Rodney that we are on opposite sides. By the way, we had a signal today that General Polyakov has been allowed to retire with a full pension and citations for loyal service. His deputy takes over and the Chairman is also changing. I will miss Polyakov, he is a gentleman, like you Rodney. Now, your third question please?'

Rodney blushed and he thought to himself that he was not having very gentlemanly thoughts a moment ago but he rallied and simply asked, 'Why are you here in my apartment block?'

'Now that is the sixty-million-dollar question. And the answer is that in the beginning it was to be an irritant to you after having me thrown out. Sort of thumbing my nose. But now, well, it's comfortable. More than convenient in a way and far enough away from the Embassy not to be bothered much by visitors, particularly some of my more obnoxious people that I have to work with day in, day out. So, unless you are going get them to throw me out, I want to stay.'

'No, please stay. When we're through this phase let's have a drink. I'd like to invite you to my pad. I am sure that we're old enough and ugly enough to keep business to one side.'

'Less of the old and ugly, young Rodney. I would like to have a drink with you and you can cook, Rodney. It's a deal.' Her Russian accent was softened.

Rodney finished his coffee and stood up. 'Until then Galena, stay safe, no more surprises please. By the way, the KGB Spetsnaz we wounded will live. No doubt someone from the Embassy will want to interview him as a Russian citizen and see the other one who was the driver, also Spetsnaz. I'm told that they're not talking, and the authorities are unlikely to ask Mr. Reid to open them up.' They both laughed.

Galena moved to him and kissed him on both cheeks. 'Off you go, Major. Stay out of trouble, if you can.'

He smiled at her. He knew that she was the consummate professional and deadly given a chance. For a lady in her middle fifties, she was still one of the most attractive women he had ever met. KGB she might be, but he didn't think of her as an enemy; he wasn't quite sure what he thought of her. Certainly, she would coldly organise his death if she was ordered to; the original Black Widow spider was his last thought. He leaned forward and kissed her lightly on both sides of her face.

'I'll say goodnight, Galena. Until the next time.'

Chapter Seventy-Four

The Health Service

Even though Rodney and Armand thought that they had arrived early in the operations room next morning, the team was already in full flow. Mr. Reid was, quietly for him, orchestrating the arrests of the targets.

The radio and telephone traffic was feverish. In the finance room the Banker, Colonel Jimmy, Pat and Andrew were preparing the boards and flipcharts that they would use to damn the Health Service Directors of the drug and equipment and supply organisation, real-estate, and clinical. Freire's men and Graham's administration team were both busy. Freire was monitoring the communication traffic and backing up GCHQ and the Metropolitan Police Control Centre. Graham's team was putting together portfolios for the Banker.

Laurie lolled in his chair, head nodding, over at the refreshment and drinks area. Clearly, he'd been up all night. Rodney made a mental note to get him support as soon as possible.

Rodney grabbed two teas and took them to Mr. Reid's area. Laurie stirred himself, followed the Major and made for a chair next to Mr. Reid where he slumped. He had got one or more of Freire's men to set him up three large monitors. One showed all the teams locations, another was focused on one of the teams with their location superimposed over a large-scale map of the area. The last screen, split to cover all the teams in play, was showing real time video of what the teams were seeing. A phone for each team was connected and sat in cradles in front of the screens.

Rodney handed Laurie and Reid a cup of tea and pulled up a chair.

'Looks as though you've got everything organised. Anything to report?'

Laurie warmed his hands on the mug of tea and nodded to a growing pile of log sheets.

'Not too much, but the intelligence is building. Did get a few meetings between a couple of the thugs but otherwise not a lot.

Importantly, no new faces from the Embassy or elsewhere contacted our targets, but it's early days, Boss.'

'Hmm. You're right of course, Laurie. Mr. Reid will give you support as soon as he has sorted today. In the interregnum I am going to get Christine from 5 and Miss Reid from 6 to sit with you.'

'That would be great, Boss, if you could.'

'Consider it done. Where is Jean Saied by the way?'

Laurie leaned forward and pointed to one of the flashing location dots on the screen. 'There he is, shacked up in the Somali Club. He's being looked after and has a room on the second floor with all mod cons. Let's just say he is a happy man.' Laurie winked at Rodney.

Rodney laughed. 'Incorrigible, both of you.' He pulled out his phone and called the two ladies that he wanted to come and support Laurie. He closed his phone down. 'They'll be here in half an hour to spell you. I suggest that until Mr. Reid moves in with his support, you and the ladies set your own schedule.'

'Will do,' said Laurie. He turned his attention back to his screens.

Rodney spun out of his chair and went and stood with Mr. Reid, waiting patiently until his deputy could free himself up.

'Morning, Major. Having trouble getting up these days?' Despite his cutting remark, Mr. Reid had a smile on his face. 'Not that I would want an officer getting too involved in the detail.' The men around him smirked or grinned.

'Right on all counts, Mr. R.' Both men laughed.' So, where are we now?'

'Well, Boss, all the teams are out collecting the targets. Most are now in the bag, just a few stragglers to pick up but for all intents and purposes the job is done. Thank goodness. Phew, got to admit it's been a trial. I've just got the presentation this afternoon and then it's back to what we do.' He paused. 'I overheard you standing up the two ladies for Laurie. Another hour or so and we will be there to back him as well. The Brigadier told me about your idea of getting anyone they put against us into a killing zone. I think that could be a plan. I did say to him that we need to start going home via his home if that's the place we decide on, and sooner rather than later so that the enemy gets used to us being at his place. He's going to talk to you later.'

'I look forward to seeing the Brigadier later then. We're going to need a day or two for tidying up and resetting the teams. I'd better go and see Graham and check that the transcripts from Neil Ashchurch don't have any surprises for us. I really do want to put this mission behind us and get on to sorting out the KGB hit teams. After that we'll see.' He turned to go over to Graham and stopped. 'Please get one of your team to get Laurie some breakfast, I would swear he is losing weight.'

Rodney flopped into a seat next to Graham.

'Good morning. What's the gossip?'

Graham groaned. 'Lots and lots but mainly we are helping John to get ready for this afternoon,' He paused. 'And then there is our guest, Mr. Ashchurch.'

'Go on.'

'Well, he's written a small book. I've had some of the team typing it up overnight. He's just about finished; another day he reckons. What he wanted was to see the typed version, so he's asked for a copy of the transcript to check through. I thought that I'd wait for you to give the nod. He claims that he has some additional titbits for your ears only.'

'Oh God, I was hoping we were at the end of this.'

'Well, if it helps your ulcers, we've been through the transcript to run it against what we know and there are no surprises. In fact, we have more intelligence than he's declared. Saying all that, he's put his in chronological order so it will help with the post mission report. And that report, I take it, you want me and my team to put together as soon as possible?'

'Thank you. That would be a huge weight off my shoulders. Now, how long before we have a couple of copies of the transcript?'

'Ready now, almost. I take it that you want to read it and take a copy to Mr. Ashchurch and hear what he has been hinting at?'

'In one.'

'Give me half an hour.'

'OK. I'll be with John.'

'OK. I'll bring it to you when the reports are ready.' Graham's attention was already diverted back to the papers on his desk.

'Hi, Rodney.'

'John. Just asking how far we are from being ready to present?'

'If you mean, will we be ready for the Health Service at two this afternoon, the answer is absolutely, so we will!'

Rodney didn't feel that he was completely up to speed on the Health Service frauds.

'Got some time to take me through what you've got?'

'Sure, walk with me and learn. The first thing to note is that what we found could have been exposed years ago by the Health Service's own audit and compliance teams, of whom there are many. They just aren't joined up. It's the same old story and quite frankly it drives me crazy. It's simply that the right hand doesn't know what the left hand is doing. Classic breeding ground for frauds.

'And because some clever dick decided wouldn't it be a great thing to mix some private health services with public health services…' He took a deep breath. 'The result is that all the possible different frauds that could be perpetrated were in both private and public sectors, albeit that they are subtly different in each case. So, the whole thing is magnified. What a scam this has been and at the taxpayers' expense. Do you know, Rodney, of all the frauds we have dealt with this one has really got to me. Just how many lives could have been saved for a few billion or how many nurses and doctors could we have employed.' He was saddened for a moment. He shook himself. 'Right, follow me for a whistlestop tour of the evidence. By the way, if you see me getting too heavy this afternoon, please raise a hand and I will know that I'm getting near to crossing the line.'

Chapter Seventy-Five

Neil Ashchurch

Graham, as he had promised, found Rodney in conversation with the Banker and Colonel Jimmy. Graham joined the three men and passed two bound copies of Neil Ashchurch's confession. Rodney thanked him and flicked through the pages.

'Quite a weighty document.'

The other men crowded round Rodney and scrutinised the document.

'Well,' remarked John Brown 'I hope that there's nothing here that contradicts what we're doing.'

'We've checked against all the stuff that we have and we can't find any contradictions.' Graham answered. 'But we're all open to any input from your team. Although I am pretty confident that we captured it all. I'll get a few copies to you, John, later today if that would be helpful to you?'

'We'd appreciate that, before one if possible.' Graham gave a thumbs up and left them to finish off.

After another ten minutes Rodney had seen what he wanted to so thanked John. 'For my part I need to go and read this confession before I see Ashchurch.' Rodney excused himself and set off. He went down to the cellars and with the permission of the guards found himself an empty cell to sit by himself and quietly read through the Ashchurch writings. He spent a good half-hour concentrating on the paper. It was really well put together and it was the first time he felt that he had a full understanding of the schemes. Frighteningly simple in the prosecution of the frauds but brilliant in its conception. Rodney was not surprised as he closed the cover of his file that the fraud had taken someone as clever and an anorak like Colonel Jimmy to bust the whole scheme into the open.

Before Rodney went to see Ashchurch he had a word with the guards. He wanted the interview covertly recorded, audio and video, but no telltale lights on the cameras etc. With a new tape which he would collect when he left.

'I want you to set up the kit, get it running, check it's recording and then disappear. I think that it would be better for your careers if you didn't know what Ashchurch was telling me. Are you OK with that?'

'If you feel, Major, that it's that important, then we will comply with your request.' The senior Officer of the guard team made it clear that he was doing Rodney a favour. 'But I will need you to write a short note concerning your request and to sign it off, so that we're covered. I hope that you understand, Major.'

'Absolutely fine. Scribble something in your log and I'll sign it when I leave Ashchurch.'

'Good, give us three minutes to set up the recording before you start in on the serious stuff.'

'OK, no problem.' Rodney saluted the chief. He thought that they liked that as the guards were mainly ex-military.

He walked down the corridor, took a deep breath and entered the room of his prisoner.

'Morning, sleep well?'

'Not bad and I want to compliment your cooks on the food, it is quite excellent. I see that you have what I assume is my report so far?' Ashchurch moved to the chair on his side of the cell.

Rodney sat down opposite him. 'I have a copy for you to study to see if you want any changes.'

'Well, well impressed that they could produce this book so quickly.,' He flicked through the 'book', as he called it. 'Hmm, your staff must have worked all night to get this, what, 150 pages, ready for me today. They say that Agatha Christie once wrote one of her books in three days. Well, hers was fiction so she needed time to think and create whereas I could just dash the information down on the pages. Still, I think that your staff did an amazing job in the time. Got to be more motivated than any staff I had, except of course our Colonel Jimmy. Is he still helping you?'

Rodney didn't answer his question and Ashchurch really didn't expect Rodney to answer any of his asides and throwaway questions. Never give information to anyone who doesn't need it. Instead, he replied, 'Are you generally in good health? I could get our doctor to see you if you need anything?'

'I am fine, isolated from the germs of the proletariat, the great unwashed. Good food, stable temperature. If only there was a view of a beach and surf I'd happily stay longer.'Ashchurch laughed. 'Still, like to get out sometime.'

'Hmm…' Rodney looked at his watch. Five minutes gone, 'You wanted to talk about people that you felt that you could not put to paper?'

Ashchurch looked at the camera – there was no light on it. 'We are not observed?' For the first time Rodney noticed a fear in the man who sat, elbows on the desk, with the book nestled in his forearms. Rodney shook his head.

'What you have to understand, Major, and my confession bears this out, is that we were able to operate in a bubble. So far so good, as far as it went. The problem was that our KGB masters and various Cultural Attachés wanted us to fund the spies or sympathisers. You can imagine that this was an additional difficulty, especially if it had to be cash.'

'I can see that that might be troublesome. So, what did you do and who were these men and women who wanted you to feed these individuals?'

Ashchurch rubbed his nose. 'Well, the first thing I set up was a UK bank account. And I, let's say, skimmed our takings from the frauds into a slush fund. I set this up with the full authority of a senior Attaché. He's dead now so there's no one who knows that the fund even exists. I built it up and up and it's now the pension fund for several of the key players in the fraud. They don't know this, so nothing is lost to them.'

'I take it,' Rodney said, 'that it would be difficult to discover from the data we have? I would guess that there is a substantial amount of money lodged?'

'Everything is relative but there is probably closing ten to twelve million on deposit and another million in an immediate access account.' Ashchurch spun Rodney's copy of his book round and wrote out the sort codes and account numbers.

Rodney thanked him. In his mind he was pretty sure that Ashchurch had another account for himself alone, but he wasn't going to push it. He wanted the names more than the money.

'You asked me about names. Let's break it into two shall we, Russians and our people. For the Russians that's easy as there is little that can be done about it. The head of the Cultural Attachés were always my immediate controllers. Of the current batch at the Embassy, Galena, who you know, is the boots on the ground. She is dangerous, Major, and commands a group of miserable thugs. Mostly Eastern European but there are at least one if not two men in the Embassy who she can call on if extra muscle is needed. They are apparently security men but they are Spetsnaz.'

'Any idea how many thugs we're talking about?'

'Well, since you lifted my two enforcers there are probably still five or six, no, six out there and they have no respect for the person.'

Rodney was pleased that at least they may have pegged the thugs and that they were under surveillance by the Somalians.

'How about these Brits?'

'Ah yes, the Brits, as you put it. You must understand that I needed the occasional politician in my pocket. Let's say, for example, to ensure that a contract went to the right company for instance. Then again, a government minister or two to look the other way. Then there was the odd Director of a quango.

'The problem with these people is that if they weren't either ideologically motivated to help us or compromised then they were difficult to control. Money was the only option. These money-grabbing individuals were a major problem; they would keep coming to the honey pot for top-ups. If we couldn't stop them with honey traps and coercion, the threat of blackmail or worse, well...' Ashchurch shook his head from side to side. 'The Russians neutralised them. The only way I knew that they'd been removed was that I never heard from them again.'

'How on earth did you manage to run this massive organisation and still do your Treasury work?'

'Not a problem. The systems were robust, honed over hundreds of years. Just try changing the procedures and processes, no chance. And the frauds, once set up, looked after themselves so apart from having to transfer money and keep the whole thing in shape it was easy when you have good lieutenants to work for you. Sad to say they are all in the bag now.'

Rodney was sure that Ashchurch was holding back.

'Bit tidy, all this. Are all your lieutenants in the bag?'

Ashchurch smiled. 'I know what you are thinking Major, but when you get to the bank accounts I gave you you'll have the whole picture. I made sure that when I withdrew funds or paid by transfer the name of the person, their title and place of work for each and every withdrawal was recorded. In your possession you now have all the information you need – foot soldiers and supporting players.'

'Nothing else I should know?'

'You have it all.'

Except, Rodney thought, *your well-concealed nest egg*. He shrugged, he had enough and had fulfilled his mission. 'Well, thank you. Please go through your book as you called it. I will get someone to collect the changes if any from you tomorrow afternoon.' He paused. 'I need to tell you how I think your future will pan out from now on.' He breathed in and let his breath whistle through his teeth. 'The data from the bank will go to the Director General of MI5 via my Boss with my recommendations. My recommendations will be, and they will be acted on, that you are debriefed by MI5 and the Fraud Squad Superintendent Freddie Howelle together. Because of the security implications re some of the men in the fraud it means that MI5 have to be involved. That you become a Ward of the State with an MI5 guardian angel who will manage your freedom. That will mean you will be able to live a near normal life with your family, including the choice to live in the European family of nations or the States if they will have you. I will recommend that you are given a new identity for the sake of your family. More than that I cannot do. I don't know if we will meet again but your further jottings in the next few days will come to me and I would expect all the names to be in this final document if you have left any out so far. I will then seek in person your freedom package with my Boss and the director of MI5 who I know.'

Without another word Rodney got up and waved goodbye as he left the room.

Ashchurch sat for a moment. He wished the Major had thanked him for all the information, but what could you expect, he was a traitor and criminal. If it went the way the Major had outlined, he would be happy enough, he had a fund that was well hidden, certainly enough for a couple of his lifetimes. He went back to his writing with a will. He would ensure that nothing was left out. Sooner done, the sooner he would get through any debrief and gain his freedom.

The guards were waiting for Rodney as he left Ashchurch.

'Everything work out OK, Major?'

Rodney nodded at the chief warden. The man could have been a bouncer in any provincial hot spot.

'Think so, we'll see. I hope to be handing him over to an MI5 handler by the way. Could be as early as tomorrow, maybe the day after but soon. Can I get the recording on my way out?'

'Sure, follow me.'

After he left the cellars Rodney went straight to the Brigadier's office, he knocked and went in as soon as he heard the Brigadier call out.

'Morning, sir, got a few minutes?'

Brigadier knew that if Rodney had made the effort to come and see him it would be important.

'Take your time, I'm free until we go and sort out the Health Service.'

'Good. It won't take long.' Rodney took Robinson carefully through his meeting with Ashchurch, and when he'd finished, he put forward his proposal. 'I believe that as soon as he stops scribbling it's time to hand him over to MI5 and Freddie. Having said that, I believe that we already have most if not all of what we're going to get. They should chase down these bank accounts and the men and officials that have benefited from them. After all, if there are men of ministerial rank, it's within MI5 and their master the Home Secretary's remit to handle any sanctions. And if they are going to relocate Ashchurch and his family for favours rendered, then MI5 need him to verify the data they get.'

The Brigadier was persuaded and had already been thinking that it was time to cut loose from this mission.

'You're right, of course Rodney. It's time we let go. I think that we've done more than we were asked. I'll go and see the DG and handover this tape and bank details. I'll take that draft book as well. Between you and me, do you think that Ashchurch has given up all his secrets?'

'Truthfully, in the context of the frauds probably as much as we will get from him or that he can remember. MI5 may finesse something, but I think that we have the vast majority of what's available. As for the rest, there may be some small change in the way of a nest egg for himself and his family, I think that's quite likely. He's a clever man and I couldn't see him not making provision for if the whole scheme fell apart. But I don't see that it's in our interests to spend more time on the man than we already have. I think that we need to move on, I really do.'

Robinson thought over what his deputy had told him. 'Happen you're right, Rodney, and anyway, it's MI5's problem as you say. Now, I am glad you called in; Sir Geoffrey is inviting the Health Minister to the presentation this afternoon. Think on balance that it's a good move and anyway the PM has sanctioned it. By the way, she's over the moon with us and the American involvement, she sees that as a big bonus. Look, you brief the team about our ministerial level guest. I'll go and see the DG.'

With that he scooped up the recording and details of the bank information along with Rodney's copy of the Ashchurch draft chronicle.

'See you in the ops room in half an hour or so. Hope that Laurie has some good food on offer, I'm hungry.'

Chapter Seventy-Six

The Final Fraud

There was an air of expectancy in the room when Rodney got back. The team knew that they were on the final run. Even so, over at Mr. Reid's team area an operation to monitor the targets was underway and a quiet purposeful atmosphere pervaded the space. Rodney saw Mr. Reid look over and beckon him.

'Hi team, any update?' Rodney found a chair next to Mr. Reid. Mr. Reid had set a couple of chairs behind the team watching and working the screens and phones. Some new screens had arrived since Rodney had been there earlier in the day and all were being monitored.

'Where we are – we 've finished with the pickup of the targets and formally handed over to Special Branch and the Fraud Squad, so we're out of the mission now unless you tell me differently. As for our thugs, well, it's just getting interesting. A few of them met up in a Turkish cafe off the Portobello Road. We're getting our first picture of them at work and it looks as though one of the targets is a leader of some sort, name of Alexander Ivanov. That leader Alexander met earlier with a man from the Russian Embassy, an attaché called Ivan Servo who is either KGB or Spetsnaz. Don't think it matters much which he is, he'll be dangerous by definition. Could be that they're on the move. Let's see what other contacts are made as the day goes on. There are a couple of things that I want to run by you. Firstly, I think that we need to begin to visit the Brigadier's home on our way home and I think we need to begin to stay in his outhouses soon as well, otherwise we're not going to draw this lot in, if in fact they do form part of the hit squad or are supporting any external force that number 2 Bolshaya Lubyanka sends against us.' He pointed to the screen. 'Secondly, I need to formally set up a twenty-four-hour watch for these desks. We can do days, but I'll need another couple of men to support Laurie overnight. I thought of Pat for a start?'

Rodney wasn't unhappy with Reid's proposal, but something was nagging at him.

'Hmm, Pat would be ideal. As for moving the centre of gravity to the Brigadier's estate, I'm happy if you have a word with him. You will, I know, have already thought about the risk of an ambush going to and from the estate. It's not ideal and I'm increasingly concerned about collateral damage to the Brig's house.' That, he realized, was what was worrying him.

Mr. Reid ground his teeth. 'I'm working on it. If we continue to track them then we shouldn't be surprised but I intend to roll in the Somalis and Jean Saied. I'm envisaging an outer cordon, sort of long stop and ambush disrupters. Give me the rest of the day and I'll get back to you.'

'Sounds good. Where's Laurie? The Old Man wants feeding in about half an hour.'

'He's sorting lunch and then I want him to crash for a few hours.'

'Agreed,' Rodney stood. 'I'd better go and give Pat the good news. He'll kick back, you know that.'

'Tell him that I want my best men on the screens and comms, any fool can fire a gun.'

'Do my best.'

Laurie looked even more knocked out than when Rodney had seen him earlier but he was valiantly soldiering on with a couple of ladies from the canteen. The smell of the food drew Rodney.

'Hello people. Looks and smells amazing, just what this old soldier needs.'

Laurie looked up tiredly. 'Hi, Rodney. Just in time.'

'Just in time to relieve you I think, before you fall over.' Rodney made it plain that it was time for Laurie to get his head down. The canteen ladies looked sympathetically at Laurie.

'You tell him, Major, it's time to stop.' The older of the ladies, Mora, was forceful. She bustled about, stacked a plate of food while her companion poured a mug of tea. 'Now, Laurie, away with you. The Major and us will sort this.' Laurie, tired as he was, gave a wan smile, accepted the plate of food and mug and shuffled away.

'Any chance that you ladies could stay for an hour or two? The boss is coming down to eat shortly; it would be a great help.'

'What, that lovely Brigadier Robinson? Of course, love. Now, what do you want to eat?'

'What do we have?'

'You choose, Laurie always orders a variety from the main menu for lunch times. How about a Singapore curry and some fried rice?'

'Yes please, great!'

The curry was so good that Rodney had a second portion and whilst he was helping himself the Brigadier joined him.

'Hi, Rodney. That looks good but I think that I might get the sack if I breathe curry fumes all over the Minister. Pork cutlets look good.'

They shared lunch together on the conference table. When Rodney asked how it went with the DG, Robinson laughed.

'He practically tore my hand off. I fancy that he's a bit jealous and bruised because of the money we recovered. I think that the opportunity to get his hands on the bank accounts and some money for his funds was irresistible. The chance of taking over control compulsive and the chance of having such a high-profile traitor as a ward of MI5 irresistible. A masterful stroke, Rodney, getting them to take on the detail work. We're officially out of it now. DG may attend this afternoon to see for himself what's what.'

Mr. Reid joined them and put his plans to them both about moving into the Brigadier's estate. The plan was simple and all agreed they would execute it that night. Rodney was still concerned about using the Brigadier's estate; he argued that they should find another solution, even though he had initially suggested the location.

They ate their meals in companionable silence until it was time to go to the finance room and meet the team.

'Timing's perfect.' The Banker welcomed them. 'We're all ready and Pat and Andrew have just gone down to collect the Minister and the Health chiefs.'

Robinson looked around the room; it was impressive. The walls were covered in the detail of the scams. Linking ribbons plotted routes from fraud to fraud and the flipcharts stood like sentries ready to be exposed. The chairs had been set out for the three Health chiefs and the Minister. Behind the targets chairs were chairs for the Brigadier, the Cabinet Secretary and Rodney, plus a few more. As on the previous day, a table was set with refreshments and snacks. 'All very welcoming. Aren't they in for a disappointment?' Rodney had a little smile to himself. It didn't go unnoticed.

'I do believe that you're enjoying this,' the Banker gently chided him.

'Could be. I'm only a few days away from resuming my convalescence on a beach in Cornwall.' Rodney had been thinking more and more over the last few days of getting back to his beach. He had tried to push it to the back of his mind but it stubbornly refused to go there. He was a little disappointed when the boss replied.

'Perhaps; dream on, Major,' the Brigadier said dryly. 'We shall see.'

Andrew and Pat arrived with their train of Health Service chiefs, with the Minister trailing behind. The Banker showed them to their seats and the Brigadier took central stage to give the opening words.

Robinson eyed the men in front of him. It seemed to him that their attitude was poor and from the body language they displayed, they were there under sufferance. Nevertheless, he acknowledged to himself, they were busy people. They were at the top of their game and at the pinnacle of their professions. Probably not used to taking orders or being criticised. Given all that, the buck stopped with them and they were being paid well to manage the NHS so he would shock them and get buy-in early.

'Good afternoon, gentlemen. I will get straight to the point. You are here to hear about fraud that is rife in your businesses.' There was an audible intake of breath from the men. 'I will also point out that whatever you hear today not directly related to your work area is bound by the Official Secrets Act and I will personally ensure you end up in the land of striped sunshine if you breach the Act in anyway. Do I make myself clear? Minister?'

He got a nod from the Minister and held the gaze of the others until they nodded too.

'Good, let's begin. My staff will take you through the scams and the cost to you for not policing your areas properly.' Like others before them, they pushed back, turning to each other, wanting to protest. They didn't get a chance as Robinson went on, 'You will have ample time to study the evidence which will be presented to you by Mr. Brown,' He paused. 'You can take little comfort that others are in the same position as you. Two more points before I hand over. First, this is a KGB-driven scam. Yes, Russian meddling in our affairs. Second, you will have noticed that several of your key staff and others are not at work today. That is because they have been arrested and are under lock and key. They are being interviewed by the Fraud Squad. In this context, I want you to be aware that some are victims who have been entrapped in some way. Others are simple chancers and villains. In closing, I want you to know about outcomes for others we have recently investigated in the construction and defence industries. Where we have discovered fraud we have both retrieved the money from Russian bank accounts and fined the companies the same amount as was stolen. In your case you will not be fined as it would be taxpayers' money that we would rip out of the system. And, positively, whatever money we have drawn back for the Russians who have been robbing you blind will go back to the Minister to be reallocated. This will be several billions in sterling.'

Robinson looked directly at the Minister. As he raised his eyes, he saw for the first time that the DGs of M15 and the SIS had arrived and sat quietly with the Cabinet Secretary, Major Brown and Mr. Reid. He gave a slight nod of acknowledgement and was secretly pleased that the DGs had come to see the fun and his team in action.

He went on, 'I advise, Minister, that you use the money wisely and invest at least some into anti-fraud and good governance measures. I think that as the afternoon develops you will begin to think that a taskforce is the answer. I wouldn't like to think in a years' time we will meet again for the same reason as today. We have some files to give you for your area of the business for you to take away. Everything that you need will be in the file and Mr. Brown will be on hand to offer you any advice and help after the meeting and for a week or two after that. You may not record or take notes in this meeting. Please hand over now any recording device you may have on your person, or any mobile phones etc. Failure to do so will result in your immediate arrest. Now.,' He smiled as two of the NHS chiefs offered up Dictaphones. He took them and handed them over to Pat, who would check them and scrub any recording so far. Then he smiled. 'Grab yourselves some refreshments and drinks and then settle down while my staff take you through the evidence.'

It took a little while for the room to settle as the Chiefs and the Minister conferred and then grabbed what little comfort from each other that they could. Once the room was silent again, John Brown stood in front of the gathering and began.

'Let me set the scene. We are focused implicitly on the KGB fraud schemes but I would be doing you a disservice if I didn't at least paint a picture of fraud in your area. The frauds are further compounded by the decision to mix public health and the private health service in some areas of your operations.

'Bad move, as you will see. In the public health service, there are generally half a dozen or so corruption scams generic to the sector.'

He held up his hands and counted them off on his fingers to emphasis the points. 'Bribery, local normally but not aways, informal payments, diverting and theft of material, pure embezzlement simple or complex, deliberate or informal waste, finally absenteeism while staff are still drawing salary, and in some cases organised individuals and teams working for others i.e., the private sector.' John had them nodding and ticking off the list in their minds. 'In the private sector it is slightly different. And mentally I expect you, with your long experience, to make a linkage where the run list of five or so private medicine frauds could with ease cross over with the public sector. Well, it does as the evidence will show. Think kickbacks to healthcare professionals. So, for the simple example that I alluded to, when your staff are absent, absent because they are working a shift offering a service to the private sector and are getting paid twice. Or stores, equipment and material being diverted and used in the private sector from your resources paid for by the taxpayer. Think on that. Where you use the private sector to help you, are all the claims fair and true? Or are they in some cases fraudulent, is there overcharging and inflation of claims? Is there research being publicly funded that is both unethical and unfounded? Is there waste between the two sectors that is driven by fraud? What about the case of deliberately buying in medicines and equipment that is near its sell-by date, obsolescent machines, so no spares are available? Let me take you back a step to buildings, major refurbishments, funding by the private sector and the buying of assets and leasing back. What a woefully miserable story we have to tell you. Have you been asleep? Too tied up in the detail of the coffee fund? Gentlemen, wake up. Are we frustrated and angry at what we unearthed in a few days of digging? You bet.'

Rodney held up his hand, the agreed signal for John to calm it down a bit. John nodded but he was seething inside. He didn't think that he was alone. The Minister's face had reddened, and the Health Chiefs' faces were ashen.

John Brown took the files offered to him by Colonel Jimmy and handed them out to the three Chiefs with a compendium of all the files for the Minister and Sir Geoffrey, Robinson, the DGs and Rodney. Rodney passed his file to Mr. Reid to get a heads up.

'Don't open the files yet. You know that fraud exists in business. We all do, but the KGB have seamlessly exploited all of the routes that I've outlined. Worse, the blending of private and public service has given them a perfect opportunity to multiply the ways they have been defrauding the NHS. May I warn you that they have been undermining the very fabric of the Health Service. The Russians, the KGB, sow confusion and moral-sapping disillusionment at every twist and turn they can. They have fingers into the unions. They are past masters of deception, disinformation and misdirection. You,' he pointed to the Minister and the three men, 'are going to get a masterclass in the methods they use and how they actually did it. I remind you once more that this is all about the Russian scams and I don't want you to in any way take from this briefing that this is all there is. False hope there, I am afraid, that nothing else is going on outside of the KGB attack. Thieves abound in every business and statistically with the large workforce you employ you will have thousands of your staff involved in minor and major fraud activities either by omission or deliberate act.' John Brown paused; he needed them to absorb the magnitude of the problem.

'Before we get into the minutiae of your business there are other matters you need to consider. Bear this in mind as we go into the detail. Writ large, we have found abuse of funding. Critical or high-cost medicines diverted to others, example, public to private and or third parties ex-UK. Certainly, corruption of officials. Accountancy fog and official and unofficial bookkeeping. In a word, more than one set of accounts. Double billing etc. There are one or two cases of the NHS buying in drugs, prohibitively expensive drugs which are being replaced by cheap counterfeit medicines and the drugs the NHS had paid a king's ransom for are being sold on to the private sector or even to other countries. These frauds kill people. It is expected that you will go after and recover money from private hospitals and private health at large where they have defrauded the taxpayer and used our money. Building material and maintenance over-charging and every trick of the trade to scam which is found in the building industry is replicated in your property divisions.'

He pointed to the fat files in the men's white-knuckled hands. He had shaken them to the core. 'Open your files. I am going to give you ten minutes to read through them and then I will allocate you individually to one of my team who will take you through your part of the business and the frauds that have been perpetrated on you. Then we will reconvene in two hours for a wash up. Now, refresh your drinks.'

Mr. Reid got a nod from Rodney and they got up, excusing themselves to the Brigadier, Sir Geoffrey and the two DGs. Rodney needed to stretch his legs. He winked at the Americans as he passed them. They had been shocked, that was for sure.

He would wander back later as the detailed evidence was presented to each of the chiefs and the Minister. As he left the room, he noticed that the two Americans who had joined in the presentation had left their seats and moved to catch up with him. Carol and Murphy mobbed him.

'Hi Rodney, got a minute?' It was Carol, dressed in typical solicitors' black garb – black skirt and black jacket with a white blouse. All very expensive, Rodney was sure. Murphy had the sort of standard FBI Suit that would disguise a shoulder holster and pistol.

'Sure, how are you guys?' Rodney could not decide if he was irritated or relieved to have a diversion.

'Another masterclass from your team. God, we are impressed. Murphy and I are off now, think we may outstay our welcome with all your guests if we hang around.'

'Hmm; you might be correct in that assumption. Come and have a coffee with me at the conference table, I think that we need to talk about the future.'

After they had grabbed coffees and a few biscuits from Laurie's food stall they sat down with Rodney.

Carol straightened her skirt and jacket. 'Ok, shoot. What's on your mind?'

'I just wanted to tell you where I think we are, leaving out the money that will filter through fairly soon now. I've asked John Brown to put our portion of the recovered money to one side and to sign over the rest to you. How you distribute it back to the countries affected is up to you, backed up of course by the data that we've already given you and will add to.' He sipped his coffee and made a face. 'Not the greatest brew. Anyway, before I move on, I need to have some idea about what you're doing to move on your villains and the other governments. Are you talking to them yet for instance?'

Carol took out her Filofax and skipped to the tab behind which she had her notes. 'Our director has spoken to his counterparts in all the countries, and he has convened a meeting with them all later this week in Paris. Do you think that Brigadier Robinson would attend if we invited him?' She paused. 'Our director is flying in tomorrow and there is a dinner tomorrow night. Just him, us and the Ambassador. We'll invite Brigadier Robinson as he might like to attend. Sort of a heads-up dinner. Then I guess that your Boss could fly out in the Director's plane with the Ambassador to Paris and back. Good idea?'

'It's certainly a plan. You need to catch the Brigadier this afternoon and ask him. I think that it's a very good idea, but it's not my shout.'

'Talk to us about how you see the immediate future, Rodney.'

'First, as far as this fraud matter goes, we handed over to MI5 and the police today. The health presentation was the last of it for us. Sure, John Brown, Colonel Jimmy and the two gurus and I guess the analysts are going to be needed for a time to close it all out and, as promised, to support you. I think that you need to get around the table with John Brown and work out how that will work. But my team has to move on.'

'What do you mean, move on?' Murphy sat up straight and asked.

'You're aware now that I got attacked?' He didn't really want to talk about it and the rule was to only tell what was absolutely necessary to get the job done. First rule, need to know. Did they need to know? Not really, but he would be gentle and he owed Murphy. 'I am certainly a target and we're convinced that they'll try again. Not just me but in all likelihood other members of the team too. They have this KGB man, Colonel Pushkin, and he hates our guts so they will come for me again. That's what I mean, we have to move on to get ourselves in a position to hit them hard so that they'll realise that the risk benefit analysis is too great for them to pursue us any further.'

Carol looked for a moment at Murphy. Murphy nodded to Carol.

'I can tell you that our ears tell us that Pushkin is not long for the position he holds. Just as well for you that he listens to the advisor Serge Karaganov, who believes that the way to win a fight in Russia is to never give in and to escalate the conflict. But our ears also tell us that Chubias, an ace organiser with an iron will, wants Pushkin on his team. Seems that Pushkin isn't being blamed too much for the loss of money and Polyakov has resigned, so you might be lucky as they'll just have too much on their plate with the potential breakup of the Soviet Union to worry about you. Fingers crossed.'

Rodney grinned. 'Sometimes when you're zeroed in on a mission it's difficult to see the larger picture. Thanks for that information. In the meantime, we'll handle the immediate threat.'

'I am sure that you'll do that very well, Rodney.' Carol stood, drank the dregs of her coffee. 'Right, Major, see you around. I'll go and have a word with your boss. Can you entertain Murphy for half an hour?'

'No problem. Murphy, come and have a look at our surveillance on the targets. Carol, could you ask Pat to come and see me?' He got a nod.

PART FOUR

Chapter Seventy-Seven

Moscow

'Let me get this straight. You still haven't recovered the money and you don't believe that it can retrieved? You still haven't found who, if anyone, accessed the bank accounts? The bankers are not interested in making up the funds that they transferred out without even referring to the account holders despite the size of the withdrawal. Very careless of them. And you want to mount another attack on Major Brown, who you blame for the situation. Do you have any proof?'

Pushkin was unfazed, but he was angry and his fists were balled tightly, skin taut, knuckles white. Typical of the man, he showed no emotion, which rankled with the General. When Pushkin responded it was calm and his reply measured.

'Taking Major Brown first, clearly with his team's action of rolling up the agents that have been built up over a dozen years he couldn't have done it without information on all of our agents. The damage is terminal. We need to move on and develop or reinforce another way of damaging Europe economically.'

'You say Europe, why not just England?'

'Because, General, we can't be sure that they don't have the information on all our similar schemes in the other countries. Certainly, the file on other countries was also accessed.'

Shabarshin nodded; it made sense what Pushkin was laying out.

'Assume that's the case. I take it that the money that was taken included earnings from all countries?'

'Yes, it does.'

'I think then on balance that we cut our losses and close the section down and use the manpower to change to an operation which is less risky but nevertheless damaging to the Europeans. Do you have any bright ideas at this stage?'

'I do have a germ of an idea. I don't have all the answers yet but it involves making Europe dependent on Russian oil and gas until they are so committed that they can't do without our energy.'

General Shabarshin laughed. 'Like it. I was going to tell you to forget Major Brown, it's becoming a diminishing return on effort. But in view of your brilliant idea, I'll allow one more attempt but that's it, Pushkin. After that it's over. Agreed?'

'Yes, General, thank you.'

'Have you chosen your team to attack Major Brown?'

'Indeed. Servo and Carla because they have been to the UK and know their way around. Supported by Dimitri Soros and Boris Bobkov. Abraham Karpickkov and Ivan Servo, who are our declared attachés in London and both KGB, will support them. And we have men off the books to back them up.'

'Good, if not overkill. Now, close down the fraud scheme immediately. Sort out Major Brown – or not. Come and see me next week with some flesh on the bones about your idea.'

Chapter Seventy-Eight

Revision

Rodney sprawled, relaxed, in the chair next to Mr. Reid mesmerised by the screens showing the targets. He was thinking about options and it showed.

'OK, Major, what are you thinking?' Mr. Reid dreaded what was coming.

'I don't know, Doug. I thought that getting the targets into a killing zone was a sound idea, but I'm worried that we're leading them into the Brigadier's house and estates. I don't think that he'll appreciate his house, outbuildings etc., being decorated with bullet holes or worse. Lady Robinson would disown us.'

Reid grunted. 'I've been thinking about that, too. I was wondering what Mrs. Reid would do to me if she came home and found that I'd offered our house up as a target and it got shot up. I still think that getting them to a killing zone is an option, we just need to find another location.'

'Needs to be isolated, near London, easy commute, defendable. A bit of land, distant neighbours.'

'Stay here with the team,' Mr. Reid ordered, 'and keep them at it. I'll have a word with the MI5 quartermaster re a safe house. Not his job, but he'll know how to get us one.'

'Tonight, if possible.'

'Yeah, tonight,' Mr. Reid growled, 'we've wasted enough time faffing about. I know that they have safe houses on tap, it's just if they have a suitable one. Be back soon.'

Rodney turned his attention back to the screens, relieved. Sharky and Mould sat next to each other and were talking about the targets, pointing at the screens. The Jones brothers were doing the same. What seemed to be exercising the team was that several of the targets were on converging trajectories.

Sharky traced the now six blips on the screen; four of them had entered Kensington Gardens and two more looked to be on their way.

He scanned the Gardens for a likely meeting place. The only place that made sense was the cafe towards the northwest of the Gardens. He looked it up on his Google map. Sharky called for silence. He reached for one of the telephones.

'Saied, this is Sharky. Think that a meet is on, possibly in the Broad Walk Cafe. Can you get a couple into the cafe before the targets arrive, any minute now?'

'Roger. Wait out.' Saied responded to the call.

'Good call, think a dozen or more Somalis mooning around the Café, if that's where they are going, might be a bit obvious.,' Rodney frowned and ran his hand through his hair. 'A meet at the cafe makes sense with the Russian Embassy and Consular buildings just up the road.'

'Bit brazen though. Let's see who the Russians send to meet them, if anyone.' Sharky was intrigued.

'All that we can do is to wait for Saied to call back.'Mould put in.

'Well,' Rodney suggested. 'You could ask Saied to get a couple of photos of the Russians if they turn up and meet the targets, and record what's said if possible.'

'On it.' Sharky responded and spoke to Saied again. 'Done.' He put the phone back on the desk.

The team was warming to the game and Rodney himself was enjoying being back in operational mode and away from the dry paperwork of the fraud mission. It may turn the likes of Colonel Jimmy on, but it left him cold. They were now doing what they were trained to do. Rodney was determined that one way or another the threat from the Soviets and their henchmen would be terminated. He sprawled back in his chair again and was joined by Pat.

'You wanted to see me, Rodney?'

'Yeah, Pat I do. Thanks for coming over. How's it going next door with the Minister and his chiefs?'

'In a word, they're shell shocked. It should all be over in another half hour and the Brigadier asked me to get you back in time for the close out with the Minister etc.'

Rodney groaned. 'OK. I'll come back with you in a minute, but I just needed to ask you to support Laurie for a few nights. I need this lot on the ground with me as we attend to the threat to us.'

'Hmm; I'd rather be back with the team, sorting the bastards out.'

'I understand that and I'd appreciate your help but Laurie is going to fall over if I don't support him and you're the best one to do that. Give me two nights and then I'll get someone to relieve you if the ground operation is still ongoing. I'm hoping that Graham, Freire and their team will be able to get out from under by then and take over the reins from you and the others. Think we have Christine and Ms. Reid tonight but not sure. Can you check with Graham please?'

Pat thought about it for a moment and then agreed. 'Fair enough Boss. Come on, let's go back and support the Brigadier and the Banker and see the end of this phase.'

Just then Mr. Reid returned, giving the thumbs up. 'Got a place from tonight. Got a housekeeper who also cooks and is an ex-Petty Officer to boot. Set in twelve acres, some forested, walled and fenced. Surrounded by farms, so ideal. Best of all, in the triangle of the M40 and the M25. Off the A12 Denham Road. A few outbuildings and cover for our team in the grounds, couple of tree copses, not a lot of cover this time of year but not a desert etc.'

'Sounds good. Can you fit in a recce before last light? I've been summoned back to the meeting.'

'No issue, I'm going now. I'll take Sgt George and Sharky with me. See you back here later.'

Chapter Seventy-Nine

Servo and Carla

As the targets settled themselves and waited for their KGB handlers in the café, they looked out at the Kensington Gardens Park. The end of winter was a miserable time for the groundworks, bushes and trees.

In Moscow, Servo and Carla were being briefed by Colonel Pushkin and introduced to the two KGB special operations officers that were to accompany them to the UK.

Whilst Servo and Carla quickly realized that it was a great opportunity to escape to the West and into anonymity, they were wondering how they could get away from the two KGB officers unnoticed or at least with no traceable comebacks.

They had all been given thirty-six hours to get ready. The morning after tomorrow they would catch the early flight from the ex-military air base, which was now the busiest international airport in Europe, Sheremetyevo.

Any weapons and equipment that they would need would be issued to them in England. They would travel as innocent businessmen and women. Pushkin had advised them that this was the only opportunity to strike a blow against Major Brown and any of his team that got in the way. He made it clear that he didn't expect them to fail.

'If you don't kill Major Brown, don't come back'.

Later that day Servo and Carla had time to talk away from the others. They discussed a plan to extricate themselves and sent a message to Laurie with the plan that they had agreed would work. It would meet the cardinal principle that they had agreed between themselves, which was that they had to get away without suspicion being aroused against them.

Laurie was just waking up with some difficulty. He stretched and took a shower to get the sleep out of his eyes and refresh himself. He turned the shower from warm to cold and the shock of the cold drenching sparked him awake. He really needed a few more hours of sleep but he had to return to duty.

Dressing, he took an idle check of his phone. He came wide awake in a second. There was a text from Servo. He shook himself and quickly finished dressing. He needed to find Mr. Reid and the Major and give them Servo's message.

Mr. Reid was still out on his recce of the safe house when Laurie returned to the operations centre. Rodney and the Brigadier were saying their goodbyes to the Minister and Sir Geoffrey. The Director Generals of MI5 and MI6 had already left along with the Chiefs of the Health Service, who were motivated to sort out their own departments. The consequences of not doing so, the Minister had told them, would be career limiting. An understatement. What the three had agreed was a joint task force as advised by Colonel Jimmy and the original two gurus from the Treasury, Dan and Shaun.

Laurie hovered at the back of the group, caught Rodney's eye and held up his phone making it clear that he needed to speak, now!

Chapter Eighty

Stand To

'What's up, Laurie?'

Rodney had eventually extracted himself from the Minister, who wanted to know more about the last ten days. Robinson took over. The Minister had had some issues with Carol and Murphy being at the presentation and it had taken much patience from Sir Geoffrey to explain their role in the mission. Finally mollified, he'd agreed that they were necessary to the global resolution of the fraud.

'We have a message from Servo. He's on his way with Carla.'

'Great, when do they get here?' Rodney was pleased and it showed. 'We'll be able to keep our promise to them.'

'It is not quite so straightforward. They're accompanied by two other KGB officers for the purpose of killing you.'

Rodney took a deep breath. Even though he had expected that they would try again, hearing it spoken rattled him. 'Bollocks.' Rodney frowned and then grinned; his equilibrium quickly restored. 'And?'

'As I say, not without complications. Servo wants us to arrest him and Carla as they pass through Immigration and make a show of it so that the two KGB officers with them can report back that Servo and Carla's cover has been blown. They arrive morning after tomorrow, first flight of the day.'

'It's a plan and it could work, but it does mean that we let two killers onto the streets. We're allowing them the opportunity to join up and likely reinforce the other targets. They'll need to be closely monitored by Saied and his teams.'

'No issue, I'll fix that with Mr. Reid and Commander Coveney.'

'By the way, Laurie, Pat will support you for a few nights and I'll try to get others in support if you need them.'

'Pat and I should be able to handle it for tonight, but I think from tomorrow night on we need some of Freire's signallers to handle the communication traffic as it hots up. I at least need to be at the safe house.'

'Agreed. Sort it with Graham but check, and I asked Pat to speak to Graham as well by the way, that Christine and Ms. Reid take a shift with you.'

'OK. Good enough. Let's eat.'

The two ladies from the canteen were still hard at it and the food had been refreshed for the evening shifts. They were glad to see Laurie up and looking better than he had earlier in the day. Laurie thanked them for all their help. They told him that they loved it and would be back tomorrow.

'Lot more interesting than our normal day. Something going on all the time. Much better here than watching the others pushing paper all day from one desk to another,' the senior one told them straight. 'Now, let's get you some food before we go.' They stacked the plates and then she told them to go and eat before something else happened.

Rodney and Laurie had a good laugh as they felt that they'd been chided by the women; it was a moment of light relief. They had hardly started their meal before Mr. Reid returned from his recce of the safe house and joined them.

Mr. Reid was in a good humour, he was in the game that was bread and butter to him and he liked it.

'I left Sgt George and Armand at the house doing a close target recce while they still have some light. Sorting fields of fire and defences. It's an ideal location for the most part. Enough room for us all and a dragon of a housekeeper. Reminds me of my Mrs. Reid – salt of the earth who takes no prisoners.' He dared Rodney and Laurie to laugh, it was all they could do not to. 'I gave her the option to leave in case there was trouble. Do you know what she said?'

'Haven't got a clue,' Rodney responded.

'She said 'What, leave? Not a chance, just give me a gun." Mr. Reid laughed till the tears rolled down his cheeks. It was infectious, they all needed a moment of relief and they roared with laughter.

Heads turned and it drew the attention of Brigadier Robinson who was talking to Graham and Freire. He smiled at the scene; it was the first sign of the team relaxing that he'd experienced in a fortnight. If his top men were happy, then so was he.

Wandering over, he asked if anyone could join in. That brought off another round of mirth, whilst Mr. Reid sheepishly tried to explain about the housekeeper. When they were back in control, Rodney explained about the safe house.

'We hope that you'll join us so that we can protect you there.'

'Good offer, but a firefight is for you younger lions. Unless you really want or need me, I'll stay in my club. Don't think that I'll be in any danger there with their security. Plus, it needs at least one of the team available outside the battle zone to manage any fallout. What do you think?'

He was giving them the opportunity to repeat the offer or stand him down. Rodney and Reid smiled and nodded.

'Guess that you're right, Brigadier. We may need a friend on the outside,' Reid conceded. 'Could send a couple of the lads to sit outside your door?'

'Thanks but no thanks, you forget that the club employs a few ex-Regiment men to keep us old boys and the great and the good who stay there safe. Besides, if they come in strength there could be ten or more from what I can make out.'

'We haven't had time to talk yet, sir, but two of the four they are sending from Moscow include Servo and Carla. We'll make a hard public arrest of Carla and Servo at Immigration at Heathrow day after tomorrow. We'll make enough of a stir that the other two will see it all and report back that our two are lost to the mission.' Rodney waited for a response, but the Brigadier was processing the information. Robinson knew that he would have talk with the Director of MI5 to find a safe house for Servo and Carla and new documents and a legend so they could blend in, assuming they wanted to make their residential abode in the UK. He had a lot to think about and not much time to do it.

Rodney mistook the Brigadier's silence for an expectation that Rodney had more to say so Rodney half guessed it was about letting the other two run free.

'Er, we will have eyes on the other two KGB men. We want to see if they link up with our other targets. More importantly, if they meet up with anyone from the Russian embassy. We're covering every which way and either way we can pick them up if necessary.' Rodney came to a halt and waited.

Robinson stirred. 'OK, I see where you're coming from. If I seemed distant it's because I was thinking of Servo and Carla and the process of keeping them safe. You go for your plan, and I'll sort out a new identity for them with the DG. The whole works and get them somewhere safe to stay until this crisis is over.' He asked Laurie if he would mind getting him a tea and some food.

He needed to talk some more. 'Mr. Reid, tell me about this house you've found and what it offers the team in way of a defensive position. I'm also very interested in what your surveillance teams have found out so far, and in general any information that I need so I can respond to questions from Sir Geoffrey, the DGs and the Intelligence committee etc. I don't want to go in half-cocked. Admittedly, I'm behind the curve because the focus on the frauds has been all consuming, but that's mainly over now, the Americans and the Banker and his boys, along with the Fraud Squad, SO13 etc., etc., all of them can run with the fraud from now on. I want to get the team safe and that means I need to know all.'

'A pleasure, Brigadier. Let me start with the defensive position that the house offers us and then we can move on to the surveillance team and where we are.' Mr. Reid warmed to his subject. 'The house itself is an old country house. Big old pile, back and side entrance. There are two outbuildings, a stable at right angles to one side and a barn again at right angles to the other. Forms a "U" looking down on it with the house forming the base. There's a gap between the house and the outbuildings, five metres, no more. The house is set in around twelve acres. The immediate surrounding area around the house is fairly clear of trees and vegetation for fifty yards or so. After that initial perimeter, the rest of the ground is interspersed with trees, copses and arable fields which are currently in grass. A two-metre-high drystone wall for the most part encloses the whole of the property. Some of the wall needs attention and a makeover. So, there's a back gate for the farmer to gain access to the fields which is a weak point. But the main entrance, the front gate, is electrically operated from the house and has CCTV. There's CCTV on the house covering approaches. Armand and Sgt George have thirty-six hours to get some additional CCTV and listening devices into the grounds to give us early warning. A couple of the copses give good fields of vision over the estate at large including eyes on the house, so we'll dig a couple of shooters into them. The housekeeper is a caretaker and cook all in one. She can look after soldiers' comforts, so that's a bonus.'

'Sounds promising, but how are you going to get the targets to come to you?' Robinson wanted to know.

'Well, that's the trick. We know where the targets are and so far, Simon's boys haven't lost any of them. They are keeping close to the targets. I'm expecting more intel from the team when we talk to them in a minute or so, specifically on the question of how we lure the targets.

'Let's say that there's no move for thirty-six hours, probably a little longer as they'll want to have the boys from Moscow with them and to come in the hours of darkness. So, we propose to publicly show ourselves leaving the building over the next two days. That's two Land Rovers with the Major, myself, the Jones brothers, Sharky, Mould and Andrew on board. We'll make a show of it. Simon's boys will track any vehicles that follow us. We've identified a couple of cars belonging to the targets and they now have trackers on them.' Mr. Reid broke for a moment and looked at Rodney. 'Thought that the Major might nip over to his flat this afternoon and make a show of collecting some kit and letting his neighbour Galena know he would be moving locally for a week until his flat was sorted out and the paint had lost its odour etc., etc.'

He got a thumbs up from Rodney.

'OK, sounds like a germ of a plan. Shall we see what the Ops team have for us?' Robinson stood and led the way over to the desk.

'Sharky,' ordered Mr. Reid. 'Brief the Brigadier on where we are and what we've done so far.'

The three bosses and Laurie crowded round Sharky.

'Let's start with organization. Teams supplied by Simon are covering the targets 24/7 and they're good at the job. No cover blown as we speak. Three cars identified and trackers fitted. Let me show you on the screens the targets, yellow blobs with name alongside and their vehicles, red blobs with registration number alongside. See, there and there.' Sharky pointed out the targets and cars on the screens, 'We had a bit of a win this afternoon. All six of the targets met in the cafe in Kensington Gardens. This is a major development as it means that they're working together, something that we couldn't be completely confident about. Plus, they were joined in the cafe by two KGB men from the Embassy and later by Rodney's neighbour.'

'I'd like to have been a fly on the wall at that meeting,' ' the Brigadier whispered, almost to himself.

'Well, we sort of were the fly. When we realised where the targets were heading, we managed to get two of our teams to put people in the café, thanks to Saied for that. So, we have two recordings. Not great by any means, but the techs are working on them to see if by combining the two and enhancing them we can find out some of what was said. As you might expect, the meeting was in Russian so I have a Russian speaker from MI6. Mr. Reid's daughter is tweaking the output from the auto Russian to English translator software. Laurie can link up; he has the best Russian of us all. Hope that we'll get something later this afternoon. Thankfully the meeting was short, fifteen to twenty minutes max. Saied's people, a man and woman, both said that they felt it sounded like an orders group or a forum for passing information. In the main, one of the Russian officers spoke for max only five short minutes and then he allowed a few questions, thought to be clarification questions from the targets. Then the meeting broke up.' Sharky again pointed out where the targets were now. 'They seem to be breaking into two teams of three men. This is good for us as if we can confirm this is the case over the next twenty-four hours, then we'll be able to release some of the Somalis who have some military and fighting experience to support us at the safe house if Mr. Reid thinks it's necessary. I hope that you don't mind, Mr. Reid, but I've asked Saied to identify any likely lads and lasses that might be useful to us.' Sharky looked at his boss.

'Hmm, good thinking Sharky, well done. Mr. Reid beamed, then gave Sharky a downer. 'Clearly some of what you're learning here is rubbing off on you, even for a blanket stacker. Still, we've done our best to give you a good training in what soldiering is all about. Accepting of course that you are a handy sniper, which is a skill we may make use of in the next few days.'

Sharky was pleased with the approval from Mr. Reid; this was praise indeed.

'Thanks for that. Don't think that I'm too rusty to stay still in a hide.'

'You may not be rusty,' growled Reid, 'but are you too soft from easy living and all the junk food Laurie has been feeding you to stick it out in a open field for a day or two? I've identified the roof for you, my lad.'

The Brigadier and Rodney looked amused at the exchange between the two friends and the other members of the team were chuckling to themselves. Sharky responded.

'As you say boss, maybe I'm of an age that I would prefer to be up in a roof space chewing on sandwiches and the like; thanks.'

'Humph, maybe. Don't push it.' Mr. Reid brought the banter to a close. 'You lot, back to work. Mould, chase up my daughter and find out how far she is on with the translation.'

Rodney turned to the Brigadier.

'Seen enough, sir?'

'Yes, impressed. I'll get out of your hair. I need to go and see Sir Geoffrey anyway to see if the PM has anything to add to what we've done for her so far.' He looked at his watch, it was already almost five. 'Where does the time go?'

After Robinson had left them, Mr. Reid took the reins again.

'Right, stand to, listen in. This is what we to do over the next few days.'

He went through the plan and explained the safe house and grounds. In addition to what he'd told the Brigadier, he allocated the team individual tasks that they were to do when they got to the safe house. He got hold of Graham and told him what he needed in the way of support for monitoring the targets, and Freire for what he wanted from a couple of her soldiers. He wanted two men to man the control room in the safe house to monitor the CCTV and other warning devices as well as to maintain a communication network that needed to be set up tonight. Freire agreed but wanted to increase the manpower to give cover 24/7.

He took Rodney to one side. 'Galena will be back home now. Take the Jones brothers with you just in case; get some stuff and let her know that you're off for a while. I am sure that you can sort that. Then get back here and we can start our plan to draw them in to our killing zone.'

Rodney saluted. 'On my way.'

Chapter Eighty-One

The Brigadier and the Prime Minister

Sir Geoffrey welcomed the Brigadier when he arrived at his office in Number 10 with a warm handshake and invited him to sit in the easy chair. Robinson took off his hat and overcoat and hung them on the old-fashioned standard-issue hat stand. He wondered idly how old it was, it was certainly showing some age and there was a time in the distant past when only bowler hats would have adorned it. Robinson took his seat and Sir Geoffrey ordered the Brigadier's preferred tea, Earl Grey, from his PA over the intercom.

'I told the PM that you and I were meeting this afternoon for a washup and that your part in the mission was done. She insisted that we see her before you leave here.'

'Of course, happy to.' Robinson was secretly pleased to be able to bow out formally. 'I wondered what thoughts there have been about us handing over the international frauds to the Americans? I did think about not doing that for about sixty seconds but then realised that the job would suck our resources, indeed everyone's, dry.'

'She's delighted, the decision to pass the file over helps cements our special relationship a little more, and God knows we need the USA. If ever we are to get a long overdue trade agreement with the Americans it is now while the PM shares particularly good relations with this President. Whilst a trade agreement is not in his absolute gift, it helps to have him on side.'

The lack of an overarching trade agreement rankled with Sir Geoffrey. He felt it was the country's due and owed. He felt betrayed and despaired that his peers and their ministers in the Trade and Foreign Office hadn't got a deal done. A deal that would at least be equitable, but he knew that the pressure groups in the Senate and the other House were barriers to be overcome.

The tea arrived; the PA poured a cup and set it on the occasional table next to his chair.

'Good, I did wonder,' said Robinson as he lifted his cup and took a sip, 'Excellent. Must be the water in here.'

'Now, tell me all. I know that I've been at the presentations and met the Americans and by now all of your team, but I'd like you to tell me where you see yourselves and any outcomes I need to know about.'

Robinson talked for a quarter of an hour and he and Sir Geoffrey agreed points and clarified positions. It was a good debrief for both of them.

'Thank you. When we see the PM, she will ask what's next for your team, so think on that. Any thoughts?'

'Several, and I'll run some by you. First, I am closing mid-seventies and it's time for me to bow out gracefully. Got to happen sooner or later. Rodney is my natural successor, but he's approaching fifty and the rest of the team are also not in their first flush of youth. Mr. Reid, who is pivotal to the team, will not see sixty-five again. With our relocation into the real estate of MI5, it does beg the question of whether we should be absorbed in the context of those members of my team that want to soldier on. I feel terribly disloyal even talking like this, but I've always been a realist. I am sure that if the team ever knew that I was of this mind they would feel, after all their efforts, that they'd been kicked in the teeth.'

'A conundrum indeed and one to wrestle with. If you don't have the fight in you, it's difficult to see how you go forward.'

'Hmm. We now have the added complication that Moscow is out to get the Major, who they see as the prime motivator for all the problems that they have experienced recently. I think that they believe he is the one person who has caused them the loss of billions of ill-gotten gains.'

'Oh dear, what does this mean?'

'It means that we're facing a backlash. They've already tried to assassinate Rodney once and they'll try again.'

'What can we do?'

'Nothing. We're handling it, and I think we have used up all the support from MI5, SO13 and the Metropolitan Police that they can afford. They have their day jobs and we certainly impinged on them this last fortnight. We have the situation covered as far as we reasonably can.'

'Are you sure? I know that the PM would resource you, if you needed, from the Regiment.' Sir Geoffrey was thinking of the SBS and the SAS.

'Knowing the KGB as I do or as well as anyone can, I think that they'll try one more concerted go at us. After that they'll move on and wait for our paths to cross again. It is true that they are moving into a different mode at the moment, more disruptive and a willingness to undermine at every turn, and they have long memories. I think that as we know that they are on their way for another go at the team, if we give them a terminal blow, they'll back off.'

'If you're sure. Let me say at least that my door is open if you need help.' Sir Geoffrey eyed the Brigadier. He wasn't showing the age he claimed, indeed none of his team did, and he still had energy. 'Do you think that if we slowed the game a little, if we were to throw a few files at the team, we might simply wind them down into retirement?'

Robinson laughed. 'Could be, could be. But don't forget the reason that we exist. Our remit is that if MI5 or MI6 feel that a problem isn't in their charter or that they could be embarrassed by a mission it's handed to us to win or fail at. You might retort that they need to stop playing games and work it out between themselves, but in many cases this has proved impossible. And of course, they see themselves as rivals at times and this almost cultural split needs to be bridged somehow. I would personally like to see a national Security Service, but I suspect that the Home and Foreign Offices would scream blue murder.'

It was Sir Geoffrey's turn to laugh. 'My God, can you imagine? The first objection would be that we can no longer divide and conquer. I would say who? Themselves or our enemies? Mind you, it would save a ton of money to combine the two. I might just drop a word in the ear of a long-held friend and counterpart at the Treasury who is new in, to sort them out after the mess Neil Ashchurch has left them in. He might be looking, and the Chancellor too, for both a win and some kudos.' He smiled to himself, and Robinson warmed once again to this clever, top-of-the tree civil servant.

'Wicked thought, Sir Geoffrey.'

'Wicked is my middle name, Brigadier.' They both laughed.

'Shall we?'

'Yes, it's time,' Sir Geoffrey looked at his watch, 'to see herself. A fortnight ago when we were with her you were plain Brigadier Robinson and now, I hear on the QT that you're referred to as the 200 Billion-Dollar man.' Robinson thought about the name tag for a moment and decided that it wasn't at all bad, but that didn't mean it pleased him. He didn't like affectation or nicknames.

Sir Geoffrey led Robinson through two sets of doors, knocking on the second one and waited for the Prime Minister to call them in. He opened the door and let the Brigadier lead the way. Mrs. Thatcher was at her desk and rose and moved towards the two men.

'Welcome; so good to see you, my dear Brigadier. Come and sit at the meeting table. Would you like a drink? I have some rather good Scotch, I hear that's your tipple, Brigadier?'

'That would be very welcome, Prime Minister.'

'Sir Geoffrey, how about you?'

'A small one, I hate to see a man drinking on his own.'

The Prime Minister gave a small laugh as she went to her cocktail cabinet and poured two glasses and a jug of spring water.

'There, try that.'

Both men took the whisky neat and sniffed and then sipped allowing the amber liquid to run round their mouths.

'Excellent,' said Robinson.

'Good, good, and now it is for me to thank you for what you have done,' She held her hand up. 'I know that many unnamed others are working hard to close out the mission and that it will take some time. But your team's Midas touch, if I may call it that, exceeds any expectations I could have thought possible a few weeks ago. It was a desperate time for me personally when that report appeared on my desk. Quite outstanding, Brigadier. You have saved my bacon and bloodied the perpetrators of the scheme. Now, what can I do for you?'

'At this time, Prime Minister, there really is nothing that we need.' The 'we' was noted by the PM.

They spent another ten minutes answering the Prime Minister's questions on the way that they had approached the mission and she wanted to know about the members of the team, who they were and what part they had played. She was interested in how it had been organised and the key tenets that had led to the success. In the end she said, 'I take my hat off to you all. Thank you. I will not forget your intervention on our behalf.'

On the other side of the River Thames, Rodney, driven by the Jones Brothers, made a fuss of returning to his flat for some kit and making sure Galena and other tenants would know that he was moving to a temporary location whilst more work was carried out on his flat. The faithful ex-soldier, Joe the concierge, would spread the word for him. He left a note for Galena explaining that the drink he'd promised her would have to wait for a few weeks until he got back from his temporary lodgings just outside London. Satisfied that he had set the scene and salted the trail if need be, he and the Jones brothers returned to the office.

Chapter Eighty-Two

The Enemy

'They say you should respect your enemy and expect the unexpected and plan for it.' Rodney had the team in front of him in the section of the team's rooms that was now known as Mr. Reid's 'operations cell.'

Before him were the men that would accompany him to the safe house set in its dozen acres, Mr. Reid, the Jones Brothers, Sharky and Mould. Hovering on the outside of the circle were Andrew, Pat and Laurie and Dr Christian. Dr Christian had joined them; he wanted to help. He had got fed up with his lab and wanted a change. An unusually quiet period for him amongst his test tubes so he had decided to rejoin the team and help out with the night shift.

Rodney continued, 'The Somali teams have eyes on three of our targets and the targets are close by together in one car. We surmise that they will follow us to where we are staying. So, two things. The first is that we as a team are moving into a final phase which is to eradicate the threat to us personally. The second is that they are, we hope, going to try to follow us home, so let's make it easy for them.

'At home working on the security of the safe house and grounds are Sgt George and Armand. That's our eight triggers against their number of eight, could be ten, if the two KGB from the embassy are going to go into the field with them. Not bad odds, but I'm going to add Saied and two old friends Carla and Servo, they need to earn their bread too. Any questions?'

'Not so much questions as points.' Mr. Reid took the centre stage now. 'Sharky, get us three extra sets of weapons for the three guests, rifles and personal side arms, and body armour. Better get a knife for Servo; I don't expect that he has his Spetsnaz wrist throwing device with him so see if the armoury has one, they should have at least one from the attack the other night. Ammunition – a hundred rounds for each gun. Mould, I want a dozen torches, powerful ones, with plenty of spare batteries.' He looked at his notebook. 'We leave in an hour, two Land

Rovers. Vehicle One driver, Sharky with passengers myself and the Major. Vehicle Two driver, Lewis Jones, passengers Fred Jones and Mould.' He looked at Rodney. 'Who's going to be at the airport day after tomorrow to collect Servo and Carla?'

Rodney thought for a moment; he had been thinking about this for a day now. 'I don't think that it should be anyone from the safe house teams as that would give me a problem in case we are spotted and recognized, it could give the game away. So, my thought is that it should be Laurie; he's not known and claims to be stir crazy, and one other.' He paused and pointed. 'Andrew, OK to go with Laurie?' He got a nod from him.

'OK, 'said Mr. Reid. 'When we get to the house, you'll be allocated rooms and defensive positions for stand to by Sergeant George. Some of the positions are in the main house, others in the two outbuildings.' He conferred with his notes again. 'Sharky, get yourself a sniper rifle and spotter kit, in fact, double up.' He looked over to Rodney, who mouthed, 'Night Vision Goggles.'

'Sharky, add sixteen sets of Night Vision Goggles to the order,' Reid added.

Rodney took over.

'Well, let's get on and sort out what we have to do and get ready to move out. We've lost the daylight but we do have time to get eyes on in the morning before we return to the office.,' He paused. 'I don't think that they'll move against us tomorrow, they'll want to wait for the team from Moscow and to carry out a reconnaissance of some sort at least. So earliest time for contact I think will be early hours two days from now, probably three. But we need to be ready for the unexpected.

'It does seem from what we can see from their movements recently that the local thugs are operating in two teams of three to cover twenty-four hours a day. This means that if they do follow us tonight, they may scout our position so there will need to be eyes on. I expect that Sgt George will have it covered but be prepared to do a stint on stag. Right, let's go guys or we'll all be in trouble with the housekeeper who has dinner waiting for us.'

He got a laugh and a stony look from Mr. Reid, that broke into a smile.

'Doug, I'd like to have a look at the screens to see where the targets are now and have a word with Saied.' Rodney moved towards the screens and Laurie pointed out the target's car, parked a couple of hundred yards down the road.

'Saied tells me that the boys have got trackers on all the cars now and as we can see they're working fine. One of the targets is on foot and they constantly change over with each other. They position themselves over the road up toward the bridge from us, supposedly looking over the Thames.'

'Good. We'll drive out of the back from the underground car park and round to the front to pick up a couple of us from the main doors so it gives them the time to get on our tails. Let's do it.'

Andrew appeared and caught Rodney's eye. 'Andrew, Laurie,' Rodney drew them to one side, 'The task tomorrow morning at Heathrow is to ensure that Servo and Carla are stopped and arrested at Immigration. I want a lot of fuss. Enough fuss and noise so the other two agents on the plane with them can't be in any doubt that they've been arrested. Moscow Central must believe that the arrest was genuine when it's reported back to them that Servo and Carla were taken by the Border Force and yourselves in a hard arrest.'

Laurie smiled. 'Going to be fun and games, that's for sure. I've got the flight details so we'll be there early. Do the Border Force and police know about this?'

'Not yet; I meant to stand it up through MI5 but I got busy. Can you do that for me?'

'Leave it to us,'' Andrew replied. 'I take it that you want us to bring them to the safe house?'

Rodney nodded.

'Time to chill and slow down now Major, or you'll be heading for a heart attack,.' Laurie added.

'Hmm, I'll try. If I can't relax going on the attack, I don't think that there's much hope for me,' Rodney answered ruefully.

Rodney looked around; the others had gone. He said goodnight to Graham and asked him to support Pat where he could. He collected his pistol and personal protection equipment from his office safe and then left, making his way down to the underground car park. It was busy. The team were ferrying arms and equipment and loading them into the two Land Rovers. He stood apart, not wanting to get in the way.

He had some doubts and reran his plan to get the targets into a killing zone against the alternative of taking them out one at a time. On balance he wanted to deal with them all at once, better to bury the bodies, he reasoned. He would risk the wrath of the authorities but he thought that they wouldn't make too much of a fuss if they could demonstrate that they had attacked the team. Their credit was riding high so he wasn't over bothered about any flak.

Rodney took off his jacket and put his body armour on over his shirt. Tightened his shoulder holster. He checked his pistol. Drew the slide back slowly, checked the bullet was home in the breech and let the slide go. He checked that the safety was on, stuck the pistol in its holder and then replaced his jacket. Straightening the jacket, pulling it round him, he felt ready.

Mr. Reid turned up with a takeaway coffee for himself and Rodney. Rodney took it gratefully. 'Thanks.' He sipped it. It was black and strong; the caffeine hit the spot and that was what was wanted.

Time seemed to run on until Rodney became aware of the vehicle's tailgates being closed. Mr. Reid came over to him. 'You ready, Major? No last minute second thoughts? ' Reid was probing. He really didn't know how Rodney was feeling about going into action after being shot up last year. 'I was just wondering if you had any reservations about pulling the trigger?'

Rodney smiled; he knew that Mr. Reid was checking if he was fit and wouldn't freeze. He knew that he was ready and had been for some months to go into action if he had to. He said truthfully, 'You have no need to worry about me, Doug. I'm ready. I don't have flashbacks and I'm reconciled to this reminder.' He ran his finger up the side of his face to the end of the scar at his right eyebrow. 'A expensive reminder to me to be more careful in future.' He laughed. 'Come on, let's sort this lot out.'

Mr. Reid slapped him on the shoulder.

'Take the front seat. I'm going back upstairs with Fred Jones. You pick us up from the front door in fifteen minutes from now. Don't be late, I don't want to be exposed for any longer than I need to.'

Rodney climbed into the front seat next to Sharky. Sharky was tapping the wheel with his ring finger to the music that he had playing on the radio.

'All right, Boss?'

'Yeah, cool. How about you and the family? I feel guilty that you haven't had time to speak or see anyone these last few weeks.'

'They're all good. Kids are costing me a fortune with extras at the sun-dome and now the wife with Mrs. Reid seems to have decided it's time for a new wardrobe; they are seriously bending the plastic.'

Rodney laughed freely. It felt good to be out with the team.

'Just make sure that all the girls' bills get to the Banker, I'm sure that he can fudge them through as necessary expenses whilst they're all in hiding. I think that it's a fair one.'

'You sure?'

'Yeah, why not, what can they do, fire me? Help me get back to my beach?'

'See what you mean. Thanks, Boss. I'll tell the ladies.'

Rodney checked his watch. 'We'd better go, or do you want to keep Mr. Reid waiting?'

'Bloody hell, no!' He fired up the Rover and signalled the other vehicle to follow him.

They drove slowly out of the garage, up the ramp into the back street of the MI5 building. The Rovers turned right, circumnavigating the building to emerge onto Millbank, turning right again to run to the front of the building.

Both vehicles pulled up and Mr. Reid and Fred Jones emerged from the building, strolled across the road and climbed into their Land Rover. Rodney made a point of getting out so that he would be seen and then getting into the back with Mr. Reid. They gave the targets plenty of time to see them, recover their man and get him on board.

They took care as they drove to drive slowly out to make sure that they didn't lose the targets' car. Once or twice when they lost line of sight to the enemy, Mr. Reid called Laurie to make sure that the targets were still following them. The journey was an easy one at this time of the evening as the rush hour was beginning to thin.

Chapter Eighty-Three

First Night

They drove down the Western Avenue, noted RAF Northolt on their right until they got the sign for the A412 and then came off at the large circle with six exits. They took the second. A couple of miles down the road they hung a right onto a single-track road. Lewis, driving in the second Rover, had been watching the targets through his mirrors, following them at a discreet distance. He called Rodney in the lead Rover to say the targets had followed them, swung onto the track and switched off their headlights.

'Not so dumb.' Rodney turned round to Mr. Reid, who grunted.

Sharky slowed down and took another single-track road on the left, turning down towards the tributary known as the Alder Bourne, which eventually fed into the River Thames. This track, some 300 metres long, would lead them to the gates of the estate. Mr. Reid called ahead to have the gate opened, that two Rovers were on their way and to close the gate as soon as the second one was through. He added that they were being followed by three triggers and didn't want them in the grounds.

As they approached the gates were sliding open and the Rovers swept through. He strained his neck to check the gates were closing behind them but it was too dark to see them properly, so he asked Sharky to stop. The other Rover pulled up behind them. Mr. Reid got out of the car and walked back toward the gate. Twenty metres from the gate he got down so that he could see against the night sky that the gate had closed. He fancied that he could see the bulky shape of the target's car up the track. He hurried back to his Rover and ordered Sharky to drive on to the house.

The drive curved round to the right and soon hid the gates from the house and its outbuildings. Even so, as the Rover's lights lit up the safe house complex now directly in front of them. Mr. Reid directed Sharky to kill the lights.

'Drive as close as you can to the front door so that we can offload the kit quickly.'

Mr. Reid and Rodney left the Rover and headed for the house.

The door was open and Sgt George stood well back from the entrance.

'Major, Mr. Reid. Come in.'

Rodney went first and shook George's hand.

'Good to see you. Any chance of a look around?'

'No problem. Full tour and briefing for all, but only after you've eaten or we'll all be in for it. Our lady housekeeper takes no prisoners.'

Mr. Reid said, 'Just let me get the team to carry the kit in from the Rovers and secure it inside. Five minutes max. Take the Major to the dining room in the meantime.'

He looked around. 'Where's Armand?'

'On walkabout, near the gate. We'll call him up later. Follow me, Boss.'

They walked down the wood-lined hall and turned right into the dining room, a large room at the back of the house with a table set with twelve chairs. On one side a curtained wall closed out the view from the back of the house. Like the hall, the walls were covered in wooden panelling. The plain walls were a signature for the rest of the house. Basic and bare. Sat at the table was one of Major Freire's signallers tucking into his dinner; he nodded as Rodney and Sgt George entered.

'Major, meet Pete. He, along with his two mates James and Will, are managing the control room. I'll show you it later, it's in the cellar and we're almost ready to roll.'

'Just as well as the targets are here.' Rodney smiled, 'Better meet the boss of the place.'

Pete quickly flicked his hand, indicating a sign, 'Better you than me.' Rodney grinned.

Sgt George motioned that Rodney should follow him through a side door in the room. They emerged into a country house kitchen with all the equipment you would expect of a stately home catering for the lord of the manor and staff. Standing at the cookers was a woman in her middle years. A natural brunette and not unattractive. Well-proportioned, neither fat nor thin. Tall for a woman and had the sort of look that questioned your reason for being. She was dressed in jeans and a shirt over which she wore an apron. Rodney approached her to introduce himself, but she got in first.

'Major Brown, I presume?' Her voice was husky and accentless. What you saw was what you got. 'Food's ready and I would appreciate it if you and your men would eat now so that I can clear up.'

'Absolutely. How would you like to be addressed?'

'Hm. They call me Ms. Blake and that will do just fine.'

Rodney had noticed several serving vessels with lids on, clearly keeping the food warm.

'Right, Ms. Blake, can we help you carry the food through?'

'Thank you. George, grab the plates from the bottom of that oven and you, Major, grab the food and ferry it in onto the table. I'll bring the silver and hot drinks. I take it we are dry?'

'Dry we are until the task is done,' Rodney said light heartedly.

'Poor you,' Ms. Blake responded dryly.

Table sorted to Ms. Blake's satisfaction, she withdrew into her kitchen as the rest of the men poured in.

'Food, help yourself. Then we can get down to business.' Sgt George joined them.

When they all had filled their plates with steaming vegetables and a steak stew and begun to eat, Mr. Reid got started.

'OK Sgt George, give us the must do for this night stop.'

'Armand will keep us safe for a while and call in if he needs help should the targets show signs of moving in. After dinner I'll show you around, your rooms, the control centre and stand to positions if we need to react. Stand to will be at first light. When we get to the control room, I have maps of the area and layouts of the house and two outbuildings so you will get an idea of what is where and arcs of fire etc., standard stuff. Eat up.'

'Thanks for that. We hope to have another three people coming in tomorrow to give more eyes on. Any immediate thoughts about likely approaches and anything else of use?'

Sgt George went on. 'I've been thinking that although we can defend and attack from this location, the weak point is the approach for vehicles. There's a slight chance of an ambush situation in the lane leading to the gates. I'll show you another way in across the field tracks and through the back gate. May be overkill but I would rest easy if we adopted that route if the stay here gets protracted.'

'I agree,' said Rodney. 'It was on my mind too that we could be vulnerable to an ambush as we drove in, need a good recce in the daylight. In truth most of us could simply stay here until this is over to reduce the risk. I do need to go back tomorrow to see the Brigadier and

I'll take two men with me, Fred and Lewis. After that we'll stay put. I take it that we have plenty of stores to feed and water us for a period?'

Sgt George nodded. 'Rations are not an issue; we could feed a small army for a month. If everyone has finished, bring your plates, glasses and eating irons etc., into the kitchen and stack the washing machine or Ms. Blake will find a way of making you suffer.' The men laughed.

Domestics done, Sgt George led them down to the cellar, which ran the whole length and breadth of the house. A mega boiler took up one corner and various cold freezers and other necessary house equipment. In the middle of the cellar was a series of desks and a battle board. On the desks were monitors and screens. One large screen showed the permanent cameras with night vision capability covering the approaches to the house and front and back gates. Another showed the cameras fixed in the halls and public rooms of the house. Another was split-screened, showing the locations of the target vehicles. The vehicle that followed them was seen as a blip on the screen a hundred yards up the track from the main gate. Another desk to the right of the runs of three desks held the communication equipment and another had a dozen sets of individual radios on charge.

Sgt George gave the team a few minutes to orientate themselves and then began his briefing.

'The control centre is run for us by Major Freire's soldiers.' He pointed them out. 'Pete, Will and James.' The soldiers held up their hands as their name was called. 'I believe that Major Freire will may join them tomorrow or sometime after that. Now, gather round the battle boards. The first one is a map of the grounds. Study it well. I will just point out the back and front gates and the track you can take to avoid the front gate.' He traced the route along the river and then breaking right up to the back gate. 'I'll make sure that I take away the chain from the back gate in the morning so you won't be locked out when you need access. On this board is the house and outbuildings. I've annotated firing positions and arcs of fire from the main house and two outbuildings. I've moved a few tiles in the main house roof which give good observation over the land. A sniper's bird's-eye view.'

George stopped to ask a question.

'Do we have a sniper?'

Sharky held up his hand, and then he asked, 'If we have enough manpower, is there a preferred spotter for the sniper?'

Mould held up his hand.

'Good. Mr. Reid, happy for you to move to the stand-to positions tomorrow but for tonight I've got a man in the stables and another man in the barn. Both outbuildings have a mezzanine floor but I don't think they offer anything better in the way of line of sight or protection than the ground floor. I will personally place the men so they have the best view possible after we finish up here. Now, the radios you will draw in a minute, have a location and 'man down' function. If you don't breathe, which is a movement, for a minute the radio will send an alarm signal to this centre. Range about two miles. We are close to Heathrow so radio traffic is monitored. You are going to have to make sure your radios are charged with batteries at all times. Your responsibility.' He paused. 'I know that it's dark and not the best time to see the ground for the first time, so study the map carefully and the house plans. You need to be able to get round the house in the dark.'

Pete called out that Sgt George had a message from Armand.

'Says that one of the men from the car has got out and is scouting the perimeter, looking in from outside the wall.'

'Fine. I'd be surprised if they didn't want to have a look. Pete, tell Armand that if the man climbs the wall to monitor him. If Armand thinks that the man is going to offer a threat to us, call me,' Sgt George ordered. 'Right, let's get to it. Mr. Reid, can we get the guns and any equipment not issued to a man down here so we can control it. And then let's get the radios issued and the men on stag shown their stand-to positions. After that I want to get the stags sorted so that we have eyes on outside tonight. I need to relieve Armand and I am asking, Mr. Reid, that you base yourself in the control room for tonight at least. There are beds down here for the signals team and a couple of spares. The rooms on the first floor have your names on the doors and the beds are made, so let's get going or we'll be here all night.'

'Right lads, let's move.' Mr. Reid sent the team to get the kit.

It took half an hour to sort themselves out and settle themselves in the house. The spare kit was stowed, radios issued. Mr. Reid had found a chair and sat with the signallers watching the screens. Rodney stood behind them running his eyes over the screens and watching the blip from Armand's tracker. The blip was steadily moving round the estate almost as far as the back gate now. It seemed at the moment that the target was going to go right round the estate, but how much he could see was limited. He would be able to see the dark outlines of the buildings but little more. Sharky and Mould had disappeared up into the roof with night vision goggles (NVG) and their weaponry. Fred and Lewis Jones were making tea for everyone from the brew kit the signallers had got themselves tooled up with in the cellar.

Sgt George took his tea and drank it as quickly as he could. When he'd finished, he handed out NVG to Fred and Lewis Jones.

'Time to recce your stand to positions.' He led them out of the cellar and took them into the hall. 'Check your weapons and make safe.' When he was satisfied that they had a bullet in the chamber and the safety catch on, he turned off the lights. 'Goggles on.' The three of them stood for a moment, getting used to the new world they now saw in a green hue. George opened the front door and beckoned them out into the night.

In the control room Rodney watched the blip for Armand continue its slow travel round the perimeter of the estate. The target was more than halfway round the estate, moving quickly.

George took them first to the stables on the right. They spent time going round the building inside and out until they were satisfied that they had the layout and noted the windows and doors that could be used to fire from using the thick stone walls as shelter from small arms fire. They then did the same at the barn. When they were happy, George wanted Fred in the barn and Lewis in the stable block.

'I want you to mount stag from here until I come and get you. I'll give you two blips on your radios or call you if the area is clear to let you know I am on my way. I know that you old, retired Welsh Guardsmen shoot first and ask questions after.' He got a chuckle from both.

Rodney looked up as Sgt George got back to the control room.

'Sgt George, just in time. Armand's signal has just started moving inwards. I have to assume that the target has entered the estate.'

George went to the communications desk and spoke to Armand.

'What's the situation, Armand?'

There was no issue with the earphone and radio throat mic that Armand had that any radio noise would be heard more than a foot away.

Armand whispered back. 'He's in the grounds but still paralleling the fence. Can I take him out if he compromises me?'

His question was on the speaker in the control room and Sgt George looked at Rodney for a decision.

Rodney took the handset. 'Armand, only if he's a threat and you think it necessary. I would prefer that he's allowed to finish his reconnaissance and to get back to the car. We have two men in the barn and stables. We'll remind them that you're still out in the fields. Roger over.'

'D'accord,' Armand replied in French. Rodney smiled.

He handed the handset back to George.

'Better warn the Jones brothers that Armand is still out and that one of the targets is in the grounds. They should have picked up the traffic anyway, but they are Guardsmen after all!'

'Roger that.' George relayed the messages.

Mr. Reid said, 'You should get some sleep, Rodney.'

He wanted Rodney out of the way so that he could get control and in truth it was the right thing to do and Rodney knew it. But Rodney wasn't quite ready.

'You're right, Mr. Reid, no place for a Rupert tonight.' He put his head to one side. 'If I promise not to interfere, I'd like to stay until the target either gets back to his mates and drives off or is neutralised.'

Mr. Reid grunted in the inimitable way he had and in his rough Glaswegian replied.

'Good enough. A brew for the workers, please Major and then sit over there and watch and learn.' He got snickers from the signallers and a smile from Sgt George.

'Thank you. Tea all round.' Rodney got a thumbs up from everyone.

In the attic, Sharky and Mould with their NVG had been watching Armand and the target move round the estate and could hear the exchanges over the radio net. Working at a distance, the NVG were not great but good enough to make out the movements on the ground. They watched the target, who was three-quarters of the way round the estate move back towards the perimeter stone wall. Clearly, he'd seen all that he wanted for that night. The man climbed the wall and legged it back to the car. They could see Armand moving quickly to keep up. Sharky called in and got a direction from Mr. Reid to keep eyes on and to let him know as soon as the car lights came on and they left.

Ten minutes later Alexander Ivanov climbed into the target's car to join Adrian Sanchin and Erast Abel.

'How did it go?' Adrian wanted to know.

'Big old house and grounds, around three to four hectares. The house has three floors and two large outbuildings, stable and barn. I could only make out outlines. There's a back gate but it had a heavy chain securing it. It was all silent, no dogs, thank goodness. I climbed over the wall about three-quarters of the way round. The wall has crumbled there and it is an easy step over, could be an entry point to think about. Anyway, shortly after I got in the grounds, I had the feeling that I was being tracked. Just after that, my skin was prickling, I was sure someone was there but I couldn't see or hear anything. Maybe I was dreaming it or it was ghosts, but I took the sensible option and got out of the grounds. The main thing is that I got a feel for the place and I'll draw it out when we get back.'

'You didn't see anybody, signs of life, nothing?' Erast, the leader of the three, was cautious. A long-in-the-tooth mercenary, his natural reserve had kept him alive. 'No noises, nothing?'

'Nothing. Quiet as the grave.' Alexander was definite.

'Hmm. OK let's get out of here and get a late meal. You can sketch the place out when we get back.'

Alexander squirmed in his seat. 'Put the heater on Erast, I'm soaked to the skin. We'll need some outdoor clothing if we're going to work in the grounds.'

'Good point. I'll sort it with the boys from the Embassy. They can pay.' Erast backed up the track.

Sharky called down that the vehicle was leaving. Armand then confirmed that the third man had got into the car. In the control room there was a sense of relief, but they all knew that it was temporary as the targets would be back, looking for blood.

It took Mr. Reid twenty minutes to gather his troops for a debrief on the night's events.

'Right, settle down and gather round the map of the house and grounds. Before we start, I want to remind you that we need to all know the proper procedures for reporting in target activity. So, I will remind you once more. The estate and house is divided into four quadrants. Front door is twelve o'clock. Clockwise plus 90 degrees, green sector. Plus, 90 degrees blue sector. Plus 90, red sectors. Plus 90, back to the beginning, black sector. Got it? Any questions?'

'No,' came a shout from the team.

'Why then, Mould and Sharky, when you were reporting from the roof didn't you report "Target going Red to Black?" Hmm!'

'Sorry, Boss; Rusty, but we're on it now.'

'OK. Point taken then. Keep it simple and we'll get through this. He grunted. 'The Major is the Boss and I am Mr. Reid.' He swung his eye round the group. 'Report, Armand first.'

'I followed the Target all the way round. He made entry, er, Red going into Black.' He got a nod from Mr. Reid. 'He stepped over the wall where it was broken down but something spooked him and he went back over the wall further down. Not easy but he managed it quite easily. I thought that he moved well for a man carrying some weight.'

'You mean he was fat?' Reed wanted to know.

'Not fat. Bulky, a strong man I have no doubt. About five feet ten or close.'

'Thank you, Armand, very clear. Mould, Sharky, anything to add?'

'Not really. The night vision goggles are not great at distance, but we could pick out Armand and the man. It was as Armand reported.'

'Thank you. Fred, Lewis, anything to add?'

'The field of vision from both our positions is OK but not great. We'd like to have a walk with Sgt George in the morning and see if we can tweak the situation, that would be helpful.'

'OK with that?' Reid looked at George.

'Fine, Mr. Reid. After Ms. Blake's English breakfast, a brisk walk will help work it off.' Sgt George smiled.

'Good, happy with that. Despite the fact that they are unlikely to be back immediately, we are now operational, so Sgt George please set the guards of the night.'

Rodney stretched. 'If you're OK now Mr. Reid, I think that I'll turn in. Tomorrow could be a big day.'

'All good. Now, get off, I'll make sure you get a call at seven.'

'One thing; the risk of an ambush still worries me. Can we recce the track in and the back way in too?'

'Leave it to me; I'll sort it and let you know when you get back from the office.'

They left it at that. Rodney said goodnight to everyone and thanked them.

Chapter Eighty-Four

Day One: The British

Ms. Blakes' breakfast was a feast – she clearly didn't think that anyone should starve on her watch. During the drive out Rodney took notice of the brush and few trees on the way and the clear fields behind. His concern about getting ambushed eased, there was little cover in line of sight and setting one up was unlikely to go unnoticed. Still, he thought that in the dark it could be possible.

Mould drove as Sharky wanted to mark his distances from the roof to various key points on the ground to ensure he had the right distances logged in for his sniping if it came to that. He closed his eyes for a moment and dozed till they got back to the underground office.

Pat and Dr Christian sat before the screens watching the targets and the Somali teams tracking them.

'Anything new, Pat?'

'Very quiet overnight. We tracked the target car that followed you and parked for a couple of hours outside your safe house. We're watching the car now. They're parked up at Heathrow waiting for the team from Moscow.'

'Any news from Laurie and Andrew?' Rodney looked at his watch. 'The plane landed an hour ago. 'Rodney was concerned.

'That's the big news. They've just picked up Servo and Carla; quite a scene according to Andrew and enough fuss to ensure that the other two men from Moscow saw the arrests.'

'That's a relief; what's next?'

'Andrew asked you to call him when you got in.'

'Better do that now.' Rodney thumbed his phone to find Andrew's number then hit the speed dial.

Andrew answered immediately.

'Hi, Rodney, we're OK. I've got the two guests in the car and we're heading for the house, ETA circa ten minutes. Spoke to Mr. Reid, he's waiting for us and will see us in.' The last sentence meant that Mr. Reid had put out a defence. Rodney would have expected nothing else. 'Just to put your mind at rest, we left the location undetected via a service gate. We weren't followed, as you'll see from the trackers.' Andrew was referring to the tracers on the target's cars.

'Good job. We'll talk later when you get back here.' With some relief he cut the call.

The others were looking on expectantly so Rodney gave them a thumbs up. He needed to see a lot of people before he went back to the safe house. As importantly he wanted to make sure that the various divisions in the office would function without the good percentage of the team that were deployed in the field. He wanted to ask the Brigadier just to keep an eye on them. His first stop was with the Banker John Brown.

As he walked into the Banker's area, he immediately noticed that things had changed. Gone were all the data to do with the frauds and instead the Banker and his staff were reorganising the domestic operation for an international one. The two FBI agents Carol and Murphy were working alongside Colonel Jimmy.

'Morning John, what's happening here?'

'Morning Rodney. We're resetting the game. All the domestic stuff has been handed over; data, files, scheme maps etc. to the Fraud Squad. They'll need it to drive the recovery of money and prosecute going forward. It's been agreed, and the Brigadier called us together last night after you left, that we'll support the Americans by developing a European hub here for the next few weeks whilst they get up to speed. After which, we'll move lock, stock and barrel to either the States for a period of time or to the American Embassy in London. More likely the latter, sad to say.'

Rodney stroked his chin. 'Well, who would have thought a fortnight ago that you'd be going global? I'm just checking for understanding, who exactly will form your team?'

'I'll keep Colonel Jimmy and the two gurus plus some MI5 analysts. I'll be sad to lose Andrew and Pat but the Brigadier made it plain that they needed to return to the main team. But that I could call on them through you from time to time if we get overwhelmed and I can't find the right assets we need from wherever to support us, like Greg for example. Greg has agreed to work with us for a little longer which is a plus.'

'What about Freire and her team for secure communications gathering intelligence in conjunction with GCHQ?'

'We have that covered. Freire will stay with us for another month, during which time Carol has to get an equivalent team set up, location to be advised.'

Rodney thought for a moment. 'How soon can you release Andrew and Pat?'

'Immediately, with the proviso that I may need them at a pinch. But I hope not to.'

'Fair enough. I'd like to take Major Freire out to see her signallers, if not tonight then sooner rather than later and get her here back the following day, if that's OK?'

'No problem there, but tomorrow might be better.' The Banker was pensive. 'It's just that we have a lot to set up today and having Freire to hand would be an advantage.'

'Fair enough, it'll give her chance to put an overnight bag together.'

'I'd better get on, Rodney; perhaps talk later.'

Rodney shook the Banker's hand. It was an unexpected gesture. 'I just wanted to thank you, John, for everything. It wouldn't have been possible without you.'

The Banker put his hand on Rodney's shoulder.

'It has been a pleasure. Don't forget that I set up a large sum aside for your operations and currently Graham has been the paymaster for the Somali team and is paying out for the ladies in hiding.' He laughed. 'Some of the bills look a bit iffy but they'll pass. I'm still countersigning them and paying the expenses so no need to worry on that account.'

'Thanks John, I've taken up enough of your time. Off you go.' Rodney waved him off.

His next port of call was Graham and his co-ordination and administrative cell; he would speak to Freire at the same time, then he needed to have an hour with the Brigadier.

Graham's team area was piled high with archive boxes and his team was working on the paperwork and handover sheets for the Fraud Squad people working with them.

'Hi Rodney, want a cup and wad?' Graham asked one of his ladies to serve the Major.

'Is this the last of it?' Rodney cast his eyes over the activity.

'Yes, once these boxes are gone, we're free, except for the Americans' needs. Then new adventures await. Maybe have a little holiday first?'

Graham was not always known for his dry wit but this was one occasion. He looked around the room.

'Everyone's been full on. I think that they've all done well. I heard that the PM is over the moon. Couldn't have done better for her if we'd tried.'

'I knew that the Brigadier was seeing her last night but I haven't had chance to see him yet.'

'Anyway, Rodney, take a seat and enjoy your drink and sandwich. Freire and I would enjoy chewing the fat for ten now that the pressure is easing.'

'Sure, why not.' He pulled up a chair and put it between Freire and Graham. 'Saw your guys last night and they seemed to be enjoying themselves.'

'All soldiers who know what they are doing enjoy working independently with no bosses looking over their shoulder.' She grinned. 'Me included. I spoke to them this morning and they filled me in. I was thinking of a visit.'

'I spoke to the Banker just now and he wanted you to hold off today but I'll get you out there tomorrow. I'm going back in an hour or two, is there anything I can do for you?'

'Not really, they seem happy enough and enjoying Mr. Reid's style of leadership a lot. "No messing Ma'am"is what they said.' She grinned again.

Rodney's phone went. It was Andrew.

'Hi Rodney, been having a chat with our guests and they say that the targets' plan is to come tonight and that they must be on the next plane out in the morning. That came from orders from on high, they told me. That's the time plan, so you need to get back sooner than later.'

'Hm. Can you put Mr. Reid on please?' He waited till Reid came on the phone. 'Doug, can you run the Saied people from your location if I bring our boys back with me?'

He waited and heard him talking to the signallers.

'Yeah, we can. Could do with some bodies to support the lads.'

'Done, and Laurie and Andrew stay with you, so put them to work.' He swilled the tea down and took a big bite of the BLT. 'Sorry, got to go. Let's catch up tomorrow.' He legged it over to Pat. 'We're off, Pat. But first get yourself tooled up if you're not already. Get Saied here in an hour and a half. We'll pick him up at the underground garage door. Draw a weapon for him, body armour and NVG for both of you and draw two stingers. Take Mould with you and I'll see you at the Land Rover. Please be ready to go. But first I want you and Dr Christian to hand over control to Mr. Reid and his band.'

'Oh Rodney, you're not sending me back to my lab so soon? I was really beginning to enjoy myself,' Dr Christian protested.

'Not yet. I need you right here in case it all falls to bits and you need to pick up the pieces. So please can you continue to monitor the situation for the Brigadier. I'll probably get Graham and Freire to support.'

'Happy with that.'

Rodney went back to Freire and Graham and gave them the news and the need to keep a satellite control going with Dr Christian. He wanted them to call for situation reports every hour so that the Brigadier would be kept up to speed. He hoped that it wouldn't be necessary but he believed in having one leg on the ground.

'So, we're watchkeepers now,' commented Freire.

'Only for tonight if Andrew is right. And no, you're not to use Christine and Ms. Reid. Now, got to see the Brigadier. Can I tell him that you've got his back?'

Freire and Graham looked at each other.

'OK,' they said and laughed.

A short time later Robinson welcomed Rodney into his office and offered him a drink.

'Single would be appreciated as it's not yet midday. And I don't think Mr. Reid would approve as we are now on full alert.'

'Sometimes the Jocks have no sense of humour. Whisky, I am reliably informed, is food anyway. Now, tell me, where are we?'

'We have Servo and Carla at the safe house, and they are saying that the hit has to be tonight as Moscow is, I am guessing, losing patience, or so it would seem. The men from Moscow centre have to be on the first plane out tomorrow. I'm pulling all the team to the estate less Graham, Dr Christian and Freire who will set up a watchkeepers' desk for you and I will ensure that they get hourly updates.' Rodney sipped his single malt whisky. The flavour was familiar. 'You must be in favour; if I'm not mistaken, this is one of the limited supply of the DG of MI5.'

'Oh yes.' Robinson held his glass against the light, 'An acquired taste.' He turned serious. 'Are you ready for them?'

'Ready as we will ever be.'

'Try not to get too many of our team hurt. Including you.'

'Do my best.' Rodney finished his drink. 'I'd very much like to get this mission finished.'

'Wouldn't we all. By the way, Mrs. T is very grateful. Please pass that on. Get this sorted, Rodney, and we can move on. Tell Graham that I'll be with them tonight except when I'm with the Americans for dinner with their FBI Director. And now I think that you should get on, but you can tell Servo and Carla that I've sorted new papers and identities for them. Location to be agreed.'

Rodney met Pat and Mould in the underground garage. 'Ready?'

'Ready,' responded Mould. Pat and Mould had their body armour on and Mould reached into the Rover cab and pulled out Rodney's set. 'Put them on Major. Mr. Reid's orders; SOP.'

Rodney grinned, checked his watch and shrugged into the body armour.

'Saied should be waiting outside for us now. Let's go.'

As they left the underground garage through the armoured roller doors, Saied appeared and climbed into the back seat with Rodney. Rodney offered a hand and Saied took it and shook Rodney's hand pumping it up and down.

'Good to be back at work.'

'Hopefully one night only, but it could be difficult.'

'Difficult, I don't think so.' He took the gun offered to him by Pat from the front seat and checked it out. 'Spare mags?' Pat handed over another four fully charged magazines. Saied tested the springs of each of them to make sure that they would feed the bullets on demand.

Then Pat handed him over the body armour, which Saied struggled into.

Mould stuck his foot down and they were soon flying through London to the outskirts. Despite heavy traffic and traffic lights, thirty minutes later they were careering down the track and through the gates. No need for caution, the targets were still in the centre of London.

They were met by Mr. Reid and Sgt George who called out as they pulled up, 'Park the vehicle in the barn with the other one, Mould, and then come to the control room.'

Reid noticed Saied as he got out of the vehicle.

'Hello Jean, good to see you, we have two old friends of yours who are very keen to meet you.'

Reid smiled and then turned to Rodney.

'All good back at the office?'

'All good. Shall we?' Rodney grabbed the stingers from the boot of the Rover and laid them on the drive. 'Thought that these might be useful.'

Sgt George nodded. 'Got just the job for them.'

In the control centre, Rodney saw a hive of activity. Extra cables were being laid in. He knew that they would be for sonic detectors laid out in the grounds and extra cameras. He saw that the operations boards were being updated by Andrew.

'Where's Laurie?'

Mr. Reid said, 'Where do you think? Helping Ms. Blake.'

'Servo and Carla?'

'We are here, Major.' Carla and Servo came from the back of the room to meet him.

Rodney grinned and hugged Carla and gripped Servo's arm. 'Well, I can hardly believe that you're here. Let me welcome you officially. And well done for getting here. I would have hoped for a gentler welcome to the UK, but your help is appreciated.'

Carla was the one who responded.

'We are fine. The arrest certainly felt real. We had a moment when we were not certain but then Laurie appeared, thank goodness. Both of us are looking forward to getting tonight over so that we can get on with our lives. We insist that we are part of the action.'

'Rest assured that's our mission too and you will play a part. I had little choice as it all happened so quickly and despite the situation thought that this would be the best place for you until we sort out this trouble. Can I ask you again what makes you think that they will come tonight?'

'It's political. Colonel Pushkin has been given orders that this attempt on you is final. After that they have to move on to other matters, so it's a last desperate attempt for him to gain some credit. But I have to say it is poorly planned and ill conceived.' Servo's English had improved measurably.

'No doubt you've talked to Mr. Reid about what you think that they'll do tonight?'

'Yes, we spoke and he has added our thoughts to the defence plan. Although it looks more like an attack from his side!'

'That doesn't surprise me.' Rodney smiled.

Mr. Reid came over. 'Sorry to grab you away but I need to talk you through the operational plans for tonight. Servo and Carla, you are welcome to come and listen. After all, you are involved.'

Chapter Eighty-Five

Day One: The Russians

In the basement of the Russian Consulate Building on Kensington Palace Gardens, crowded round the meeting table, were ten men huddling over a large-scale map of the safe house and grounds. Alexander Ivanov was explaining what he had seen the night before.

The other men listened in silence. It would be fair to say that they were still off balance because of the apparent arrest of Carla and Servo. The two men from Moscow had witnessed the aggressive arrest of Servo and Carla at Immigration that morning. The picture of the heavily armed police remained in their minds as a warning that, they could be next.

Servo had cautioned the Colonel at the meeting in Moscow that the British had facial recognition systems that might pick Carla and himself out if they had been flagged as undesirables, but the warning had been dismissed.

'By the time they react you will be on the plane returning to Moscow,' he had retorted.

What worried the two men from Moscow, Dimitri Soros and Boris Sidankco, more was that their images would now be on the facial recognition database and the chance of the Border Security Force linking them to this evening's planned attack. Hopefully the timing would not give the authorities time to react. Their plan was predicated on this. So, time from the attack to escape had to be minimised.

Even though Ivan Servo and Abraham Karpickkov, the two resident KGB officers, had been told directly by Moscow to get involved in the attack to make up the numbers, they were far from happy. Their normal remit was agent recruitment, the running of the agents and any disinformation and administrative mayhem they could manufacture. Add to this covert tacit support, technical aid to activists in the UK, not excluding the trade unions, which was seen as a high priority. And, of course, the supply of funds to the activists and union members that could facilitate mayhem and disinformation.

When Alexander had finished, Ivan Servo, the elected leader of the mission, thanked him.

'What I propose is that we use two vehicles, five men in each. One vehicle drives to the main gated entrance and parks up where Alexander, Adrian and Erast did last night. The other vehicle takes the tracks here.' He traced the course along the tracks to the back gate. 'The gate will be easy to climb. Vehicle One manpower. The men go anticlockwise to the point where Alexander said that the wall was broken down and make entrance into the grounds. Your responsibility is the outbuilding on that side and the house. Vehicle Two manpower. This group will climb over the back gate and move to the outbuilding on their side and cover the first group as they assault the house. Questions?'

Alexay Shchusey had a question.

'Don't you think that it might be prudent to leave one man with the car in case we need to get away quickly?'

'Our problem is that because we haven't been given the luxury of proper close-target reconnaissance, we don't really have any idea how many men are there and what they are armed with. All that we know is that two Land Rovers went into the property and what you saw when they left, so we can assume there are anything from six to ten men in the house. With all due respect to Alexander's report that he saw no one last night, we are still the attacking force and military wisdom dictates that usually we should have a three to one superiority. We don't have that luxury, far from it. Now,' Ivan turned to the two local KGB officers. 'What arms and ammunition can you offer us, perhaps the fire power can redress the balance?'

'We've got hold of four SR-3 short barrel and suppressors for each gun, two 9x39mm round magazines. They fire subsonic rounds so the noise profile will be mitigated. One KM with a GP-25 Grenade Launcher and a 30 mag of 7.62. Noisy, so we should only use it if we have to. We also have ten handguns, 9mm GSh-18, two 18 shell magazines for each. A gun that will pierce most body armour, good for close combat.'

'Hm, no hand grenades or smoke?'

'Sorry, no. What we have is the best that we could put together in the time we had.'

'OK. We are where we are and a bonus is the amount of ammunition for each gun; well done on that.' He looked round the table, 'Any more questions?'

Dimitri wanted to know who was in each of the two teams. Boris stood forward.

'May I suggest Ivan and Abraham, with Alexander, Adrian and Erast, for Vehicle One. Front gate area. The rest and I for Vehicle Two. Back gate area.'

There was a shuffling of feet and nodding of heads around the table. The proposal was accepted unchallenged.

Ivan thanked Dimitri. 'Not quite last, but for one reason at least, Dimitri and Boris need to be at the Airport by 0700hrs to get the first flight out, so we need to be away from the target area latest 0500hrs as they'll need to clean up and change. So, we hit them at 0200hrs; if we're there an hour later we've failed and we need to make a run for it. Not that I expect us to fail. Last chance for questions?' He waited. He expected that each man was thinking of his part to come and if he would come out unscathed, 'No? OK, let's get to the weapons and practise until I'm satisfied that you can strip and assemble the weapons and clear a stoppage in the dark and change a magazine in less than three seconds.'

He looked round at the team in front of him. He was relatively sure the two men from Moscow and his sidekick from the Embassy would be effective, but as he cast his eyes over the six Eastern European mercenaries as he thought of them, he saw only thugs out of their comfort zone. He didn't doubt their commitment and knew that they were ruthless but still, soldiers they were not. That was why there were two KGB trained men in each team.

Chapter Eighty-Six

Afternoon with the British

Mr. Reid had everybody in the cellar for their final briefing. He stood in front of the battle boards with Sgt George off to his right. There was an air of expectation in the room, bordering on excitement by some of the people. Others, more experienced, were serious and mindful of the bloodiness of a battle and only too aware that things don't always go to plan.

For most, there was an underlying urgency to get out on the ground.

He called for quiet. 'Thank you. Mission is to eliminate the attacking force, believed to be up to ten enemies. Aim is to prevent any enemy reaching the main house and outbuildings at all costs.'

He repeated the mission and the aim. He let that sink in and then continued, 'I will now confirm deployments. Listen in, I won't keep you long. I'll be located in the control centre with the signallers, less one. You've all been out with Sgt George and been given areas of responsibility and arcs of fire. You've all been given a refresher on the weapons that you've been issued with. I am now confirming deployment.

'Andrew, Servo and Saied, in the tree copses in Sector Green, responsible for arcs of fires covering the Sectors Green and Blue.

'Major Brown, Armand and Sgt George, in the tree copses in Sector Red, responsible for arcs of fire covering Sectors Blue and Black.

'Lewis and Mould, located at the barn, responsible for Sectors Green and Blue.

'Pat and Fred, located at the stable, responsible for Sectors Black and Red.

'Roof snipers: Sharky, gunner, and Ms. Blake, observer, Sectors Green and Blue.

'Sniper Corporal Pete, observer Carla, responsible for Sector Black and Red.

'I will repeat.'

Mr. Reid went to the battle board and with his pointer confirmed everyone's positions again.

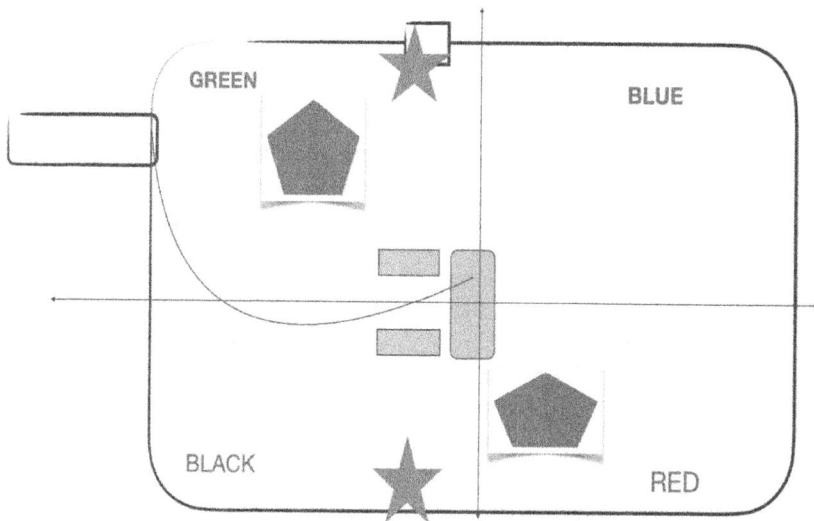

He gave them a moment to focus on his schematic.

He then pointed to the schematic. 'Potential enemy approaches. Obvious approaches back gate and the broken-down wall that was broached last night. Could be they split their forces. Could be they don't. I would go five and five. Even if they split up and take the easy entry points the only thing we can be sure of is that they will see the need to come through the front door. Be prepared for anything and any variation. So eyes on the sectors you command.'

It was a long speech for Mr. Reid, but he had felt he had to set the scene. He continued. 'Other tasks. Stingers: Fred and Lewis are to deploy the Stingers at last light, one on the track to the back gate a fifty to hundred paces before the gate, and the second one a hundred and fifty paces along the metaled track leading to the main gate. Now, general, communications and administration.'

He paused. 'General, you must be in your location by last light. You are to patrol your general areas to familiarise yourselves with every rise and fall in the ground and every bit of blocking vegetation. You are to finish preparing your fire positions.

'At this time of year, the foliage cover is light so your hides in the copses must be undetectable. SOP: no shine, no outline no unnatural shapes etc., you know the drill. Think camouflage, it can save your life.' He smiled. 'Clothing: courtesy of Commander Coveney. Padded black overalls, waterproof black jackets for warmth and balaclavas. Black combat boots.'

Mr. Reid continued. 'Your call signs are as supplied on the radio net plan issued by the signals cell; No change.'

'Lastly,' Mr. Reid raised his voice. 'Administration: as you leave here, pick up your cold rations from Ms. Blake. I will then carry out an arms and equipment check as you leave the building. Sharky, you are to carry out arms check of the sniper rifles and small arms.

'Weapons disposal external forces: each will have an HK MP5 with three magazines and Sig Sauer P226 Browning high power, three magazines. House forces, two sniper rifles and all personnel will carry a side arm, the Sig P226.' He stopped and looked at Servo.

'Whilst you'll be wearing body armour, be aware that if the enemy has Russian Special Forces weapons your body armour will help, but at close range all bets are off so don't let them get close.'

Then Mr. Reid gave his final warning.

'They've come to kill you and will spare no-one to tell the story. There must be no hesitation; shoot to kill first. That is an order for which I take full responsibility. Any questions?'

There were none. The mood was now sombre, tinged with a pent-up excitement to get on with the task, and get it over with.

Doug Reid dismissed them characteristically with a flea in their ears.

'Now go, and earn your pay.'

His Scots accent was evident in the last statement, leaving no one in doubt that they were here to kill the enemy on sight.

Chapter Eighty-Seven

End Game

It was a long afternoon and evening for Mr. Reid's team out in the field, for some a wake-up call that they were not as fit as they thought. But they all mucked in, supporting and helping out where they could and taking a grim satisfaction from their efforts.

Team play was built quickly. Defence was improved around the stables and barn to improve protection from the various chosen fire positions and to give the best possible observation over their arcs of responsibility.

In the copses, led by Andrew, they had finished off the hide giving them line of sight on the back and front gates whilst being invisible from the front and side.

Over at Major Brown's copse, there was a dilemma; the strong feeling was that the enemy targets would come from the broken-down wall to their front right. It was an easy entry but obvious. They still had a responsibility in addition to Sector Black with an arc into the Red and Blue Sectors for covering an attack from that direction. Albeit they thought it a slim chance because of the terrain at the back of the house, they had to cover it, so they made two hides, one to the front covering the expected enemy advance and one to the rear right of the copses covering the red and blue Sectors.

As the day wore on Mr. Reid did his rounds and grudgingly approved each defensive position. After a few hints as to making them better, he felt that he could do no more, it was up to them now.

He wandered back to the house and went into the kitchen to find something to chew on. He found the housekeeper sitting at the kitchen table, checking her pistol.

'Still sure that you're up for this?' he asked her.

'All the way, Mr. Reid.' She looked up. 'And you, what do you want?'

Mr. Reid smiled and responded. 'Obviously I want everyone to walk away whole. And I could do with some comfort food.'

'Meat pies in the fridge over there. Stick some in the microwave for a few minutes.'

Even with all of his experience, Doug Reid hated the waiting and was reluctant to leave the kitchen to go and sit idle in the control room.

'How about you Ms. Blake? Is there anything that we can do for you?'

'Matter of fact, there is. When you lot disappear tomorrow, I have to set up this place for a posh meeting. That means that I need to get the silver, paintings and the rest of the best house stuff back up from the cellar where it's locked up. Problem is, I've broken the key in the lock. If you could work your magic and get the door open, I'd be grateful.'

'Where is this door?'

'Far end of the cellar; there's a steel door behind some furniture. Sort of camouflaged you might say. Can you do it?'

'Not a problem.' He thought for a moment. 'Not only that, but if there's not too much drama overnight then we'll bring the stuff up for you.'

'Deal. Get your pies and I'll show you the door.'

In the cellar he helped to remove the furniture covering the door. True enough, on inspection he could see the end of the key broken off. The toolboxes were raided, and Mr. Reid triumphantly held up a drill. It took no time at all to drill out the barrel and the door swung open on a treasure trove of paintings and silver from the governments stockpiles. Reid wandered round looking at the paintings – Goya, Sorolla, Turner and others. He was amazed. He saw the housekeeper's sly smile and blushed.

'Some collection eh!'

'Blown away.' Mr. Reid thought he had given away enough of his emotions and said gently, 'Thank you for sharing this and now we need to get back to work.'

'OK I am back upstairs. See you when this is over.' With a cheerful wave she left him.

As the evening light gloomed, the last food and drink was taken in shifts. In the gathering darkness the 'Stinger team' went out and laid the two Stingers. By the time they got back, the others had settled into their positions, and all was quiet. The evening was cool, but it would get colder, and the dew had already begun to form. The sky was clear, and the stars and a half-moon gave enough light once their night vision had been established to see the ground clearly for the distance that they would need. The night vision goggles, along with the night optics on the MP5s, turned the world from dark grey into green and good enough to see great detail at a hundred yards and more.

The Russians packed the two cars and left London at one o'clock in the morning. The aim was to be on target at 2am to commence the attack. They would stop a few miles short of the target and confirm timings.

In the cellar the signals team and Mr. Reid watched the trackers begin to move on the map. He put out a call to all to the teams in the fields to tell them the targets were on their way.'

The Russians had worked out that when they split up, the car led by Ivan would take exactly fifteen minutes to get to the back gate. The car with Alexander would take only five minutes to get to the road leading to the back gate. Ivan gave them ten minutes to park the car and hustle to the broken wall.

They got to the point on the road that they had chosen as a forming up point and jumping-off point without incident, it was twenty-five minutes past one. The road was little used in the daytime and deserted at night. Ivan thought that it was quite safe for the men to get out of the car, have a last check on weapons and a smoke. A word of encouragement and confirmation of the timings. Ivan gathered them around him; he needed to endanger a sense of urgency as the Eastern Europeans in particular seemed sluggish and were milling around aimlessly; many were stamping their feet to keep warm.

Ivan felt that they had been on the side of the road long enough and that he needed to grip them.

'Listen carefully and snap to; cigarettes out.' He looked at his watch, 'It is now sixteen minutes to 2 am. At 2 am, no matter what happens, in groups or as individuals, if necessary, we press home the attack from the broken wall and the back gate at the same time. Don't stop for anything or anyone or we will be lost. Mount up. Good luck. Remember, 2 am, not a minute before or after. Go!' There was a scramble as the men ran for the cars. Ivan smiled.

'Awake at last.'

In the control room, Mr. Reid was fretting over not having had the manpower to put scouts or sentries further out to give early warning. He shrugged. He had professionals out there, the best of the best. He had Laurie spare and he sent him to patrol the ground floor and it gave him some modicum of comfort

He had walked round the positions before last light and was satisfied that all approaches were covered. In the hides, no one was sleeping; the early morning time was the most dangerous. Everyone was fully aware that the next few hours would confirm if they were coming or not.

As the car carrying Alexander turned into the track road leading to the front gate, he switched off the headlights and drove on sidelights. The occupants of the car felt rather than heard the tyres being shredded. The car seemed to sink, and they could see Alexander fighting with the wheel. They came to a stop at an angle, slewed across the road. Alexander switched off the side lights and the engine, swearing. He felt some responsibility but not much. He got out in the dark and felt the wheels and the tyres. He knew that they'd been subject to a Stinger attack. He looked round but could see and hear nothing.

'We're not going any further in this car tonight, we'll need to use their Rovers afterwards. Let's go now or we're going to be late, and we need to be on time.'

The signaler and Mr. Reid were watching the screen and saw the tracker become immobile on the road leading to the main gate. He called up Rodney.

'Stand by target on the approach road to the main gate.'

Five minutes later the other car, which was negotiating with some difficulty and rocking up and down and through mud up the farm track leading to the back gate, ran over the Stinger on the track. The driver, Daniil Litvinenko, felt the steering become very heavy and fought with the wheel until he could control it no more and the car dug into the track. He switched off the sidelights and the engine. He climbed out, while the others tried to see what was going on. A quick examination by Daniil soon found the shredded tyres.

'Got to leave the car, the tyres are gone.'

When Reid saw the second vehicle go static, he called up Andrew and told him to stand by.

'Targets approaching the back gate. Stand by, stand by.'

Ivan looked at his watch. Three minutes to go.

'Come on, we have to go now or be late.' The rest tumbled out of the car, grabbing their weapons.

Ivan slung his machine gun over his shoulder and carried the rifle with grenade launcher at the trail. Trudging along the muddy track he called, 'Make ready, safety catches off.' He could hear the heavy breathing of the men around him. They were making a meal of getting the machine guns ready for battle but they got to the back gate two minutes later, out of breath. Ivan led them over the gate. Once inside the grounds he went down on one knee. The rest joined him and fanned out, also dropping on to one knee.

At the same time, in equally ragged order, Alexander's group began to tumble through the broken-down wall. Like Ivan's team they went down on one knee to scan the strange landscape in front of them, bathed in starlight and weak moonlight.

Both teams could pick out blocks of buildings, black against the landscape and clumps of black trees. A night mist was rising from the ground. They wished that there was more of it to disguise their approach over the open ground.

All was quiet, too quiet for Ivan on the other side of the house. He closed his finger on the grenade launcher trigger. The plan was simple – arrive together at the house. Ivan would use the grenade launcher to blast open the front door and blast out the lower windows and then they would assault using the shock of the explosion and with speed overwhelm everyone in the house. No quarter was to be given.

In the roof space, both snipers acquired enemy targets. Both, out of instinct, chose the man on the far left and right respectively. They would wait until the ground teams opened fire.

In the control room the cameras set out in the grounds picked up the approaching Russians. The signallers and Mr. Reid hardly dared to breathe.

Major Rodney Brown felt his guts tighten as the shadowy figures advancing became distinctively men with guns. Now or never.

He opened up, the first leading the fire storm. He took out the man on his right with two aimed shots and then the next one. Armand and Sgt George took out the next two and the sniper, the Corporal from the Signals, took out the last one.

The man was Alexander. He was down and dying but still had the strength in him to get off a half magazine before his lungs filled with blood and he choked to death.

Sharky had told the signaller to aim for the body mass and he had done just that but had had to fire twice as the man had fallen to one knee after the first round and was still functioning. Before the second sniper round finished him off, the man had fired a long burst towards Rodney's group, instinctively aiming at the muzzle flashes. The other enemy personnel had died almost immediately but some got shots off as they died.

One bullet caught Rodney in the top shoulder. He felt the bullet rip his top muscle. He groaned and swore but gathered himself. Not a time to give into a minor wound. There was no pain, but he knew that the heat would build until his shoulder was on fire. What would Mr. Reid say at this point to motivate him? – 'Man up and dig in.' Another shell, fired by Alexander as he died, skinned across Armand's knuckles making him drop his rifle. Rodney's team recovered from the light hits quickly, but it didn't matter, the enemy on their side of the house were dead.

In Andrew's sector, the fire-fight was equally ferocious and immediate. A split second after Rodney fired, Servo and Saied let rip, taking out three men immediately. Andrew, slower from lack of practice, took careful aim at a man. The man was Ivan the leader. In the roof, Sharky was equally quick as Servo and Saied and took out the man on the far right.

Andrew unfroze and fired at Ivan, hitting him in the chest. Ivan swung towards the copses that they were in and pulled the trigger of the grenade launcher; he got off two rounds before Saied riddled him with bullets. Both grenades whistled through the copses, taking out small branches before exploding 300 or 400 yards away.

Then there was a silence. The silence was deeper and colder than the night. None of the enemy moved, there was no sound from them. The shock of the violence had overcome the immediate rational thought and relief that at least for now that the threat that they had been living with was over.

A group letting-out of breath could be discerned by those who had regained their hearing after the noise of the fight. There was no talking; men who in other circumstances might have been allies had been sent to their death by a man who cared nothing for them, only his blind revenge.

Rodney, silent for a moment, knelt on the ground, exhausted. The stress of the last few weeks overwhelmed him. Then he switched on and came back to life. He sent his group to check that the enemy were all dead. They collected the enemy weapons and any identifying documents they could find. Where an enemy gun hadn't had chance to fire, Sgt

George put a burst down the barrel. When they were satisfied that there were no lingering issues they made for the house.

On the other side of the house Saied had gone forward to check the dead and then signalled Servo and Andrew forward to collect any identity documents and weapons. In the same way that Rodney's team had fired a burst from any unused guns, they did the same.

As Rodney was passing the stable and barn blocks, he called the Jones brothers, Pat and Mould over and asked them to sort themselves out and to patrol the dead until relieved. He took off his NVG, swept his uninjured hand through his hair and ruffled it.

The night was back to normal with the distant sound of the M25 and the noise from jets leaving and arriving at Heathrow.

Reid looked up as Rodney entered the cellar. Rodney's left arm was bleeding badly but he still felt no pain, that would come later. He smiled tiredly at his mentor.

'All done, Mr. Reid. All dead. Injuries on our side, my shoulder, not serious and Armand had the skin of his knuckles skinned by a stray bullet. Not serious.'

Mr. Reid showed no emotion.

'Good. I'll let the team at base know that they can close down, and I'll get the Brigadier on the phone. You need to speak to him now.'

'OK. Put him on.' Rodney spoke to the Brigadier for ten minutes and the Brigadier agreed that he would alert Sir Geoffrey and the Home and Foreign Secretaries. He would also get the duty officer at MI6 to send over an officer to deal with the dead Russian nationals. Rodney agreed to phone Commander Coveney at the Anti-Terrorist branch straight away in order to close the site down from prying eyes.

Rodney made the call. The Commander was not pleased at being called at three in the morning but immediately came awake when he knew it was the Major.

'Rodney, do you know what time it is?'

'Only too well, Commander. We had a situation. There was an attack on us at the safe house. There are a number of dead, not on our side, thank goodness.'

'How many?'

Rodney could hear the wheels turning in the Commander's head. One or two could wait till the morning and he would just send a couple of men to secure the site tonight.

'Ten and some are Russian nationals.'

'Jesus, Rodney. I'll be there in... Where is there?'

Rodney told him. 'I'll be there in half an hour. Stay where you are.'

'One other thing, Bob; we need recovery trucks to take two cars. Their tyres are shredded.'

Rodney thought that it had gone well. He had had the idea that putting a few rounds through each of the enemy's guns that hadn't had the chance to fire a shot in anger had been a good move. They all knew the routine.

He asked Mr. Reid to get the Stingers in as soon as possible; he didn't think that the Commander would be pleased if his car got 'stung.' In the event, he found out later that it had been taken care of immediately after the fire-fight by the Jones brothers at the prompting of Sgt George. They also knew the form.

Reid had a cup of sweet tea ready.

'Drink that down, it'll settle you.'

'Thanks, but I feel fine. A little fatigued, like everyone else. Just need to get my arm seen to. Oh, I put the outbuilding teams on patrol and guarding the site of the fight.' He looked at Mr. Reid.

'I know Rodney, I'll sort it from here. Ms. Blake is not only a retired Petty Officer in the WRNS but a retired nurse too amongst other things. Get her to sort you out. I've got her and Laurie cooking an early breakfast in the kitchen. Now fuck off. I don't want to see you until that shoulder is bandaged up. Let me get some work done at least and prepare for a very pissed off Coveney. I told everyone that I need a written statement by 0700hrs and that means you too. The rest, apart from the outside guards, are stood down, milling around in the dining room telling each other war stories. And I hope writing up their account of the night's activities, brief though it was, well done to them for that. Don't forget to get us some rations down here sharpish. Now, once again, fuck off Major, I have a lot to do.'

For Mr. Reid to swear Rodney knew that he was secretly pleased.

Chapter Eighty-Eight

Epilogue

A lot had happened in the four weeks since the fire-fight. A Colonel Pushkin, they found out, had been given his marching orders by the new General of the First Directorate and been sent to St Petersburg to make a nuisance of himself there as some sort of military attaché to the civil authorities, whatever that was.

The Somali force had been paid off and Rodney had a call from Simon in Mogadishu who was pleased and wanted to know if his brothers could be of assistance in the future.

'Goes without saying,' responded Rodney.

The Banker and his team had been shipped off, along with Pat and Andrew, to the FBI headquarters in the States for an unspecified duration.

Major Freire's team were back in barracks and had a tale to tell over a few beers. They were all mentioned in the Brigadier's report to their Commander with thanks, along with a letter of commendation for Sgt George to the Commander of Special Forces.

The mess at the safe house had been cleaned up by the Home and Foreign Office and Rodney's men were never there, it seemed. A tragic motor accident accounted for the death of four Russian nationals and an underworld inter-territorial gang fight had taken six undesirables off the street. Seemed tidy to Rodney.

Servo and Carla had been rehoused with new names and would initially take jobs in the Civil Service in Glasgow, after a paid holiday with Rodney in Cornwall. In Glasgow they would be processing something or other. No accounting for taste, but they were happy. Saied had faded back into his anonymity.

The overly high expenses incurred by the wives forced into hiding for three weeks had been paid and Mr. Reid, Mould and Sharky reunited with them. Mr. Reid was forced to take a break.

The team were all now on enforced leave except for the Brigadier, Rodney and Graham, but before anyone went on leave, they had all mucked in for two days to revamp the office and reset it for another mission. It gave them chance to unwind and have a few beers.

Now, only three men sat at the office conference table. Rodney's shoulder was stiff, itchy and it ached. He would get over it.

The Brigadier chaired the small meeting. They reviewed and closed out items for an hour or two. Then the Brigadier brought out from his old-fashioned battered hide briefcase a bottle of single malt and four tumblers as Dr Christian arrived and joined them. The Brigadier poured a generous measure into each glass.

'I thought that I would toast you all and by the way, commendations all round. Herself insisted on it, plus a gong or too. But we shall see. A week in politics is a long time and, as ever, last week's heroes are soon forgotten' The Brigadier smiled. 'Now, there's something that we need to discuss. The Banker seems to have found some more fraud money in the form of gold bullion. It's safe from discovery as the Banker had it moved to a local friend's secure site, so he says. It can stay where it is for a month or two, or even more. But we have to go and collect it and bring it back here. Cheers!' He poured another large tot.

'Are we talking about a lot of gold?'

'Around fifty billion at today's rates. Could be more tomorrow.'

'Who's was it?'

'KGB, of course.'

'Can't we just have it sent?' Graham had a bad feeling.

'Regrettably not.'

'OK, I'll buy it. Where is it?'

'There's the rub.'

Later that afternoon, Graham sat alone in the cavernous office suite of two rooms with the rest of the bottle of whisky that had been left behind for him to finish off. He gazed around. It was so quiet and a lonely, lifeless place without the team buzzing around. To be fair, Graham had been offered some leave, but he felt that there was more to do in the office. As he was acting as support hub for the Banker and others in the States and for those on leave, he would stay at the wheel. After all, who would look after and protect old Doctor Christian?

Major Rodney, well, he was being driven back to Cornwall, where he rejoined Servo and Carla, who were having a great time with Jane. The Brigadier had ordered Rodney to take four weeks' rest and recuperation with Jane in the cottage by the beach. This was to give him the time to think about a scheme to retrieve the gold, of course, even though Robinson had admitted that it would be a difficult extraction. He had a passing thought – they still had Major Vasily in deep cover in the KGB and then there was of course Galena, the beautiful KGB spy mistress and his neighbour. Nothing would be ruled out. He just knew that the mission would be challenging.

End

THE SPYMASTER SERIES - SYNOPSIS

THE SPYMASTER SERIES BY ROGER BENSAID

SPYMASTER ADAGIO ISBN 978-0-7552-0734-3. 426 pages; 163K words

An old-fashioned, cold war, soldier-spy story, with an underlying vendetta that is set to continue. The story moves from South Africa after a spy device is stolen through to London, Moscow and on to action in Central America which tests friends and foe alike. The middle part of the book is a flashback to the time when the antagonists first went up against each other. Finally part three of the book cements the vendetta for all time between the protagonists.

(Authors own art used on the cover)

SPYMASTER ALLEGRO, ISBN 978-78507-610-7. 408 pages; 162K words

For a second time this special Section of the British Secret Intelligence Service faces the Russian Spymaster. In the sequel to Spymaster Adagio, Major Rodney Brown meets his opponent again in a race to prevent the KGB General Tsygankov wreaking havoc on the British Army. The action takes place in London, Afghanistan, Moscow, Somalia, Split, Southern Ireland and Libya with a climactic ending in the tranquil British villages of the Wallops. There is a final face-to-face between the antagonists at the General's dacha in Southern Russia. This story also sets the scene for the third and final book of the first Rodney Brown trilogy where he still has the support of Brigadier Robinson, the master of deception.

SPYMASTER ACCESO ARMAGEDDON ISBN 978-1-78719-563-9, 418 pages

In this final book of the First Spymaster Series, Major Brown once more faces General Tsygankov of the KGB. The race against the General and his contract killers has to be won or the consequences to the British economy will do untold damage. the action takes place between Russia and the UK with fast moving situations that have to be dealt with by the British team if they are to save the day. Back from the dead an assassin is sent to eliminate Major Brown and his team and a new battle is on. Brigadier Robinson, as the head of the secret service team, again plays a vital part in support and facilitates Major Brown's efforts to save the country from ruin.

(Authors own art used on the cover)

SPYMASTER MIDAS 2023 ISBN
978-1-80369-837-3, 410 pages

The fourth Major Rodney Brown Spymaster Story. The Major is recalled to duty by Brigadier Robinson after Rodney's physical injuries have healed. Reluctantly mentally unready, once again the Major gives his all to take down an invidious disruptive fraud spanning key national interests in construction, defence, and the health service.

Failure would mean that the Prime Minister and her government would almost certainly fall. Out of his comfort zone Major Rodney Brown and his team find a way through a morass of government departments and businesses being defrauded by a KGB scheme instigated by his nemesis General Tysgankov to weaken the economic base of the country.

A mandarin in the treasury leads the fraud, supported by KGB thugs he runs roughshod though the economy ripping millions out of the country. As Rodney's team begin to roll the frauds Colonel Pushkin KGB takes up a vendetta against Rodney. The Colonel wants vengeance never more so when Rodney discovers that the fraud model has been exported to the USA and other European neighbours. A crunching climax to the story which is Pushkin's last chance to assassinate Rodney.

(Authors own art used on the cover)

Printed by BoD™in Norderstedt, Germany